Dog Logic

Lyrical, Satirical, Genre-defying

Hertell Daggett has just discovered a time capsule. Only this one is full of people, and they've been living beneath his pet cemetery since 1963 due to some bad information they got about the end of the world. Hertell leads the duck-and-cover civilization into the glorious, mystifying, and often dismaying modern world. What could possibly go wrong?

Dog Logic

A Novel

Tom Strelich

Owl Canyon Press

Copyright

Copyright © 2017 by Tom Strelich

All rights reserved.

Library of Congress Cataloging-in-Publication Data

Strelich Tom.

Dog Logic -- 1st Ed.

p. cm.

ISBN: 978-0-9985073-2-3

2017906358

Owl Canyon Press

Boulder, Colorado

Invitation

Free Audiobook

I hope you enjoy reading *Dog Logic*, and if you'd like a free audiobook edition of the novel for those long drives, walks, bike rides, or airline flights, just point your smartphone or tablet camera at the QR Code below to copy...

Dog Logic Audiobook

Praise for Dog Logic

"Strelich's shaggy sense of humor is the motivating force..."—NY Times

"Strelich writes comedy that is fresh and vigorous and his language is both clever and elegant."—LA Times

"I would kill to direct a movie adaptation of this absolutely magnificent book. Bravo!" — Sam Irvin, Director of *Elvira's Haunted Hills*

"*Dog Logic*...will evoke a wide range of emotions, from outright laughter to shock, indignation and everything in between..."—Readers' Favorite"

"...Clever, funny, and wickedly satirical, loved it!"—Proprietor and Head Mechanic, A&E Automotive, Goleta, CA

"Strelich has the dramatist's gift for dialogue, the poet's feel for space and time, and a prophet's vision of history's currents and human folly. *Dog Logic* is a mordant romp on the fault lines of American progress... Strelich is a first-class

American fabulist."—The Deming Headlight, New Mexico

"*Dog Logic* is a thinking person's novel with a hahah funny bone and a jazz musicians sense of going left when you expect to be going right. Mr Strelich is a true original."—Artistic Director, Next Stage Repertory Theatre

"... tells a tale that is special, cautionary, sometimes mind blowing, surprisingly emotional and current... unforgettable characters and experiences that make this a great ride."—Artistic Director Repertory Theatre of St Louis

"This book has everything a seasoned reader might desire: powerful, evocative characters... dialogue that is wise, wacky and wonderful, and a plot worthy of Edgar Allan Poe. This is a work for the ages... totally aware of where we've been, and it teases us with the mystery of where we might be going."—Artistic Director Vertigo Theatre Factory.

Chapter One

An Odd-sized Casket

It was an odd sized casket, a smallish one that would have been about right for an average nine-year old boy, but there was no boy inside. The casket was carried by four Kern County Sheriff deputies. There wasn't room for the usual six pallbearers due to the small size of the casket, and it would have lacked dignity to have six deputies jammed together, shoulder-to-shoulder, crowding around an under-sized coffin—like a clown car, but in reverse. So, the two extra pallbearers tagged along behind the procession filing past the ranks of a good fifty other deputies standing in rows beside a small open grave. They all wore small black bands on their badges—the traditional sign of respect and mourning for a fallen comrade.

Hertell Daggett watched the memorial service from a respectful distance. He had forgotten to shave that morning and didn't think it proper to be too close to all that spit and polish and grief with a day's worth of stubble. He rubbed his cheek, or had it been two days? He couldn't remember. "What's today?" He realized they were the first words he had spoken all day.

The deputies didn't hear him. They didn't even notice Hertell standing alone on a nearby hilltop watching them from a respectful distance. Even if they had, their professional appraisal would have been simply: Adult male Caucasian, approximately 6 feet, 180 pounds, light hair, brown eyes, dark pants, light shirt.

But if they'd observed him more closely they would have seen much more: that his hair wasn't light at all, but was actually soot black and merely hiding beneath a layer of tawny dust, he was wearing Levi's and a Boy Scout belt, his shirt was a Hawaiian shirt but very old and faded, and that there was something about his eyes and curve of his cheek and the corners of his mouth that made his face—at least when he was lost in thought, or asleep, or confused, or simply blank—look kind.

He was not what he used to be: he'd once been married, he'd once been a physicist, and he'd once been shot in the head in a celebratory New Year's Eve accident, or possibly the 4th of July, he could never quite remember. The doctors got most of the bullet out, but a few microscopic specks of copper remained floating inside his brain, connecting parts that are no longer connected in the rest of us, filaments of species memory going back to the beginning of time. He knew how animals thought and remembered the sounds of dinosaurs, and the dry humor of mastodons, and the rubbery smell of trilobites. He'd once had a future, but he lived now on the outskirts of Bakersfield, California, a damaged caretaker of a run down, failing pet cemetery.

From his vantage point Hertell had a good view of the open grave, the approaching casket, and of the bagpiper that was poised up on Whisper Hill, some distance from the gravesite.

The pallbearers completed their mission and joined the ranks in formation as some words were spoken and some guns went off. The lone bagpiper began playing "Amazing Grace". One of the deputies reached up and put his arm around the shoulder of an adjacent pallbearer and patted it awkwardly. Even from a distance Hertell could see the man's shoulders slightly heaving. The grieving deputy was a massive affair and loomed over the other pallbearers. The fallen warrior being so honored was only 28 years old. In dog years. His name was Wiley, and he'd been killed in the line of duty at a meth lab north of Bakersfield.

Hertell watched the ceremony and contemplated his handiwork. All considered, the grave was well formed. Normal cemeteries, for people and so on, generally use a backhoe for such things, but Hertell dug graves by hand, with a shovel which wasn't as precise or symmetrical as ones made with a backhoe, but he felt that hand-wrought graves had a certain old-world charm.

It had taken him most of the morning to dig the hole. The first foot or so had been pretty easy, mainly dry dusty topsoil and an occasional smooth river bottom rock. At about two or three feet he hit Caleche, a reddish clay as hard as concrete. A pick was the only thing to use on that since the shovel would barely nick it. He usually tried to get down to about four or five feet to get out of coyote and coon range—they'd never actually eat the dead pet, but they'd dig it out for sport.

At about four feet the Caleche was particularly hard and Hertell thought briefly about using the family bulldozer to finish the job. The D6 could make an enormous pit in a matter of minutes, big enough to swallow a freight container. But the image of all those grieving deputies clustered around a tiny, flag- draped casket, engulfed at the bottom of a massive road cut seemed grossly out of proportion, so Hertell completed the grave by hand shortly before the funeral party arrived.

Hertell would periodically use the D6 to smooth out the dirt road that led from Highway 178 up to the Li'l Pal. The whole area east of the 178 was mudflow and alluvia from the Sierras and hadn't changed much since late Pleistocene. Hertell remembered the Pleistocene vividly, the smells, the sights, the sounds—Mastodons had a sound very similar to an AME Gospel choir, only louder. He was convinced that was why Gospel music got to people the way it did, because we remembered it way down in our dinosaur brain. What was left of it, and he knew that all of those brains were still in there, each brain built on top of an older brain: the man-brain, monkey-brain, the dog, the turtle, the lizard, the snake, all the way back to the beginning of time, back to when we were all just a bunch of amoebas floating around eating each other all day. So even though he'd been shot in the head, he nevertheless considered himself to be very lucky. Not to be alive, there are lots of people alive, but to have those parts of his brain, those prehistoric, primal, Precambrian parts of his brain connected to his reason and his language and his soul, if there was such a thing.

A jet flew high overhead. Hertell looked up and searched the sky and spotted the tiny shining speck dutifully pulling its contrail across the red sky and watched it disappear as its sound faded away. He was struck by a thought, and looked down at the gravesite. The deputies were all gone now. He didn't remember them leaving. This had been happening more often lately. He rubbed his cheek. Maybe it had been three days.

He looked out over Li'l Pal Heaven, 40 dried-up, burnt-out acres of little dead pets on the outskirts of Bakersfield. Hertell had a wife once. He thought of her often and hoped that she was happy. He had a father too, but his father had taken most of the previous September to die and was buried over near Wiley. He had a mother, much younger than his father, but she had left long ago when Hertell was nine. His dad always insisted that she was dead, but Hertell knew that she actually lived up in Sacramento. He had no sisters or brothers or aunts or uncles or cousins. The whole family tree ended on his leafless branch. Like those long extinct Mastodons he remembered so well.

He stood motionless and savored the silence for a moment: no jets flying high overhead, no highway noise, no birds or wind, no barking dogs or leaf blowers, just the still air above and the mute hillside below and the blessed silence in between.

And it was during that silence that he first heard it, distant, faint, and just out of reach, but definitely there. It wasn't the remembered gospel calls of Mastodons this time, but something much more recent. He turned his head to listen, it was reedy and elusive, he could almost identify it, but then the wind picked up and carried the sound away.

He told himself it was probably just the copper specks again, tuning him into solar storm or plate tectonics or something like that. He turned and headed toward the house. It was time for a shave.

Chapter Two

Mister Frostie

I t was the sound that got his attention; only it wasn't a solar storm this time. Hertell had been clearing the weeds away from the graves over on the dog side of the grounds. He liked to keep the dogs separated from the cats—dogs over on the east, cats over on the west. He'd move the flowers, the tennis balls, the cracked and curled photos and other offerings left there by the bereaved pet owners to a safe distance from the grave—usually a whole row at a time—then lay waste to the dingy brown weeds with a 2-stroke weed-whacker. He was just returning the flowers and tennis balls to their rightful graves when he heard it. The distant, distorted, music box sound of an ice cream truck.

He climbed to the crest of the dog hills and looked south toward Highway 178. There was a weather-beaten ice cream truck making its way up the dirt road toward the cemetery. He could tell by the way it was bouncing that it was time to start up the D6 and smooth out the dirt road again.

The music was getting louder but would occasionally drift in and out as if carried on the breeze. Hertell carried the weedwhacker back toward the house since he knew that was where the ice cream truck would stop.

The house had been built by Hertell's father back in the '50s specifically for his young bride. It was spacious and airy for the time—a nice little ranch style with all the modern conveniences and a special sewing room just for her. The estate had been much more impressive back then: green grass and fountains and little ponds and trees. But they were long since dead and dried up like the dinosaurs and their beloved swamps—the county changed the zoning from agricultural to mixed commercial- residential, so Hertell couldn't afford to irrigate anymore. The grass and ponds went first and then the trees. And now all that was left were the graves and the headstones and the weeds to be cleared. Hertell propped up the weed-whacker by the back door of the house as the ice cream truck rolled to a stop.

The driver let the song continue while he finished his cigarette. Hertell was quite familiar with the tune and was glad the driver didn't stop it in the middle since a sense of foreboding could often color the rest of his day if the song stopped before it had resolved itself.

The tune concluded, and the driver killed the engine before the music box started again. Hertell approached the truck. He smiled and waved at the driver and then dutifully stood at the service window on the passenger side of the truck to make his selection. "Whatcha recommend today Mister Frostie? Drumstick or Fifty-fifty bar?"

Mister Frostie thought for a while, then took a long last drag on his cigarette. "Fifty-Fifty's too non-committal, doesn't know what it wants to be. I'd recommend a lime paleta." He flicked his cigarette away. "It is what it is."

They sat on the ground and ate their lime paletas in complete silence in the shade of the ice cream truck. Mister Frostie was slender as a length of rope, and of indeterminate age, but definitely older than Hertell. His hair was thick and mostly black with a sprinkling of gray that always reminded Hertell of Harris Tweed. Hertell stared at their feet as they sat in the dirt and reflected on the fact that his legs extended several inches beyond Mister Frostie's and that although Hertell knew himself to be the taller of the two, that Mister Frostie had always projected a larger presence somehow. Perhaps it was his voice.

Hertell finished his Mexican Popsicle first and put the stick in his pocket. "Excellent suggestion, very refreshing."

After a good five minutes of silence Mister Frostie finally replied, "Yeah."

Hertell didn't care because he knew what Mister Frostie was doing. He could tell by the look on Mister Frostie's face, he could tell by the way he was breathing that Mister Frostie was somewhere else. He was thinking up a prayer and Hertell didn't want to interrupt.

Hertell had never even been in a church himself. His father had only bad things to say about churches and religion in general; at least until the last few weeks of the previous September when he'd had a sudden and extreme change of heart. He said he kept hearing Jesus talking to him at night, telling him not to worry, that he was not lost, that God would find him, and that God doesn't sweat the little shit. His father found a great deal of comfort in that as he slipped peacefully and silently away. Hertell was convinced that it wasn't really Jesus but just the sound of the swamp cooler in the blackness of night, and that the same way you can see faces and landscapes in knotty pine paneling, you can hear the whisper of God in the rumble and hiss of white noise.

Mister Frostie got up and stamped the dirt from his boots. It was time to go to work.

Hertell stood at the open back doors of the ice cream truck, looking in as Mister Frostie dug through one of the freezers. Hertell watched him for a moment. "How many you bring today?"

Mister Frostie found what he was looking for under the drumsticks. "Only three, two dogs and maybe a cat." He pulled out a black garbage bag and handed it to Hertell. "This is the cat. I think. Coulda been a small dog. Kinda hard to tell sometimes." He moved on to the next freezer and began digging. "I got the dogs in here. I like to keep'm separated."

Hertell nodded an agreement. "Logical."

Hertell and Mister Frostie spent the rest of the afternoon digging three small graves in the Lost and Found section of Li'l Pal: the section furthest up the hill that never received dead pets or their visitors or plastic flowers or tennis balls. It was too steep and inaccessible for the regular graves and was inconveniently located on the far side of an arroyo and required a hike and a climb to reach, but Hertell had established this as the Lost and Found section because there was a good five or six feet of easy topsoil and substratum before you hit the Caleche. Other than Hertell and Mister Frostie, no human foot ever touched the lost and found section. It didn't need plastic flowers or tennis balls because it had the thickest cover of poppies and other wildflowers in wet years. But it was October now and the poppies and wildflowers were long gone. Just short patchy mats of brome grass.

Hertell noticed that Mister Frostie's shovel blade was cracked, no doubt from historical campaigns on Caleche down in the dog and cat grave sections. Hertell had never bothered to establish bird and fish and lizard and bunny and rodent sections since most people disposed of them in their own unique and typically informal ways.

He held out his shovel to Mister Frostie. "Lemme trade you. That one's got a cracked blade." Mister Frostie silently exchanged shovels with Hertell and they continued digging, until three small graves stood open before them.

Hertell solemnly moved from grave to grave, respectfully lowering a single black bag into each. He then stood opposite Mister Frostie. He bowed his head in reverence, but kept his eyes open so he could watch.

Mister Frostie stood silent and still for a moment. Then his eyes began to blink as if he were about to sneeze. Hertell leaned slightly forward in anticipation. Mister Frostie took a deep breath and from deep within began:

> Merciful and Loving God, receive these tiny friends who soil our carpets yet give us unconditional love. Who now find themselves in Your presence due to their complete ignorance of both inertia and the redeeming blood of Jesus Christ that brings them life everlasting. You see

them now naked, broken, torn, flattened by a driver's momentary inattention, poor hand-eye coordination, or simple indifference: may they be precious in Your loving sight.

Great and Everlasting Father, You knew their last moments, their fear and confusion: the sanctuary of the gutter and the safety of the sidewalk beckoning, salvation in sight but not in reach, instinctive, futile darting to and fro, from certain death to certain death, or frozen by dog logic in the path of the great, looming mystery that roars like the rushing wind, only to crush them remorselessly beneath steel-belted radial angels of death.

O blessed Redeemer, grant them comfort and peace in Your ever expanding procession.

Lord High King of Heaven, would that You will grant us, the waiting, the lost, the condemned, that same loving comfort and peace, when we pass from life to mere matter and find ourselves before You as they: naked, broken, torn, from a lifetime of darting pointlessly, or frozen in fear, ignorant and rejecting of the sanctuary and salvation that is ours... for the mere asking.

Hertell watched. Mister Frostie appeared to visibly swell as he concluded his prayer...

And now, may this prayer, here softly spoken, muted and muffled by this veil of flesh and clay, resound throughout the planets, galaxies, and parallel universes, so that every molecule and atom in Your Creation's wake rings with our unconditional love!!... AAAAAAMENNNNNNN!!!!!

Hertell stood quietly as the."Amen" faded away into the hillsides. He took a satisfied breath.

Mister Frostie lit up a cigarette. "Okay, we can cover'm up now."

Hertell knew the past, from Precambrian to the Mesozoic, from Jurassic to the Neolithic, but he didn't know the future. It never occurred to him that he would never see Mister Frostie again.

Chapter Three

The Funeral Barge

A Deputy named Orbin found the ice cream truck abandoned off Rancheria Road on the north side of the Kern River. Odd place for an ice cream truck, and there would normally be no need to patrol this stretch of road except for some recent pot farming further up Rancheria in the National Forest. They'd occasionally find a dead Mexican in a sleeping bag further up the road: typically, an illegal forced to work in the fields and then killed by the cartel at the end of the harvest as a cost control measure. No dead Mexicans in a sleeping bag this time though, just an ice cream truck. The doors were open but the engine was cold. He checked the plates and it wasn't reported as stolen, so he closed the doors, filled out a citation and stuck it on the bent radio antenna. The registered owner would receive a notice of abandoned vehicle in a few days.

He went back a few days later and the truck was still there. On the lane nearest the truck, there was a greasy grey stain with little bits of matted fur: probably a possum or coon by the looks of it. He walked along the side of the road for a few hundred feet in front of the truck. Nothing, just the usual debris you find on back roads—plastic cups, hats, scratched CD's, a single boot. He returned to the truck and looked inside. It smelled like cigarettes and melted sour ice cream. Not his problem. He went back to the patrol car, but something told him to search the area around the abandoned ice cream truck.

He found the shovel first. The handle was broken off; it was just the blade sitting in the dry drainage ditch about a hundred yards from the truck, a little further up the ditch was an old safety vest that had probably blown out of the back of a pickup. Nothing unusual really, there were some new grape fields nearby, so a shovel wasn't necessarily out of place and safety vests were always flying out of pickups and were a fairly common sight. He continued down the ditch for a few more car lengths looking for the handle, though he wasn't sure why. That was when he smelled it.

He could see what appeared to be a small trash heap at the edge of the featureless low bluff overlooking the Kern River. It was a windless day, so there was no staying upwind of it. He got close enough to confirm that it was what he thought it was. It was. And it wasn't. It wasn't recognizable as a person in any case; just a pile of blackened rags. The only other color was what appeared to be a bright green bracelet on the wrist of what was once a hand.

He remembered the boot he had seen a few hundred feet up from the truck, so he guessed it was a hit and run. And what the drag down the pavement started, the coyotes finished. Even though he knew it was a person, it didn't look like one anymore.

Orbin stood and looked down on the former person and said a prayer to himself. Nothing fancy, short and sweet. He noted how far the remains were from the road. The impact and the dragging would have left him on the road. What was left of him. Might have been the coyotes; they might have dragged him away for a little privacy, or the poor guy might have tried to crawl away from the road so he wouldn't get run over again. The will to live was an amazing thing. But most likely the hit and run driver panicked and dragged him off the road like it never happened.

Hertell was in the quarry when he found out. It wasn't a quarry actually; just an open area by the leach field where they had a bunch of flagstone and other assorted rocks to use as headstones. For some reason he always thought of his wife when he was in the quarry, and he would often stand and look at the ancient stones and think of her and the life he'd lived before the bullet fell from the sky and left him with little copper specks floating in his brain. He missed his wife. The sound of her voice, crackly and tart. He missed the smell of her -- a happy smell that reminded him of young puppies: clean, pure, uncomplicated.

He was trying to reconstruct his own history again, but it wasn't clear if the specks came before, during, or after his wife life. That was their only downside, at times the specks made his world a confusing scrapbook: Jurassic period and the sounds of dinosaur voices, marriage and Kaye's voice and smell, Devonian epoch, boy scouts, September, lost and found—he was just getting them sequenced when an SUV rolled up.

"Hertell Daggett?" A CHP officer with a manila envelope was easing out of her seat. She was very nice, and he wondered what had attracted her to this line of work. Hertell stared at her blankly for a breath, as the smell of his wife faded away, "what?"

"Are you Hertell Daggett?"

He looked at her. "Junior or Senior?"

She pulled some papers from her manila envelope. "Not sure, stand by, checking," and began leafing through them.

Hertell watched her for a moment and then pointed out into the graveyard. "Hertell Senior is out there, buried between the little pyramid and the grieving angel..."

He trailed off because suddenly it was September all over again, and the swamp cooler was whispering comforts to his father in his final days: "God will find you, you are never really lost, God doesn't sweat the little shit..."

"Junior," she said. "If Senior is deceased then it's Junior." She handed Hertell a driver's license. "Do you know this individual?"

Hertell looked at the license carefully. It was Mister Frostie. Mister Frostie had a real name, North Dakota Hill, and he was much older than he looked. Hertell would have called him North or even Dakota in preference to Mister Frostie had he known his real name, but Mister Frostie seemed content never to correct him on it. He returned the license to her. "Yeah, this is Mister Frostie. Is he in trouble?"

She seemed to soften. "Excuse me," she said. "I have some pretty sad news about your brother."

For once in a long, long time, Hertell's mind didn't drift to the Precambrian or the dynasty of Thutmose II, but instead stayed focused on the CHP officer. He looked at her for a long time. "I... don't have a brother," is all he could offer.

She continued. "You were listed on the ICE form at his trailer park, and it's got 'brother' in the 'relationship' box." But her voice faded into the distance. He remembered seeing her mouth moving and he remembered nodding politely, but they were all just words to him.

It was a very nice trailer; about eight feet wide and thirty feet long with a round window on the door that vaguely resembled a porthole on a cartoonish spaceship or submarine. A faded and tattered awning shaded the front door and a small picnic table. An old coffee can and a debris field of cigarette butts sat in the gravel beside the table, the top of which was barren except for an old Popular Science magazine that sat open, a page turning occasionally in the breeze as if Mister Frostie were still there catching up on ion propulsion's bright future.

The Trailer was probably from the '50s based on its lines, rounded and streamlined. Hertell sifted through the big envelope looking for the keys. Mister Frostie had left the Ice Cream truck and all of his possessions to his "brother", Hertell. Mister Frostie had no relatives, and certainly not a "brother", but Hertell had always wanted to be a brother, and grew into the role.

The interior of the trailer was surprisingly tidy. The wooden paneling and cabinetry was the most beautiful birch he had ever seen. There was a tiny TV on some brick and board shelving along with an assortment of books, an old Kenwood receiver, some stained speakers and an old Sony cassette deck. The bed was made. The bathroom was clean. The fridge was empty except for some "D" cell batteries and a root beer.

The forward end of the trailer, the sunny room overlooking the hitch and propane tanks, was stacked full of boxes of varying strata and epoch. Hertell worked his way through them and lost track of time as he descended through the generations; an unheralded and unknown dynasty now in cardboard boxes of forgotten photos, christening gowns, trinkets, keys to long forgotten luggage, bridal veils, cake knives, cracked tea cups, and strings of old Christmas lights, the kind that bubbled, and it all ended on Mister Frostie's now lifeless branch. The sum total of who he was and who they were, encapsulated in a 1950 Owasso Traveleer, like prehistoric ants in birch amber. And now Hertell was the only living person who knew or cared that such people ever even existed.

"You the brother?" A woman resembling the bride of Frankenstein stood in the tiny doorway of the Traveleer looking in on Hertell who sat in a cinder cone of opened boxes and their effluvia. It took Hertell a moment to return to present time and place. It evidently wasn't fast enough because she asked again, "You the brother?"

Hertell tried to talk, but couldn't yet. "Dakota talked about you when he'd come to the office to get his mail, you the one with the Pet Cemetery? The brother?"

Hertell stood up and looked at her. "Yeah." He looked down on the dynasty of boxes. "I'm... I'm the brother."

The D6 made quick work of the grave, which was big enough for a freight container. Hertell slowly and reverently maneuvered the Owasso Traveleer containing Mister Frostie's ashes to the edge of the grave with the D6 and then gently eased the trailer down to the bottom. He thought of Mister Frostie's prayers as the clods rained down on the funeral barge. It was an odd sized casket, too big for a man, too small for a Pharaoh, but big enough for a dynasty.

Chapter Four

The Old Deputy

atrol deputies usually didn't get involved with investigations, though Orbin had done it all: patrol for many happy years; scuba when he was younger, mainly recovering drunks from the bottom of the Kern River and the various canals that wandered over the valley floor; bomb squad for a while, jailer, court bailiff, internal affairs, search and rescue, homicide, rural crime unit, everything. He'd established the SWAT team back in the '80s and was generally venerated and referred to as 'Obi Wan' by the younger crop of deputies.

The best job was K-9. Every day was different, and there was no caseload to catch-up on, no calls to return; you started every day caught up. It was kind of funny, peoples' response to dogs too. A lot of times all they had to do was shout out that the dog was there or that the K-9 unit was rolling, and the meth-head or wife-beater, or whatever would immediately surrender. They'd run sometimes, and that usually came to a comical end. That or they'd try to hide.

He and Wiley would find them in a variety of unusual places since people can get very creative in a panic: port-a-potty, swamp-cooler, chicken-coop, a chimney though there weren't many in Bakersfield; one time a guy was hiding in the wall behind a fridge since evidently, he'd been planning for such a contingency. Wiley just kept barking at the fridge until a couple of Deputies shoved it aside and found the guy curled up and squinting in the light like a newborn, only with tattoos and bad teeth.

But Obi left K-9 after Wiley was shot because it didn't seem respectful to continue on with a new dog so soon. It seemed like getting married again right after the first wife dies. Maybe in a couple of years, after a suitable passage of time, but not yet.

So he was back on patrol now and alone with his thoughts, and it didn't add up: the ice cream truck, the pile of black rags so far from the road, the boot, the broken shovel blade. He had called it in when he found the remains but left after the Coroner arrived and the CHP got there to take over the accident investigation. He kept thinking about it, because, he wasn't sure why. That's why they called him 'Obi Wan'. Eventually, he'd spot one of the investigators in a hallway or a men's room and find out what happened, but for now the radio was quiet, he was out east of town driving through the foothills above the Kern River oil fields, and besides he was in the neighborhood so he decided to visit Wiley's grave.

Orbin was a large man, with a bullet shaped head shaved to obscure his male pattern baldness. He had a sweet soft voice and tired eyes. A bit thicker around the middle now that he was of a certain age, but with shoulders enough to compensate.

He was the issue of a gritty pod of dustbowl Okies who blew into Bakersfield back when Steinbeck was trolling the lower depths of Lamont and Weedpatch for protagonists. They lived in the Hoovervilles on the north banks of the Kern River at first but then moved into Oildale to a more respectable shack somewhere in Roosevelt's second term. This was twenty years before the dam went in up at Isabella, so there was still water in the river back then and there was a family legend that grampa Orbin, Obi's namesake, and some of the uncles even panned for gold in the Kern which is how they got into the upscale shack in Oildale.

All of the cousins ended up working in the oilfields, mainly as swampers and roughnecks but never as drillers. After the war they moved out of the shacks and up onto the bluffs south of the river with real streets and sidewalks. The area was called College Heights in honor of the freshly minted Bakersfield Junior College, and all the streets had the names of famous colleges: Harvard, Loyola, Occidental, Purdue. Names that were essentially meaningless to the Okies that lived on them. Obi was the first one of his family to ever go to college, even if it was just for a year and even if it was just to Bakersfield Junior College. It was enough to get him out of the oilfields and into the Kern County Sheriff's Department.

Hertell watched as the Kern County Sheriff patrol car drove up the dirt road, a much smoother approach since he had graded it with the D-6. He nodded to himself for a job well done. "MmmHmm," even though there was no one there to hear it.

He was in the midst of moving a bunch of old TVs from the garage to a shed some distance from the main residence and had just finished getting the first load stacked in the back of his dad's '74 Chevy Stepside when he spotted the patrol car turn off Highway 178 and head up the dirt road up to Li'l Pal right up to the open garage where Hertell stood with all the TVs.

The deputy stopped his car and addressed Hertell. "Nothing official, I'm just gonna visit... a grave." Hertell had seen this many time before: a first visit. "Yeah, I know, who you're here to see, just go to the right when you get to the pyramid, and then right again when you get to the grieving angel."

"Pyramid, grieving angel, right and right. Thanks." The deputy drove off. Funny guy, he thought, what a job. The place was deserted, as you'd expect for a cemetery, especially a niche cemetery, for pets. But it was also desiccated and decrepit, words he'd picked up from."30 Days to a More Powerful Vocabulary" during his yearlong idyll at Bakersfield Junior College. Hard to see how a few dead dogs and cats a year could cover the operational costs. Perhaps they'd invested wisely during its heyday, presuming it had one.

Orbin stared down at Wiley's grave. It had a very nice laser-etched image of Wiley on the headstone, but was otherwise unadorned. He'd kept the collar and wanted to put it on the grave. He'd seen similar artifacts on some of the other pet graves when he was leaving Wiley's funeral and had resolved to return and leave the collar as a final goodbye. It was the collar Wiley had been wearing when he took the shotgun

26

blast that was meant for Orbin. It was partially shredded where some pellets went through. It was stiff and stained a deep mahogany brown from the last seconds of life seeping from Wiley.

It was Orbin's job to keep Wiley out of kill zones as dogs don't know any better and will heedlessly charge in as if chasing nothing more dangerous than a tennis ball. Knives kill the most dogs: an instinctive primal response to an equally primal threat. Guns are used much less commonly for dogs but are instead reserved for two-legged targets like Orbin. They'd been told that the house had already been cleared and it was just a drug sweep, otherwise Orbin would have kept Wiley under closer control. That's what he kept telling himself anyway. Of course, if he had kept Wiley under control, it would be Orbin's collar perforated and stiffened with dried life.

Orbin was familiar with Li'l Pal Heaven since there was a massive wooden cross on a barren hilltop at the Western edge of the property overlooking Highway 178 that for many years was used for Easter sunrise services for easily a thousand or more people. At least it looked that way to him—he'd gone with Gramma Spencer and a bunch of cousins on several shivering mornings when he was a young boy. Everyone would park on the side of the 178, get out of their warm cars and walk the short distance to the foot of Calvary. They'd all sing. "The Old Rugged Cross." as the sun broke the horizon.

So I'll cherish that old rugged cross,
'til my trophies at last I lay down...

At the time, due to his youth, Orbin didn't realize that it wasn't the actual cross that Jesus was crucified on, and he was comforted that the beams and bolts and shackles used in its construction were exactly like the ones used in the oil derricks over in the Kern River oil fields where his dad and uncles worked—as if to sanctify.

> *I will cling to that old rugged cross,*
> *and exchange it someday for a crown.*

But they all stopped going to the old rugged cross after the one motivated grandparent died. An older and helpful cousin eventually corrected Orbin's misconception about the cross, and confirmed that it was in fact made from salvaged derrick parts from the Kern River oil fields but that Jesus wasn't killed on it, or even in Bakersfield, but actually a good distance away, out in the desert somewhere, way past Mojave.

The Easter sunrise services tapered off slowly over the years as the old Okie Baptists died off and were replaced by Mexican Catholics who evidently didn't like getting up that early on a Sunday and besides they could get communion anytime between 7am and noon on Easter. There hadn't been a formal service on the property since the second Clinton administration and the old rugged cross was now just a distant curiosity to the drivers looking to the east on Highway 178.

Thus he let his mind wander as he stared down at Wiley's grave, grateful for any distraction that would keep him from contemplation: of his imminent retirement and the black terror of what he'd do with it, of his own end and what comes after. Playing the cards he was dealt, he placed Wiley's collar respectfully on the grave, and then stared blankly into the middle distance where something attracted his attention. He noticed an enormous rectangle of disturbed earth, as if someone were grading for a foundation, and he didn't like the idea of the hallowed site of Wiley's burial to be in the shadow of some shack or shed going up right next to it.

"So what are you planning on doing out here?"

Hertell was stacking TVs in the shed when the question was posed. He patted the top of the TV he'd just set down on a pallet. "I'm just moving these old TVs from the garage to out here, 'cause they've been interfering with my sleep and I'm repositioning them further from the house to diminish their effect."

"No, I mean out there, in the cemetery. What are you planning on doing out there?"

Hertell considered the question and brushed a cobweb from his hair. "Out in the cemetery?"

"Yeah."

"Nothing special, just burying the dead pets, the usual."

Orbin pointed out toward the grounds. "Looks like you're grading out there, you planning on putting a structure out there by the graves?"

Hertell shook his head. "No, we're not. I mean, I'm not building anything anywhere."

He was clearly uncomfortable, and Orbin could tell. "So then what's with the grading out there?"

Hertell paused. He didn't really want to say since he wasn't sure if it was legal to bury a whole trailer on your own property, especially if it had Mister Frostie's ashes in it. And technically it was a pet cemetery, so you probably weren't supposed to bury actual people in it either. His father was buried under the Pyramid, and besides, it could be dismissed as a simple mistake or oversight to do it once, but not twice and Mister Frostie made it two actual people buried out there, even if it was just their ashes in some old Tupperware and an Ice Bucket.

Due to the millisecond it took Hertell to answer, Orbin knew that whatever came out of Hertell's mouth next would be a lie.

"Just playing around with the D-6," walking and pointing toward where it was parked. "Moving some dirt around, not much else going on around here." Hertell gestured back toward the road leading up from the 178. "And then I graded the road down there."

Orbin smiled and followed along. "Yeah, you did a good job on the road. Lot smoother than when we came up here for the funeral." He knew he was clearly onto something and followed along in silence behind Hertell who continued his nervous chatter, walking and pointing again. "And did a little up here too, to mark off the sections, you know the dog section and the cat section, dogs on the East, cats on the West."

But it wasn't actually nervous chatter. Hertell had almost immediately forgotten about the buried funereal barge and Mister Frostie's ashes, and was now happily engaged in conversation. Something he hadn't had since the previous September, and he had no more control over it than he would have over a long-suppressed sneeze. "Hey, did you know that the earth's magnetic poles have reversed? That the North Pole is actually a magnetic south pole, and that the South Pole is actually the magnetic north pole?"

"No, but I don't watch the news much anymore, so I didn't hear about it."

Hertell stopped to pull a weed. "Oh but this happened like a million years ago."

"That's probly why I missed it, then." They now stood before the D-6, but it was what was parked next to the D-6 that had Orbin's attention.

"Yeah, but it's a well-known scientific fact. A comet with a significant ferric component and a strong magnetic field went past Earth back then, and came close enough to flip the earth's magnetic field over, and reverse our magnetic polarity."

Orbin took out his phone and took a photo. "Boy, you don't see that every day."

"Yeah, like I said, it's about every million years or so, and that comet's coming back too."

"What a classic ice cream truck." Parked right next to the D6 was Mister Frostie's Ice Cream Truck.

Hertell fell silent and then spoke from far away. "Yeah, it's my brother's."

Orbin watched him out of the corner of his eye. "Pretty cool. Still work?"

Hertell stood for a moment, remembering how the ice cream truck came to its final resting place. It arrived on the back of a flatbed and was dumped in its present location for no other reason than that was where the tow truck driver felt like putting it. It was as good a place as any, so Hertell left it where it was and parked the D-6 next to it as a kind of guardian, after he'd finished grading the road down to the 178 and burying the Traveleer, and Mister Frostie. But something was vaguely calling for Hertell's attention now. "Hmmm?"

"Does it run?"

Hertell thought and finally shrugged. "I don't know. I don't have the key."

"Yeah, well, been nice talking to ya," heading back to his patrol car, "Gotta get going, but I'll be back." Hertell watched as the Deputy walked away, finally calling after, cheerfully, "Ok, I'll be here."

Orbin checked in on the radio and then drove back down to the 178. He was totally serious about coming back. Yeah, funny guy, he thought, skin and teeth were still ok for a Tweeker, and what a perfect place for a meth lab.

Now it all made sense. He mapped out the whole operation on his drive back down to the 178: isolated lab with a good view of the one road in and out of the cemetery; ice-cream truck to get the product to town and sell it; D-6 cat to dig pits to bury the empty barrels and propane tanks and starter-fluid cans and assorted debris. Don't need too many dead dogs and cats to cover costs when you've got that kind of cash flow. The place where he found the Ice Cream truck wasn't that far away, maybe a mile as the crow flies, just across the river and you could probably see Li'l Pal from it, so now the pile of black rags he found was probably a homicide and not a simple hit-and-run.

Chapter Five

The Machinery That Runs the Earth

H ertell finished moving all the old TVs some hours after the grieving deputy had left that afternoon. Most were just junk from '70s hotels, but many were beautiful old classic TVs from the '50s and early '60s that his dad for some reason had been collecting: Philco, Emerson, Magnavox, but all had been homes to the field mice for many years and were full of fluff and pellets and crystallized urine. The garage would be much more pleasant without the TVs, but it wasn't the smell that was interfering with his sleep, or the scratching of the field mice, it was the voices. He'd been hearing them since the Sheriff Dog funeral.

He didn't hear them all the time, and it was unpredictable when he would, but when it was a quiet, windless night, he'd hear them sometimes. Not the swamp-cooler voice of Jesus like his dad heard, but instead, a pod of voices, muffled and reedy, vaguely harmonic and far away coming out of seemingly silent air. He couldn't make out individual words or voices; it was almost like the sound of the ocean or the freeway, only with voices. It was pleasant and kind of comforting in its own way; nevertheless, he felt that hearing voices, however enjoyable, was probably something to be minimized if possible.

He'd given it a lot of thought and came to the conclusion that it must be the TVs—that every show that was ever on them, was still in them, vibrating in the wires, down in the atoms, the faint final echoes of Gunsmoke, and *Lucy*, and *Friends*. The same way those special telescopes out in the desert could hear all the way across the universe for the faint echoes of the big bang, the little copper strands swimming in Hertell's head made it so he could now hear what nobody else could, even if it was just old TV shows.

Even as a small child, he'd often heard what sounded like Morse code when he'd put his fingers in his ears as a way to be alone with his own thoughts. First was a low rumbling that sounded like heavy machinery, and at the time he thought it was the machinery that ran the earth and all the people on it and all the rules they lived by. But when he listened closely, up above the rumble, he could hear the faint and distant pattern of the codes: rhythmic, purposeful, possibly of cosmic origin. He made what he thought was a reasonable assumption that it must be the universe trying to communicate with us, to tell us the answers to all the questions we've ever had, and ever would have. When he was older, he realized that the codes were simply tinnitus, and the low rumble was merely the sound of his own blood flowing and not the heavy machinery that moved the universe. In any case, he learned to ignore the sounds, until now at least when they were joined by the TV voices.

Unfortunately, moving the TVs seemed to have no effect.

Presuming that he hadn't moved the TVs far enough away, Hertell decided to conduct an experiment to find the optimal relocation site for them. The weather was now warm enough at night, so he set up a camping cot at a fixed distance from the TV shed and moved it every night over a period of days to see the effect of range on the voices. They seemed to be diminishing the further he got from the TV shed, at least until he got to the Western edge of the property under the big wooden cross where the sounds were swallowed by the grumbling of Highway 178 and the hiss of the high-power lines sagging overhead.

Since he was at the Western edge of the Li'l Pal, he decided he would continue his experiment at the same distance but over on the Eastern side of the property for the next few nights. He dragged his cot up Whisper Hill where there was a large flat slab of granite that would be radiating heat for most of the night. He had camped out on it with his Cub Scout troop many times when he was little, and they would scare themselves into the bottoms of their sleeping bags with stories of hook and chainsaw wielding madmen lurking at the edge of the light.

It was called Whisper Hill because there were some old capped oil wells in the dry wash that ran behind it, and when the wind was just right they would create the unmistakable sound of whispering. Whoever capped the old wells didn't do a good job since they weren't completely sealed and you could feel the air softly blowing out of them when a low-pressure front moved through. They weren't production wells, just some old test wells that his dad had drilled with some wildcatters back in the '50s to see if there was any oil on the property. But even though the Kern River oil fields were only a few miles away, there was no oil under Li'l Pal Heaven. His dad must have been very determined to find oil because the property was dotted with the old, poorly capped test wells, and all of them would whistle and wheeze under the right circumstances.

This night, there was no wind, and no sound except for an occasional motorcycle opening up as it cleared the mouth of Kern Canyon for the long straightaway south toward Bakersfield. He lay on the cot and listened for a while and looked up at the stars. It was the same cot that he had slept on during his father's last days. His father had started having night terrors, so Hertell would drag the cot into his father's room every night and listen to his dad's stories until he'd finally drift off into a murmuring sleep.

Kidney failure was giving his dad hallucinations, or it could have been the liver disease, or the dementia, or the meds that the hospice people brought for him. "There's people. Living out there under the big wooden cross. Living under the ground."

Hertell knew that very soon he wouldn't be able to engage his dad in any kind of conversation at all, and he decided he would cherish what remaining few they would have however sad and delusional they might be. So he'd lie on his cot with Yappy, an ancient buttermilk lab, and follow wherever his dad's conversation went. "A lot of people?"

"Hundreds of'm. Hundreds and hundreds of'm. Not exactly sure how many."

"What do they do down there all day?"

His dad answered brightly, "Oh, 'bout the same as up here, all kinda different stuff I guess."

"Why'd they want to go live under the big wooden cross?"

"Well they aren't under the big wooden cross exactly, but more in the general vicinity."

"Ok, that makes more sense." Hertell fluffed his pillow and looked up into the knotty pine ceiling.

"President Kennedy told'm to go down there, and then he went and got his head shot off, and then couldn't tell'm it was ok to come out again. So they been down there ever since."

"This whole time?"

"Yeah, living in these big lava tubes, whatever those are, but that's what they live in, and they got atomic power down there, toroid power, whatever the hell that is. And swimming pools, sun-lamps, and movies, and everything that people could ever want, except the sky and the ocean and dogs."

Hertell patted Yappy. "Yeah, I'd miss dogs. How'd you find out about'm."

"Young guy used to come out here, tell me about'm. I thought he was crazy, finally took out a restraining order on him, but then, maybe all the drugs they're giving me now or something, I've just become more ... open to possibilities... shit's only crazy until it actually happens you know, then it's not crazy anymore, it's just... how it is."

His dad fell silent as if calculating a number in his head.

"They're probly all dead by now. All those people President Kennedy sent down there. That's why they killed him you know—not the dead people but the other people, you know CIA and Forestry Service, and BLM and those kinds of people... Because of shitty fucking ideas that Kennedy had."

He coughed for a while and then continued, "Probly." He fell silent for a few minutes and then continued in a conspiratorial whisper that Hertell had to lean in closely to hear.

"And when I worked for the Government, for Kennedy, for Jack, 'cause I knew him from the Navy, did all kinda jobs for him after the war. I helped all the chin pullers make the atom bombs over in New Mexico, and I also saw the flying saucers and all the dead aliens over in Roswell."

"What'd they look like?"

"Well they were kinda burnt up a little bit from the crash and everything, so the one I saw looked kinda like a big piece of beef jerky, only with eyes and a mouth and stuff."

"What kind of jerky, regular jerky, like teriyaki or habanero, or more like a 'Slim Jim'?"

His dad's face clouded as he fixed his gaze on Hertell. He then began to slowly nod his head. "You know, actually, now that I think about it, he really was more like a 'slim Jim', only bigger, you know, an alien-sized Slim Jim, with the big round knobbly eyes like I was saying... at least I think it was a 'he', if it was a she then her titties musta come off in the crash or something, or she didn't ever even have'm 'cause she was an alien and everything, I mean aliens may not even have titties like we do..."

Hertell laughed and rubbed his eyes. "Yeah, good point."

"Hey did I tell you about the people who live on the bottom of the ocean?

38

Hertell rolled over on his side toward his father. "Yeah, I think you told me about'm yesterday, that they're called Oceanoids, and that they'll trade you gold for Styrofoam, because Styrofoam is the rarest thing on the bottom of the ocean, just like gold is the rarest thing up here."

"Yeah, yeah that's right, and me and mom and President Kennedy, and Jackie too sometimes, would smash up old Styrofoam ice chests and take'm to Morro Bay, actually more up toward Cayucos, and trade them Styrofoam for gold... which is why we have so much money and six thousand acres going all the way up to Mt Adelaide... and you never have to worry about anything, because... you'll be, you'll be taken care of by... President...Kennedy...and... Oceanoids... and... lava tubes... and..."

Hertell watched him drift off to sleep.

In many ways it was reminiscent of their New Year's Eve tradition when his dad would get drunk and tell stories that had similar elements: that the big wooden cross up on the hill overlooking the 178 was good insurance. "Just in case all this God shit is real." Hertell felt that if the God shit was real, and He really was Omni-Everything, He probably knew that Dad was gaming the system and that it wouldn't sit well with Him, unless He was a really good Sport about that kind of Thing. But when his dad was drunk, it wasn't worth exploring the issue. Once the blood-alcohol got to the appropriate level, he'd move on to the topic of Hertell's mother and start blubbering about how beautiful she was, and how much he hated her accordion, and how she drowned on the beach in Cayucos.

Then at midnight, when the rest of the world was singing "Auld Lang Syne" and kissing to the twelve chimes, his dad would be shooting his Luger into the air, shouting whatever came into his head. "Happy New Year..." "Close cover before striking..." "Hemorrhoid sufferers..." "May cause Drowsiness..." "But wait, there's more!"

On his last few nights, his father didn't tell any stories, he just related what Jesus was telling him from the swamp-cooler. "He says, don't worry." Then he would pause as if listening, and then start again evidently after he'd gotten another earful from Jesus. "Everybody is with Him, Mom, Kennedy, everybody and everybody makes mistakes, I'm not in trouble, 'cuz God doesn't sweat the little shit. Nobody is so lost that He can't find'm, even the people underground under the big wooden cross, He'll find'm and roll away the stone so they can all join Him in Heaven..."

But that was last September, and Hertell was alone now on his cot under the stars. Even Yappy had died in the months since and was buried near his dad, so Hertell looked at the moon and thought of Mister Frostie, and the ice cream truck, and the Rapture and Ascension that Mister Frostie would always talk about. And he stood by the big wooden cross and watched as all the little dogs and cats, and the flat, stiffened road-kills rose up out of the ground beneath his feet, and all of their owners following behind rising up into the night sky, and then the mastodons and the dinosaurs, and the amoebas and blue-green algae going all the way back to the beginning of time, only they weren't playing harps like you'd think, they were all playing accordions—all the classics, Lady of Spain,

Peg o'my Heart, Little Nash Rambler, Bali Hai, scales too, and he could hear every note even though they were all playing different songs, and he was cold...

The sun was still below the horizon when he woke up, but the sky to the east was already bright. It was cold, and he was damp but there was no mistaking what he was hearing, accordion music. It was faint and muffled, but it was unmistakable. He rose off his cot and scanned the horizon. Maybe somebody was stopped down on the 178 to take a leak and had the accordion channel on Sirius cranked up really loud. Only the sound wasn't coming from the highway to the west, it was coming from behind him, down in the wash below Whisper Hill.

He moved toward the edge of the large granite slab. He moved slowly and as quietly as he could so he wouldn't lose the sound. The wind was starting to pick up, as it always did with the rising sun, and the rush of the breeze momentarily masked the phantom sound. He looked down into the wash where the capped wells were barely discernible on the far side. He hadn't visited the capped wells since his Cub Scout days when he and the rest of the pack would gather around the wells to feel them breathe and hear them whisper, and occasionally pound on them with rocks because that's what boys do. The more cautious scouts would stay at a safe distance as they'd heard many stories about kids that had fallen into abandoned oil wells never to be seen again, and how the parents would just drop flowers down the well and then go off and have some more kids.

The wind died away for a moment, and he could hear the accordion again. He moved down the dry wash, but it was hard to negotiate in the shadows. He slid most of the way down and ended up below the wells and had to scuffle back up the sandy wash and up the opposite slope to reach them. He was winded and couldn't hear anything over the sound of his own breathing, and it took several minutes for his breathing and the sunrise breeze to die down.

The sun was above the horizon and he could see the capped wells clearly now. He kneeled down near the larger wellhead and listened carefully, but he couldn't tell if he was really hearing an accordion or if it was just the wind in his ears and his imagination. He pressed his ear to it. It was cold with a feathery patina of rust that was gritty to the touch. It wasn't breathing, and it wasn't whispering, but he could hear something. He pressed his ear closer and listened patiently as the sound emerged from the depths. He knew this sound. It was the sound of the machinery that ran the earth and all the people on it and all the rules they lived by.

Chapter Six

Wind Shift

Two deputies watched Hertell's nocturnal experiment for several nights from a dirt road on the north side of the river above the weir and the power substation. They had a clear view of Li'l Pal Heaven, and what they saw through their night-vision binoculars confirmed their suspicions.

Roy laughed and adjusted the focus. "What a dumbass." He was a benign but excitable man, and reminded his sons of Thomas the Tank Engine: a keg like body, a perfectly round face, a bright smile, and big bulging eyes like he was always in the middle of taking an epic crap.

Roy's comment was non-specific so Ruben felt no urgent need to respond; besides, he was trying to finish a text message.

Ruben resembled one of those Aztec princes in the velvet paintings found in low-end Mexican restaurants: defiant chin, Dick Tracy nose, hooded eyes, sloping forehead leading up to a plume of feathers on his head, carrying a nubile and unconscious, or at least swooning, virgin to be thrown into a Volcano or have her heart cut out or whatever it was that Aztec princes did with virgins.

"Must be a butt-load of chemicals in there stinking the place up if he's moving that far out to stay upwind of it. Gotta be a good five hundred yards from the house to where he was at the big cross last night, wouldn't you say? Gotta be at least a quarter mile."

Ruben continued texting. "You got a rangefinder in that thing, what does it say."

Roy took a gulp of his diet Coke. "The range finder only tells you how far you are from the thing you're looking at. It doesn't tell you how far things you're looking at are apart from each other." He thought for a moment. "Unless you're one of the, you know, things."

Ruben looked up from his cell phone. "Good point." looking toward the big wooden cross. "Yeah about five hundred yard."

"Ya know, if the smell is strong enough to drive him all the way out to the big cross, I'm surprised we can't smell it from the highway. You'd think we could smell it from here even, but I don't smell anything. Do you?"

Ruben returned to his text message. "Just the wild mustard. And the river."

Roy took a deep breath. "Yeah, smells good. Love the smell of the river. The willows." He returned to his binoculars.

"I think he's been cooking this whole time. At least as long as we've been out here watching him. Nothing's gone out. Probly not since he killed his Ice-cream truck guy anyway. This could be a big one if he's been stockpiling it all while he's trying to find a new ice cream truck guy."

He watched through the binoculars as Hertell loaded his cot onto an old Cushman cart and bounced to the distant edge of Li'l Pal. "Looks like he's setting up his cot over on the east tonight, wind musta shifted."

Ruben looked up from his text message, and reached out into the evening air. "There isn't any wind tonight."

Chapter Seven

The Velvet Fort

I t was a very disorienting time for Hertell. He spent several days down in the wash below Whisper Hill. He wasn't sure why since the accordion sounds had faded away in the light of day only to be replaced by the random whispering for which the hill was so named. He sat quietly at the capped wellheads for most of the morning until they were in the full sun, as if the day could somehow explain the night.

He inspected them closely, something he hadn't done since his Cub Scout days, and he noticed several subtleties he must have missed when banging them with rocks as a youth. For one thing, there was no relief valve or pressure gauge, not surprising since it was never a production well. The casing of the adjoining wellhead didn't seem to be ferrous, but instead some kind of aluminum alloy since it had a white powdery oxidation and not the traditional red rust.

They were also of differing diameter and height, the powder grey aluminum wellhead was narrower and extended several feet above the squat, rusty steel one, and their arrangement reminded him of the prairie dog towns he'd seen on the Discovery Channel. He also found a large collection of cigarette butts that littered the ground around the wellheads. Just the filters remained, bleached and weathered, since the tobacco and paper were organic and probably long since gone to compost.

He remembered how Mister Frostie, after burying an assortment of road-kills with Hertell, would often spend hours ranging over the hills praying aloud, smoking cigarettes, and singing hymns in his deep, Latigo voice ...

Just a closer walk with Thee,
Grant it, Jesus, is my plea...

Out past the quarry.

Precious Lord, take my hand,
Lead me on, let me stand...

Out past the Lost and Found...

Made like Him, like Him we rise, Alleluia!
Ours the cross, the grave, the skies, Alleluia!

And far into the dry hills east of the Li'l Pal where his voice and his singing would fade to a murmur indistinguishable from the wind and the highway and the Mourning Dove.

Partly out of curiosity but mostly out of instinct, Hertell decided to visit all of the old capped test wells his dad had drilled with the wildcatters back in the '50s. From the old rugged cross, to Whisper Hill, to Everlasting Slumber, to Snuggle Bottom, to Lost and Found, he wandered the Brownian length and breadth of Li'l Pal, and at each station, he found that the well heads had the same Prairie Dog Town configuration he'd found in the wash below Whisper Hill. He also found Mister Frostie's cigarette butts. Perhaps Mister Frostie had heard something too.

By the end of the day, Hertell had returned to the wellheads at Whisper Hill, tired and sweaty from the hours traversing the hills and gullies. He sat in the dirt and felt his breathing slowly dampen, and his sweat begin to cool. He leaned back and looked up into the sky and tried to remember when Mister Frostie had first appeared at Li'l Pal.

It was probably late Pleistocene since he clearly remembered Mister Frostie bringing in mastodons and how it took him nearly all day with the D-6 to dig a pit big enough to bury the massive roadkill... He stopped himself and sat up.

He sat there frozen, motionless for a long time, scarcely even breathing, and slowly surrendered to a confused acceptance. It was now official, he was descending into the same vortex that consumed his dad in his last days, only this time it was accordions, and voices, and the machinery that ran the earth, and not the reassuring whispers of Jesus.

Hertell decided he would ignore it. He would not yield to it as his father had, so he kept busy cleaning the house every day and doing various projects, such as organizing the garage now that the TVs were gone. He found his mother's accordion while so engaged.

It had started out innocently enough. He was sitting on a box shared with a collection of paint cans, looking through some old high school yearbooks, at the hope-filled, shining, happy faces peeking out from behind the attitude and the bangs and the facial hair of the time. He didn't recognize anyone, even himself. In fact, he had to look himself up, and spent a long time staring at his own face, as if at a long-lost relative from the old country, searching for the recognizable jaw line, or squint, or cupid's bow, and wondering what the person was like. He resumed flipping the pages but then stopped. He recognized someone.

She was cute and freshly scrubbed and looking back over her shoulder and upward toward the future, and he realized that he had once been married to this beautiful girl. The name below her photo was Kaye Kerf. "That's right," he thought, "That's right... she used to love me, very much, back then." And her picture was signed in the buoyant hand of a young woman and the words "total love" with little hearts and exclamation points. For an instant he could actually smell her again, but then something shifted and she was gone. Replaced by the dust of the garage and the flinty smell of the old paint cans. He thought for a moment and then came to a decision. He took out his Swiss army knife and carefully cut Kaye's picture from the page, but at the last snip, her picture fluttered to the ground, repeatedly eluding his grasp.

It was while kneeling on the ground, blowing the dust off of Kaye's picture that he noticed what he'd been sitting on. It was a big square suitcase type affair from back when suitcases were hard and rectangular and had spring-loaded latches with locks and were built for fathers and porters to carry, in the days before overhead storage bins and rolling luggage and Velcro. Only this wasn't a suitcase.

It was his mother's accordion case that he'd spent many happy hours inside when he was quite young. She would practice her scales, never songs, just scales, and as the metronome ticked away the happy hours, he would crawl into the empty case with some toy dinosaurs and soldiers and close the lid on himself to make a little fort, and breathe in the mysterious black velvet smell in the subconscious hope that if he smelled like an accordion, perhaps she would hold him as much as she held it.

Hertell moved the paint cans and drop cloth off of his mother's accordion and opened the case. Yes, it was his mother's Sonola accordion alright. He wondered if he would recognize her as easily as he recognized her accordion, or if he'd even recognize her at all. There were no photographs of her around the house, his dad had taken care of that, so all he had to go on was his memory of her through a nine year old's eyes, but the memory was malleable and constantly alloyed with images of other mothers, mainly from TV shows and commercials, so over time she became an intoxicating punch of paper towel moms, rock band moms and his real, accordion mom and he was never really sure where she stopped and the other mothers began.

He lifted the accordion from its velvet well, rested it on his thigh and tried to put it on, but couldn't get the shoulder straps much past his elbows. He adjusted the straps and attempted to ease his shoulders under its slender, padded arms, and after a few tries finally stood in the sunshine, yoked to his mother's accordion. He decided he would try to play one of the scales he'd seen her practice so many times. He picked one of the white keys toward the top, and much to his surprise and delight, effortlessly played a scale, though he didn't know which one it was. "Now that's interesting."

He tried it again, starting with one of the black keys and achieved the same result; his fingers seemed to know where they needed to go.

He continued playing scales for much of the afternoon, starting with a different black and white key each time, and with each scale he tried to remember his mother's face, which was kind of odd since he remembered the trilobites and their clicking sound and rubbery smell, but he simply couldn't recall his own mother's face.

He marveled at how easy it was for him to play scales, and wondered why it had been so difficult for his mother, and why she had required so much practice. He pondered several explanations: perhaps he'd observed her more carefully than he'd thought and subliminally absorbed the musical ability at a particularly receptive stage in his development; or perhaps he'd learned the accordion at some point in his life as a way of confronting his abandonment issues but then forgot about it because he'd been shot in the head; or perhaps the copper slivers had connected the fine motor functions of his cerebellum to some kind of primitive accordion player brain which lay hidden amongst the trilobite and alligator and dinosaur and all the other brains he knew to be resident in his head, and everybody else's head for that matter; or perhaps it was a combination of all of the above.

In any case, he quickly progressed to picking out tunes and haltingly singing along...

"This old man... he played one...he played... Knick knack... on my thumb..." because now he had a plan.

He'd recently, as part of his campaign to resist the vortex that had consumed his dad, begun whistling and talking and singing aloud more of the time. It was a very effective way to drown out the accordions and voices and machinery that ran the earth, at least during his waking hours. Now, armed with the accordion, he would fight fire with fire. He would drown out the phantom accordion sounds he'd been hearing with those of his own making—all the classics, "Twinkle Twinkle Little Star", "Lady of Spain", "Peg o'my Heart", "Bali Hai".

After a few days, he mastered the left hand, his fingers traversing the ranks and rows of buttons to find the right ones to complement whatever tune he was attempting and by the end of the week he was giving heartfelt concerts to all the little dead pets buried in the dry hillsides of the Li'l Pal.

"And now for your listening pleasure, 'Somewhere Over The Rainbow'." Hertell stood between the D-6 and Mister Frostie's Ice Cream truck and played a few more tunes, and he'd just finished playing a passionate version of "What a Wonderful World" when he heard someone clapping.

Chapter Eight

The Funeral Piper

"Hi, my name's Doug, and I'm the bagpiper that played up here a few months ago?"

The clapping surprised Hertell and he turned around, fully expecting to see his long-lost mother, but instead he saw a man wearing a tool belt. The man was of middling age and middling height and middling weight and completely average and forgettable except for his eyes. They reminded Hertell of Yappy.

The man continued. "The bagpipes for the dog funeral with all the deputies, and I was up on the top of a hill."

He paused for a moment to let Hertell respond. Sensing Hertell's embarrassment at being caught mid-concert, Doug gave him some cover by pointing into the distance; "I noticed a really interesting geological formation on that hill over there when I was playing here."

Hertell followed his gaze over toward Whisper Hill.

"And I was wondering if I could go give it another look, take some pictures." He tapped on the geologist pick hanging from his belt. "And maybe chip out a sample, if that's ok with you?"

He seemed like a very nice man. "Sure. Yeah that'd be fine. You a geologist?"

"Yeah, well, used to be. I'm a psychologist now." He fished a card out of his pocket and handed it to Hertell. "You play the accordion pretty good. Been playing long?"

Hertell eased himself out of his mother's accordion. "Nah, just about an hour or so."

"No, I meant in general, not just today."

"Oh. I dunno, maybe a week or a little less, I just found it a few days ago and started messing around with it. It was my mom's. She didn't play it really, mostly just scales, I think it was mainly just something to keep between her and dad." He laughed, and then laughed again at the realization that his joke was probably the better part of the truth.

Doug smiled, not sure how to respond. "Yeah, well... you play pretty good after just a week, you must be a natural."

"Yeah, kinda surprised me too."

Hertell accompanied the man on his excursion, chattering happily the whole way.

"So anyway, they're called Oceanoids, they live on the bottom of the ocean, hence the name, and they'll trade you gold for Styrofoam, because Styrofoam is the rarest thing on the bottom of the ocean, just like gold is up here."

Doug took out his camera as they walked. "Makes sense when you think about it."

"Yeah, and President Kennedy was involved, but I forget exactly how. It's funny what people talk about when they're dying. Space alien titties, lava tubes all kinds of stuff..."

He watched as Doug stopped and took photos of the surrounding hills.

They reached the top of Whisper Hill and were standing on the big slab where Hertell had slept so many nights as a cub scout and where he'd first heard the accordion. He watched as Doug took out his GPS, captured the coordinates of the interesting formation beneath their feet, and then knelt down to examine the slab.

Hertell moved a few feet so that his body could shade Doug from the afternoon sun. "Yeah this is called Whisper Hill because of the old well heads that..."

Hertell stiffened and fell silent. He'd been successful so far in keeping the vortex at bay, but he could now faintly hear the accordion starting to penetrate his story and his thoughts. He would fight it.

"There was a guy on the radio one night talking about parallel universes, and there's a lot of them, an infinite number of them in fact, and he said one of'm is where all the old TV shows are, in a parallel universe. Only in that one, all the TV shows are real, and we're all pretend..."

"Now, that's interesting." Doug was kneeling and examining one of the flakes with his hand lens. "This formation isn't granite, it's not even rock." He looked at another chip with his hand lens. "It's actually concrete with little flakes of iron mixed in, so it... looks like Granite. Like the way they'd camouflage some of the old World War Two coastal artillery bunkers around Goleta, but they were just painted to look like rock; this is actually mixed into the cement. Was this place ever an Army base or anything?"

Hertell grew more agitated as he urgently told the history of the area hoping to keep the vortex at bay. "Well, it all used to be on the bottom of the ocean for a long time."

Doug nodded in agreement. "Yeah, several times in the Jurassic and then again in the..."

"Yes, I remember the Jurassic distinctly." Hertell took a few steps and gestured to the north. "These mountains weren't here yet, and it was all swamp to the south, and there weren't any wild flowers back then, no poppies and no wild mustard or fiddle neck because they hadn't evolved yet, and not any grasses either, only tree ferns and sago palms and sauropods. And this area where we're standing was on the western migratory path of the pterosaurs and the sky would just be black with them in September and again in April, only they weren't called September and April back then because we didn't have names for time yet either. But I don't think there was ever an army base here."

Doug laughed, and then realized that Hertell was serious. He looked at Hertell for a moment, searching his eyes for the telltale signs of a man gone off the rails.

Hertell watched as the expression on Doug's face changed at his memory of the Jurassic, and then, as if to explain: "I got shot in the head once. And it makes it so I remember things, and play the accordion too I think."

Doug's face softened. "That's too bad. How'd that happen?"

"Well, I just found the accordion under some old paint cans and then took it out and..."

"No, I mean, how did you get shot in the head?"

Hertell took off his hat and showed the top of his head. "New Year's Eve gun shooting in the air I'm pretty sure. At least I think that's what it was. Mighta been 4th of July though, or maybe Vietnam. You mix things up sometimes after you get shot in the head.

"Yeah, I'll bet. You're way too young for Viet Nam, though you might be the right age for Iraq or Afghanistan since those went on for so long, but you're probably right about New Year's or 4th of July." Doug examined the top of Hertell's head. "You ok now?"

"Yeah." Hertell put his hat back on, "They got most of it out, but there's still some little specks of copper in there, floating around, connecting things that aren't connected in the rest of you anymore." He watched as Doug knelt down to resume his examination of the curious chips. "They make it so I remember all kinds of things that everybody has forgotten 'cause you all got disconnected when that big comet went by and reversed the Earth's magnetic poles."

Doug nodded in agreement and squinted through his hand lens at another flake. "I didn't know about the comet, but yeah the poles have reversed a lot of times in the last four billion years, every million years or so, give or take. It's a fairly common thing, no big deal really."

"Yeah, but people weren't here that whole time, it's only happened once since we've been here. And you figure a couple million years of human evolution, and then the poles switch? It's like going from DC to AC, only we're not wired for it."

Doug lowered his hand lens as if considering Hertell's assertion.

"We forgot things, forgot who we were, forgot how everything is connected, how it's all one big... thing."

59

Doug tilted his head in contemplation.

"And that comet's coming back too, and it's gonna flip the poles again, and we're gonna forget everything we've learned since the last time."

Hertell could see and sense that the geologist was clearly troubled. "We're gonna be a bunch of cavemen again, only in three piece suits this time, holding cell phones we won't know how to use, or even what they're for."

"Hold on for a second." Doug looked up at Hertell and raised his hand as if calling for quiet. "What is that sound? I hear... Is that... uhh... is that... an accordion?"

Hertell felt tears of relief welling up beneath his eyes as an overpowering feeling of redemption and resurrection lifted words to his lips. And for the rest of his life he would never understand why he answered the way he did.

"I... don't hear anything."

Chapter Nine

The Great Warm Slab

For several days Hertell crisscrossed Li'l Pal in the Cat D-6, clawing away at the bases of the capped test wellheads that dotted the property. He noticed that all of them were in narrow, protected washes with the taller cap always peeking just barely above the crest.

At each site, the first few feet of overburden were quickly removed by the D-6, but at about 6 feet the casings began to angle inward toward the centroid of the hill itself so that the deeper he dug the more difficult it became. He initially presumed that it was just the clumsiness and haste of the wildcatters his dad had hired back in the '50s and their primitive drilling techniques. It was only after two days of repeatedly excavating and giving up as the casings retreated deeper into the hillside that he noticed the consistency of their presumably random tilt. They all seemed to be angling toward Whisper Hill, which he decided should become the focus of his exploration.

It was a simple, straightforward proposition. He decided to find the edges of the great warm slab on Whisper Hill. The D-6 started right up and Hertell maneuvered it up to Whisper Hill while carefully negotiating his way through Lost and Found. He made good progress scraping away yards of earth with each pass, and each pass took him deeper and deeper into the hill. By dusk he'd excavated most of the lower portion of Whisper Hill, creating an immense pit, and he still hadn't unearthed the edge.

Finally, just at sunset he hit something, something apparently immovable. He backed up a few lengths and made another run with a little more inertia, but just as he reached the slab the D-6 hesitated and then went silent after a brief death rattle. "Well fuck me dead," he said out loud. Though he rarely used such language, Hertell had often heard the expression used by Mister Frostie while chipping through Caliche, and while it was uncharacteristic of Hertell, he was kind of pleased that the words had come to him, as if a small testament and memorial to Mister Frostie.

He climbed down from the silent machine to investigate the new obstacle and scuffled down to the slab over the freshly disturbed earth he'd created. It was a difficult descent as he was hungry and dehydrated from a full day of digging and the slab was gritty and slippery with the residue from the overburden he'd scraped away. He lost his feet on the way and slid all the way down to the fresh pit and twisted his ankle on the uneven bottom. The sky was now a beautiful pink due to some high clouds to the west. He limped over to where he'd found the buried obstacle and started digging with his square-blade shovel.

After a few minutes of shoveling he hit something that made a metallic clang. He presumed it was some long abandoned and forgotten oilfield equipment left by his dad and the wildcatters. He began scraping the dirt away in the fading light and saw that the mysterious metal object was beginning to take on a shape. It appeared to be some kind of pipe or possibly a rail, but it was well past sunset now, and he was starting to get a headache.

He had just turned to head back to the house for a shower and some aspirin, when he smelled it. There was a slight breeze from the west and he knew this smell. It was the smell of happiness and promise and youth. It was his wife.

It was dark now and he could see her silhouette shimmering in the distant headlights. He ran toward her in the dark as fast as his limp would allow, but his pace slowed as he approached the light until he'd slowed to an almost imperceptible crawl—as if a dream that would dissipate should his movement disturb the air. He finally stopped in the darkness and watched her in silence.

She called his name. Her voice was different now, not like before, it was a harder voice, and sadder somehow. He didn't remember exactly, but he knew that, somehow, he had contributed to that hardness and the sadness at its core.

Chapter Ten

Code Seven

The deputy knocked on the door. She waited the traditional three-count and then knocked again with the butt-end of her flashlight. She checked her watch, and then, on a hunch, tried the doorknob. It was unlocked and the door swung open. She shook her head and took out her cell phone. "Typical." The house was dark, so she walked back toward the patrol car while keying in a number and then waited, and was rewarded with the piercing 3-tone the-number-you've-dialed-is-no-longer-inservice-please-check-the-number-and-try-again haiku.

She checked out the garage, where the old Chevy Stepside was parked, and then walked the perimeter of the house, shining her flashlight into the windows. They were sparkling clean, as was the rest of the house which she discovered upon inspection of its interior. The fridge was clean and well stocked, the kitchen spotless, the furniture in good repair, the magazines recent, the bedrooms tidy, sewing room idle but well organized. Though nowhere to be found, the occupant had obviously been taking care of himself and the property.

There was even a Lava Lamp gently roiling in the living room next to the big-screen TV.

She returned to her patrol car and checked with dispatch on the '74 Chevy registration and confirmed that there were no additional vehicles for this address. It was during this conversation that she felt someone watching her. She completed her radio call and then stood, looking out into the darkness. She cupped her hands over her mouth. "Hertell?"

She moved into the darkness, sweeping her flashlight in an arc as she went. "Hertell?" She stopped and listened for an answer—nothing, just the wind and the faint hiss of the highway. He might be hurt, she thought, he could be out there with a broken leg, dying of exposure, turning into ant food. She followed the main path toward the cemetery, calling for Hertell as she went. She finally stopped by the big pyramid and stood in silence next to it. She knew this place, the pyramid and the kind man beneath it. She turned her flashlight to some of the adjoining graves, and moved down the row, sensing the unconditional but long-forgotten love that was buried mere inches beneath her feet.

She was close. Hertell could almost reach out and touch her. She was angular, as she was when they'd first met, with short copper colored hair, and eyes that always reminded him of Junior Mints. She had a square jaw and a broken nose that was softened by her Shirley Temple dimples; nevertheless, she would never be a Disney Princess. She was short-waisted and walked with a confident stride, and there was something about the turn of her legs and the tilt of her pelvis that always appealed to Hertell, and though every strand of his being wanted to cry out. "I miss you, and I'm sorry for whatever it was I did!" all he managed to say was, "I'm right here Kaye, you don't have to yell."

Kaye was obviously well trained since a flashlight and pistol were aimed at Hertell before he'd even finished his sentence.

She took a deep cleansing breath to let the adrenaline fade, and then holstered her pistol. "That's a good way to get shot Hertell."

Hertell held up his hand to shade his eyes from the flashlight. "Oh. Why, you working tonight?"

She looked at the man squinting in the beam. He was dusty and weathered, but still handsome, as he'd always been. "No, well, actually yeah. Technically I'm at lunch."

"Code seven huh?"

"Yeah." Her voice momentarily softened, "Code seven." She could sense the presence of the boy she had once loved. But she quickly recovered and lowered her flashlight a few degrees. "Why didn't you answer? When I was calling out here?"

Hertell thought for a moment as he stared down at the flashlight beam at his feet. "I ... wasn't sure if you were real."

"I'm real Hertell." She swept her flashlight over the cemetery. "This's all real."

"Then I didn't want to scare you away."

She turned off her flashlight. "Well that was very considerate of you, but as a rule you should answer when somebody's calling out to you."

The moon was finally peering over Mt. Adelaide, and Hertell could now see Kaye in the moonlight. "Especially when it's dark, and they have a gun?"

Hertell heard a sound, it wasn't hard anymore, and it wasn't sad. It was a sound he remembered. It was Kaye's laugh. "Yeah," she said, "especially when it's dark and they have a gun."

He breathed in her sweet laughter. "You want some mac'n cheese? I was just gonna make some back at the house." She paused, then turned and started walking back toward the house remembering why she'd once loved him so much. "Nah, I gotta get back."

He followed her at a trot until he caught up with her. She noticed his gait. "Why are you limping?"

Hertell tried to even his pace. "Fell in a hole. Kind of an occupational hazard in a cemetery."

Kaye continued walking and smiled to herself. She stopped suddenly. "Where's Yappy?"

"Dead." He stood watching Kaye who said nothing. "Buried him right next to dad out there at the pyramid."

"When'd he die?"

"Right after Dad. Yappy, just kind of... well you know how dogs are, very emotional, they take these things personally. He used to sit outside Dad's bedroom. I mean, the room is still full of the man, only he's not there, to be seen, anymore. Dog has one of the most precisely logical minds to be found in nature. Death doesn't make any sense to a dog, he has no appreciation of it. Like we do. He doesn't know it's coming for him too. If he did, he'd just say, 'what is this shit, who's in charge here, what's the point?"

"So you're alone out here now?"

"I guess. In the traditional sense."

Kaye resumed walking. "You know your phone's been disconnected."

Hertell followed. "Yeah, been getting too many robo-calls from old movie stars telling me who to vote for and stuff." He was just about to tell her about the call he got from Johnny Depp when he was struck by a thought. "Unless you've been trying to call me. 'Cause I can have the phone hooked up again if you've been trying to..."

Sensing where it was going, Kaye redirected, "Did a guy come out here and talk to you?"

Hertell walked in thought for a moment. "What kind of guy?"

"I don't know, just a guy. Any guys been out here to talk to you?"

"Talk to me about what?"

"I don't know. Whatever they're out here to talk to you about I guess. Anybody been out here to talk to you?"

They reached the house and stood for a moment near the back door. Hertell could see her clearly now in the soft orange glow of the bug-lite above the back door. He studied her face. He could see each individual eyelash as she blinked at him.

"Not since Mister Frostie. But he's dead now. Well no, yes. There have been a coupla guys out here, not counting people here for funerals and stuff. There was a psychologist that wanted to look at some rocks, and propane Ray from CalGas, he's getting married, and Bobby from FarmFuel to fill up the skid tank, only he's getting divorced." Hertell stopped. "No, that was before Dad died. And then there was a guy who wanted to buy the property to put up a Casino..."

"Yeah, that's the guy, what'd he say?" The hardness and sadness had returned to her voice.

"He said that this was Indian land 'cause there were some dead Indian fossils out here and they want to build a Casino for all the people on the way up to Lake Isabella, so I gotta sell it to him or they'll just take it 'cause they're Indians and we owe it to'm."

"He said that?"

"He used a lot more words at the time, but that's pretty much all he said."

"Did he give you a number?"

Hertell saw his opening. "Well, I think he left a card... it's in the house, you wanna look?" He pushed open the kitchen door and then politely stepped aside to let her go first. "We can look for the card while the mac'n cheese is cooking. For your lunch, for code 7."

Time stood still as Hertell imagined the familiar rapture of being in the kitchen and chatting with his wife as dinner cooked on the stove. Time resumed abruptly.

"No, not a phone number, a dollar number. How much did he offer for the estate?" There was a new sound in her voice that Hertell didn't recognize.

"What do you mean, 'estate'?"

Kaye folded her arms and tilted her head slightly. "This 'estate' is one third mine Hertell. Your dad left it to me too."

Hertell fell silent for a moment. "He did?"

"Yes, he did."

Hertell finally looked up at her. "You knew my dad?"

For all her hardness and control, this was the thin blade that could always slip between the plates of her armor. Her throat began to ache. She'd covered this ground with him before. "Yes, I knew your dad."

In fact, she knew the father before she knew the son. Hertell Senior had officiated at the funeral of her beloved cat Pudna when she was in 5th grade. Her own father was unmoved by the death of the cat and was unwilling to dig a grave for it in their dirt backyard, and suggested she throw the dead cat into the Beardsley canal—a short walk and determined heave from their rented home on Monache Drive. Her brothers were very excited about the prospect.

Indignant and determined, she rode her Huffy bicycle the sixteen miles from Oildale to Li'l Pal and the old Rugged Cross where she'd watched the sunrise every Easter morning of her life. She arrived with a stiffened cat in a lettuce crate, borderline heat exhaustion, and penniless. Hertell Senior gave her a wet towel for her head, a big glass of lemonade, and then had her lay down on the floor and rest while he prepared the burial site. She lay on the cool tiles of his kitchen floor and looked up at the knotty pine paneling and the faces and animals and landscapes hidden in the grain, unaware that many years in the future she too would disappear into its swirls.

He gave the cat a beautiful service and even managed to get Kaye to laugh through her grief. He gave her a ride home to Oildale with her Huffy in the back of his pickup truck and asked her about her school and her mom and dad and what she wanted to do when she grew up. She forgot what she answered, but remembered what he said: "Tell you what kiddo, anybody stubborn enough to ride 16 miles on a one-speed coaster bike under a September sun in Bakersfield can do pretty much any damn thing they decide to do." Anything but remain married to Hertell junior, as history would eventually show.

She didn't meet young Hertell that day. They met a few years later at North High. She mere trailer trash with a latent Okie accent having difficulty in math, and he the math tutor, the smartest boy in the school, smarter than even some of the teachers, shy but destined for greatness. Though too young to formally date, they nevertheless became inseparable spending many happy hours together ranging over Bakersfield and Oildale and the verdant hills of Li'l Pal Heaven. They savored and celebrated the origins and progression of their relationship, and determined that they could have met years earlier at Pudna's funeral had not Hertell been out with his mother that day, buying back-to-school clothes—it was also the last day he would ever see his mother. And in the years that followed, Hertell would marvel at how the routine can become the pivotal with the slam of a car door.

Hertell looked away for a moment, searching. "Were you at his funeral?"

She took a deep breath and started slowly and evenly at first. "Yes, I was at his funeral. I gave the eulogy. I talked to all those people, his Shriner friends, and the ancient Elks and the Rotarians. I was here all last September."

Kaye in fact spent every night praying over him in his final and fearful last days. She and Yappy would sleep on a cot and would whisper reassurances to Hertell Senior when he'd wake with night terrors, telling him about Jesus, and how he was not alone, and not lost, and how God would find him, and how God didn't sweat the little shit.

"Last September, remember?" And even if Hertell didn't, she did, and her pool of patient sadness and grief began to slowly rise to the surface. "I helped you take care of him, remember?"

She in fact was holding Hertell Senior's hand, as he died that September morning. His hand was cool and waxy and weakly gripping hers. She was with him as he took his last, random, ragged breaths, and it was while gazing into his scared, rheumy eyes that she felt and saw his soul falling away. There were a few fluttering blinks of panic that ultimately surrendered to a steady gaze that she could never quite identify. The old man gave her hand one final squeeze, as if to say, "Gotta go, see ya" and then he was gone. She felt Yappy's chin resting on her knee. All in all it was a good way to leave this life she thought. Hertell Junior couldn't bring himself to look and sat in a chair in the corner of the room staring into the knotty pine ceiling.

Her tears were in full flower and her voice was now cracking. Kaye, wiped her nose and cleared her throat. "I helped you take care of him because he was my dad too! For twenty fucking years he was my dad too!"

The turn of events would not permit Hertell to share his mac'n cheese with Kaye that evening.

Chapter Eleven

The Ant Farm

It was a long night for Hertell. He couldn't bring himself to eat his last box of Mac'n cheese, so he just ate some frozen corn while watching the Weather Channel and dozed off in the big Lazy Boy his father had inhabited up until his last September on earth. He lamented the big gaps in his memory and was tortured by the knowledge that they caused Kaye so much sadness—she was sobbing and apologizing as she left.

They weren't gaps so much as they were black holes, because they couldn't be filled. The face and voice and smells and thoughts went in, but the gravity of her memory was so strong that they couldn't escape, and he could never bring them back to hold and cherish. And every time he went in search of her, he'd be consumed by the black hole only to find himself not with Kaye's memories but somewhere else entirely—with the Mastodons, or the Egyptians, or the Trilobites.

So as the TV murmured about Hurricanes, Hertell concentrated on Kaye's face and her voice, to keep it from disappearing into the black hole. If he could just keep her face or her voice in his thoughts, he could use it as a lifeline into the black hole and never lose her again. But her face was fading: first into the faces of the hospice people who had come to help his dad, and then into the faces of the people on TV, and finally into the grain of the knotty pine above the TV, just like his father's soul had done the night he died, and her voice faded into the rumble and hiss of the swamp cooler. She was gone again.

A loud commercial woke him up; he was confused at first, but then realized where he was and that it was late, since the ad on TV was for the "Ab-Scrambler." He blankly watched the rest of the ad, and the shimmering young athletes who were all seemingly exhilarated by the use of the device. It was followed by another ad, but Hertell's thoughts had sufficiently cleared that he could ignore it. He tried to think of Kaye as he sketched a diagram of Whisper Hill and the slab and the pit and the rail on an old engineering pad that his dad used as a coaster. The pages were warped and crinkly, but good enough for Hertell's purposes though he eventually dosed off after his last random note. "Costco—mac and cheese, Advil... Sonola, ab scrambler..."

He slept in and didn't return to Whisper Hill until almost noon. The 550-gallon skid tank that his dad had purchased back when the quarry was established was still about half-full from its last filling, so Hertell topped an old Jerry can, and struggled to carry it out to the dry D-6 at the foot of Whisper Hill. His ankle was still sore from his graceless slide to bottom of the pit the day before, so he would stop every hundred feet or so to flex his ankle and give his hand a rest. He emptied the Jerry can into the D-6 and then drove it back to the quarry for a top-off at the skid tank, which only had a hand pump, so it took until almost mid-afternoon to get it filled.

All of his recent practice on the D-6 had given Hertell a mastery which he now used to gently clear the dirt from not just the one pipe he found the night before, but from three more parallel pipes for a total of four pipes extending below the lowest edge of the slab. The Cat also allowed him to easily expose the top edge of the slab, just below the summit of Whisper Hill and also the edges on either side down to a depth of about three feet where he hit what appeared to be identical abandoned culverts. Satisfied with his progress, he shut the machine down and spent the remainder of the afternoon in the pit with the square-blade shovel painstakingly and carefully removing the dirt from the freshly discovered pipes as if at an archeological dig.

His excavations eventually revealed that it wasn't so much a slab as it was a massive wedge, which came to a crude almost plow-like edge just above the now exposed pipes which he presumed to be some kind of oil field pipe manifold which was curious since there was never an actual production oilfield on the property, just the taunting test wells of his dad and the wildcatters.

He began clearing earth from beneath the plow-like wedge and braced himself against one of the now exposed pipes for leverage. The presence of the culverts was confusing too since you don't need culverts for drainage at the top of a hill and he thought through the possible explanatory scenarios as he dug, and it was while digging that he felt something odd. He felt it in his leg first, the leg that was braced against the exhumed pipe. It felt almost like it was ticking, only it wasn't.

He stopped digging for a moment and put his hand on the pipe. It was still warm from being in the sun for most of the day, but other than that, nothing. He scissored over the pipe to get to one of the parallel pipes and felt that one as well. Nothing unusual, just the fading warmth of the sun, which had disappeared behind a layer of high cirrus that had moved in from the north. It might peek out again just before it set, but it would be a starless night.

For some reason he began to feel uncomfortable in the pit, so he climbed out and hiked back to the top of Whisper Hill and the D-6 where he'd left his water and snack. He sat on the freshly exposed top edge of the slab to survey his handiwork and sipped from his old Cub Scout canteen and chewed his tortilla and cheese as he watched an ant struggle with a small piece of cheese he'd put down for it. He wondered if it was a descendant of one of his own personal special ants.

It was the last Christmas before his mother left, and he'd gotten an Ant Farm, a bunch of other stuff too, but he mainly remembered the Ant Farm. He immediately sent away for the special, ant-farm-ants. He lovingly tended and nurtured his ants. He even gave them names, even though they were of such uniform character that he couldn't really tell one from the other; he would nevertheless, amaze his Cub Scout friends and identify them by name. "That's Larry with the bent antenna, and that's Curley the fat one, and that's Moe who always bites the other ones..." The ant farm was bright green with snow-white sand and the ant-farm-ants were happy and thriving, and then one day they were gone. Escaped while he was at school.

He spent many afternoons after school out in the Li'l Pal searching for his lost ants, and, at the time, was quite tortured by the thought of his precious, innocent, and overprotected ant- farm-ants wandering, lost in the cruel wilderness. Strangers in a strange land with no green plastic windmills and no snow-white sand, but only sky and sun and hard cracked dirt, at the mercy of the elements and the native fire ants and black ants that ruled the night, and totally unprepared for life in the real world.

It was while watching the ant that Hertell realized that he hadn't heard the accordion for a long time. Not since he'd begun excavating the slab. He then felt a slight tremor and then everything went black.

Chapter Twelve

Busy Bee

"**B**oy he's been keepin' busy."

Ruben clipped his nails as Roy scrolled through downloaded images collected by some game cameras they'd positioned at the mouth of Kern Canyon on a hilltop above Li'l Pal Heaven. It was a perfect spot with an excellent field of view over the meth lab complex.

They'd mounted the cameras some weeks before on a power line pylon that was accessible from an old forestry service road. The road continued up the hill for a few hundred feet before melting into a firebreak that finally petered out some miles away near the peak of Mt. Adelaide. Roy was familiar with the road and told Ruben the story of the time he once fought a grass fire on it back when he spent his summers as a seasonal fireman. A pre-dawn drunk had crashed his camper right into the canyon wall at the first curve and started the fire, which quickly spread up and east and over the canyon to the dry chaparral and grassland beyond.

"So me and Johnny Ray, who's a jet mechanic up at Lemoore now married to a high school principal, and uh...

I forget the other guy's name, but he was a fat stump-kicker from Earlimart I think, and I don't know what ever happened to him, let's call him Numbnuts. So we park the jeep down on the 178 at the mouth of the canyon, and the fire looks like this big white hot glowing horse shoe, and its growing up over the top of the canyon, and we want to get out ahead of it to set a firebreak. So we grab our shovels and Pulaski's and canteens, and this is before Camelbacks, this's with the old tin and canvas canteens, so we looked like a buncha prospectors, only without whiskers and burros, and we just start climbing up the hill in the dark. And so we're climbing and climbing and sliding back and climbing again and saying 'fuck' like some kinda machine gun, and we finally get to the top, and what do we find? A road. And so Numbnuts says, all kind of indignant, and like he was ready to start crying..."

"There... was... a... ROAD!"...

Roy looked up at Ruben who was still clipping his nails. "Yeah, how'd you know?"

"You already told me this story."

"I did?"

"Yeah, you told me on the way up there to set the cameras, 'cause that's how you knew the road was there, and again when we went up there to get the cameras, and you threw in what the fire looked like, and you're telling me again right now."

Roy fell silent for a moment and stared at the screen. He then took a deep cleansing breath as if satisfied. "Good story though idn'it?"

Ruben couldn't help but laugh, he'd grown to love Roy's delivery. "Yeah it actually is a pretty good story. And you change it up a little bit each time, like you called the fat guy 'Fucknose' the last time, which I greatly prefer."

Roy considered Ruben's critique. "Yeah, you're probly right, 'Fucknose' is better. It's got a certain... flair. And actually, his nose did look kinda like a weenie."

They silently resumed scanning through the images, and Hertell had indeed been busy. The images were kind of comical when viewed in time-lapse mode with the D-6 cat darting back and forth across the property from sunrise to sunset, digging pits for hiding the meth lab detritus.

"Ya know what'd be a great soundtrack for this?" Roy thought for a moment since it had never occurred to him that surveillance imagery would benefit from a music track. "No."

"That Benny Hill theme song." Ruben folded his nail clippers and began his approximation of the song: "Buh dibuh dee dee diddle dee, dee dee diddle dee, dee buhdee buhdeebuhdee... that one."

Roy shook his head, but didn't look up from the images. "That's the Hamster Dance song."

"No, hamster dance is, dibby deedie dibbydeedoo, dibbiediedo dibbydoo, and so on and so forth..."

"I'm always impressed at the level of intellectual conversation between you two skid marks, and it's not the Benny Hill song either, it's 'Yackety Sax' by Boots Randolph."

Ruben and Roy swiveled around to see Orbin leaning over the cubicle partition. "Obie Wan", Roy pointed at the screen. "Good call on this thing. I bet they got a lotta meth up there for all the trash pits he's digging."

Orbin leaned forward and squinted to see the screen. "That's what he's doing? Isn't he cooking too?"

83

Roy turned back to the screen. "Probly in one of the structures, but we can't see if he's cooking really. Not with these cameras anyway."

Ruben returned to his nail clipping. "IR camera mighta picked that up a little bit."

"Yeah, true." Roy turned to Orbin as if to explain, "but we haven't looked at any of the thermal images yet. Wanna get through these first. And he's mainly just digging holes. See? He's been a busy little bee."

Orbin grabbed a chair from the adjoining cubicle and dragged it in to join them. "More like a busy little ant for all the digging he's doing." He watched Hertell and the scurrying D-6 and thought of the Uncle Milton Ant Farm he'd gotten for Christmas right before they moved from the shady forts of Oildale to the upscale treeless dirt subdivision on the bleached, dry bluffs of College Heights—his dad called it garbage heights since the area was a landfill before it was developed for Bakersfield Junior College and the surrounding subdivisions.

"You ever have an Ant Farm?"

Ruben looked up from his nail clipping. "Huh?"

Roy laughed at the thought. "Yeah I had a Ant Farm once, but I was too cheap to send off to Left Nut Oklahoma, or wherever it is, to get the special ant-farm-ants, so I'd just go out in the yard and get some fire ants and throw'm in there with some bread crumbs and shit, and then watch'm for a few minutes and then get bored and go off and do something else, and then come back in a few days and they'd all be dead 'cause they were too dumb to eat the bread crumbs. I mean, the bread was right there, all they had to do was eat it but, you know, what the hell, they were ants."

Ruben held up his cell phone for their benefit. "There's an Ant Farm app... this what you're talking about? I'm downloading it so..."

Roy was annoyed at the interruption of his boyhood reverie. "Aww fuck, get away with that thing. These were real ants in a real plastic thing with little green plastic windmills and a real plastic farmhouse and a real plastic barn up on top, this was not some fake thing on a phone..."

The discussion was interesting, but Orbin had to go out on patrol soon. "So where's he getting the chemicals?"

Ruben kept working on his cell phone but immediately caught Orbin's intent. "There was a pretty good load of ammonium nitrate stolen from a duster strip east of Wasco, like, a ton, literally."

"Bulk or bagged?"

Ruben confirmed with Roy, "It was bagged wasn't it, it wasn't bulk? It was a coupla months ago, you know."

"Yeah it was bagged. And there was a thousand-gallon nurse tank of anhydrous ammonia, full, stolen from the Superior yard over in Buttonwillow, so there's that too..."

Orbin watched the screen. "Nurse tank would fit in one of the holes that Cat is digging wouldn't it?"

"Yeah, that's where we think it is. I mean nothing's gone in or out since we been watching, unless we see something in the rest of this download. So he's got plenty of stuff for cooking."

"How much could he cook with that much stuff?"

Roy thought for a moment, mentally calculating. "Well... uh..." and then approximated, "a butt load, maybe, more depending on how much of the other chemicals he's got."

Orbin crossed his arms and leaned back in his chair and thought for a moment. "Imperial butt load or a metric butt load?"

Ruben stretched and yawned. "We only deal in Imperial butt loads around here. Roy's kinda old school."

"Anything on the dead guy, the Ice Cream truck guy?"

Roy stopped the time-lapse for a moment to look at an image. "Not really, there was a restraining order on the dead guy back in the '70s I think, mighta been the '80s, he pissed off the pet cemetery guy or something so he couldn't get within a hundred feet of the place, but nothing since then."

Roy resumed the time-lapse and leaned back again. "It's a perfect setup. The whole valley fulla the chemicals he needs. I mean, everybody's watching the 99 and the 5, but the 178 is a decent north-south route too, take it right over Walker Pass to the 395 and you got a clear shot up to Reno. And nobody's watching."

"How long you been watching him?"

Roy shrugged. "I dunno. Since you told us about him I guess. Spent a coupla days and a coupla nights watching, and then set up the cameras a coupla weeks after that, cameras been out there for like a month. So a coupla three months?"

"A coupla three months?"

"Yeah, we got a case load we gotta deal with, it's not like TV. We had a lab out on Panama Lane, then a smaller one in a trailer court over on Edison Highway, bunch a little shit but we still gotta deal with it, you know. But this's probly the best one we have, biggest too. Biggest I've ever seen. Wouldn't you say so Ruben? Ruben?"

Ruben looked up from his cell phone. "What?"

"This is the biggest operation we've seen isn't it, at least in Kern County?"

Looking back at his cell phone, "Oh yeah, totally, this's gonna be a big one. Huge. Like, Drudge Report huge."

Orbin checked his watch; he still had time. "Unless he blows himself up first. All those chemicals buried all over the place and he's such a total tweaker, all jumpy and telling me about separating dogs and cats and the North and South Pole switching places and, just weird shit. I'm waiting for the fireball."

Ruben looked up from his cell phone. "I don't think he'll pop it. He's kind of a brainiac, or at least he was. He may be a tweaker now, but he has like a PhD from Berkeley in some kinda science, I forget exactly what kind—not political science but you know, a real science you know physics or something like that, so cooking meth should be way inside his skill set."

Orbin rubbed his hands on his legs, something he'd done since he was a child when deep in thought. "Hmmm. Interesting." There was a long silence as they watched Hertell erratically scratching and digging at the earth. "How's he getting his money? He's spent a least a grand just on the diesel he's burning up driving that cat around."

"Trust fund," Roy said. "Plus whatever he gets for the dead dogs and cats. But he hasn't made a dollar on the meth since we've been watching, 'cause nothing's going out. Unless we see something here," he said, indicating the images.

"He's a trust-funder?"

"Yeah. I mean we haven't drilled down into it yet but I don't think we need to, not until the trial anyway, we got plenty to go on for now."

"Trust fund," Orbin nodded. "Pretty smart."

"We didn't see much when we were watching from over by the weir, a guy coming up to visit a dead pet, so we ran the plates on him and they were clean, but then there was a propane delivery, so we checked with CalGas and found out that he's been using a lot of propane, probably for the cooking and then he started sleeping outside to stay away from the stink."

Ruben leaned back in his chair. "Nothing in this batch of pics yet, mainly just him running around digging all day, but it turns out his mom owns a couple of apartment complexes up in Sacramento that've had meth labs in'm, so there's that connection too."

"What about the cooker? Anything on him?"

"No, he's clean, no record, nothing, 'cept for getting shot in the head."

"That was him? I knew something happened out there, but I didn't know it was him."

Ruben kept working on his cell phone. "Yeah they were shooting off guns on the 4th of July or New Year's Eve or something and he ended up standing under one of the bullets. I mean what are the odds, he oughta go buy a lottery ticket."

Roy shifted in his seat. "And then there's the whole wife thing," shaking his head. "That could complicate things for the department."

"What about the wife?"

Ruben grabbed his head in dismay. "Aww shit, Roy..."

Roy looked at Ruben. "Aw shit, we weren't supposed to say anything about that."

"What you mean 'we' white man? I didn't say anything."

Roy stood up to look over the cubicle and make sure the room was clear. "Ok, damage done, I'll tell Lance that it's my fuck up, and Orbin, you're part of the investigation now." He sat down again and his voice went into a softer, almost soothing register. "The cooker's wife is..."

Ruben cut him off. "Ex-wife, will you get it straight?"

"Yeah, ok, ex-wife, get technical. Anyway, his ex-wife is Kaye Daggett."

Orbin stared at them blankly. "You gotta be shitting me."

"Nope. Sergeant for the Kern Valley substation, right up the 178 from there."

Orbin shook his head. "I thought she was over in Tehachapi...", and then as if to confirm, "Kinda cute, but a little dykie right, her?"

"Yep. Cute..." Roy looked back at Ruben to confirm. "But kinda dykie. Not that there's anything wrong with that."

Orbin began rubbing his hands on his legs again... "Well. It is what it is."

They all fell silent again, and Ruben returned to his cell phone now that the crisis was over.

Roy clicked the mouse and opened another folder. "Let's see what the IR camera got for us." They all waited quietly as the images loaded in the viewer, Ruben with his cell phone, Roy with his mouse, and Orbin with his thoughts. He thought about Wiley and about all the meth accumulating in pits of

Li'l Pal Heaven poised to etch the teeth and scar the skin and damn the souls of the poor dumb Tweakers, and he took comfort that the last bust of Wiley's would be a big one, Drudge Report big, and nearly a year after he took the pellets meant for Obi Wan. He was troubled that it might take a deputy down with it, but life goes on. He checked his watch and stood up, it was time to go on patrol.

"This Ant Farm is a great fucking game, man. Why didn't you tell me about this before?" Ruben looked up and gestured with his cell phone and then fell silent along with Roy and Obi Wan who stared, motionless, at the screen.

Ruben put down his cell phone and moved his chair closer to the grainy infrared images slowly scrolling on the screen where pale grey, ghostly forms were seemingly rising from the black earth.

They all watched in silence. Orbin finally spoke. "Are those... people?"

Chapter Thirteen

404 File Not Found

An ice cream truck was approaching. Doug wasn't a piper today, and not even a geologist, but just another faceless dad sitting in a Karate dojo watching his youngest daughter practice her kempos or katas or whatever. No kilt, no sporran, no bagpipe or geologist pick, nothing to distinguish him in the procession, just another faceless, middle-class, middle-aged man shuffling through life. The ice cream truck was getting louder, loud enough for some of the others waiting in the dojo to hear. He noted the Pavlovian response to the tinny music-box chimes coming from his phone. It was more pronounced in some than in others, some would look up and out the window for the truck, others would simply smile in recognition as they continued texting on their phones or reading their Kindle or an actual analog magazine or book on rare occasion, and some would be completely oblivious.

It was the usual pod today waiting in the dojo, except for one older man, who appeared to be in his high 70s to low 80s, high-mileage but fit, and presumably a visiting grandfather. Soul-Patch-with-faux-Celtic-tats was slouched near the door leafing through Autotrader, Middle-management-comb-over was perched near the display case pecking at his laptop, Yoga-mat-step-mom was sitting in her usual spot working on her Sudoku, and a few others not worth noticing like Qiana-Mood-Ring.

Doug knew nothing of Yoga-mat but her surface layer and apparent devotion to physical and mental fitness, but as a student of humanity he couldn't help filling in the rest: probably a personal fitness trainer or Pilates instructor who never had or wanted children, due to their deleterious impact on the female body and attendant compromise of her value-proposition, with a 6th sense of net worth who landed a 50-ish VP or CEO or law partner in the terminal phases of a 30 year marriage complete with a debris field of toxic ex-wife and conflicted grown children and one pre-teen straggler, probably a last-ditch effort to save the marriage, now practicing kempos or katas or whatever, that Yoga-mat now had to chauffeur to private school and ballet and piano and karate lessons where her Sudoku concentration was challenged by phantom ice-cream trucks.

Satisfied with his observations, Doug fished out his cell phone and silenced the ice cream truck. Calm returned to the dojo as he turned his attention to his cell phone and touched it to life—he now blended in with the rest of the pod.

It was an email. He had set his ringtones to be identical for all incoming demands for his attention whatever their source or conveyance as a way of preserving at least some element of mystery and surprise. The phone sounded the same as a text, or an email, or an actual person, always the cheerful approach of an ice cream truck.

92

The email was addressed to "webmaster@lapsedgeologist.com", but Doug wasn't a webmaster so he wasn't sure why it came to him. He presumed it was spam at best and phishing at worst and was just about to mark it as 'junk' when he noticed the salutation in the preview pane. It was from a regular contributor to his blog, a geologist who was typically a short-tempered flamer who, with the least provocation, would inevitably blame homophobia or George Bush as the cause of Western decline. It was a short email which simply said, "Your domain is down. Got 404. Faggot."

Doug was confused, not about "Faggot," since this particular contributor always signed off his emails that way as a point of pride, or even about the domain being down, but about who had crowned him webmaster, which conjured up images of yeasty twenty-somethings in black t-shirts and sneers. He typed in his URL, www.lapsedgeologist.com, and up came the "404 - Not Found" page just as Faggot had warned—he'd once suggested that the blog contributor choose a less provocative handle but was immediately accused of homophobia, so "Faggot" he remained, with defiant fist held high.

He holstered his phone and leaned back in thought. The 404 was probably due to a backhoe going through a fiber-optic cable, so he figured the site would be taken care of eventually or at worst in a few hours which was essentially the same thing. He resolved to check again when he got home from karate.

He looked up to see how is daughter was doing. They were doing forms now, the ornate and almost ritualized responses to multiple unseen assailants. He turned his gaze to the waiting pod to see if any were actually watching their students. All heads were down, except for the visiting Grampa who was actually staring right at Doug.

The old man's face was expressionless and free of the usual creases and asymmetries suggesting partial, I-know-you-from-somewhere, recognition. This was expected, as Doug had long since resigned himself to being one of those people who were so congenitally forgettable with a persona and face so vaporous and bland that even a flicker of recognition was not worth pursuing, and there was no flicker of recognition. The old man kept staring directly at him even after Doug made eye contact, so he was probably ex-military since they never look away.

The Grampa finally smiled slightly and nodded his head. Doug did likewise and looked back into the dojo where all the pre-teens were now suiting up for sparring in shiny crimson rubberized armor. Doug could still feel Grampa's eyes on him, so he got busy with his cell phone as a diversion and to blend in again. The "404—Not Found" message was still there, so he decided to refresh the page to see if the problem had been fixed.

It hadn't. He wondered if the ISP was down, so he checked one of his bookmarks. The "Drudge Report" was up and running and evidently some UFOs had interrupted a soccer game in Brazil again. Following a hunch, he soft-keyed his work website URL into the address bar—he'd set up his work website at the same time and with the same ISP as his geology blog so they were probably served from the same data center, so if it was a backhoe-vs-fiber-optic-cable deal it should be down too. It wasn't, it came right up with his graphics and logo.

He hated when he did this, but he reached between his legs and pulled out his laptop. It was official now, he was one of those people whose time was far too valuable to be wasted savoring, in his short time on earth, the fleeting, ephemeral, radiant youth of his precious daughter, never to return for the rest of time. But this would only take a minute.

He quickly established a chat session with the ISP tech support geeks.

Rangefire > what's the problem?

GeoPiper > www.lapsedgeologist.com is getting 404's, what's up?

The status bar indicated that 'Rangefire' was typing a response. Doug waited for what must have been a voluminous reply. It finally came:

Rangefire > call 877 827 4376

Doug stared at the response for a moment. "Odd," he thought:

GeoPiper > is there an issue?

The answer came back much more quickly this time:

Rangefire > 877 827 4376

He closed the laptop, but left it on his lap as he thought. He looked up at his daughter; she was sparring with a slightly larger girl and had just received a point for delivering a well-placed kick to the larger girl's solar plexus. He looked back at the pod. Grampa was now on his cell phone, apparently listening intently to something. Yoga-mat was working on her Sudoku. Soul Patch was texting on his phone. He glanced back into the Dojo. His daughter was done sparring, and was bowing to her larger opponent. She returned to the wall awaiting her next call into the arena, so no harm done if he slipped outside for a quick call. He refused to make cell calls in confined spaces feeling that it was akin to farting loudly in an elevator, at best disrespectful and at worst disruptive.

He leaned against the planter outside the dojo and navigated through the phone system. "Press 1 for English, etc.". He glanced back into the dojo where the pod sat. Grampa was still on the phone, and was looking at Doug again.

"This is Justin and this call may be monitored for quality control, how may I help you?" Doug was jolted back to the present. "Uhhh, my website... I'm getting a 404, and tech support said to call this number."

Justin asked all the pertinent questions and then asked if he could put Doug on hold for a brief moment. They were still sparring in the dojo, so he still had time. "Sure," and as Doug listened patiently to the Kenny G he wondered what Justin's real name was, Rajive or Subrata possibly.

"Thanks for your patience, your site kept getting flooded by a DDOS attack and so we just removed your domain from the DNS."

Doug was surprised that the hold actually was for only a brief moment. "Uhhh, I know what each individual word meant, but I'm not sure what they mean all together, what's a dee-dee-oh-es?"

He could literally hear 'Justin' sneering through the phone. "DDOS is a distributed denial of service attack, it's when a bunch of computers try to access your website all at the same time which makes the server crash."

"How many computers?

He could hear 'Justin' typing. "I'll see if it's in the report, but it's probably ten thousand, maybe twenty thousand."

"Twenty thousand people?" This was news to Doug since his site had a regular but small core of followers that was certainly in the hundreds, but nowhere near a thousand, and hadn't had ten thousand hits in its whole existence.

"No, not twenty thousand people just their computers, it looks like there was a pool of about twelve thousand that were flooding your site and the data center had to keep resetting the server every few minutes, so they finally just took your site offline."

Doug had more questions like, "Why would someone want to take down my website, and how do I get it up again?", but his daughter was now in formation and Front Position with the rest of the students, signaling the imminent conclusion of today's lesson. "Thanks Justin."

"Have you got time for a quick quality service poll? You get a free..."

Doug was already heading back into the dojo. "Nope, sorry, not this time, gotta go."

He returned to his seat still holding his phone as the karate students kneeled down for their final meditation. Doug sat silently and tried to make sense of the recent conversation as he watched the sweaty karate students slowly calm and cool down. He glanced back into the pod. They were mostly emerging from their distractions and getting their car keys out, Yoga-mat was closing her Sudoku app, Middle-management was bagging his laptop, and Soul Patch was stretching and yawning. Grandpa was still on his cell phone and staring directly at Doug. Doug smiled awkwardly, but before he could glance away, Grandpa stood and with eyes drilling into Doug, spoke. "Interesting geological formation you found."

Doug looked at the older man in stunned silence as the class was dismissed and the sweaty karate students flooded into the waiting pod. He watched as Grandpa moved toward the door. "Not the Mesozoic diorite you'd expect around here." And then he was gone.

Doug followed his daughter across the parking lot in silence, his, not hers. She was sputtering about the upcoming blue belt test. "And they make you do push-ups on your knuckles until you throw up and then they make you do leg lifts until you throw up again and then they make you… Da, will you answer your phone? It's right in your hand." The ice cream truck was indeed demanding his attention again. It was another email addressed to 'webmaster@lapsedgeologist.com', with a subject line of "We should talk…"

Chapter Fourteen

Are You A Mutant?

Hertell couldn't see where it was coming from, but it was a woman's voice, and it sounded scared. He tried to move but couldn't and decided that it was a reasonable enough question that deserved a sincere answer. He thought about it for a moment since it could be a trick question, and then laughed, but it didn't sound like a laugh, it sounded more like, "Mmmrrrphm".

It was black except for a narrow strip of lighter black seemingly suspended, alone and abandoned far away at an odd angle. He wasn't sure what woke him up since there was no commercial for Ab-Scrambler and no TV and no LazyBoy and no light except for the lighter black black. He presumed he was still sleeping, so he relaxed to enjoy the dream and the quiet and the darkness, and darker darkness.

The voice asked again, "Are you a mutant?"

It wasn't scared as much as it was young and curious. It also sounded kind, and somehow it made him feel safe and totally connected with the rest of the universe. He turned his head toward the voice. "No more than anybody else."

A blinding light flooded the dream. "Are you the one that's been trying to dig down to us to eat us?"

Hertell covered his eyes and squinted, and, with some difficulty, answered, "No. Just trying to see where the accordion music is coming from." He waited for a reply as his eyes adjusted to the bright lights, but there was only silence. This seemed rather odd to him since events typically go a lot faster in a dream.

"Do you like accordion music?"

The voice had moved. It was behind him now. Possibly another trick question. "Well, everybody likes accordion music."

His vision was adjusting. He was flanked by a folding chair and a hassock and an accordion and a music stand a few feet away. The ceiling, if there was one, was high overhead and beyond the reach of the light that was blinding him.

He could almost see a silhouette in the darkness, but it may have been his imagination.

"How did you get in here?"

Hertell felt that honesty, especially in a dream, was called for. "From my dad's Lazy-Boy Recliner."

"Oh." The answer seemed to satisfy her curiosity. "You were just laying here when I found you. And not in a chair either, just on the floor like you are now."

Hertell raised himself on one elbow. He was lying on what appeared to be a wide ramp, or really more of a broad, flat tunnel that sloped up toward the distant slit of lighter dark. He could clearly see a faraway shape in the darker darkness down below at the opposite end of the great hall. "How did you get in here?"

She answered very matter-of-factly. "Walked over from Egypt."

Hertell considered her answer. "Musta been a long walk?"

"Not long really, but uphill most of the way." She was moving but still beyond the edge of the light, just a teasing shadow.

He could see a shape in the darkness. "Does this place have a name?"

"No, not yet. It's just a pressure buffer where I can get away to practice the accordion. It's got excellent acoustics though."

She was right. Even though her shadow appeared to be at least a hundred feet away, she sounded like she was close enough to touch. She had a familiar and sweet accent. It sounded like an Old Spanish accent from Northern New Mexico or maybe Southern Colorado and could only be detected in certain words. Mister Frostie had a similar accent, which Hertell recognized from a graduate professor he'd known back in the Jurassic period.

"Haven't practiced in here for a while because of all the noise of the mutants trying to get in and eat us. You're not much of a mutant."

"Thanks. That's good to know."

"Your rad count is fine and nothing is broken. You're much more bilaterally symmetrical than I would have expected for a mutant. I've already given you a complete exam. You have multiple abrasions on your face and extremities, a contusion on your occipital lobe and a nasty one on your coccyx. Your testicles are large but otherwise normal and I noticed you've been circumcised; I'm glad to see they're still doing that, much more hygienic, and streamlined."

Hertell nodded. "Streamlined." He was imagining his penis with fins like a '57 Chevy when his thoughts were interrupted by a figure emerging from the darkness.

He could see her clearly now. She wore bejeweled horned rim glasses straight out of a Gary Larson cartoon and had the most lustrous black hair he'd ever seen outside a shampoo ad, and eyes the color of coffee, and luminous alabaster skin, and she seemed to live every word she spoke—it was a hypnotic joy just to watch her talk. She was beautiful and ageless and the crystalline confluence of every woman he'd ever seen or known. She wore a pink cashmere sweater, a tasteful pearl necklace, and a skirt straight out of "Grease" only without the poodle, and penny loafers with white ankle socks. She reminded him of a '50s TV mom from some long-forgotten black and white TV show that never got picked up for syndication, only younger and closer to his age.

Her name was Virginia, after the state. They had a long and far-ranging discussion about accordions and the great nuclear war that destroyed civilization and the Broadway Musical as his eyes adjusted: the key targets and primary, secondary, and tertiary exchanges, the global wind patterns and radioactive fallout dispersion, and the inevitable extinction of mankind as its institutions dissolved, and it fed upon itself, and Rogers and Hammerstein.

Since he'd told her he liked accordion music, she sat in the small chair and lifted the massive accordion onto her lap. Hertell sat at her feet like a preschooler as she played her accordion—no scales, just songs—and sang him an assortment of old show tunes: "Bali Hai", "Stout Hearted Men", "Wouldn't It Be Loverly", "If I Loved You", "Surrey With

The Fringe On Top." She had a beautiful voice that made him happy and connected to everything that ever was, just like with the copper specks only less confusing because he stayed where he was and wasn't suddenly walking with mastodons or swimming with trilobites.

Between songs, she told him about Nikola Tesla and Oceanoids and Kennedy and the great underground world that stretched out in the darkness below toward Egypt and India and France and how they had atomic power, and swimming pools, and movies, and lights to make daytime, and bowling alleys, and miniature golf courses with the history of the world, and that they would all one day emerge into the sunlight to restore civilization, after the radiation levels were low enough.

She scanned him with an old yellow Civil Defense Geiger counter just to make sure he hadn't suddenly become radioactive. "So who finally won?"

Hertell was confused at the question. "Won what?"

"The war."

"Which one?"

"The one we've been talking about, the atomic war, the one that destroyed civilization, and the Broadway musical. Who finally won?"

"Well... nobody."

She scanned the soles of his shoes. "Then it turned out just like we thought, no winners, just mutant survivors fighting over fetid scraps, running around killing each other all day. Just mutants and cockroaches and lawyers... oh my!"

Hertell laughed at the "Wizard of Oz" reference. "Well it's too dry for cockroaches out here and I'm not a lawyer so there."

She finished with the Geiger counter. "Well, ok, but you're still a mutant."

Somehow that was good enough for Hertell. "Clearly." Nevertheless, he felt obligated to correct her misimpression of recent history.

"But just so we're clear on this, the big nuclear war never happened, the button never got pushed. The rockets never flew, nobody was vaporized in the fireball, no shadows frozen mid- stride. Nothing like that, just the '70s and bell-bottoms and disco, and the '80s with the evil empire and shoulder pads, and the '90s with commies fading into the internets and stuff. So I may be a mutant, but not because of a big nuclear war."

She was unconvinced. "Are you sure? Were you paying attention? Sounds like there were a lot of distractions."

"Well, yeah. I mean, I wasn't there the whole time, but I'm sure I would have heard about it and I would have noticed the lawyers and cockroaches at least. The world didn't end. It's still out there."

She took off her big Larson-lady horned-rims, bowed her head and closed her eyes. He sat motionless on the floor looking up at her face, lit from a light within. She was moving her lips slightly, but he couldn't hear what she was saying. Then the light caught something and a tiny twinkling star fell on the accordion, then another, and another. Her face was calm and serene as the cascade of tiny stars escaped from her closed eyes and fell and haltingly rolled down the glossy black face of the accordion and collected in the decorative lettering on its face: "Sonola".

He marveled at how everything comes together in a dream and reached up to comfort her. He could hear her now, she was softly whispering, just like the hill they were inside.

"...When amidst earth's closing thunders, saints shall stand before the throne, God has promised, Christ prepares it, there on high our welcome waits, we are not alone, we are not lost, God will find us."

Hertell felt strangely comforted. "Yeah, and I hear that He doesn't sweat the little shit either..."

Her clasped, prayerful hands rested on her lap, and Hertell remembered that he was in love once. He remembered how, after he fell in love with Kaye, how all of the love songs he'd heard through his whole life, suddenly made total sense to him—no longer mere words, they had meaning and mass. And he wondered if it was like that with God for people like the beautiful woman sitting above him, and Mister Frostie and Kaye, and all those Okies that used to shiver in the dark on Easter mornings all those years ago as the sunlight touched the big wooden cross; that somehow, they'd been granted a glimpse of God or something, and all of a sudden the hymns and the prayers and the grief and the joy and the machinery that ran the world and all the people on it, made total sense. He couldn't remember exactly, but he was sure he'd somehow envied that in Kaye, and how it hurt her that he didn't, and couldn't, and wouldn't even try to fake it.

He was trying to remember Kaye's face and voice and smell when he had a vague feeling of something needing his attention, he wasn't sure what. Thoughts of love songs and hymns and prayers and Kaye dissipated as his attention was drawn back to the pleasant dream he was having.

"What's that?"

He looked up and was immediately struck speechless by the sight of the beautiful woman in prayer.

She was radiating a golden light and had a halo about her head and shoulders, just like in the church windows. She was squinting and blinking from the brightness of her own beatific radiance. She raised her hand to shade her eyes and pointed straight ahead. "What's that?"

Hertell turned and squinted into the rising sun, which had transformed the former lighter-black strip into a blinding shaft of sunlight. It had been going so well up to that point: an otherwise perfect dream where nothing was scary or threatening and everything connected and everything made total sense. Only now it slowly dawned on Hertell, that this wasn't a dream at all, but quite the opposite in fact.

And as he looked back at the beautiful woman struggling to see in the shaft of blinding day, he was overcome by a feeling he'd never felt before.

He stood up, shading her with his body. "That's ... that's just the sun, the light of our world, and it's ok, it's out there every day."

She looked up at Hertell, now framed in a corona of sunlight, and smiled. He didn't see her lips move, but he distinctly heard her say,

"Show me."

Chapter Fifteen

Mustard Seed

I t was almost time for the last patient of the day, but it was
still a few minutes before he or she arrived—Doug didn't
know which it would be since it was not only a new patient
but also an appointment he'd apparently forgotten—his
scheduling software reminded him of the appointment as he
was attempting to shut down his computer for the day. Kern
County had experienced a spike in military enlistments in
the days after 9/11, and Doug was seeing a belated spike in
PTSD patients. It wasn't his specialty, but the patients didn't
seem to care and they seemed generally satisfied with the
results and their word of mouth kept a thin but steady stream
of young vets coming his way in addition to the hoarders
and cutters and divorcees and children of divorcees and
teenagers preparing for the SAT.

He considered himself a general practitioner MFT who had
a knack for getting people to talk to him, a knack he'd had
since childhood. He'd once been told by a patient, wife of
a prominent Buttonwillow dairy farmer, that his voice was
a soothing Smurf blue, and that his face was reassuring and
nonjudgmental— just like a Jersey cow with big, kind eyes,

sympathetic, but not necessarily comprehending. He'd taken it as a compliment and had long before resigned himself to the fact that he would forever be a sounding board whether it was in a bar, or his office, or in line at Costco. So he might as well make a living of it.

It had been an interesting route from geology. The energy crash of '86 prompted Golden Bear to consolidate all of its exploration organizations to somewhere up in the Bay Area—a futile, damage-limiting operation that ultimately failed to save the company. For some reason Doug's wife, at the time, would simply not consider a move from her beloved Bakersfield, and her job as a medical office assistant, to move up to Milpitas or Concord or Hollister or whatever. So, Doug quit his job as a Golden Bear Geologist 2 and sought another; however, due to the crash of '86, there were no geologist jobs of any number designation, so he decided to change careers.

Psychology was a good fit and he noted a great deal of similarity with geology—fault lines great and small lurking patiently below as the tensile stresses and shearing strains build, and then, without warning yield, sending waves of jagged destruction up to the thin veneer of civilization above; tectonic plates that collide and grind against each other silently miles beneath the surface, roiling lakes of magma created from their friction occasionally boiling and bubbling to the surface, spilling out of volcanoes and vents to bury whole species and cultures or tunneling underfoot in miles of lava tubes; three types of people: sedimentary, igneous, and metamorphic—and his job was to identify the strata and log the wells to identify the pools of self-discovery to be tapped, the veins of insight to be mined, the pockets of hidden toxins to be purged. And his wife was very supportive of his career change.

She encouraged him in every aspect: night classes, weekend workshops, and she would often have dinner waiting for him, even if it was a greasy bag from McDonald's, when he'd arrive home after a full day working his bridge job at Sears, so he could go directly to his night classes. He was truly a blessed man—up to the point he learned his wife was fornicating with the M.D. she worked for and would ultimately marry, his first; her second.

And even though it was an illusion, it was a productive, happy and life-affirming illusion, and Doug was of a personality type, metamorphic by his estimation, such that he nevertheless cherished the memory of this period in his life because, for the most part, he considered illusion the basis of life itself since perception is the only way we can actually know reality. It was a very philosophical epoch in his life and he likened his response to the illusion and the humiliating betrayal it masked, to a good movie, where even though you know the sets are fake and the dinosaurs are fake and the spaceships are fake and the people are fake and the blood and the money and everything you see is fake, the movie nevertheless made you feel happy, and strong, and resolved to be a better human being.

An ice cream truck was approaching. It was his scheduling software, letting him know it was time for his next appointment. He silenced the wobbly tune, smoothed his slacks, took a quick inventory of the office—Kleenex box, note pad, pen, water bottles—as he crossed the room and opened the door to the reception area. It was not what he expected.

Evidently, his last appointment of the day wasn't an appointment at all. It was a hack into his scheduling software thanks to a security vulnerability in Outlook that made it possible. Doug sat in his office with two visitors. The younger one, probably the hacker, was big and pale and lumpy and silent and seemed to be taking notes on his iPad. The other visitor was none other than 'Grampa', of the Dojo. Evidently, he wasn't at the Dojo to watch his granddaughter—in fact he didn't even have a granddaughter, only grandsons, all grown and in the military. He was there to watch Doug that day, and he now sat in Doug's office in the Big Chair between the Kleenex and the water bottle.

Grampa was leathery and creased, and even for his age he had a terrier's build with big wrists and massive forearms covered with a carpet of gray hair. He had bright blue eyes that were overhung by eyebrows resembling small birds' nests. He consulted his notes, rubbed his crew cut with his hand, and then fixed his eyes on Doug.

"Does the word 'Mustard Seed' have any significance to you?"

Doug thought for a long moment, considering the question. "No... Not really."

"It's in the Bible."

Doug was confused by the comment but not really surprised since there were a lot of things in the Bible he didn't know—he'd been raised in an old school Catholic Parish that had clung to the spooky Latin mass long after it had been replaced with less demanding English, and guitars and altars facing the wrong way; consequently, he knew almost nothing of the actual Bible and stopped going to mass when his parents stopped taking him when he was still in Junior High. Though he knew he'd go back some day, as all Catholics do.

"Hmm. Didn't know that. Haven't been to church for a while. Sorry."

"No apology necessary. You know what a lava tube is?"

It was a rather abrupt and confusing change in direction, but Doug pivoted. "Well, yeah, I... I know what a lava tube is. I was a geologist back in late Pleistocene. I've never actually seen one, though, except in photos, if that's what you're asking."

Generally, it was Doug who asked the questions during a session, but this was a decidedly different counseling session.

"That's interesting." Grandpa took a Kleenex from the box and proceeded to fog and clean his glasses. "Because I didn't ask if you'd seen a lava tube. I asked if you knew what they were. So I'm puzzled here. Why did you tell me that you had never seen one, when I didn't ask you that?"

"Well it seemed like it was important to you for some reason, especially since it came so closely behind the Biblical question, so I decided to provide as much information as I could to move the conversation along."

Grampa checked a lens for clarity and then fogged and polished again. "How do you think the conversation's going?"

Doug laughed, and hoped that it didn't sound nervous. "Well, for an unusual conversation I think it's moving along pretty good. I mean, I recognize you from the Karate studio, you were on the phone, I was on the phone; you said we should talk. I have no idea who you are, or your... friend, or why you're here."

"Well... my name is Carl Balkey, and I work for... the Government." He gestured with his glasses toward the hacker. "And this is uhh..."

The hacker didn't look up from his iPad.. "Rusty."

"Yes, and this is Rusty Broacha." Carl had always been better at last names. "And Rusty works for the Government as well." He put his glasses back on and looked at Doug. "And we're here because we're curious as to why you posted some GPS coordinates on your blog?"

Another abrupt and confusing change in direction—Doug conjectured that, where in his chosen profession one tried to tease out and follow congruent or at least parallel filaments of thoughts and associations on the path to self-discovery and illumination; whereas the chosen profession, whatever it was, of Carl and Rusty relied on orthogonal, ad hoc, and seemingly chaotic lines of inquiry to achieve their ends.

Nevertheless, Doug was forced to ask, "What GPS coordinates?" But at least he was asking the questions now.

"The coordinates for the pet cemetery."

Now at least Doug was starting to see a strand of thought emerge. Grampa, Carl, had mentioned the Mesozoic diorite in the Dojo, and more recently the lava tubes, and now the pet cemetery, so there was a geological thread.

Doug also heard the faint trace of an Old Spanish accent in Carl's voice and wondered if he was from one of the small towns in southern Colorado or northern New Mexico like Pecos or Glorieta where Doug's mother was born.

She was the eldest of six and lived in Glorieta until she was in her teens when the war drew her family to Los Alamos where she met Doug's father, a B-24 pilot returning home after VE-Day, who drew her subsequently to Bakersfield at the war's end – depression baby, war bride, '50s mom, and now, a memory, like his father who died peacefully in his sleep on Valentine's Day.

Doug thought of his parents, and their generation, the greatest, often: he vividly remembered his father's hands, they looked... gentle, there was no other way to describe them, he remembered the dense forest of fine black India ink stains on the back of his father's left thumb—his father was a geological draftsman when Doug was a toddler, back in the pen and ink days before CAD/CAM, and had the habit of brushing his Koh-i-noor rapidograph on his thumb to get the ink flowing. And then, at day's end, after whistling up the driveway, he'd sit and smoke a filterless Chesterfield and tell Doug stories about the lines on the back of his thumb. "This one is named Jo-ko-po-ko -oh-no-ro-no, and he's looking for his pet boy..."

His dad never talked about the war, except for one time—funny stories about flight school and basic training and night clubs in Midland Texas yes, but the war itself, never. Except for one time. They were flying back from his grandfather's funeral. It was before deregulation, so flying on an airliner was still something you got dressed up for, before flip-flops and tank tops and sweat pants, people actually dressed up with ties and heels and white gloves to sit between the great throbbing Wright Cyclone engines and traverse the continent. Doug was very young, a few months shy of his fifth birthday. His sisters were in high school and not inclined to be inconvenienced by a midweek funeral a thousand miles away.

Doug was a surprise baby and the only boy. His mother was in her late forties when he was born, and his father was five years north of that, so he was essentially an only child with older parents. He wasn't in school yet, so he accompanied his dad on the trip, and he had never been in an airplane before. He had the window seat and was looking out the window at the solid layer of clouds below. "Is this what it was like in the war?" He watched as clouds crawled along miles below. He asked again. "Is this what the war was like?" His father was sitting next to him, but wasn't answering. Doug finally looked up at his father. "Is this..." His father still had jet-black hair back then; his eyes were red and unblinking.

He was looking right past Doug and staring out the window at the wooly layer of clouds below. He spoke very softly. "There was a guy named... 'Pinky', he was a bombardier. I always had breakfast with him, it was kind of a good luck ritual, knew him from pilot training but he washed out, so he'd ended up a bombardier, that's what happened back then, you'd wash out of pilot school so they'd send you to bombardier school and if you washed out of that, navigator school and then gunner school and if you washed out of that, a Higgins Boat on Normandy. We called him 'Pinky' because he was... pink. He was in Milk Run. I'd flown it on a couple of missions, we all had, good plane. It wasn't like in the movies where you'd fly the same plane every mission, you flew what they told you to fly. The planes were interchangeable. Just like we were, crew number six. We were coming up on Bielefeld,

114

I was low element, and Pinky and Milk Run were at the 10 o'clock."

Doug's father pointed out the window. "An ME-109 flew up out of the clouds just... exactly.... like those down there and settled in between us, dropped his gear to slow down to our speed. I could describe that plane in every detail, every smudge and rivet." Doug didn't know most of the words his dad was saying, but he understood the story. "Did you shoot him?" His father shook his head. "Couldn't shoot'm 'cause we'd hit our own planes. I could see the pilot talking on the radio, telling the gun crews down below our altitude so they'd be ready for us. Then he waved to me and did a split-S and dove and disappeared into those clouds again, just like down there."

His father's breathing was shallow and short. "Flak wasn't that bad, seen much worse, but Milk Run took one right in the chin, right where Pinky was sitting getting ready for the bomb run. The whole thing pitched over into a fireball and disappeared into those clouds. There weren't any parachutes." He stared out the window in silence at the clouds below. Doug, followed his father's eyes and looked out the window at the clouds as well. And then young Douglas, sympathetic but not necessarily comprehending, said, "I bet clouds seem pretty different to you now." His dad nodded. "Yeah. They are. Sometimes."

Doug told the Pinky story to his mother shortly after his father had died, and she told him that she first met his dad when he had come to visit Pinky's parents in Glorieta. She was also sure that it was the sound of the engines that took him back to the war—they were still flying the old Martin

404's out of Bakersfield back then—because he never seemed to be bothered by the clouds or the war in all the jetliner trips they took around the world in their later years.

As a professional Doug would always marvel at the human ability for time-travel. Something that in popular fiction requires a massive machine like the Large Hadron collider or a mystical talisman with ancient symbols and incantations. When, in reality, we do it in our own heads a thousand times a day, almost like breathing in its regularity, as Doug was doing just now, thinking of the ink stains on the back of his father's thumb and fleecy clouds from a long-ago war while otherwise engaged in a Brownian conversation with two seemingly serious men.

Though still puzzled by the biblical question, Doug decided to focus on the geology and described how he'd discovered an unusual rock outcropping while playing the bagpipes at a police dog funeral and had later returned to revisit the formation and do some field work, take a specimen and put it on the 'name-that-rock' challenge on his Blog. He was in the midst of explaining how he always included GPS coordinates as a courtesy to help his readers solve the mystery when he was struck by a thought.

"You read my blog?"

Rusty shook his head but kept looking at his iPad. "Not exactly."

Doug would later learn that in one of those randomly named Government programs, like Predacious or Talon or Mail Pouch, that no one ever heard of, an algorithm was diligently doing deep packet inspection, sifting through the entire contents of the daily traffic of the internets looking for... whatever it was told to look for. And it had been told to look for literally millions of things over the years.

In this case it was looking for coordinates—in a variety of coordinate schemes: LLA, UTM, WGS84 or any of its earlier variants, or ECEF—that corresponded to a localized point on the outskirts of Bakersfield. The target values matched, the alarm was tripped and the information routed to the appropriate fold of the benevolent, caring Government where Carl and Rusty toiled to keep us safe.

What made these coordinates such an important and unusual artifact was that nobody knew why they were important. They were classified at the highest security level, above TS/SCI, above SAP/SAR, and had been that way since the Kennedy administration. They had also been totally forgotten since that time and lay buried in the electronic equivalent of the cavernous Government warehouse at the end of *Indiana Jones*, the artifact and its enigmatic DNA passed silently and automatically from generation to generation: from BCD to EBCDIC to ASCII, from paper to tape to disk to flash, until discovered again under the unblinking eye of the Predacious algorithm and brought to the surface and the eventual attention of Carl Balkey, who had specialized in the forensics and disposition of numerous Government special access classified programs, projects and associated artifacts that had been forgotten or otherwise abandoned over the decades—it was actually a very common occurrence due to damaged/destroyed document logs, lost/misfiled DD254s, retirement, and death.

Carl had been brought out of retirement to investigate this prehistoric enigma and otherwise support Rusty, his web-enabled counterpart and eventual successor. Rusty was a borderline Asperger software practitioner and he rejected the term 'engineer' since it lacked geek street cred and considered all of these events to be a memory leakage problem just like you'd have in a buggy program—memory is allocated from the pool, used, and then forgotten instead of being deallocated and returned to the pool, so it just floats disconnected and isolated in intergalactic cyber space where no one can use it, until there's no memory left in the pool anymore, and nobody knows where all the memory went, and the program crashes—and could consequently be resolved in much the same way one would solve the equivalent problem in a buggy, crufty, leaky C++ program.

However, in this particular buggy program, the information was insufficient for Rusty to use his preferred methodology, since the only information they had were the coordinates themselves, the project name, "Mustard Seed", the security classification and some marginal and essentially useless copies of smudged and scarcely readable redacted documents where, according to the old yellowed document log, the originals had been destroyed in the days after the Kennedy assassination. It therefore required a more traditional, shoe-leather approach, which explained why Carl was sitting in the Big Chair between the Kleenex and the water bottle noting Doug's every subconscious movement, pause, blink, and vocal inflection— cues and indicators that were utterly invisible to Rusty who throughout his life was simply unable to read people, so he read software instead. It didn't blink and it never got its feelings hurt.

"Your Blog brought something to our attention." Carl unscrewed the cap on the water bottle. "And we're just following up on it." He took a drink from the bottle and never took his eyes off of Doug. "What was unusual about this formation?"

Doug began explaining about the iron flakes and the cement when he was interrupted again.

"You play bagpipes, are you Scottish?"

It took Doug a moment to process the question. "Uhh, no. Mexican and Croatian... In any case, I just figured it might be an interesting thing to use for my name-that-rock challenge..."

"He's telling the truth." Rusty finally looked up from his iPad.

Carl laughed since he knew Doug was telling the truth since the lava tube question. It also meant that they were at a dead end.

"I am? How do you know?"

Rusty pointed to his iPad. Evidently, he had an app that could determine such things as truthfulness, which explained the confusing assortment of unrelated questions.

"Oh, I guess that makes it official then."

Carl took another drink of water and then put the cap back on the bottle. "Well, thanks for your time." He put the bottle in his pocket and then stood up. "We'll just do a direct deposit to your bank account for the session—we have all the information we need."

Somewhat surprised, Doug sat looking up at Carl for a moment. "Can you tell me what this is about?"

Carl checked his watch. "Probably nothing, but probably better the less you know. Sorry."

Doug noted that he felt vaguely used, and smiled to himself and shook his head in recognition of his instinctive response to his sense of rejection. He stood up to be at Carl's eye-level, another instinctive response which he recognized in himself. "Well, sorry I couldn't be more help."

Rusty stood but was still looking at his iPad. "He's telling the truth again."

Carl nodded and led them out of the office. "Thanks, Broacha that's good to know." Doug, ever the gracious host, followed them out. "You know you might want to talk to the caretaker out there at the pet cemetery, he might know something. About whatever it is you can't tell me about."

Carl acknowledged Doug's suggestion as he crossed the empty reception area toward the door, but didn't really hear it. He was thinking of a six-hour drive to the Veteran's Home up in Yountville.

Carl had spent several weeks sifting through the "Mustard Seed" files, analyzing the worthless, redacted documents and had determined that the program seemed to involve some of the folks who worked on the Manhattan Project and some of its spin-offs—no names since they were blacked-out under the redactor's pen, but Carl's sense was that they weren't the top-tier folks, but further down the food-chain, all brilliant no doubt, but otherwise unremarkable.

One of the only documents that wasn't fully redacted were some Travel Orders for an Airman 3rd class Craig Sweetser who was now in his 80s and a Yountville resident. His 201 file indicated that his years of service overlapped the "Mustard Seed" document destruction, his MOS was blacked out but all of his duty stations, assignments, and TDYs were listed, and though he'd been read out of all the programs back in the late '60s he had all of the appropriate clearances to work in some minor role, probably admin or clerical, possibly logistics, on Mustard Seed. He'd retired from the Air Force in the '80s and Broacha's digital shoe-leather tracked him to Yountville, a six hour drive from the Psychologist's office in Bakersfield, a six-hour drive with Broacha. Perhaps they could take separate cars, or perhaps Broacha would see that his time could be better spent in a cubicle somewhere, or anyplace where he didn't need to interact with people, like now with the Psychologist who was following them out into the parking lot telling them about the Pet Cemetery caretaker.

"Funny guy, I don't think he gets out much, and he'll talk your arm off." Doug laughed at the thought. "He was telling me about parallel universes where the TV shows are real and we're pretend, and Indian Cave Paintings, and Oceanoids and gold and Styrofoam and Kennedy and lava tubes and all kinds of stuff, a real character, so you might be able to get something out of ... him." Doug trailed off, slightly embarrassed at his motor-mouthed jabbering. He recognized it as just a nervous discharge from the subconsciously stressful interview he'd just completed, totally natural but nevertheless embarrassing.

Carl and Rusty were both staring at him now since one of the few things discernible in one of the most sensitive and heavily redacted, smudged and scarcely readable project documents, was the word, 'Oceanoid'.

Chapter Sixteen

A Well Lit Abyss

Virginia held Hertell's arm and covered her eyes as he led her up the long and steep incline to the narrow strip of daylight ahead. "Just look down and keep your eyes closed as much as you can until you adjust to the light, and don't look up until I tell you."

"Okay." Her voice sounded like coiled joy.

He put his hand over her eyes as well, just to make sure. "We're almost there." The ramp now had deep stair steps cut into it, and he spotted his Cub Scout canteen, which had evidently fallen in with him but hadn't accompanied him the additional hundred or so feet to the bottom of the ramp. As he stepped over his canteen, he realized that the steps they were walking up were actually part of the great warm slab.

Her pace slowed and her steps shortened as they approached the consuming light, not out of fear or apprehension, but just the normal hesitation in the face of a prophesy come to pass. She finally stopped and stood in the narrow strip of warm daylight with both hands cupped over her eyes, hunched like a child on Christmas morning, savoring the last delicious moments of promise and potential. "I know this place."

They were framed in a low rectangular opening just below the crest of Whisper Hill. Hertell turned her to the south and away from the sun. "Okay, you can open your eyes but just look at the ground until your eyes adjust.

She opened her eyes and looked at the ground. "I know what this place is."

Hertell watched her blink-rate stabilize and slow as she adjusted to the light of day. The sun had broken the horizon and was painting an altostratus layer to the south in breathtaking red and gold. "Ok, you can look up now."

"I know this place." She hugged herself. "It is the resurrection and the light."

Hertell, didn't really hear her, he was just watching her emerge into the day. She was even more beautiful in full daylight. "Uh-huh, you can look up now. It's a really pretty morning."

Virginia lifted her head and looked up into the beautiful southern sky. She then took a deep rasping breath and froze in terror. "I'm going to fall in! Hold me! I'm going to fall in!"

Hertell put his arm around her shoulder. "No, you won't fall in, it's just the sky. You won't fall into the sky..."

Like a drowning swimmer clawing at her savior, she didn't hear a word he said. She grabbed him around the waist, squeezed the air out of him and buried her face in his chest. "Don't let me fall in! Hold me! Don't let me fall in!"

Hertell struggled to keep his balance and was patiently explaining about gravity and the sky, as she climbed on him in a panic, and how she couldn't possibly fall into the sky, when he lost his footing.

She clung to him as they slid down the great warm slab. "We're falling into the sky! We're falling into the sky!" and into the pit Hertell and his D-6 had dug at the foot of Whisper Hill.

They slowly skidded to a stop at the bottom of the pit, dusty and torn from the trip down, her arms still clasped across his chest. He could feel her heart beating; it felt like a hummingbird in his shirt pocket. She opened her eyes as her face slowly emerged from his chest and looked up into the jolting sky. "Are we in the sky?"

"No, we're still down here and the sky's still up there. See, we're fine. We're right here, we're not going anywhere." He noticed that her skirt was covering his arm.

The skirt had evidently slid up past her waist on the long slide down the slab, revealing the most beautiful, shapely, smooth creamy thighs in all Christendom, and topped off by white cotton high-top panties that hadn't been seen on earth since Sears Catalogs of the early '70s. He felt a stirring he hadn't felt in a long time. He stared in rapt wonder at her snowy legs for a few more trembling heartbeats, and felt her warmth, and then dutifully and gently took the hem of her skirt and restored it to its proper, modest position. He tenderly brushed away some of the dirt and foxtails it had collected on the way down Whisper Hill. "We fell, or actually slid, but not into the sky. We fell in a more normal direction, down, and not up. Into the sky."

"What's that?" She was looking up into the sky where a jet contrail was arcing toward the north.

Hertell followed her gaze up to the silent airliner. "It's just an airplane, probably going to San Francisco or Seattle or something."

She repeated his words. "An airplane going to San Francisco." She shook her head. "It can't be going to San Francisco." She pointed toward the centroid of Whisper Hill. "San Francisco is down there, way past Egypt and over by the Ponderosa."

Hertell watched in amazement as she slowly reached up, childlike, to touch it, her fingers gently, clumsily grasping at it. "It's really far away, you can't reach it… you can't touch it from here…"

"It's so small. How do they do that? How do they get the people inside?"

Hertell looked into her upturned face. "It's not small, it's just far away." He did a quick mental calculation. "Probably six or seven miles away. Up close it's really big and the people in it are the same size as you and me."

She stared into the sky and shook her head in amazement. "Well, fuck me dead."

Hertell was unsure how to respond, but his confusion was overcome by events when a shot rang out from up above.

"Mutant! Get away from her!"

A lone figure stood at the top of the hill. He was a distinguished looking black man wearing casual attire of the early 1960's, and while definitely an older gentleman, he also had that ageless quality that some people achieve when reaching a certain age, and could have been anywhere between his late 60s to the high 90s. He also bore a striking resemblance to Nat King Cole; only he was holding Virginia's Geiger counter in one hand and a pistol in the other.

"The rad counts here are minimal, so there's no problem with decontamination. Just get away from him so I can get a clear shot."

Hertell and Virginia had already scrambled to their feet on the uneven ground at the bottom of the pit, and stood awkwardly like two teenagers caught in the back seat of a Buick Electra. Fearing collateral damage, Hertell edged away from her, but she closed the distance immediately and took his arm—still concerned about falling into the sky.

"No, Pop it's ok. He said there wasn't any war..."

"You can't believe what he says..." The man was squinting and struggling to see in the blinding light and was awkwardly attempting to shade his eyes with his pistol hand. "Mutants and lawyers will tell you all kinds of lies."

"But I saw an airplane up in the sky and it was only this big," she gestured with her fingertips as if holding a tiny fragile insect, "because it was far away, and it was full of people, people the same size as you and me and it was going to San Francisco. And so it must be the real San Francisco, not the one down by the Ponderosa where the Cartwrights live!"

"You can't believe what you see either, it's all lies up here. We knew there'd be a few stragglers left but they'll kill each other off in a few more years... Now get away from her mutant!" He fired another shot into the air and winced painfully at the noise. "Damn, I forgot how loud these things are. Lot louder than I remember."

"You shouldn't shoot up into the air like that." Hertell lowered his head to show the entry point of the bullet, "I got shot in the head once that way, see?"

"Yeah, or you might hit one of those tiny airplanes." Virginia pointed up into the sky. "Look Pop, there's another one right now. It's going the other way!"

The older man looked up and sure enough, there was a southbound speck and its contrail crawling across the morning sky on its way to LA or San Diego or Mexico.

He lowered his gun and his Geiger counter and stood staring, uncomprehending into the sky.

Virginia stood at the bottom of the pit looking up at the silent, southbound airliner, and then let her gaze fall down to her father standing at the top of the hill. She watched him for what seemed an eternity to Hertell. It was a pleasant enough eternity. She was still holding his arm and he felt the warmth of her skin. And then he felt something else. It was coming right through her skin, he could feel it going up his arm and into his chest and into every part of his aching body. And then she spoke.

"We made it Poppy? We're here." She pointed to the great warm slab. "The stone has been rolled away. It's the resurrection and the light. We can start the world over again now. It's our time."

The old man finally looked down from the sky toward Hertell and Virginia at the bottom of the pit. Even at this distance, Hertell could see that the old man's eyes were a well of tears. He finally spoke.

"Well, fuck me dead."

It turns out that the expression was one of general exclamation, passed down from generation to generation within the underground colony until it completely lost its original meaning and was, to them, completely free of any vulgar cachet or interpretation. It was on par with the traditional "Well, I'll be", or "Well, how 'bout that" or "Well, what d'ya know" but was reserved for only the most extreme exclamations of surprise—such as those that morning on Whisper Hill, but Hertell wouldn't learn this until much later because it didn't come up on the short but dusty ride in Hertell's Cushman cart.

Virginia seemed to really enjoy the trip from the great warm slab and Whisper Hill down to the main house. She sat beside Hertell and continually pointed out things of interest to her father along the way, a bird, a buckwheat plant, a pyramid, an ice cream truck.

They had an unusual exchange as they went inside, which Hertell wouldn't understand until some time later. It happened just as they entered the kitchen via the backdoor, as the front door to the house and the living room hadn't been used in decades. Virginia stopped in the doorway and stared into the kitchen.

"What's all this back here?"

Hertell went into tour guide mode. "Well... the whole rest of the kitchen, the kitchen is where we make all of our..."

Virginia was confused. "Right in the same place, right next to the door?"

"That's how they do it up here Ginny," her dad offered blankly. "They put the door right next to the room it goes into. Funny, but that's how it is up here. As I remember."

This seemed to satisfy Virginia. "Ok, kinda makes sense though."

So as she pondered the close proximity of the kitchen to the kitchen door, Hertell made lunch, his last box of mac'n cheese, and patiently explained the history of the world since the assassination of JFK to Virginia and her father, Miles.

Hertell organized it into three main thrust areas: technology, geo-politics, and popular culture. Only a few things seemed to register though: that we landed on the moon since that was a JFK promise; that Reagan had been President since they knew him from the movies and one of the founders had actually worked with him on a couple of westerns; that the Soviet Union had collapsed, but was otherwise unchanged; that their clothing was back in style again because of a popular cable TV show; and that there was no great atomic war.

That was the hardest one for them to absorb, so Hertell turned on the TV and cycled through hundreds of channels to prove that the world was still out there: Mexican soap operas, Brazilian soccer, Japanese game shows, music videos, WWF. He turned on the radio to a talk station where they were ventilating about the debt. He put his cell phone on speaker and called a number at random. "A and E Automotive, this is Sanford."

"Oops, sorry Sanford, wrong number." Hertell hung up the phone and turned off the TV and the radio. "See? It's all still out there."

Virginia was exhilarated, but Miles was troubled and was staring silently at the milk and graham crackers they'd been presented for dessert.

Hertell dipped his graham cracker into his milk and took a spongy bite. "I mean, the world didn't end the way you thought it would, with nuclear bombs and stuff, and there's a whole buncha new possibilities now, asteroids, carbon, viruses from the jungle and the computer..."

Virginia watched Hertell dipping his graham cracker and followed suit. "But if there wasn't a war that destroyed civilization, then what happened?" gesturing toward the TV. "Where are the flying cars? Where are the dome cities on the moon? This seems like more of the same, only faster, and louder."

Though feeling obliged to defend the modern world, Hertell couldn't disagree. "I don't know. I guess the priorities changed."

The copper specks had long ago enabled Hertell to realize that just because you're breathing now, doesn't mean that you're smarter or more evolved than someone who was breathing a thousand or even ten thousand years ago—a million years yes, but not as recently as ten thousand years ago. He would often wonder what the ancients would think of us if they could watch us on a reality TV show. He was doubtful they'd see it as an improvement. The people hadn't changed, just the priorities.

Miles took a big drink of milk, swallowed and stared silently at the now half empty glass. "Milk..." his voice softened, "from... a cow." He put the glass down. "Should we tell the rest of them?"

Hertell looked at Virginia. "There are more?"

Chapter Seventeen

Extremely Low Frequency

T hey had become a fixation of the spoon-bender, late night AM conspiracy radio demographic back in the mid-'90s, and when the cattle-mutilations, Bigfoot sightings, Face on Mars, cold fusion and other suppressed inventions, and UFO abductions with plumber-snakes up the butt simply weren't enough, they'd trot out HAARP and mind control, and the Taos Hum as evidence that the Government was up to something.

The signals had been detected as early as the mid-sixties. The initial assumption was that it was a Navy black program for talking to our boomers; however, an investigation determined that there was no Navy project using the ELF band and none of the Three-Letter-Agencies either, so the most reasonable conclusion was that they were Soviet communications to Russian Boomers, probably just bell-ringers to bring them up to buoy depth where they could receive operational instructions for nuclear Armageddon from Mother Russia at a higher data rate. The signals were scarcely above the noise floor and very difficult to detect since, at 53 Hertz, they were nestled between the two power transmission frequencies used throughout the world—very clever those Russians.

The bell-ringer had an agonizingly low data rate, just a character every five minutes or so, and it could easily take a day or more to complete a transmission, sometimes transmissions could go on for a month or more, so the spook community determined that it definitely wasn't any kind of tactical or operational communication, but otherwise had no idea of its source, target, or objective, and eventually wrote the signals off as just an expensive attempt to mess with our heads by Soviet Psyops.

So the mysterious signals were characterized and cataloged and punched on cards and read onto DASD peripherals on the old IBM 360/65's that defined state of the art at the time, where long ago, in the days before the web and email and Bayesian search algorithms and cluster analysis and data mining, legions of transcriptionists would diligently convert recorded conversations, intercepted cables, news clippings, mail, and all manner of documents onto punched cards to be read onto DASD peripherals where they could be compared and correlated with other data fields on other DASD peripherals by the mighty IBM 360/65. And there the mystery lived; slowly receding from memory and relevance while simultaneously preserved and ultimately engulfed in the ocean of data to be consumed and digested by a succession of insatiable analysis platforms over time—SLCSE and CAVS on IBM, Haystack and Voracious on VAX, Voracious II on SUN, TESS on SGI, and currently Predacious on racks of commodity GPGPUs. All in the hope that someday somehow the signals and their source and their purpose would emerge into the light of day and have meaning and value.

Due to solar storms and sunspots and the like, and their effect on the Earth's magnetic field, the signals would tend to localize occasionally and create a characteristic hum which was noticed with some fanfare in the UK in the '70s and the US in the '90s and, because of the internets, pretty much everywhere else in the time since—the equivalent of telling ghost stories around a campfire and convincing yourself that the normal noises of the forest are an approaching mental institution escapee with a hook for a hand.

Because they were ELF signals, and at such a low frequency, they basically used the whole earth as their antenna, so they seemed to come from nowhere, and everywhere, at the same time, so there was no way to determine where they were coming from or who they were talking to, and certainly no way to determine why. When the Berlin Wall came down there was a cursory sip from the tsunami of released or otherwise exfiltrated Soviet documents, but nothing about the mysterious ELF signals.

The messages were plain text in the clear and without any encryption to speak of except that on occasion they would be in Russian Morse Code rather than the usual western version. Regardless of which coding scheme was used the messages were a random assortment of words, phrases, and sentences—happy birthday wishes, Christmas lists, recipes, eulogies, farm reports, sports scores, lyrics from songs, quotes from noteworthy figures, even knock-knock jokes—but all of them, whatever the topic, ended the same curious way, with a string of alphanumeric characters "3526N11846W" followed by two words, "Mustard Seed."

Chapter Eighteen

Main Street USA

They had created a beautiful world beneath Li'l Pal Heaven, and they led Hertell patiently through it explaining as they went. And much like Miles' and Virginia's introduction to Hertell's world above, only a few things seemed to register: that the half-life of the most dangerous radioactive isotopes required about thirty thousand days to decay to marginally safe levels; then something about toroidal accelerators and infinite energy, the founding mothers and Disney Imagineers, full-spectrum light and production design.

It was all too much for Hertell to absorb as he was led back through the pressure buffer where he'd met Virginia, which, now that he could see, fanned out into a dozen or more narrow passageways at its furthest edge. Virginia explained how the pressure buffer worked as they proceeded down one of the dimly lit passageways, which seemed to zigzag down at a gentle slope.

They emerged into what appeared to be an Iowa cornfield, but with a much lower ceiling painted a beautiful blue with puffy clouds. Virginia and her father nonchalantly flapped their arms like flightless birds as they proceeded down a row of corn, explaining that there were no insects for pollination, so they did it themselves. The cornfield led into a beautiful, gleaming gymnasium and basketball court straight out of an old "Leave It To Beaver" episode, and then on to an absolutely adorable miniature golf course with a little Eiffel Tower and Pyramids and Big Ben, Wind Mills and the Roman Coliseum. Off to the side he glimpsed a great hall that appeared to be an immense Cathedral with ornate carvings in the salt and pepper colored rock, and a Crucifix, almost as big as the Old Rugged Cross overlooking Highway 178, only with a pierced and dying Jesus artfully nailed to it, looming above the altar.

Almost every direction he looked there were wide passageways leading into bright and inviting chambers and everywhere there were enormous lights, like from old movie studios, lighting up ceilings and walls in beautiful colors and textures.

The floors were all flat and polished, and if he hadn't actually walked into it, he'd never have guessed he was in a cave.

They finally walked into what appeared to Hertell to be a cross between Disneyland's Main Street USA and a Norman Rockwell painting. It was a timeless small-town square from some mythical past with a flagpole and a cannon and a bell and bandstand, and ringed with stores and offices and streetlights and park benches. From the lighting, Hertell guessed it to be late afternoon.

Miles asked Hertell to sit and wait on the park bench. Virginia sat down beside him. "I'll stay with him."

Miles excused himself and disappeared.

They sat quietly for a moment, which allowed Hertell to puzzle over a sound he was hearing. "Do I hear... birds?"

Virginia listened for a moment. "Yeah, it's the atmosphere track, there's crickets too." Hertell listened. "Oh yeah, I hear'm. You have crickets down here?"

She sighed wistfully. "No, just the sounds. They ate all the crickets a long time ago, before I was born."

Hertell nodded thoughtfully. "Oh, well I'm glad you kept the sound though." They were sitting across from what appeared to be a Malt Shop straight out of "Happy Days" and he could faintly hear music drifting from its open door. It sounded vaguely like Dick Dale. There was a movie theatre next to the malt shop, and according to the marquee, the main feature was "The Nutty Professor." He could smell popcorn.

Hertell inquired about what appeared to be a twenty-foot tall, two-headed insect poised above the bandstand at the center of the town square. Virginia was in the middle of her explanation about the Zeiss planetarium projector when a new sound captured Hertell's attention, it was distant and faint, but it was unmistakable: a distorted, music box sound. Hertell gripped the seat of the park bench, as if to reassure himself that it was real. "What's that sound? Is that... a music box?"

Virginia listened and then smiled in recognition. "No, that's Mister Frostie's ice cream truck."

But before Hertell could react, the birds and crickets and Mister Frostie went silent. There was a crackle of static and then Miles' voice filled the air.

"Will everyone please come up to Main Street, USA? We have an announcement to make."

It was a very difficult discussion down on Main Street USA. The initial shock yielded to suspicion since Hertell was presumed to be a mutant after all. It was followed by denial and rejection, though repeatedly rebutted by Virginia and Miles who vouched for Hertell and his story, and eventually settled into sullen skeptical acceptance, accompanied by a lot of "well-fuck-me-deads", which still greatly confused Hertell, and was concluded by an assortment of random questions: "Are there flying cars? Are there colonies on Mars? Do people live under the ocean? ..."

However, it was the last question that would affect Hertell the most. It was a voice that came from the darkness. It was a woman's voice and it was choked with emotion. "Are there still... dogs up there?" Hertell was unable to speak, so he just nodded into the darkness and thought of all the beloved dogs buried above their heads for all these years.

The people had arrived from every direction: some emerged in doorways, others rode up on bicycles, some walked right into the town square, and others remained at a distance.

From the discussion, Hertell gleaned that the oldest ones, like Miles, were a venerated, but small and shrinking group, the "Founders" all in their late 80s to what appeared to be high 90s and were the last remnants of the initial group that had abandoned the world above in 1963 for the one they now had beneath Li'l Pal Heaven. Everyone else, who was either born beneath the Li'l Pal, like Virginia, or a small

140

child when they went to live in the world below, was referred to as the "Future" which puzzled Hertell initially until he finally got the context. Collectively, the Founders and the Future seemed to be referred to as the "Generations" which appeared to be an aggregate term for the entire settlement.

The climb to the surface was slow going. There must have been over a hundred people in the fact-finding delegation, of all ages from infant to ancient, and races including a smattering of blacks and Asians and various blends, all in casual attire of the early 1960's, and all in varying levels of disbelief, apprehension, and excitement. It was a long way back through the zigzag passages into the pressure buffer and then up the slope leading to the steps cut into the great warm slab.

Presumably out of respect, the Founders led the way. They were very old and many were quite frail with some only able to take small, shuffling, uncertain steps which set a glacial pace for the last few hundred feet as they ascended the slope toward the great warm slab. The thing that Hertell found most astonishing was that he didn't hear a single grumble or even an exasperated sigh from the younger population, which followed patiently and quietly behind. They simply took it in stride as if that's the way it should be and didn't seem to begrudge the inconveniences of old age. Hertell had totally lost track of time as he led them up into the world, and it was dark as he emerged from beneath the great warm slab.

There was a high cirrostratus overcast that night and no moon, so it was a starless and otherwise uninteresting night. The glow of Bakersfield was clearly visible in the distance and there was an occasional set of headlights on Highway 178. Hertell stood at the rectangular opening above the great warm slab and guided the Founders away from the slippery slope he and Virginia had slid down when they were falling into the sky, and led them up to the top of Whisper Hill. The Future followed and eventually the entire top and upper flanks of Whisper Hill was covered with people. They all looked up into the sky and out toward the horizon, and Hertell was quite relieved that none were afraid of falling into the sky.

The Founders were silent as stone, but some of the older members of the Future were grumbling. One of the leading skeptics, a man in his fifties, finally said what many of the rest were evidently thinking. "This isn't the world. It's just a bigger pressure chamber that we didn't know about. It's big, I'll grant it, but it's not the world." There was a general consensus of relieved agreement: it needed better lighting to see its full extent, but it was just a very large pressure buffer.

Hertell tried to address the whole hilltop to explain. "Those are the lights of Bakersfield over there, and you can even see the rotating beacon at Meadows Field." He walked a short distance and pointed to the west. "See, there's the white flash... and just wait for a second and you'll see the green... and there's the green!" He noticed some headlights coming down the 178. "And that right there, that's a motorcycle coming down the 178 you can hear the engine, he's got it wide open for the straightaway."

He turned back toward the disbelievers again. "This isn't a pressure buffer, you're outside; you're looking at the world!" But several of the older Future were unimpressed, saying it was no different than San Francisco, the one down below past Egypt near the Ponderosa, with the same kind of tiny lights serving for Oakland across the bay. One of the younger Future took a few hesitant steps toward the lights of Bakersfield, and reached out to touch it, just as Virginia had done with the airliner.

Hertell kicked at the dirt and pulled up a tuft of Brome grass. "This is real dirt, this is a real rock, this is a real plant."

There was laughter as someone pointed out that they've got real dirt and real corn in the cornfield. They had just begun discussing how to best utilize the newly found pressure buffer, perhaps as another cornfield or possibly a larger miniature golf course or possibly a new site for the planetarium, when everything changed.

A small airplane, a Cessna, flew directly overhead from east to west. It was low, only a thousand feet or so above their heads and lit up like a Christmas tree with green and red position lights shining and strobes dutifully flashing as it followed the river west toward Meadows field. The entire Future fell into silence and struggled to comprehend what they'd just witnessed.

They didn't get much time to struggle because the moon was now peeking up from behind Bear Mountain and was illuminating the underside of the cirrostratus layer turning the sky into a bright undulating silver sheet stretching from horizon to horizon and crisscrossed with several ragged contrails from long gone airliners but now visible in the moonlight along with the distant Greenhorn mountains to the east and the Tehachapi's to the south and the lumpen hills and gullies leading west towards Bakersfield.

Hertell looked at the hillside staring silently into the great yawning moonlit sky, he felt vindicated, triumphant. "See! This is the sky! This is not a pressure buffer! This is the world, this is the sky!" There was silence except for the fading drone of the Cessna. Hertell caught sight of the Founders. They were all looking up into the sky in awe and loving remembrance. Some had tears in their eyes. And then it started.

It started spontaneously and spread like fission. "I'm going to fall in!"

It was a small boy, maybe nine or ten years old who was hugging his father around the waist. The father, a man of probably forty, looked panic stricken with his wife and at least three children now clinging to him. He looked down at his wife and children and then up into the sky and then reached out for the nearest Founder. "We're going to fall in, help us, we're going to fall in!" More voices joined the chorus. "I'm going to fall in... help me... hold me... don't let me fall in!"—until the entire Future was a terrified knot of people desperately clinging to each other in a blind panic with the aged and frail Founders trying to comfort the whole Future, their grown children in their fifties and sixties trying to hide their own fear, and comfort their younger children in their thirties and forties who were trying to hide their fear, and comfort their younger children, like the ten year old boy that started it all.

It reminded Hertell of that fairy tale where all the people got stuck together because of a goose of some kind and made a sad princess laugh or something. Only nobody was laughing on Whisper Hill tonight and their fear was so focused that they couldn't and wouldn't hear Hertell's frenetic and sincere assurances that they were in absolutely no danger of falling into the sky.

It was then, like a top wobbling and losing momentum, that his urgent circling explanations of the world and the sky began to dissipate as he became focused on a sound that was emerging from the chorus of woe. It was a humming sound, not like those humming cities in the desert, but the humming of a human voice. It was faint and difficult to distinguish beneath the appeals for salvation and sanctuary, but it was there and getting stronger as more voices gradually joined in until eventually everyone on Whisper Hill was motionless and all humming the same note—everyone except Hertell who stood staring at them all as if gazing into a campfire. Someone began singing...

This is my Father's world,
And to my listening ears,
All nature sings, and round me rings,
the music of the spheres...

And then, like a school of fish changing direction, at the hint of a predator, in perfect silvery formation, the hilltop began singing in perfect pitch and harmony as if they'd done it a thousand times before.

This is my Father's world,
I rest me in the thought

Of rocks and trees, of skies and seas;
His hand the wonders wrought.

All of them, of every age, the ancients, the infants, and everyone in between now calmed and at peace, and singing the hymn that Hertell remembered as one of Mister Frostie's, one that he'd often sing as he wandered into the bleached hills east of the Li'l Pal with the mastodons and the trilobites and the Mourning Dove.

This is my Father's world,
I walk a desert lone,
In a bush ablaze to my wondering gaze
God makes His glory known

There was something in their voices, something that made Hertell think, for the first time in his life, that even though it was illogical and irrational, that for the first time ever, he thought there might be a God.

Chapter Nineteen

A Heartwarming Reunion

The Founders and the Future all agreed that they should return to their lower world and make preparations for their return to the upper world. They'd quickly grown accustomed to the sky that night and after a short time were actually able to laugh at their initial response as they relived the experience over and over again, mixed in with an assortment of discussions about the future and their plans for it. A woman in her 60s was sobbing for joy at the prospect of actually being able to hug and hold a puppy again, something she hadn't done since she was a tiny child before the first generation escaped into the world below Whisper Hill the day after Kennedy was assassinated. She was surrounded by a likeminded group that rhapsodized about hugging big squirming bouquets of puppies and kittens and it reminded Hertell of the "Grapes of Wrath" when Grandpa Joad wanted to smush grapes all over his face.

They'd also spent much of the night singing, and not just hymns, but everything you could think of: a fantastic medley from *Oklahoma*—they even made the clip-clop sounds for the horses in "Surrey with the Fringe On Top"; an inspiring doo-wop interpretation of "Sixteen Tons"; and a heart-rending version of the old Marty Robbins hit, "El Paso", where the cowboy dies just as he reaches the Mexican girl he loves, and all of it completely a capella and all with a faint trace of Old Spanish.

What was odd though, was how they'd start. It was just like in the old musicals. There would be dozens of simultaneous and unrelated discussions, and then seemingly at random, a word or a phrase would trigger someone to start singing and they'd almost immediately be joined by the rest of the hilltop, and then at the conclusion of the song go right back into their conversations.

Aside from the odd genesis of the singing, it was their actual sound that completely captivated Hertell. He couldn't place it. It seemed to be a combination of Madrigal and those Sing-AlongWith- Mitch-'60s-TV-variety-show type singers with a little Gregorian chant thrown in, but the predominant, unifying force was full-throated, joyous AME gospel, just like with the dinosaurs. Hertell later learned that their unique sound was attributable to a cherished and venerated Aunt Tawney, a negro, which was their preferred term when used at all, and the matriarch who taught all the grateful generations of the Future to sing, and to play the piano and the Hammond B-3 organ.

The Founders took one last look into the sky and then began their return to the lower world. The Future followed along behind, though it took much longer since they were forced to proceed single file through the rectangular opening which was much smaller now due to a large volume of loose dirt that had fallen into it during the Falling-into-the-sky episode. However, it was still passable, and Hertell watched as the last of them disappeared back into their world. Whisper Hill was quiet once again.

Hertell sat for a while as the sounds of their voices faded back into the earth. The sun was just rising when Hertell left Whisper Hill and drove the Cushman back to the house. He took a shower and shaved and made a list of things to get. He then left a note on the kitchen door in case they emerged before his return, and then drove his dad's truck to Costco where he spent most of the morning getting provisions: mac'n cheese, sunblock, graham crackers, milk, from a cow, bags of apples and oranges, paper plates and cups—not nearly enough for everyone below, but a start. Hertell had never had this many visitors before and he was resolved to make their transition into the world-as-it-is, as gradual and pleasant and safe as possible.

He wasn't sure how much the Costco excursion was going to cost, so he'd gotten some money from his dad's safe. It was a massive affair, with an "Atomic Energy Commission" emblem on the front that his dad evidently got at an auction back in the '70s. It had been tucked into a closet in his mom's sewing room and was hidden by boxes and bolts of fabric from long abandoned sewing projects, but his dad had given Hertell the combination and showed him how to open it during the last September of his life, and told him, with some gravity, that it was all his now. It was mainly full of old cigar boxes and papers, but there were also several shelves of money toward the bottom.

The clerks at Costco seemed unperturbed by someone of Hertell's aspect and demeanor thumbing through an inch-thick bundle of cash to pay for the two fully laden dolly carts. The truck was old and slow and Hertell made it his practice to stay off the freeway, as it tended to frustrate the other drivers, so he would usually take surface streets. He turned off Rosedale Highway at Buck Owens Boulevard and followed it up through Oildale. There was no radio in the truck, so Hertell was alone with his thoughts on the drive home from Costco. His thoughts mainly cycled over the provisions he'd gotten and the various scenarios for their consumption: a picnic out by the quarry or possibly a hike down to the highway to watch the cars and trucks and motorcycles and RV's go by.

His thoughts quickly progressed beyond his immediate plans and he made mental notes of various things he'd soon be needing: a large bus for transporting the group to various events as they became acclimated to the current world; building materials for constructing new houses for all of them, and he could think of no better use for the Li'l Pal than to build the homes of those who had once dwelled beneath all the little dead pets, so that they could now dwell above them. He'd put in streets and lights and playgrounds and there was plenty of money in the safe to do all of that.

It was nearly noon by now and a very sunny day. Hertell was squinting in the bright sunshine as he drove and felt around on the bench seat for his sunglasses. He couldn't find them but immediately recognized that sunglasses would be essential for the return of the Founders and the Future when they emerged into full daylight.

There was usually an assortment of vans with merchandise for sale on this particular stretch of the 178 as it carried both the fishing, boating, and jet ski traffic up to Lake Isabella and also the local commuter traffic that ran between the entrepreneurial areas of southwest Bakersfield and the high-end, for Bakersfield, gated communities of Golden Hills Estates, Rio Bravo Country Club, Tuscan Sol and so forth that had sprouted in the early '80s in the north east near the river. The vans sold a variety of items: velvet art, Bonsai trees, pottery, flowers on occasion, and always an assortment of sunglasses. Hertell, stopped and bought out the inventory of one lucky vendor and headed for home where some people were waiting for him, but it wasn't who he'd expected.

Kaye was accompanied by a woman in her 60s or possibly well- preserved 70s. Kaye was without her flashlight and gun and uniform on this visit but was instead dressed in a floral sundress and armed only with a manila folder. The other woman wore a khaki skirt and a starchy white blouse. Her every movement was accompanied by the jangling and clanking of her bracelets, necklaces, broaches and rings. The two women stood at the back door and read the note Hertell had left.

Getting victuals.
Kitchen door is open and leads directly into the kitchen!
All other doors work the same.
Make yourselves at home.
Be right back.
Hertell Daggett Jr.

The older woman stared blankly at the note. "Did he know we were coming?"

Kaye shrugged. "I don't know. I guess." She looked at the older woman. "You wanna go in? It's very tidy, he cleans it like every day or something."

The older woman shook her head. "No." She escaped to the sanctuary of her cell phone and turned away from the note, the kitchen door, and the house. "I'll wait in the car."

They didn't wait long.

The Chevy Stepside turned off of the 178 and began a dusty trudge up to the house. The truck appeared to be heaped to overflowing with sunglasses, and it came to a stop directly in front of the rental car. Kaye was leaning against the fender and nodded in acknowledgement at his approach. Another woman sat in the passenger seat, but Hertell was unable to see her face.

Hertell revved the engine just as he shut it down, a habit he'd acquired in his teens, as had Kaye when both learned it from Hertell's dad. Kaye smiled in recognition of the automotive tic they now shared and watched Hertell exit the truck. "Got enough sunglasses?"

Hertell was momentarily confused by the question but then remembered all of the sunglasses he'd recently acquired and lashed down over the Costco provisions. "Yeah, I think so."

"Were you expecting us? We read the note you left, but didn't go in."

Hertell stopped in his tracks. "No, the note wasn't for you it was for all the people under Whisper... no, it wasn't for you. I didn't know you were coming."

Anxious to change the subject, Hertell pointed at the truck. "Look, this isn't a very good time for me. I gotta lot of stuff to do right now. Can we interface some other time?"

Kaye thumped the fender. "We're here right now, let's just take care of it, it doesn't need to take that long. But we gotta just deal with it."

He was now looking at the older woman still sitting in the car. "Is that your realtor?"

Kaye shook her head. "No it's..."

Hertell addressed the woman in the car. "It's not for sale."

The older woman in the car sat motionless, unable to make eye contact. Kaye finally spoke, "Hertell, it's your mom. It's Anita."

He hadn't been expecting this. It was almost as remote an expectation as finding a whole civilization living under his feet. He took a few steps closer and bent down for a better view into the rental car. The absence of family photographs had achieved its desired effect since he recognized nothing about the woman, and she bore no resemblance to any of the

153

TV and commercial moms he'd forged her memory into. He waved at the woman. "Hi Mom."

The woman nodded in acknowledgement and got out of the rental car. She was bleached and botoxed and surprisingly small, as he'd remembered her as towering figure the last time he'd seen her, shortly before the car door slam took her away.

Hertell watched her exit the car and then stand awkwardly beside it. He looked at her for a long time in complete silence and then tilted his head slightly. "You look different."

She seemed unsure how to respond. "Well, it's been... thirty something years."

The voice he recognized.

For a moment he was once again in the velvet fort with his dinosaurs. He looked at her, nodded, and then thoughtfully replied, "That must be it then."

His mom laughed. "Yeah, must be."

He remembered the laugh too, though he'd heard it rarely as a child. "Heard you were dead."

Anita shrugged. "Those reports were premature."

Hertell laughed and rubbed his head and determined that the heart-warming reunion part of the program had run its course. He didn't know this woman, and even though he shared 23 of her chromosomes, he could not care less about her feelings. He bore her no grudge, but he had a whole civilization that needed him and he wanted to get back to them and his new life. "Look, I know why you're here, and it's not for sale, and I don't care how many dead Indians are buried out here."

Kaye took off her sunglasses. "It's not your decision Hertell. We all own a piece of this estate and the consortium has made a very generous offer that we need to discuss and ..."

Hertell decided it was time to lay down some guilt-laden covering fire. He pointed out into the cemetery. "Things are buried out there. Precious things. Things that were loved. Not the way we do it with each other with exclusions and unlesses and contingencies, but unconditionally loved, cherished things!"

It was a credible initial volley and Kaye and his mother immediately tried to reassure him that they could just dig up the dead pets and move them somewhere else like Tehachapi or Bodfish or Walker Basin and that he'd have plenty of money to buy another Li'l Pal, several of them in fact.

"What about Dad?" There. That should shut them up and send them packing.

Kaye fell silent, but Anita filled the vacuum. "We can dig him up too, we can put him down wherever you want."

Hertell stood with his arms folded staring down the two women. "I will not allow these sacred grounds to be dug up, paved over, or otherwise desecrated for nickel slots, Texas Hold'em and all-you-can-eat-buffets. There is an obligation that we have to the things that we have loved, an obligation which I cannot abjure. It is not for sale. There's nothing to discuss."

Kaye held up the manila folder. "It's a done deal, Hertell. We're selling Li'l Pal. There's nothing you can do about it. Hate to put it that way but that's the way it is."

Hertell looked at Kaye. He recognized this voice too. It was final, non-negotiable, almost like a car door slamming.

Anita was stunned. "Boy you cut to the chase, I wasn't..."

"Yeah, the least you could do is pretend, humor me a little."

Kaye considered his comment and reflected on the many times she'd made a similar argument to Hertell when he would mock her faith in the redeeming blood of Jesus Christ. She then shrugged and fulfilled the role she'd been assigned many times in her life. "Yeah, we could go round and round about the dead pets out there and how you were abandoned by her and divorced by me and shot in the head and everything else, but it won't change anything."

Anita was wishing she was still sitting in the car, or actually sitting in a car in Sacramento.

Kaye then softened a bit and addressed them both. "I've had a lot of experience in these matters, and with you Hertell in particular, and it's best to just deal with things as they are and do what's needed, and cauterize if you have to."

Hertell was silent and looked out toward Whisper Hill. He was trapped now. His dead pets gambit didn't work, nor his dead dad under the pyramid topper. They were no match for an Indian Casino and the riches it foretold.

"You've got a chance to walk away and start a new life. You should take it."

Hertell felt suddenly tired but steadied himself on the fender of the truck. "But Kaye, I've got a new life now."

He moved past them and pointed toward Whisper Hill and it all came flooding out of him. "My new life is out there, there's people out there, living underneath Whisper Hill, hundreds of'm, I don't know how many exactly, but I found them and I have to take care of'm now. They're depending on me. We can't put a casino on top of'm no matter how much money the Indians give us!"

He stopped suddenly realizing that he'd said more than was prudent and how it could be perceived. He stood a short distance away from them and tried to collect his thoughts and how to recover from what he'd just said.

Anita said nothing but was clearly troubled. She was however inwardly relieved. It would be much simpler to secure the property if he were judged incompetent and much harder if he were a rational person.

Kaye finally broke the long silence. "When was the last time you slept?"

Hertell wasn't sure how to answer her question, as he hadn't really been paying attention. He thought for a moment. "I... don't know, what's today?"

Kaye shook her head. "You tell me."

Hertell tried to reconstruct events of the past few days. "Well, uhhh... Friday? It's ... Friday."

"It's Sunday Hertell."

Hertell contemplated the implications of her answer. "Oh, ok... I lost track...it's been a coupla days... then." Seeing where Kaye was going, he decided to put her suspicions to rest.

"I'm not sleepy and I'm not crazy and even though I've been shot in the head I'm not, I am not imagining this. There is a large group of people living in a huge, bunker cavern type thing out there underneath Whisper Hill. And I fell into a... a hole basically on, I don't know, probably Monday maybe, and I was knocked out for a while, I don't know how long, and I met a woman down there, named Virginia, after the state, like 49 other people living down there with each one of'm knowing the entire history and vital statistics of state they're named after, and then I met her dad, Miles, and he wanted to shoot me, but I talked him out of it, and then they introduced me to everybody else down there, and they've been down there since President Kennedy got shot because they thought there would be a big atomic war, and it's huge place and they have toroid power and miniature golf courses and houses and cathedrals and neighborhoods and parks and sound effects and cornfields, and it's... unbelievable... but it's true. It's all... true."

He'd never heard himself say it all out loud before and he could tell by their expressions that it was not working as he'd hoped. "Look, I can see you don't believe me, so just come out there with me and I'll show you. You can see for yourselves."

Anita finally spoke, but she didn't look at him. "That's not... necessary, I don't need to see it. I believe you."

Hertell looked at her. "Of course you do. It'll make it easier to get this place sold if I'm just some crazy person you can scrape off like overburden." He was beginning to get agitated. "Only I'm not crazy, so just come with me out there and I'll prove it to you!"

Kaye walked over to the Cushman and sat down in the front seat. "Ok, show me."

Chapter Twenty

The Shallow Ditch

I t was a pleasant ride up to Whisper Hill in the old Cushman. Hertell drove and recounted how it had all started with voices which he thought might be coming from all the old TVs only then it turned into accordion sounds and how that led to the discovery of the underground civilization and the funny story about how they were all afraid of falling into the sky the first time they saw it and how they calmed themselves by singing a song that he recognized. The two women rode in silence.

They reached the foot of Whisper Hill and the great pit that Hertell and the D-6 had made of its western slope. They parked in the shade of the D-6 where he'd left it and walked the rest of the way to the top of the hill. He pointed out the great warm slab, freshly exposed on their left, and the curious galvanized culverts that angled off of it, and the excavation around the old test well-heads in the adjoining gulley on their right as they trudged up the hill. "Those are air ducts, see how one is a little taller than the other, just like in Prairie Dog towns? They're all over Li'l Pal, all the way up toward Mt.

Adelaide. And they all lead down into a big pressure buffer which'll be the first room we go into."

For all of his explanations, Kaye saw the air ducts for what they were, capped test wells that Hertell's dad and the wildcatters had drilled back in the '50s, as she'd been told many times over the years. She also remembered the hill as the site where she and Hertell had sex for the first time when they were still teenagers—a warm summer night a thousand years ago during a meteor shower on an old boy scout sleeping bag, a night when she'd never felt more loved.

Anita vaguely remembered the hill from her stint as a Cub Scout den mother—she was fine doing craft stuff around a kitchen table but refused to sleep outside and tramp around in the pet cemetery with the boys and the snakes and stinkbugs. She'd left shortly thereafter.

They finally reached the top of Whisper Hill and looked down over the great warm slab.

Anita watched Kaye who watched Hertell who seemed to be staring, uncomprehending into a long shallow ditch that ran the width of the great warm slab. His breathing was ragged and his hands were now shaking, and then, as if trying to explain it to himself. "This... this is where it was... it must've caved in or something, from all the people..." He fell silent.

It looked no different to him now than it did to Kaye and Anita. He was seeing the same thing they were, nothing more than a shallow ditch. He folded his arms to dampen his shaking hands and stared into what only a few precious hours before had been a portal to a new life. "I gotta think about this....

Maybe this is the wrong hill..."

160

Anita was already walking down the hill toward the Cushman. "I gotta go, let's go."

Kaye stood beside him and looked into the ditch. "Come on Hertell, we've all seen enough now. Let's go back to the house."

Hertell stood motionless staring, almost catatonic.

She looked away from him toward Anita, who was still negotiating her way down the hill past the culverts, and called after, "We'll be right there Anita, hold up." She also took the opportunity to wipe her eyes and her nose as she accepted that whatever remained of the Hertell she once knew was now gone.

She took a deep breath and squared her shoulders and turned back to Hertell. "I'm gonna take your mom down to the house, ok? But I'll come right back. She doesn't know how to work the Cushman, so I'll take her, but then I'll be back. Okay?"

Hertell didn't respond. He was silently accepting that he could no longer distinguish between the past and the present and the imagined for they all seemed equally real to him: the mastodons and trilobites, Virginia and Miles and the world under his feet, and now his mother and Kaye and the shallow ditch. He felt something, warmth.

Kaye's hand was on his shoulder. She spoke tenderly to him. "I'll be back. Okay."

Hertell looked up. "What?"

"I said I'm gonna take your mom back to the house." She looked over toward Anita who had stopped midway down the hill and appeared to have taken an interest in one of the culverts. "But I'll come back in a little bit."

Hertell nodded and smiled at her. "Okay..." He looked back down at the ditch. "I'll be here."

Kaye lifted her hand from his shoulder, turned and proceeded down the hill. She hadn't taken more than a dozen paces when she felt her bowels trembling. She stopped and started a quick inventory of what she'd eaten that day, but before she'd even gotten through her breakfast review, she felt the trembling under her feet and immediately recognized that it was just an earthquake and not food poisoning. Quite a relief.

There was a shout from down the hill, and Kaye saw that Anita had reversed course and was heading back toward them and higher ground. She was also waving and pointing at the culvert, which was now trickling water onto the great warm slab.

And then with a roar like the rushing wind, the culverts that simply had no reason to be where they were, exploded into raging torrents of water, washing over the great warm slab and spilling down its face and into a roiling river of mud that coursed down the gulley and the steep watershed emptying into the distant Kern River.

And as suddenly as it started, the water stopped. The roar faded away into a cheerful trickling drip-drop. The great warm slab was now completely exposed, and it was massive—at least the width of a five-lane freeway, and possibly twice as long as it was wide.

Kaye looked down toward Anita who had stumbled up to higher ground and was now hugging herself. "You okay?"

Anita nodded and looked back at the revealed slab glistening in the afternoon sun. She shaded her eyes from its blinding reflection. "What the fuck was that all about?"

Kaye looked up toward where Hertell stood. From the way he was facing she presumed he was staring into the shallow ditch and seemed oblivious to the event, which had just occurred.

She was about to ask him if he was okay, when she heard something, it was almost a loud ticking sound, but then immediately grew into a shrill metallic chattering and finally into a scraping, grinding, and deafening rumble as the massive slab, in one sudden and fluid motion, slid down the hill like a glacier calving an iceberg and leaving a huge, yawning vault where the entire hillside had been only seconds before.

Kaye had instinctively dropped to the ground at the deafening rumble and was now cautiously getting back to her feet. She looked back toward Anita who was similarly engaged further down the hill. She looked up toward the top of the hill, but the top of the hill was now gone and Hertell was nowhere to be seen.

"Hertell!" Kaye sprinted, as best she could over the uneven dirt and the wedge espadrilles she was wearing that complemented her church sundress, up the hill toward Hertell.

She found him on all fours, peering cautiously over the precipice and down into the glistening, wet, rectangular crater. He looked up at her as she approached. "Do you hear it?"

She hadn't been expecting a question. "What, the whole hill caving in? Yes I heard it!"

He scrambled to his feet, and raced past her down the hill. "Not that... Listen! Can you hear it?"

Kaye heard him ask his mother the same question as he stumbled past her on the way down to the bottom of the former hillside.

From her vantage point, roughly where the shallow pit had been, Kaye could see that the hillside formerly known as Whisper Hill now resembled a large airplane hanger or perhaps a Walmart loading dock, the great slab now formed a large apron overlooking the valley floor to the south, with a gentle incline leading up to the big rectangular opening directly below her and into the darkened interior.

Hertell reached the bottom of the former hill, slogged through the mud and was standing on the large glistening apron. He was jumping up and down like an excitable child and waving up to Kaye and his mother. "Listen! Can you hear it now?"

Kaye cupped her hands and shouted, "Get out of there! The water might start again!"

She was just inflating for another shout at Hertell when she noticed Anita who seemed to be transfixed and was expectantly leaning forward looking into the dark interior as if waiting for a bus. "Anita what is it?"

Anita held up her hand indicating she wanted quiet.

Kaye began making her way down the hill and had halved the distance to Anita when she heard a sound welling up from the great open vault. It was distant and distorted but it was unmistakable.

Hertell stood at the far end of the apron and looked directly into the opening and let the sound wash over him. A river of voices was issuing up out of the earth, a steady, harmonic, beautiful chord of a million voices echoing and reverberating out of the darkness and getting louder and clearer with each breath. He could see movement in the darkness now and could finally start to see them clearly. The Generations had obviously been planning for this day for a long time.

It seemed to be a procession of sorts as they were swaying and solemnly walking in a tight formation and were wearing what Hertell presumed to be radiation suits, long silvery reflective coveralls, almost like robes that covered them from head to foot except for their faces. The sunglasses he'd bought that morning were clearly unnecessary as all of them were wearing dark goggles as if witnesses at the Trinity atomic bomb test.

And as the first rank of them stepped out of the shadows and into the sunlight, the entire formation began singing...

In the cross of Christ I glory,
Towering o'er the wrecks of time...

The bright afternoon sunlight reflected off their silver suits creating a beautiful starburst corona that grew larger and larger as rank upon rank emerged into the day. They were walking in that rocking step that Hertell had seen black church choirs do on the Sunday morning TV shows that he'd watch with his father during his last September on earth.

All the light of sacred story
Gathers round its head sublime

They clapped in unison to punctuate each verse and it sounded like the gunshots from the Sheriff Dog funeral.

Hertell thought that every sound ever issued from the loving lips of human kind was woven into it. It wasn't so much the notes or the harmony; it was a palpable and unmistakable sound of... grace.

Anita, meanwhile, and true to her character, had beat feet back toward the house as soon as the singing started and was halfway down the hill before the end of the second verse.

Kaye didn't notice Anita's exit but had been overcome by the sound and the blinding light of the singing angels and had fallen to her knees.

When the sun of bliss is beaming
Light and love upon my way...

Completely overwhelmed by the spiritual shockwave, she fell forward onto all fours, sobbing for joy and barely able to support herself, as she looked past the angels in their blinding silver robes, and just over their heads, in the distance was the old rugged cross, its patience finally rewarded.

From the cross the radiance streaming
Adds more luster to the day.

Kaye, based on her religious upbringing, had, upon first beholding the chorus of singing angels in their blinding silver robes, immediately assumed that she was witnessing the Rapture and Ascension, and even though what she saw didn't exactly match her expectations since there were no flaming chariots or souls streaming upward to the Heavenly Father, the end-times were a far more probable explanation for the events unfolding before her eyes than that several generations of misinformed subterranean atomic war refugees were returning to the surface world.

Through her joy, Kaye also had to acknowledge and resign herself to the implications that arose from the fact she was merely observing the event and not actually part of it: she was not rising to heaven with all of the other saved souls, but was instead among those doomed to be left behind. So maybe God did sweat the little shit.

A great shadow passed overhead. It was the angel of death—only it sounded... kind of like a helicopter.

Kaye looked up as a helicopter reared to a hover at the top of Whisper Hill and discharged a helmeted and heavily armed SWAT team.

The billowing dust and downwash blinded her immediately and before she could clear the grit from her eyes she was pushed to the ground and handcuffed. She could hear shouting and sirens in the distance.

Chapter Twenty-One

Drudge Report Huge

A nd it all had started out so well.

Orbin, Ruben and Roy were positioned at the entrance of Li'l Pal along with several cruisers and SUVs, and a gaggle of deputies all smartly attired in tactical gear and assault rifles, and accompanied by what was essentially a tank, plus a flatbed trailer with a Bobcat Excavator on the back for exhuming the Anhydrous ammonia nurse tank buried near the grave of Wiley.

The radio murmured softly as the various units checked in with locations and ops normal reports—the incident commander checked to see if the recon team was in position at the far end of the property. It wasn't, but was still trying to get through a locked gate on an adjoining grapefield. Orbin focused his binoculars on the house in the shimmering distance and waited patiently for the last tactical team to get into position and for the Drudge huge events of the day to unfold. A red wing blackbird was calling nearby and had been doing so continuously for what seemed like an hour to Orbin, even though he knew it had only been at most ten minutes they'd been in position. Orbin listened to it and fought the impulse to search the landscape for it.

The bird went silent as a distant roaring that seemingly came from nowhere filled the air. And then stopped as suddenly as it had started. The general consensus, as they scanned the skies, was that it was probably a low-flying Navy jet from Lemore on a training run up Kern Canyon, which happened on occasion.

They waited quietly, checking and re-checking their equipment and sipping from their Camelbacks since it was important to stay hydrated when under stress.

"Boy will you look at her go?" Roy adjusted his binoculars and laughed at the sight. "Like the Road Runner... meebeep!"

Orbin was watching as well but was already on the radio calling in the SWAT team since obviously something significant was breaking—the recon team would have to miss all the action and remain in the grape field on the wrong side of the locked gate.

"We have movement, all units insert now..."

While somewhat amused by the comical sight of Anita, literally leaving a dust plume in her wake as she sprinted over the hip of a distant hill toward the house and car, Orbin nevertheless preserved his professional demeanor.

"Repeat, insert now... ground units to kitchen, air unit direct ant-farm!"

The helicopter was laagered a short distance away and effectively hidden behind the flume below the old Merle Haggard estate, awaiting its call to take wing. The radio crackled with the call from Orbin, the turbines obediently spooled up, and the helicopter lurched into the air. The SWAT team sat in the open doors of the helicopter.

They were in full dress black battle regalia, BDU's, helmets, tactical body armor, kneepads, and an assortment of stubby black rifles and shotguns, their jack -booted feet braced against the skids as the earth fell away beneath them. The right-seat pilot shouted back to them over the slapping blades, "All your base are belong to us!"

The whole operation had been well planned, but had been put into action quite suddenly due to a confluence of events: the ghostly IR images that Ruben, Roy, and Orbin had seen; a snitch at the Lerdo honor farm confirming a rumor of a big meth deal in the works, and some assorted floor sweepings. The clincher however had come in the form of some coy inquiries from a federal agency, which meant that it had knowledge of the size of the operation and wanted to shoulder their way in and take the Drudge-Report-huge credit. All of which led the team to the inescapable conclusion that all of the principals would soon be co-located and could be confronted and captured in the context of their crime which would make for a stronger case in court and a great photo-op. The day's triggering event was a report from a trusted source that the mother and the rogue deputy were en route to the remote meth lab.

The operational planners had selected a logical enough location at the entrance to Li'l Pal just off Highway 178, but it was nevertheless limited: it gave Orbin and company an excellent view of the old rugged cross and tactical control of the only exit route from the property, but Whisper Hill was not visible from their vantage point, being concealed by the aforementioned hill that Hertell's mother was now traversing at high speed.

Orbin watched her notable performance through his binoculars and determined that she was one of those menopausal women who sought sanctuary in triathlon or yoga or dressage as a way of denying the passage of time and its effects—possibly clocking an Olympic trial steeplechase qualifying time, or at least a personal best. A shadow passed over.

The helicopter swooped in low; no more than 50 feet over his head, ducking beneath the high-power transmission lines that bisected the Li'l Pal and up the wide draw leading toward Whisper Hill. The radio was alive with chatter now as the various units and strike teams revved their SUV's, cruisers, and tanks and charged into the Li'l Pal. Orbin's SUV had just rounded the hill at the approach to the main house when he heard something, and he could tell from the background noise that it was from the helicopter. Typical radio chatter in such circumstances is generally simple declarative sentences: commands, position reports, and status, and that's what made this particular piece of radio chatter stand out. It was a question: "... Are those... people?"

It was a reasonable enough question, the same one Orbin had asked when he and Roy and Ruben first laid eyes on the ghostly IR images a few days before. "Yeah. Looks like." Roy paused the image for a moment. "I can't see where they're coming from. There aren't any cars; at least we didn't get any coming in."

Ruben cracked his knuckles loudly. "Must be a back way in there, unless they're just coming up out of the ground."

Orbin rubbed his thighs. "Is it a rave or something?"

Roy resumed the imagery. "Looks like it to me. Evidently they're still partyin' like it's 1999."

"Meth at a rave though? Never heard of that one before." It was a valid observation since Orbin's experience had been that X, or whatever its current street name was this month, was the preferred drug of the classical raves of the '90s, and even into the new century—unusual but not unexpected given the entrepreneurial nature of the recreational drug-prison-industrial complex.

"Kinda makes sense when you think about it." Roy fast-forwarded the IR imagery. "Good way to move a lot of product fast. Like a little tweaker team-building retreat: get people motivated, create a market, set up distribution channels, like with Amway or Tupperware..." Roy was suddenly struck by a thought. "In fact, I got some grape seed extract I want you to try Obi, really good for your heart and shit."

Orbin considered the curious juxtaposition, but said nothing as they all fell silent again watching the black hilltop as the shadowy wisps of glowing people scurried around like ants on a vandalized mound.

"You know what'd be great here?" Ruben leaned forward with a look on his face like he had a great joke to tell, and then with great ceremony tapped the screen of his phone.

The "Benny Hill" theme started. All three laughed. Orbin a bit harder than the other two. Not so much because he found the joke funny, but rather from the relief and satisfaction that he'd been right about the Tweaker he'd met the day he'd visited Wiley's grave.

Ruben was very pleased with himself. He'd downloaded the song right after Orbin had given him the correct title and shortly before he'd downloaded the "Ant Farm" app, and the song did work surprisingly well with the speeded-up footage they were now watching. Their laughter died out as they witnessed a great stillness overtake the hilltop—all the scurrying shimmering figures suddenly and almost miraculously formed one large mass and then seemed to stop moving.

"Hmmm. Never seen anything like that before." Ruben turned off "Benny Hill" as it no longer seemed appropriate.

A subsequent check of the database indicated that there was a spike in meth use in northern Nevada, Reno in particular, which coincided with Kaye Daggett's transfer to the Kernville substation, thus validating their conjecture of the Highway 178 to 395 supply line theory. It all made total sense. They would draft an op plan.

Orbin, Roy, Ruben and the tactical team advanced from their position at the entrance of the Li'l Pal and swarmed over the house and adjacent structures, made a quick sweep for people, paraphernalia, environmental hazards, and weapons, and then brought in the K-9 team for a sweep. Anita was already in custody and thoroughly confused in the back of a cruiser.

The operation was going like clockwork and according to plan, except that they weren't finding anything. Nothing at all, and Orbin's instincts were telling him that they would have seen something by now if there were anything of a Drudge Huge drug bust to be seen.

"Excuse me! Excuse me officer!" Anita was calling to Orbin through the closed window of the cruiser. "Can you tell me what's going on please?"

Orbin was preoccupied trying to follow the radio chatter coming from the SWAT team and took a few steps away from the cruiser, and the indignant inquisitor, to give the radio his full and undivided attention.

"Why am I in this car? Excuse me! I didn't do anything... What am I in this car for?"

The helicopter orbited at the far end of the property where presumably the SWAT team was taking the suspects into custody. However, Orbin could tell by the radio chatter coming from the SWAT team that events were unfolding in a decidedly non-traditional way just a short Cushman ride over the rolling knolls to Whisper Hill.

The SWAT team had used Google Earth to plan and rehearse the mission, and they marveled at how perfect the Li'l Pal was for an industrial scale meth operation: a lot of the property was hidden from view from the highway. They geo-referenced the location of the main residence; Placemark named "kitchen" and the rave hilltop named "ant-farm" on their Google Earth MyPlaces and flew the insertion scenarios several times in the flight simulator.

The SWAT team had a good view of the area of interest from the doors of the helicopter and watched the scenery pass beneath their feet as they flew in low for the shock and awe insertion. They flew east up the draw, which was flowing with water and quite unusual for the time of year, toward the rear of the property. The copter banked and doglegged around a low knob that was one of their mission rehearsal landmarks and then heeled around toward the north and came upon a large quarry on what was remaining of the eastern slope of the large fold that formed the hillside.

The pilots were temporarily blinded by reflections from what seemed to be a thousand signal mirrors in the base of the quarry, but quickly recovered and reached the flattened summit of "ant-farm". The speedlines were spooled out as the pilots pulled into a low hover, the SWAT team fluidly rappelled down to the ground and quickly ringed the open pit on the eastern and now gaping side of Whisper Hill.

Whisper Hill wasn't so much a freestanding hill as it was a rather prominent limb angling off the south flank of the Green Horn Mountains, which rose steeply from the Li'l Pal up to 7000 feet on the Eastern spur. The part of the limb that Hertell had historically referred to as "Whisper Hill" was a low, shell-like flattish area just far enough above the valley floor to make it exclusive and attractive to wildcatters, and cub scouts and bagpipers, but not so far as to make it inaccessible or otherwise not worth the effort.

This was both good and bad: good since it was visible from the power line pylon where Roy and Ruben had mounted their surveillance cameras to observe the ghostly rave; bad because it was otherwise hidden from the highway, and even from the entrance of the Li'l Pal by a line of hills terminated by the Old Rugged Cross on the hill overlooking the highway.

Consequently, Orbin and his cohort at the gates of the Li'l Pal were ignorant of the torrent that flooded and freed the great warm slab since they'd decided the sound was that of an unseen Navy jet. Neither were they witness to the truly extraordinary opening of the earth and the emergence of the spectral choir of the resurrection. Their assumptions remained unchallenged and intact, as there was no evidence to disabuse them of their belief that this was merely a rather large drug bust and not the pivotal event it eventually became in all their lives.

Chapter Twenty-Two

A New Custom

"**G**et on the GROUND! Get on the ground NOW!"
The SWAT team crouched at the perimeter of
the pit, aimed their weapons, and then filled the air with
overlapping shouted commands.

The Generations had stopped singing when the whirlybird
flew over their heads and landed on the hill above and
now looked up in smiling appreciation of the celebratory
cheers and exhortations being shouted down to them from
the curiously attired men who stood above them on the
ramparts.

Hertell was running the length and breadth of the
shimmering formation trying to shield the Generations from
the SWAT team with his body—his torso was aglow with laser
sights.

"It's ok, they're the good guys! They just got here! They've
been living underground!

His calming explanations were mere white noise, lost
and unnoticed in the thumping of the helicopter orbiting
overhead and the crescendo of repeated and stern

commands: "GET ON THE GROUND! GET ON THE GROUND NOW!"

Virginia removed her goggles and smiled and waved. "Yes! Thank You! We're here! On the ground! We're on the ground now! We're on the ground! And we're happy to be here!" The others joined her and removed their goggles and cheered and waved up at the heralds on the parapets.

They'd never seen a SWAT team before and had no concept of their purpose. Some of the Founders were neither cheering nor waving and were clearly troubled by being surrounded by what appeared to be Nazis—the iconic helmets and the black uniforms of the Waffen SS, the stubby Schmeisser submachine guns. However, their concern was overwhelmed by assurances that they couldn't be Nazis since we had won that particular war and besides, they were cheering the arrival of the Founders and the Future and that the machine guns were there to protect them from the mutants—in general the group had considerable thought inertia and it would take some time to fully absorb that the nuclear apocalypse hadn't happened, nor produced the resultant mutants.

Hertell however had seen SWAT teams before, on TV and YouTube, and knew their purpose. He understood fully what was expected of the Generations and finally abandoned trying to explain things to the SWAT team and decided to try to make the Generations understand what they were being commanded to do and to obey. He turned to the shimmering chorus and tried to make himself heard above the shouts from above, the thankyous below and now the orbiting helicopter issuing commands from its PA system.

"They want you to lay down on the ground! They want us to lay down on the ground!" He crouched down and spread his arms and demonstrated.

The SWAT team leader watched Hertell and decided that the people below obviously didn't understand English and that it must be a human trafficking operation in addition to the meth factory since the people were simply smiling and nodding and saying "Thank you" as he'd often seen the illegals do when caught, and probably the only English they knew. The pilot switched the PA commands to Spanish to similar effect, more smiling, waving and thank-yous. This was the last straw, the defiance, the contempt for authority of the mob standing quietly and respectfully in formation below—in stark contrast to the obviously agitated, shrieking SWAT team and its helicopter churning in the air overhead.

The Generations were genuinely confused. Not so much from the spectacle of the helicopter and the heralds cheering their return to the surface world, who were now cheering in Spanish, but rather from Hertell's admonitions that they all lay down on the ground. Some of them even laughed at the silly and frivolous request.

"It's really important! You all need to lay down on the ground... I'm totally serious... right where you're standing, just lay down on the ground!"

And then, Virginia did the most unthinkable thing in the face of armed and determined authority. She put her hand on Hertell's shoulder, and then asked him, "Why?"

The Generations had lived their whole lives, organized their affairs and interactions, and resolved their conflicts through argument and retort, studied rhetoric of the classic

Greeks, and had depended on rational, defensible reason and objective facts to decide issues at every level of their society, outside the nuclear family at least. Authority was a liquid commodity which pooled around those best able to present and defend a convincing argument, even an issue as simple as laying down on the ground when they were otherwise perfectly happy standing upright on two feet. They'd simply gotten out of the habit of blind obedience, and Hertell wasn't sure how to answer the question.

"Priddy!" A toddler pointed to a tiny red dot that was dancing on her mother's chest.

Hertell froze, horrified and powerless as he looked around at the bright red dots sweeping over the shimmering choir.

"It's a custom! It's a sign of respect for the world! It's a custom! Like shaking hands! With the world!"

Virginia looked at her dad and nodded her head. "Logical." Customs were an important part of their lives and they were eager to adopt those of their new world. The entire congregation began to follow Hertell's lead and lower themselves to the ground, as the instructions and rationale propagated through the Generations: the children fell immediately to the ground since it seemed a rather playful custom; the adults, slower and somewhat amused by the odd ritual, helped ease the ancients and the aged to the ground.

Hertell looked up at the SWAT team and held his hands out as if in supplication to confirm that they were cooperating and doing as they were told, which seemed to have a calming effect on the SWAT team as they were no longer agitated and shouting commands.

"Ok it'll just take a minute, so just stay down on the ground like that until I can explain to them who you are and they decide that you haven't done anything wrong, and you can... get up... again."

He was shocked at the words he heard coming out of his own mouth. And he was ashamed.

He looked down at the Generations, now prostrate on the ground, some lying on their sides chatting to their neighbor, some looking up into the sky and the orbiting helicopter overhead—no doubt a very interesting introduction into the modern world. The red dots now skipped and darted over them, but, due to their now horizontal orientation, they effectively formed an irregular but multi-faceted mirror, which now positively bristled with reflected laser beams.

Hertell winced as one of the reflected beams caught him in the eye, causing his shame to flash directly to rage. He shot to his feet. "Turn those fucking lasers off! You're gonna put somebody's eye out!"

The SWAT team leader had a similar observation noting the laser-bedizened people shimmering in the pit and the resultant laser show worthy of Las Vegas as the reflected beams danced over the flanks of the pit and even on his own black BDUs.

Several SWAT team members had by now slogged across the muddy wash and clambered up onto the slab and were now approaching Hertell in that somewhat comical, Groucho Marx crouch walk they use when pointing guns at people.

Rubbing his eye, Hertell indignantly strode toward them. "Hey! Stop pointing that gun at me, there's little kids here! Where do you get off coming in here pointing guns at us and telling us to get on the ground? We didn't do anything! So get outta here! And that fucking helicopter you rode in on!"

He was surprised, but inwardly pleased with his response and the things he was saying and doing, and he couldn't help but acknowledge that it all seemed to be so out of character for him. It was as if he was channeling Mister Frostie who would often go on passionate and typically vulgar tirades on a variety of topics.

Remembering his circumstances, he turned back toward the Generations. "Pardon my..."

But before he could finish his sentence, a police dog named Ringo clamped his jaws on Hertell's elbow and brought him to the ground.

Chapter Twenty-Three

Slightly Excessive

"I think we need to call Risk Management, and tell'm to bring their check book." The SWAT team leader removed her helmet and addressed the confused trio: Orbin, Roy, and Ruben. She had to shout to be heard over the din of the Bobcat Excavator, which was noisily clawing yards of overburden from the anhydrous ammonia nurse tank beneath their feet. A hazmat containment team was standing by in case the tank was breached.

Orbin cupped his hand behind his ear. "What?"

The SWAT team leader, took a deep breath and bellowed, "We... fucked... up!"

Between the "we" and the "fucked up", the Bobcat struck something with the back hoe and went to idle, which gave the SWAT team leader's high decibel final appraisal a comical topspin. Nobody laughed.

Instead, the SWAT team leader described what they'd found over at the Ant Farm shortly before: absolutely nothing, except for the big hole and all the people and what appeared to be a rather over-produced choir practice, and one guy that they had to Taser, a few times. There was a

185

suggestion that they search the big hole the choir came out of, but the idea was quickly dismissed since there was no probable cause, yet. So they stood and watched silently as the Bobcat gently scraped the dirt away from the buried artifact and desperately hoped that a stolen anhydrous ammonia nurse tank would emerge.

A pair of patrol cars approached from the direction of Whisper Hill and crunched to a stop next to Orbin and the others. Hertell was cuffed and sitting alone in the back seat of a cruiser, as was Kaye in the adjoining cruiser.

It had been a long and humiliating ride from Whisper Hill for Kaye: indignant, mortified, she rode in stony silence at the treatment by her fellow deputies, all of whom she knew. She didn't say a word, and neither did the deputy driving since both knew it would just complicate whatever was to come next. She had seen the SWAT team interfacing with Hertell and the radiant choir of the resurrection as she was being taken down the hill to the squad car—stripped of their blinding silver robes to reveal... people. No Cherubim or Seraphim or the Four Living Creatures praising God, just ordinary people, in trendy casual attire of the early '60s.

She was glum and disappointed that she had not witnessed the Rapture and advent of the End Times; however, her gloom was overwhelmed by the joyous relief that she was therefore no longer among the damned to be left behind for the torment of the Tribulation and the reign of the Antichrist—like waking up from a fever dream to learn that you hadn't killed anyone, or that your teeth hadn't fallen out. She nevertheless, saw it as an omen to be heeded. Maybe it wasn't the real thing, but it was probably the closest she'd ever get, so best not be ignored, and in fact had the fingerprints of a Divine hand. She would henceforth sweat the little shit, just in case. Consequently, all she was left with on the ride down the hill was humiliation and the knowledge that Hertell was mixed up in some serious shit, and that now it was on her.

Hertell's ride from Whisper Hill was quite different. He had settled into a state of complete and almost catatonic shock: awash in guilt and self-contempt at his helpless inability to protect his precious newborn world from the procedural indignities and instinctive deference demanded on the surface; tortured and tormented by the final images of the Founders and the Future as he was being driven away—herded like cattle for processing, stripped of their glittering robes, now strewn in piles and heaps, patted down like airline passengers, fearful and traumatized by the stern, helmeted SWAT team, menaced by the barking dogs—the first ones they'd seen in over fifty years.

"Never seen a dog do that before."

It was the deputy driving the car. He had seen Hertell brought to the ground by Ringo who then almost immediately released Hertell's elbow and rolled onto its back batting his paws playfully. The deputy had been totally mystified, as were the rest of the SWAT team at Ringo's behavior—not only did Ringo release, Ringo's handler had to collar and restrain the whining dog as Hertell was subdued, cuffed and dragged away, the whole time shouting "They didn't do anything! They just got here!"

Hertell swallowed. It tasted salty; he could feel that his lip was swollen and bleeding, as he'd evidently bitten his cheek when he was Tasered. He cleared his throat. "What?"

"I've never seen a dog do that before, you a dog trainer or something?"

"No." He was remembering a face.

It was the face of the 60-ish puppy woman, and he saw her face change from childlike excitement upon seeing a dog, a real dog, to confusion, to horror as Ringo brought Hertell to the ground.

"They didn't do anything."

"Don't start that again. Forget that I even asked." The deputy was right since Hertell had continued shouting that phrase for most of the ride from Whisper Hill and had lapsed into his catatonic mode only moments before.

Hertell felt his swollen lip with his tongue and looked out the window at the Grieving Angel as they passed by. There was a cluster of people and cars and a backhoe up ahead, and as they rolled to a stop, Hertell could see that they were exhuming Mister Frostie's funeral barge. His guilt was now redoubled in recognition that his own actions, burying Mister Frostie and his Traveleer on his own property, in obvious violation of some county ordinance or zoning law, had precipitated this rather excessive SWAT response from the authorities and that he, therefore was directly responsible for the trauma visited upon Virginia and the Future as they emerged into the world. The guilt lodged in his throat, and lingered as the cruiser coasted to a stop. He could see Kaye in the back of the other car, her shoulders squared and her head held high. He knew this pose, she was praying.

The deputy got out of the cruiser, slammed the door, and approached a knot of deputies and SWAT guys standing a short distance away near what appeared to be an Army tank.

They were talking amongst themselves and would occasionally look back toward Hertell who watched as a Hazmat suited person lowered himself into the shallow pit with a square- blade shovel.

Hertell had lost track of time again. He was almost positive it was the same day that he'd gone to Costco and gotten all the sunglasses, and Kaye and the other woman came to talk to him about the Casino, but so much had happened that he kept thinking that much more time had passed. The Tasering had evidently energized his copper slivers, which contributed to his confusion.

The car door opened and he was invited out. The deputy helped him out of the car and led him over to the excavation and the archeological party. Hertell recognized one of them, he had visited the grave of the police dog and Hertell remembered that they had a very pleasant and wide ranging conversation.

The group was looking down into the pit expectantly. Most of the dirt had been cleared away revealing the scratched and scarred roof of the Traveleer where a Hazmat suit stood and then called up to them with his professional appraisal.

"It's a trailer!"

Hertell addressed the group. "Well of course it's a trailer! What'd you think it was? It's why you're here isn't it?"

They all turned and looked at Hertell.

"It's Mister Frostie's trailer and his ashes are inside it, in an ice bucket along with all of his other stuff, and if there's some law against burying dead people's ashes—which I don't think there would be since people are always dumping ashes out in the ocean and out of airplanes and stuff, so I don't see why this'd be any different—so just write me a ticket and give me a fine or whatever. You don't need to do all this!"

Since he was still handcuffed, he thrust his chin at the tank and then up at the helicopter that was circling overhead.

"Doesn't this seem kinda excessive to you?"

The SWAT chopper was long gone and had been replaced by an Action-TV News chopper that was now orbiting overhead, beaming the event into the gaping maw of the 24-7 news cycle: shaky aerial shots of people in a large pit, standing meekly in rows, amid piles of glittering costumes and SWAT team members and their dogs. Accompanied by the confident play-by-play conjecture of the reporter.

"It appears to be a large group of what appears to be people, well over a hundred by my estimation, possibly a thousand, in what appears to be an amphitheater of some kind. We're not sure what they've done, but it must be something serious based on the police presence and show of force. It appears they're being searched for weapons..."

Hertell shouted over the helicopter, "I mean for hell's sake, where's your sense of proportion? All those people on Whisper Hill you yelled at and pointed guns at and treated like shit. For what? For coming up out of the ground, like there's some law against coming up out of the ground?"

He stopped suddenly, struck by a thought.... "Are the Casino Indians behind all this?"

Orbin looked at Roy and Ruben, and then Hertell. "I can assure you, they are not. You are now looking at who was behind all this." He stepped behind Hertell and busied himself removing the handcuffs. "You are the owner of this property I presume, Hertell Daggett?"

"Hertell Junior, yes. Hertell Senior is dead."

"And we've met once before haven't we?"

"Yeah, you came to see your dog and we talked. And we had a very pleasant and wide-ranging conversation."

"Yes, I remember it well." Orbin, finished removing the handcuffs and then stood before Hertell and looked him in the eyes. "We seem to have made a mistake Hertell, and you have our sincere apology. You are free to go."

Hertell rubbed his wrists, nodded at Orbin, and then with complete and unmistakable sincerity said, "Thanks, and nice seeing you again too," and then took off in a sprint in the direction of Whisper Hill.

Other than that, it was a good plan, and well executed—no injuries, except for one dog bite, no shots fired, no property damage. If only it had been a training exercise.

It took the rest of the afternoon to complete the dust-off and apologies and explanations. Public Affairs arrived in anticipation of the press, and since Mister Frostie's trailer was already pretty much exhumed, it was decided to go ahead and winch it out of its pit for a quick check and dog sniff just in case. It was somewhat crumpled with minor water damage, but otherwise intact and legal and would also make good B-roll footage for the news crews.

Roy and Ruben explained the mistake to Kaye, who seemed distracted but fairly receptive since she'd been in their position several times when she worked rural crimes over by Taft and Fellows, and she acknowledged that a Drudge Huge meth lab was a much more probable explanation for the events they'd observed, than an over-produced choir practice. She even helped explain the situation to Anita who was not receptive at all.

Anita took the rent-a-car and left soon thereafter. Kaye stayed and accompanied Roy and Ruben and Orbin up to Whisper Hill, because, even though it wasn't the radiant choir of the resurrection, it was still a very good choir that had affected her deeply and might need another second alto.

The shimmering robes were returned to the people of Whisper Hill, and the Sheriff himself came out to apologize for the confusion and to welcome the new arrivals to Kern County, though he'd missed the part about them coming up out of the ground, and the past, and just assumed they'd come from out of state.

Hertell had already explained the event to Virginia and Miles and the Generations but was joined by Orbin and the Sheriff who gave an encore explanation of the mistake and apology, though none of them knew what Crystal Meth was, so the explanations were essentially meaningless to them, but they all got to meet and pet Ringo, so some of the damage was undone.

Hertell watched with foreboding as several local news crews arrived and Public Affairs explained the unfortunate mistake. But the press wasn't so much interested in the SWAT team's fuckup as they were with Hertell and the shimmering people of Whisper Hill who'd been seen and broadcast to the world by the news copter. For some reason, maybe the Tasering he'd received, Hertell kept thinking of the ants in the Amazon and the locust in Africa that sweep over the countryside and devour everything in their path. He didn't know it at the time, but Virginia was right about the mutants. The cameras and microphones were approaching, like an amoeba; they were all about to be consumed.

Chapter Twenty-Four

The Amoeba Tour

I t started very modestly, just a few reports from the local media that had actually made it out to the Li'l Pal that afternoon, or flown over it, but then quickly progressed into the global media flash mob it ultimately became.

The unspoken and instinctive storyline was to have been the grievous mistake that law enforcement had made since it promised a target-rich environment for spin-off stories about excessive use of force, sloppy police work, traumatized worshipers, terrorized and degraded victims of mistaken identity seeking psychological counsel and legal recourse, possibly some human interest features. They didn't realize that the epic story that awaited them was just a short hike up Whisper Hill. But they would have to deal with Hertell first. They turned their cameras toward a man walking down the hill toward them. He was disheveled and his sleeve was torn off, but he was smiling.

Virginia was among a line of excited, chattering people waiting to pet Ringo when she noticed Hertell having an animated conversation with some of the soldiers—the older ones who had welcomed them to Kern County and explained how they thought the Generations were making dangerous chemicals and were very sorry about the mistake. Hertell was gesturing toward the people with all the lights and movie cameras and trucks who were down at the road below Whisper Hill, and though it seemed to be a very serious discussion, it was now her turn to pet Ringo who was really sweet now that he wasn't biting Hertell's arm.... "Doggie Doggie Doggie!"

The high decibel commotion around Ringo momentarily distracted Kaye from the conversation she'd been having and her gaze happened to fall on Hertell as she assessed the tactical context—instinctive situational awareness developed over her years on patrol and something she couldn't turn off even if she wanted to. The SWAT team was long gone, but there were still a few deputies enjoying the interactions between Ringo and the Choir, several others down on the big slab at the bottom of the pit talking to some of the older congregants. The PAO was down at the bottom of the hill spinning a line of ass-covering gossamer to the TV news.

Though she wasn't close enough to overhear the conversation Hertell was having with Orbin and the Sheriff, she could tell that they seemed to be in agreement with whatever Hertell was saying as he shook their hands. Satisfied, she returned her attention to the conversation she'd been having.

She'd been talking to a nice woman named Peggy about the Choir and was in the middle of being told the funny story when temporarily distracted by "Doggie Doggie!" It was the story of how they were all afraid of falling into the sky the first time they saw it.

Her story captivated Kaye, at first, thinking that the woman was speaking metaphorically about how she had come to her faith, that she'd lived in artificial light her whole life buried beneath the material world and had never seen the sky in all its glory, but had finally emerged into the light of the world and the kingdom of God.

But that wasn't what Peggy was saying, Peggy was saying that she had really, no kidding, lived underground with everybody else in the Choir that Kaye wanted to join as a Second Alto, and that none of them had ever seen anything as big as the sky before, and they were all, literally, actually afraid of falling into it, and that the whole thing had happened only last night. Several nearby Choir members chimed in at the retelling, laughing at the memory and confirming to Kaye that this wasn't a metaphorical emergence, it was an actual physical emergence and that these people were exactly who Hertell said they were: Not the singing angels of the resurrection, not an off-brand Pentecostal church with a great choir, but a tiny seed of Western civilization that had been living under the Li'l Pal.

Hertell finished his talk with the Sheriff and the dog funeral deputy, Orbin, and was now walking down the hill toward the skirmish line of TV crews and cameras and lights that were wrapping up their interviews with the Sheriff's Public Affairs Officer, and were now marshalling their forces for the assault up the hill toward Virginia and Ringo and the Generations.

As he approached the news vans and lights and the cameras and the sound booms and satellite masts and blow-dried microphone holders, he thought of those old battles in the Dark Ages, where there were archers and Pikemen, and

197

cavalry, each one with a different role but all dedicated to smashing the enemy line and meting out a crushing and humiliating defeat to be immediately followed by the customary pillage.

Hertell walked directly toward the biggest camera with the brightest lights and the woman reporter he recognized from the TV news and stood patiently in the glare of the lights as they encircled him and thrust their microphones and shouted questions at him.

Traditionally targets of such media attention typically seem to be in a hurry to flee from their exposed position in a parking lot or stairwell or driveway and escape to the defilade and safety of home or car or office. However, in this case Hertell was already on his own property and indeed had no compulsion to flee since he was already at home. Consequently, the shouting went on for quite some time and Hertell listened quietly and respectfully as the frequency and amplitude and urgency of their questions slowly dissipated. It reminded Hertell of dogs and how they act after the car they've been chasing stops—they'd typically continue to bark at the parked car for a while and then get distracted by another car or a squirrel or a scent on the breeze and on occasion wander off into the path of another car and end up in one of Mister Frostie's black plastic bags.

"Felicity Spector Action News!... What can you tell us about... News Hole Six on the scene reporting!... Was anyone injured...Who are those people!... News Copter Four at seven and eleven!... Are you a religious cult?!... How do you feel about... Berkeley Stone Impact News!... What do you have to say... Is there any truth to the rumor...Can you comment..."

It was then that Hertell did an unforgivable thing, a thing that would inflame the indignation of the assembled media. He got the giggles. He simply could not stop laughing: possibly due to the bizarre narrative that the overlapping chorus of questions formed and how oblivious they were to the significance of his discovery, or possibly due to his Tasering and cuffing, or possibly due to the burden of responsibility that he now shouldered. And every time he'd try to compose himself, he'd start giggling again, which would initiate new flurries of indignant questions.

In his head, Hertell was saying "This is private property. And you are all trespassing on it, which I cannot forgive. And these people are fragile and precious and I don't want you eating them. So get out of here before I call the SWAT team on you!" However, what was actually coming out of his mouth was.... "This is..." (laughter). "This is private..." (laughter).

He felt a presence. He'd felt it many times since he'd been shot in the head, always benign, just above and slightly behind him, just out of his peripheral vision, but he had long ago stopped turning to see if there was anything there as he'd been so often disappointed. There was never anything there, until now. He felt a hand on his shoulder and heard a voice; it was Kaye. "This is private property. You are all trespassing."

Kaye stood beside Hertell and addressed the cameras.

She'd forgotten how tall he was, well over six feet. Even in her wedge espadrilles she had to look up at him. Though still silenced by the giggles, he nodded to Kaye in acknowledgement.

"You are directed to leave immediately or you will be escorted off the property by law enforcement, you will be cited and fined to the maximum extent of the law if you do not leave these premises immediately."

She'd seen this behavior in him before, on the eve of his father's death Hertell had gotten the giggles; he was horrified by them and ashamed, but nevertheless could not stop laughing. She presumed it was due to his being shot in the head since he'd certainly never exhibited it while they were together and she later learned from a neurologist that her diagnosis was probably correct, that extreme emotions could sometimes express themselves in inappropriate ways after a brain injury, such as being shot in the head for example.

Kaye saw fewer and fewer displays of any kind of emotion in the final spasms of their marriage, which was long before he was shot in the head. Their first decade together, from high school through Hertell's first PhD, was as deliriously happy as anything she'd seen in the movies, with all of the traditional emotions, both appropriate and inappropriate, for their ages. The second decade was a process of gradual and then sudden decay—she was still just a dumb Okie, while he was a rising star in academia. She got a phone call one day when Hertell was at a conference in Brazil, which she'd hated ever since. She remembered that she was very excited since he rarely called from conferences anymore, in fact she couldn't remember the last time he'd called her from the road. She asked him where he was and how the conference was going. His answer was short.

"I've met someone. I'm not coming home."

And yet now, here she stood beside that self-same man. What a dumb Okie, still. But now, at least, she had their attention. "However, if you behave yourselves and stop yelling, we will welcome you as guests and answer your questions as best we can and as time and circumstances permit."

Together, they led the media amoeba up Whisper Hill to the Great Warm Slab where they introduced Virginia and Miles and several of the Future—most of the Generations and all of the Founders had already gone back below because Ringo had left. In broad strokes Hertell told their story to the assembled media, many of whom were unapologetically dubious. Some even went so far as to strike their lights and cameras and head back down the hill thinking the whole thing a waste of time since they had their lead, the Keystone-SWAT-team-debacle, so why compromise their journalistic credibility on a bogus ragtag, storefront, Jesus freak, end-of-the-world shaggy dog story.

After the doubters had left in a noisy, indignant huff, Hertell invited the remaining camera crews to accompany him down into the world below. Though it had grown a lot in recent years, Bakersfield still had only three local TV stations, the same ones that had been around since the 1950's. The two remaining TV news crews, one was a Spanish language affiliate the other was from one of the legacy networks, plus a couple of stringers for the local print and internet news sites followed Hertell, Kaye, and Virginia into the great dark yawning portal and down into the pressure buffer with Miles and a few others from the Future trailing along behind.

Kaye, like the TV crews and stringers, was awestruck at what she saw, and followed silently as the crews filmed and Hertell and Virginia explained what they were seeing—the cornfield, the gymnasium, Main Street USA, the beautiful vaulting sky of rock above. Singing could be heard in the distance. It was the evening Sunday service. Hertell was leading them past the Church that was on the town square when one of the TV reporters asked to go inside to hear the singing and see the service, but it was explained that it was just the door to the Church on the town square, the actual Church was where they were going. None of the reporters, or Kaye for that matter quite understood, but followed Hertell to the swelling sound of the singing.

They entered a massive hall, easily big enough to house a jumbo jet, where the entire population of the settlement was gathered... well over five hundred people by the look of it. Virginia quietly explained that it was kind of a farewell service and the last one they expected to have down in the settlement now that they'd emerged into the surface world and that from now on they'd worship in the world above. Kaye began singing along...

> *And Lord, haste the day when my faith shall be sight,*
> *The clouds be rolled back as a scroll;*
> *The trumpet shall sound, and the Lord shall descend,*
> *Even so—it is well with my soul*

One of the stringers was taking notes and wanted to know the name of the song. Hertell recognized it as one that Mister Frostie often sang as he wandered the hills of the Li'l Pal, but he didn't know its name. Another reporter answered. "It Is Well With My Soul." It was a woman Hertell recognized from the local TV news, but she wasn't looking at the other reporter or Hertell or even the TV cameras, she was focused on the service and the choir and the now standing worshipers. The Hammond B-3 was at full throttle, the Leslie speakers spinning their Doppler tremolo, the Generations began to sway and clap with each tidal verse. Swept along by the force of it, the reporter joined in...

it is well... it is well,
with my soul... with my soul,
It is well, it is well, with my soul.

Chapter Twenty-Five

Oceanoids

I t broke on Drudge that night, and in a matter of days
Whisper Hill and most of the Li'l Pal was covered
with news vans and bristling with satellite masts. Hertell
was amused by it all since it reminded him of one of
the more traditional media feeding frenzies with bleachers
full of correspondents from every corner of the globe
surrounding the abandoned well with the toddler stuck at
the bottom—only in reverse this time, and he concluded that
maybe that was part of its appeal in a man-bites dog sort of
way, since all reporters got to go into the well this time and
didn't have to wait for anybody to die. Or be rescued.

This second and much larger wave of camera crews flooded
over the great warm slab, through the pressure buffer and
down into every corner of the colony the following week,
dragging their cables and cameras and microphones and
lights and blow- dried hair and blinding white smiles into
its depths, led by Hertell. Like the Aztecs welcoming Cortez,
Hertell was proud of the world beneath the Li'l Pal and what
the Generations had preserved and now wanted to share their
accomplishment with the world above; how they had lived,

and taken care of each other, and triumphed over sickness and famine and despair; how faith and music and duty had sustained them, how they had planned and managed their lives to provide for the future generations that they would never know but who would someday inherit and restore the toxic wasteland above.

Interviews with the Founders and the Future were on every broadcast, cable, and live streaming feed along with countless podcasts, magazine covers, blogs, and websites. Background, profiles, and feature articles were done on many of the principals: Hertell, Miles, Obi, Kaye, Virginia and several of the outliers like Roy and Ruben, Ringo, and several of the SWAT guys.

Tours of the warehouses, machine shops, labs, banks and businesses, print shop and bindery, libraries, cathedrals and temples, health clinics, parks, pools, fountains, sewage treatment and power plants, sound stages and sets, neighborhoods, living quarters, planetariums, gymnasiums hockey rinks, basketball courts, rivers, waterfalls, quarries and mausoleums were given to any and all interested reporters/researchers and were broadcast the world over within weeks of the SWAT team's embarrassing mistake.

And as he conducted the tours Hertell explained all he had learned from the Founders: that the concept had started as a classified whitepaper under Truman, advanced to a feasibility study under Eisenhower, and then went on to become the most highly classified black program under Kennedy to utilize a massive network of several hundred miles of cavernous lava tubes beneath the southernmost rump of the Sierras to preserve a tiny seed of the human experiment in the event that it all went horribly wrong.

The project was developed and staffed by a group of scientists and engineers salvaged from the remains of the Manhattan Project. This particular group of renegade physicists was focusing on the weak nuclear force to get the lowest energy nuclear reaction, one able to produce almost infinite energy without the Chernobyl downside of ionizing gamma radiation and nasty nuclear waste by-products. The team perfected the technology in the late '50s and then, on the day of Kennedy's assassination, took it and all knowledge of it with them down into the ground where it was to power their world until it was safe to emerge into the light of day.

Hertell also pointed out that the by-products of OSCNOIDS, Orthogonal Symmetric Collimated Normalized Toroids, but typically written and pronounced 'Oceanoids', were quite beneficial. In addition to the primary product, heat, for driving steam turbines for electricity, there was also a significant amount of gold, and lesser amounts of other Platinum group metals, generated as a byproduct of the complex reaction sequence. Up to a kilogram a day depending on the size of the reactor. Since impurities in the gold produced left it with trace amounts of non-ionizing alpha and beta particle radiation that could be absorbed with a thin layer of cellulose, it would typically be injected into Styrofoam blocks for storage until stable at which time the Styrofoam would be rendered in a brine solution leaving the gold as a precipitate which would then be processed for use—primarily for wiring the extensive movie studio lighting system in the colony and for a quarter-wave ELF antenna for communicating with Mustard Seed's assumed Soviet end-of-the world counterpart.

The camera crews loved it down there since the entire world below was like an MGM musical set, and lit like one: they could shoot entire segments at F16 with classic '50s production design, saturated colors, key lights, Cucoloris shadows, and smooth floors for dolly shots. It was magnificent in HD and the 3D IMAX versions were breathtaking and ran at the Smithsonian for many years after.

The History Channel did a well-received multi-part series on Mustard Seed. It started with the feasibility phase conducted under Truman and how the large cadre of logisticians from the Rand Corporation mathematically modeled the closed-system dynamics for post-nuclear war subterranean survival populations with initial sizes of 100 to preserve the Senate and Executive branch; 1000 to accommodate the legislative, executive, and judiciary branch plus wives, children, and secretaries; and 10,000 to supplement with administrative and domestic staff, athletic trainers, actors and musicians necessary to support the first two sample populations. However, each episode ended with the mathematical models predicting a tragic and unsatisfactory end to each of the sample populations primarily by murder, starvation, cannibalism, and under-age smoking.

A&E had a competing multi-part series, on alternate nights with *Flip You*, emphasizing that while technology was necessary for survival, it was not sufficient since the goal of 'Mustard Seed' was not merely survival, but rather the preservation of a culture, based on the atavistic and exclusionary value judgment that any particular culture was worth preserving. Subsequent episodes stressed that social cohesion, genetic diversity, economic incentives, and a plethora of non-technical factors had to be addressed. The concluding episode focused on the final approach taken by the Mustard Seed project in which, rather than trying to preserve a particular random population, such as elected officials living in Georgetown and Chevy Chase, they decided instead to preserve what amounted to a small town, its population and all of their associated institutions in vivo such that it would be self-sustaining and self-sufficient for at least a century when given adequate technology and resources—essentially a time capsule of early '60s small-town America.

And Lifetime did a dramatization of the inspirational story of how a small and isolated boomtown in northern New Mexico was selected as the archetypal community to be preserved: how the various roles and responsibilities of its inhabitants were cataloged and categorized by the scientists and then, based on a now modified Rand simulation integrating all the non-technical factors, the optimal population composition was calculated and determined to be the entire Mustard Seed program staff, including of all the scientists, engineers, and their immediate families, since they not only satisfied the population composition selection criteria, but also had full knowledge of the program, its technologies, logistics and its very existence and vulnerabilities—knowledge that would need to disappear with them in the event that the unthinkable happened, knowledge that could lead plundering survivors and mutants directly down to the precious and fragile Mustard Seed.

The B-plot dealt with how the remaining population, another hundred or so, were drawn primarily from the inhabitants of the archetypal northern New Mexico town: Aunt Tawney the seamstress, Mister Frostie and his ice cream truck, Domingo the plumber, Alvino the stone mason, plus carpenters, retailers, bankers, and gardeners. There was also a smattering of Disney Imagineers, and grips, gaffers, and production designers from Hollywood—all of them interviewed, psychologically screened, selected based on minimal extended family ties, and briefed into the program, with the understanding that if things went horribly wrong, they would enter the earth without question or complaint and live beneath Li'l Pal Heaven until it was safe to emerge and restore the world—which they did, and there they all remained until Hertell (played by Johnny Depp) found them and coaxed them to the surface.

Hertell seemed to enjoy the attention and respect being paid to the precious world he had discovered, at least at first. He wasn't seduced by the celebrity or entranced by the fame since he saw that for what it was.

What he found most gratifying and in fact inspiring, was the fact that everyone in the surface world seemed to feel a degree of ownership or at least validation of their worldview which led to an almost instantaneous viral spread of the Mustard Seed phenomenon: everybody saw something important and often reaffirming in some aspect of it and was emailing and forwarding and posting and tweeting everybody else.

Even the local Casino Indian tribe claimed that the emergence of the Generations from beneath Li'l Pal Heaven was the fulfillment of an ancient prophesy in which one day the earth would open and the spirits of the dead would arise, and even though the dead didn't actually arise, it was close enough, so the entire population of Mustard Seed, the Founders and the Future were made official members of the tribe by the end of their first week in the surface world.

Hertell also learned that he'd been a fairly notable Physicist prior to getting shot in the head, and also learned a lot about his father—that he'd been a shipmate of President Kennedy's on PT-109 and had worked at the highest levels in his administration prior to settling in Bakersfield and opening Li'l Pal, and that the Li'l Pal property was actually much more extensive than he'd ever imagined.

But what began to trouble Hertell were the questions he was being asked. Not by the reporters and lesser media feeders, or the sociology and economics researchers or the government investigators, or the Casino Indians, or the contractors and county planning officials, but rather the questions he was being asked by the Generations and the Future.

Simple questions really; nevertheless, questions he didn't really know how to answer. He noticed that while they quickly grew accustomed to and even mastered the technical innovations they found on the surface like ATMs, talking cars, bigger TVs, Skype, GPS, and watching movies on your wristwatch, all things that were classically futuristic; they were much slower however to recognize and internalize what was generally considered social progress and cultural growth: some of which they considered comical such as baggy pants

211

with underwear showing, some of which they considered vulgar such as butt cracks, and feminine hygiene ads on TV, but most of which they considered toxic and not only questioned but openly rejected.

They would be studied by academics and their technologies would disrupt the world economy. They were like one of those lost tribes that stumble out of the Amazonian jungle into civilization, only in reverse this time. This time it wasn't the lost tribe who were overwhelmed by civilization, but very much the other way around. And they would pay for it.

Chapter Twenty-Six

The Enchanted Trailer

"**H**ow big is it inside?"

A small group of the Future had gathered around Mister Frostie's streaked and stained and crumpled trailer. They stood before it at a slight distance, huddled as if afraid to go any closer, pointing and whispering amongst themselves in an almost reverent manner, as if before a shrine.

Things had progressed in a fairly linear fashion at first, and Hertell would look back on those first few precious afternoons with particular fondness in his final days: events had proven him to be not delusional at all, which was a great relief. He'd discovered a civilization preserved within the amber hills and was now its guardian and simultaneously part of a huge extended family that had been close but unknown to him for his whole life on earth, so he was not now, and in fact never really was, alone. Kaye was back in his life, and, though he didn't realize it at the time, he was in love with Virginia.

After the TV crews had left that first day, but before the second wave of media and subsequent cultural tsunami overtook them, Hertell and the Future would simply loll about on the parched, golden slopes above what was left of Whisper Hill watching the clouds and the airplanes flying to the real San Francisco and the real other places, even the real Egypt probably, maybe. They were fascinated by the buzzing high power transmission lines slung over what looked like towering four-legged giants marching in a long line headed south and across the hills near the old rugged cross.

He took large groups on foot expeditions of the Li'l Pal pointing out and identifying the weeds and washes and holes and tracks and scat piles of the various life forms that shared the surface with Hertell and the rest of the world. He led them down to the main house so they could see how the outsides led directly into the insides, and how that was normal in the world above ground. He took them to see the D-6 and Mister Frostie's Ice Cream truck, and the shed with all the old TVs.

He took smaller groups out on bouncy rides in the Cushman or in his dad's '74 Stepside pickup to explore the Li'l Pal, which was a lacy network of dirt roads stretched over the dry hills: the Lost and Found, the Old Rugged Cross, Everlasting Slumber, Snuggle Bottom, and even down to highway 178 on one sunny afternoon to watch all the cars and campers and retired baby-boomers go past on their Harleys. And it was at about this point that things started to go non-linear, slowly at first and then suddenly and relentlessly chaotic.

Hertell had taken about a dozen of the Future in the back of the Stepside down to Everlasting Slumber to look at the pyramid and grieving angel. He was pointing out Yappy's grave to some of them when he noticed that Virginia and a small group had separated and wandered up to the diggings at Cherished Friends, and the great pit from which Mister Frostie's trailer had been so recently exhumed, searched by Deputies, sniffed by Ringo, and found to be free of criminal content.

"It's Aunt Tawney's house." Virginia and the rest of the group had moved within arm's length of the trailer by the time Hertell reached the gathering. "We saw it almost every day when we'd go for our music lessons." The rest of the group voiced their excited and unanimous agreement; it definitely was Aunt Tawney's house and they'd all seen it thousands of times in a framed photo prominently displayed on her Hammond B-3—she was younger and standing with her husband in his Air Force uniform and smiling in front of the tiny little house with the round window in the door. They patted the sides of the trailer as if to reassure themselves that it was real and not their imagination. No, there was no doubt about it, they all stood before and were now touching their beloved Aunt Tawney's ancestral home on surface earth.

"Well no, this is actually Mister Frostie's house and his ashes are inside 'cause he died. And up here, these kinds of houses are called trailers and are very common, particularly in Bakersfield, and many other places, especially wherever they have tornadoes."

"How big is it inside?"

215

Virginia's question was echoed by several others as they'd imagined it to be quite large and spacious from Aunt Tawney's descriptions and they were curious how such an immense household could fit in such a small space.

"Well, the door's open. Go ahead and take a look if you want." The door was hanging by a single hinge—the other hinge and door handle having been sheared off in the hasty breaching by the deputies for Ringo's search. Hertell held the door for them as they filed in to look around.

"Look at anything you want, touch anything you want, just be careful you don't knock over the ice bucket. It's got Mister Frostie's ashes in it."

Hertell encouraged them to explore the Traveleer primarily as a way to disabuse them of the notion that the trailer was Aunt Tawney's honeymoon cottage since they'd only find Mister Frostie's furnishings and effects inside; however, several returned with artifacts they claimed to recognize from Aunt Tawney's descriptions—an old Roi-Tan cigar box full of keys, a cook book, some Christmas tree lights, the kind that bubbled.

It was at that point that Hertell decided he needed to broaden their exposure to the outside world: beyond the scrub and chaparral and rodents and reptiles who skittered across and under the Li'l Pal on four legs, to include the larger life forms who roamed the asphalt and plastic of earth on two legs.

He loaded them all back in the truck and took them, for the first time, off the Li'l Pal property. He took them down the 178 to Comanche Lane since he knew there were several trailer parks down by Edison Highway and he could prove to the Future that the world, particularly on the outskirts of Bakersfield, was abloom with trailers just like Aunt Tawney's, though most not as old nor suffering the effects of being buried for a few months. He drove them past the oil fields that gradually gave way to the orange groves and then the grape fields as the land leveled out below Edison Highway on the way to Arvin and Lamont—'vineyard' was never used in the Central Valley as it was considered a pretentious coastal, NorCal, and essentially metro-sexual term.

They all enjoyed the ride immensely, particularly the triplet of Founders since one of their fondest memories from their long-ago life on Earth was bouncing and sliding around in the back of a pickup truck with the wind and the laughter and the sunshine. But just short of the trailer court that Hertell was seeking, they heard a siren.

Chapter Twenty-Seven

Moving Violations

"You've got about eight... no nine Vehicle Code violations going here..."

Evidently it was no longer legal for people, or even dogs, to ride in the back of a pickup unless they had a leash or a seatbelt or were in some way restrained, for their own safety. The Founders were deeply troubled that there could be a law against such a small and simple pleasure.

The deputy was understanding and knew of the group through both the local TV coverage and also through Orbin since they shared the same patrol area and had adjoining lockers, so he'd heard the whole story. This was fortunate since trucks full of people on back roads paralleling major north-south corridors are typically presumed to be illegals.

The deputy examined Hertell's driver's license, and then looked up at the occupants sitting in the bed of the pickup. "Any of the rest of you have ID's?"

He was answered by silence and blank looks from the bed of the truck. None of them had any form of identification, and in fact were confused by the question since they had no concept of needing any, as they knew everyone in their world and everyone knew them—the triplet of Founders vaguely remembered driver's licenses as a much-sought after talisman but had long since forgotten them or their use and were presumed to be vestigial artifacts, like a tailbone.

"I didn't think you would, so now I'm letting you off with a warning, I'm not even gonna write this up, but you need to get these people down to DMV, but not in the back of a pickup, and get'm ID's, 'cause they're undocumented, and that's something you don't wanna be."

He handed the driver's license back to Hertell, and then escorted them back to the Li'l Pal so they wouldn't be stopped again.

After the initial misadventure in his pickup truck with Deputy Tom, Hertell decided that he would need help. His days were already full and were becoming increasingly crowded and chaotic, a vortex of TV crews, interviews, logistical discussions with the Founders and their ideas for returning to the surface world, and now taking the Future on tours of the world beyond the gates of Li'l Pal Heaven.

In the days since the story broke, Orbin had offered to take Hertell, the Future, and some of the more active Founders, on guided tours of the outside world. He'd felt an obligation to provide a more balanced and less traumatic introduction to the world above since he'd been basically responsible for the initial one they'd experienced with helicopters and guns and dogs and Tasers and TV cameras. He also had a California CDL and access to the school bus from his church, for taking anywhere from a handful to over forty people on expeditions out and about in the wild kingdom of greater Bakersfield.

Hertell welcomed Orbin's help as it would allow him to take larger groups out than if it had just been him alone in his truck, and would also allow him to focus on being the tour guide, answering questions and otherwise explaining the world to the Generations and the Future without the distraction of driving. Kaye had also offered to chaperone as well since she'd joined the Mustard Seed Choir.

Hertell initially considered driving the bus through the portal down into the pressure buffer to save the Generations the long steep walk up the ramp from the manifolds. And while the depths of the pressure buffer had ample room to admit a fleet of buses with plenty of room to maneuver and turn around, the opening itself wasn't quite big enough, and he'd noted that while the mouth of the opening itself could conceivably but barely admit the bus, the further you went into the passageway, the narrower it became before it gradually widened out again. It had something of an hourglass shape to it, like a Venturi tube. So as much as he'd wanted to spare the Generations the climb to the world, he knew the bus would get stuck if he tried. So he bought some golf carts, which seemed to do the job and everyone down there loved driving them up to Orbin's waiting bus.

The Future loved Orbin. He gave them nicknames like Spunky, Professor, Smiley, Beeswax, Tadpole, Larry, Moe, and Curley, after the three stooges who had been the comedic North Star in the world below. Orbin asked them lots of questions about their lives beneath the surface and what they wanted to do now that they'd emerged into the larger world. And though he tried on several occasions to walk down to look at their world, his claustrophobia wouldn't allow it. Each time he reached the pressure buffer he'd start to hyperventilate, so he contented himself with their descriptions, and the footage that was now all over the internets, and also by taking them on their explorations of the new world above.

The first trip was to the airport to watch the airplanes, and was followed by a series of excursions over several days to a shopping mall to watch the people, a dog show at the fairgrounds, various neighborhoods, and a large horse farm up by Shafter. They were totally unprepared for the fact that horses had a smell and for how physically intimidating they could be. It was a hot day, so the rancher, an old friend of Orbin's, encouraged the kids and the adults, including Hertell, Kaye and Orbin, to run through the sprinklers in a freshly mowed alfalfa field. They screamed and laughed and got soaked as they darted to and fro between the cool sweeping arcs of the Rainbirds. The day ended with a Tri-tip BBQ and some ranch type activities. Hertell sat on the rear bumper of the Christ Victory bus and watched Kaye and Virginia playing Horseshoes with Orbin and several from the Future while the rest shot Daisy Red Ryder BB guns at some old soup cans. He absently picked at some body rust and congratulated himself; things seemed to be going well.

But the next excursion, a tour of the old Bakersfield downtown to see the Fox Theatre and the Nile and the Padre Hotel, was where the Future made a most unusual request. They asked to go around the block again, and specifically down the alley behind the theatres and restaurants and storefronts. And then they asked again, and then again.

As they circled the block the third or fourth time, Hertell realized the Future had lived their entire lives seeing only the façade fronts of buildings: the malt shop, the movie theatre with "The Nutty Professor" on the marquee, so the backs of buildings were endlessly fascinating and he could not stop laughing about it—laughter that was just a fraction too hard, laughter that had a sad, almost tragic feel, as if laugher could be in a minor key, and nobody noticed it, not Kaye and not Orbin since they were laughing too, and not even Hertell, because his was laughter tapping into some deeper and forgotten folds where there was snow-white sand and green plastic barns and windmills.

Chapter Twenty-Eight

The Crazy Man

"**W**ho's that?"

They were on their way to the Bakersfield Speedway to watch the races and were passing through an area of big box stores, a vaguely industrial, but consumer friendly stretch of North Chester. They were stopped at a notoriously long red light, when Virginia asked the question.

Virginia had noticed a man sitting on the corner. He was sitting in a folding chair and holding a poorly hand-lettered sign that read, "GOD LOVES, GOD FORGIVES, CHERISH LIFE!"

Hertell had seen the man many times before, so many that the man was as invisible as a light breeze. The man had been a fixture on that corner for as long as Hertell could remember, since the Reagan administration anyway and maybe even before. Hertell had witnessed the man age over the years on that corner. He stood at the corner of East Galaxy and North Universe waving his signs at the passing cars for many years, and as he grew older he settled into the folding chair in which he now sat smiling and waving at the big blue Christ Victory bus as it made its way past his outpost after the light finally changed. He was probably in his 70s now, worn and weary and weathered and wearing a big floppy hat to protect his leathery skin from the sun, a Hawaiian shirt, and chalky cargo pants and waving the sign. "GOD LOVES, GOD FORGIVES, CHERISH LIFE."

"Him? He's just a crazy guy. He's been on that corner forever."

Hertell typically gave much more thought to his answers, particularly when answering questions posed by the Future, but not in this case. It this case, his answer was given with no thought at all, almost as an instinctive, involuntary response and he would later decide that it must have been God's will, or at least fate if there wasn't a God, since his answer prompted a succession of questions that would prove pivotal in Hertell's philosophical trajectory.

"But the words make sense. God does love. God does forgive. People should cherish life. How is he crazy?"

Hertell went on to explain that the man was crazy because he'd spent the last thirty or so years on that same corner with his anti-abortion signs and that it didn't make any difference because abortion was legal and everything. And as Hertell mouthed words like "choice" and "reproductive freedom" and "women's health", he noticed the effect of his explanation on the faces of the Generations within his earshot.

They certainly knew of miscarriage and stillbirth—Hertell knew they'd lost many members of the Future that way during their fifty odd years beneath the earth. They knew what abortion was of course and that it had been practiced in some form since ancient times; but in their world, where life was so precious and its preservation so essential, the concept and the manner of its execution had faded from their consciousness and was as unthinkable to them as slavery or human sacrifice—just a sad historical artifact to be acknowledged and ultimately regretted.

Orbin was driving and couldn't hear the exchange but noticed how quiet the bus had become, he watched as best he could in the rear-view mirror, as much as the responsibility of driving permitted. Kaye was sitting a few rows up and was staring out the window.

Kaye watched the crazy man with the signs scroll by as the bus passed him. She remembered how the signs had moderated over the years. When he was a younger man, the signs were very accusatory and graphic, but eventually they converged on variants of the words and phrases being explained by Hertell that day on the bus to the Future.

The man was strategically placed at an intersection with one of its major tributaries flowing into and out of a light industrial area where a number of health care providers and practitioners had congregated in the '80s, such that anyone venturing in would see his signs. He'd once been interviewed by a local reporter who was curious why the man had taken up this particular cause and persisted with it for so long for no discernable effect. Evidently the man was a prosperous business owner who'd had an epiphany while watching a "Horton Hears a Who" production at his daughter's school, and had taken its refrain, "a person's a person no matter how small" to heart, and to his quixotic corner. But the reporter was merely a stringer and the story never got published. The man had been routinely threatened and beaten several times by protective boyfriends and even shot on two occasions from passing cars: once with a paintball gun and once with a real gun, but it was only a .22; nevertheless, he was far enough away that he was violating no restraining orders but still visible and unavoidable to any potential customers seeking reproductive freedom.

Kaye knew this to be the case since she'd once been one of those customers, turning down the wide lane leading into that very industrial park.

She'd been so excited and relieved when Hertell had called from out of the blue that day from his conference in Brazil. She'd had such exciting news, but before she could even utter a word past 'Hello', she heard a flat voice from a thousand miles away say, "I've met someone. I'm not coming home."

She drove herself that day, and circled the block many times but finally took the road past the man with the signs. She was carried by rage and sadness and grief and fear and every other ineffable emotion that torments the human heart.

Her son or daughter would be in their teens now, studying for their SATs, learning to drive, sitting in the kitchen with their friends as Kaye made spaghetti for them, if she'd let them live. But she didn't, and they would never exist and would never feel the weight of a blanket or the warmth of a hand or the comfort of a mother's whisper. She was now in her 40's and single and would never ever have children of her own or make spaghetti for them or their friends. So she stared out the bus window at the crazy man and his sign, God Loves, God Forgives. Kaye certainly hoped so.

"They must be very ashamed."

The observation had come from behind Hertell. He turned to face the voice and was taken aback by the look of such sadness on the woman's face. It was Peggy, the one who asked about dogs that very first day. She was a handsome woman in her sixties with a pageboy cut and green eyes, but she wasn't looking at Hertell, she was staring at her lap.

Hertell attempted to comfort her by explaining that they probably have a lot of different reasons, but that shame probably wasn't one of them.

"Sometimes, it may be that they have too many kids and can't afford another one, other times they don't want the kid because they broke-up with their boyfriend or whatever or to get even or something like that, it's really hard to say, and then sometimes it's just not convenient, but I don't think shame figures into the equation much anymore."

Satisfied with his explanation and hoping that it provided at least some comfort for Peggy, Hertell turned and faced forward again. "Orbin, how long to the Speedway?"

Orbin held up his hand. "Five minutes or so." Hertell noticed that Kaye was rubbing something from her eye.

"No, not her."

It was Peggy again, she was staring out the window at all the people in the parking lot of the big box stores. "The people that let it happen. They must be very ashamed."

"Oh, them." Hertell thought for a moment as he'd never actually thought about it that way before since shame had kind of faded from the palette of primary human emotions in recent years, replaced by the more active vapours like outrage, indignation, pity, envy, and embarrassment but never ever something as adhesive and persistent as shame.

It was as if it had disappeared from human consciousness, from language as well.

One of the strongest strands in the cable of human relations, social order, culture and ultimately civilization—more than fear, more than hate, maybe even more than love, because it is internal, relentless, silent and inescapable, patiently waiting to hold you accountable, for as long as you draw breath, and possibly after. Only now faded away to a mere curiosity of western civilization, a relic of a less enlightened and more judgmental time, to make shelf-space available for self-esteem, participation trophies, rights to choose, and social justice. Hertell knew from TV and the internets that it still carried freight in other, less evolved parts of the world where people obsessed about face, whatever that was, and killed their daughters for wearing eye makeup and so forth, but in his corner of the globe it was last season's laughable fashion and even worse, lacked sophistication.

He knew that shame must still exist since he'd felt it deeply the night his father died: it washed over him in waves of self-contempt with each inexplicable and inappropriate spasm of insuppressible laughter which finally stopped when he saw his father's soul fall away from his motionless form and then drift lazily across the room and then up, where it lingered for a time as if saying goodbye, only to fade slowly into the knotty pine ceiling directly overhead. Hertell traced his behavior to the fact that he'd been shot in the head and that his giggling was probably a vestige of the neurological trauma he'd experienced, which comforted, but did not absolve.

He also knew, from the copper specks, that animals felt shame, some more than others, depending on their phylogeny: invertebrates were too simple and solitary to feel anything, much less shame since they couldn't care less about the opinions of some other gob of protoplasm, though most arthropods felt it to a small degree, but the higher animals, especially those with four-chambered hearts, whether predator or prey, felt it deeply and instinctively. The dinosaurs and later the mastodons that roamed the Li'l Pal in times past had highly complex rituals and conventions for earning and showing respect and avoiding shame. Only the advent of rational intelligence was able to convince its possessors that it was no longer relevant, or that it even existed—we'd long since convinced ourselves that there was no heaven, and no hell, and no hurry in any case. And now, no shame either, quite an accomplishment.

He turned his head toward Peggy, but didn't look at her. "Nope, nobody ashamed yet... Maybe someday."

"Ladies and Gentlemen boys and girls will you please put your hands together and welcome the folks from the land that time forgot, the visitors from another planet, please give a big 'ol Bakersfield welcome to the Li'l Pal Future!"

Thus was their arrival at the Bakersfield Speedway duly noted and heralded by the race announcer since they'd been on the news and all over the internets for at least the last 72 hours and probably longer for those paying attention, plus they were a local phenomenon and therefore a source of civic pride.

Orbin knew the Speedway General Manager since his Bakersfield Junior College days, so he'd called to let him know they were coming, but that was just to get some good seats, and he certainly didn't expect the reception they got. They were met by a delegation of Civil Air Patrol cadets who led them down front and center to the VIP seats directly overlooking the pits.

It was a family crowd, and still early in the evening so the blood alcohol levels were still low and the crowd waved warmly and shouted their welcome and cheers to the Future who were pleased but puzzled by the reception.

The crowd whistled and waved and almost everybody on the aisles reached out to shake the hands of the Future as they descended the stairs with a chorus of suggestions and observations. "You shoulda stayed down there man, it's crazy up here!... If you got beer and X-Box down there, sign me up!..."

They reached their VIP seats, just as the National Anthem was announced. Now here was something they recognized.

"Will you please stand for the cadets of Civil Air Patrol Squadron 121 cadet honor guard who will present the colors for our national anthem!"

The revving engines were silenced, everyone stood, hats came off and hands went over hearts, some of the older men saluted as did some younger ones. And everyone began to sing. The Future was relieved as everyone around them began to sing, and they joyously joined in.

Hertell trailed off in mid-verse as they sang and just watched and listened. Many people within earshot had a similar response, and the announcer, similarly captivated moved his microphone closer to them until the Future was just an island of voices surrounded by a silenced and almost reverent sea of listeners— several people captured it on their phones that day and it would become the first of many million-hit videos of the Future on YouTube.

And the rocket's red glare...
the bombs bursting in air...

The Future had a sound, partly it was their harmony, and partly the clarity of their voices, but mostly it was the sound of open-throated purity, and though Hertell didn't know it, what he and everyone else in the stands that day was hearing, was the voice of Aunt Tawney.

The song finished and the engines started, but Hertell was already lost in thought. Well not lost in them so much as just unable to escape them. He was reflecting on what it must be like for the Generations trying to reconcile the issue raised by the crazy man on the corner, an issue that had been accepted or at least accommodated in the surface world for many years: they'd just emerged from a place in which the preservation of life was the only reason for existence, for anything else really, and it must be difficult for them to comprehend a world so otherwise ordered.

So maybe it was up to him to not only preserve their world, but also to promote it, evangelize it. He resolved to reproduce the little world they had so lovingly created below, on the surface above, on the dusty dry hills of the Li'l Pal—the topography was perfect, just the right mix of elevations and contours and slopes and gullies that was roughly consistent with the configuration below. It would be a charming, close-knit community, a village with a center and a heartbeat, but also with solitude and space, with a real sky and sun and stars overhead, not artfully lit rock; and with real church doors that actually led into a real church, not just backstage; and the crickets would be as real as the wind and the mourning dove, and dogs, lots of dogs.

Superficially, it would be just another gated subdivision on the outskirts of Bakersfield, only instead of being called Tuscan Sun or Sonola Hills, it would be called Mustard Seed V2.0. It would be like Colonial Williamsburg, only everything is real and the people aren't re-enactors. They're the real people and they're still living in 1963 only they're doing it now, today. So it would be more than just a teachable moment, it would be a teachable landscape where they could reintroduce the lost surface to its not too distant past. Mustard Seed V2.0 would change people since people just ignore bitter old men ventilating about how things have gone to hell in a hand basket, but having a living, breathing, talking, time capsule to show, not necessarily what was, but more what could have been, would be reassuring and motivational to some, and deeply troubling and shaming to others.

And it could really work since there was plenty of capital for the project thanks to Oceanoid by-products and the necessary skills of the architects, designers, Imagineers, and tradesmen. But the planning, permitting, environmental impact analysis, and construction would take time, so they would have to content themselves to live below while exploring the world above, and this is what was causing Hertell the most concern: The Future's exposure to the modern world. He would need to prepare them but would need specialized help that neither he nor Orbin nor Kaye could provide.

"Hertell?" He felt a tapping on his shoulder that drew him from his thoughts. "What?"

Orbin was looking at him. "The race is over, time to take the kids home."

Chapter Twenty-Nine

P2TSD

"**P**re-Post Traumatic Stress Disorder?" No, Doug had never heard the term before, but it was an intriguing notion. Kind of like those diseases and syndromes that only exist to justify a heavily advertised pharmaceutical cure.

It was a term of Hertell's invention, conceived in response to the Future's immersion and ultimate absorption by the modern world, and it kind of made sense as Hertell explained it.

It had been some time since Doug had visited the Li'l Pal, though it seemed like it had been in an earlier geological epoch since so many things had happened since—his daughter got her green belt in Karate, they'd gone to Disneyland, he'd been questioned by Government investigators, a small civilization had been discovered under the hills northeast of Bakersfield.

Doug had vaguely recognized the Old Rugged Cross from the photo on Drudge, under the flashing red headline "Duck and Cover Colony Emerges after 50 years", but didn't immediately make the connection. It had been scarcely a day since the visit by Carl and Rusty and he would have followed the link regardless, but for some reason he sensed that this would be different: not just a curiosity to be noted and then forgotten like the last Japanese soldier limping from the jungle or the UFO over the soccer match in Brazil, a headline for a day or two before fading into a footnote or a wiki page asking for input, or a web archive.

Doug would routinely wander the internets several times a day, usually between clients, but often while multi-tasking at home when there was nothing good on TV or during commercials for drugs curing restless leg syndrome, as was the case the night the story broke.

He had email and several browser windows open, Drudge was in the background, obscured by search debris: mainly about 'Mustard Seed', some wiki pages and a variety of Christian web sites. His wife glanced over his shoulder as she reclaimed the remote, and noted the particularly religious nature of his searches; "You're not going Catholic on me are you?"

Doug answered as he always did. "No, not yet. Just want to be ready for the final."

Apparently satisfied, she sat down beside him on the love seat and switched to a Public Access channel where the County Board of Supervisors was debating a new Indian casino. She'd grown up in Reno and hated gambling, and gamblers, and was resolved to oppose the Indian Casino at every opportunity.

Doug noticed that the Drudge page had just refreshed and had a new headline, so he clicked it to bring it to the foreground where he saw the flashing red headline and photo. He followed the link to the story, which was primarily a video report from a local Bakersfield news station. That was the first surprise.

After the usual banner ads and flash promotions, the report proper started. "Felicity Spector, Action News..." Doug immediately recognized the reporter—surprise number two.

It was Yoga-mat-step-mom; at least she had a name now. He never watched local TV, mainly cable channels like Discovery and History, which explained why he didn't recognize a local celebrity. She went on about the meth lab drug bust that was a bust, the usual clever wordplay that passed for news reporting of late.

There were overhead shots of a large crowded pit from News Chopper 4, some B-roll footage of a large trailer being exhumed, some shaky group shots of people in the distance in casual attire from the early '60s, and finally some extraordinary images of the underground corn field, and the main street, the singing, clapping choir, and finally Hertell and a woman in a sun dress addressing the press.

"I know that guy!" Third surprise.

Hertell stood with Doug on the Great Warm Slab. No longer a geological curiosity, it now formed the broad approach to a time portal leading back into the ancient world of the Kennedy Administration. Hertell explained his concerns about the effect of the world above on the people below based on the early excursions to the horse farm and the alley behind the Fox Theater and the crazy man on the corner and the races at the Speedway, and even though he knew Doug as a geologist, the card he'd left Hertell at their initial meeting identified him as a psychologist, and the only one in fact that Hertell personally knew. And now he was being asked to help Hertell prepare the Future for the world.

Doug had been watching the story unfold from a distance and had seen all of the initial interviews and special reports on TV during those first few weeks. His devotional interest in the story wasn't so much that it was a local story, or that he felt a degree of ownership since he'd actually met and talked to Hertell before the story became a story, he was captured by it in the same way and for the same reasons that the rest of the nation, and to a varying degree the rest of the world had been snared. Doug was by no means alone.

It was a chance to observe an alternate future; it was time travel. Only this time what was being revealed was that the dystopian destiny we'd all been expecting at some point in some fictional future, was actually our present—a present no worse than any other past present, but definitely not what was promised, or even expected, certainly by comparison to the past as represented by the civilization beneath the Li'l Pal. It was almost like being able to attend your own funeral, only in reverse. And it had a tragic quality, and everyone sensed it, everyone except the Future. And now Doug was part of it, brought in to ease, explain, and help them make sense of the present.

Hertell lead Doug beneath the remains of Whisper Hill.

"I've got a bunch of those IMAX guys coming down here again pretty soon, and then I have a meeting with the county after that, so I won't be able to give you the whole tour,

240

but everybody else can take you around and show you everything. I mainly want you to get, you know, started."

Doug didn't answer. He was speechless at the sights and textures and the lights and the sounds, and the smell of the earth—just as Yoga-mat-step-mom and her contingent had been on that first day, and as would all of the subsequent cameramen and soundmen and PA's and press and academic researchers and assorted strap-hangers upon their first exposure to the civilization beneath the Li'l Pal. The footage he'd seen on TV and on the internets didn't prepare him for what they'd done.

The lava flow origins of their world, and a million or so years of torrential water flow, gave the ceilings and floors a natural, cove quality, gently curving domelike over their heads, horizonless and seemingly infinite, and lit for the illusion of clouds rolling across the sky—it was like an enormous ride at Disneyland, only you weren't in a boat with pirates shooting cannons over your head, you were walking past storefronts on Main Street USA, and Leave It To Beaver's house, and Virginia City in 1880, looking up side streets that stretched into the distance, only they didn't go into the distance, but only an arm's length or so. It was all palpably artificial, yet fascinating and strangely, but undeniably comforting, like an intricately detailed train set or doll's house or Nativity Scene.

"And so most of these doors we're walking past, don't really go anywhere, they're just, you know, doors." Hertell opened one to demonstrate. It was the door to a Painless Dentist office on the Bonanza/Virginia City set, diorama, whatever it was, and just as Hertell had promised, it led directly into rock.

"One of the things you're gonna have to help'm on is that doors lead to real places usually, not always, but usually; because they've either forgotten, or more likely they just never really learned that doors mostly lead to real places up in our world. In their world they learned that doors mainly led nowhere. Kinda like religion up there in our world."

Doug reflected on Hertell's observation. "Doors must seem pretty different to you now."

Chapter Thirty

Aunt Tawney

O ver the next few weeks, while Hertell was dealing with news crews, network executives, reality TV show producers, politicians, Casino Indians, and the county planning commission; Doug was wandering through Egypt and the Ponderosa and Washington DC and the rest of their world with the Generations, sometimes in pairs but usually singly, doing very much the mirror image of what Hertell had done on the surface, only in reverse as Doug wasn't explaining, he was doing what he did best. He was listening.

He used essentially the same technique he'd developed, or more accurately stumbled upon, for his more traditional PTSD patients, the combat veterans of overseas contingency operations or whatever they were calling it this election cycle. Only instead of exploring the geological formations of Kern Canyon and Tehachapi as the metaphorical vehicle and psychological side-entrance to their subconscious landscapes, Doug was exploring the remote and sometimes secret passages and chambers in the lava tubes beneath the Li'l Pal and traversing the surprising inner landscapes of the Generations and the Future.

They'd developed an extraordinary oral tradition and had elevated double Dutch jump roping into an Olympic-level art form, not so much for the athletic benefit but primarily for the rhythms and rhymes which they used to memorize what seemed to Doug to be the entirety of western civilization; they jumped rope and chanted the Constitution and Bill of rights, Churchill's speeches, Dr. Seuss, and also Pindar in Greek, Virgil in Latin, Dante in Italian, and Goethe in German, Shakespeare in English, and Burns in Broad Scots until it was part of their muscle and bone and sinew.

Since Doug was the product of the California public education system, he recognized none of what he heard, except for the English and German, and had to ask what he was hearing, much to the amazement of the jumpers who couldn't imagine anyone over say the age of ten not recognizing Pindar in Greek. Their library was immense and well used and had been collectively memorized over the last fifty years by the Generations. They believed that Jesus was a real man, and didn't seem to know or care whether he really was the Son of God or just a regular son, because it didn't really matter: it worked and it was a better way to live and the music made them happy.

Doug also learned that it was no utopia: they were human and had the customary flaws, there was jealousy and envy and deception and greed and gluttony and sloth, adultery, neglect, cruelty, drunkenness, hypocrisy, the usual. There were also consequences for them, scorn, regret, shame, punishment which seemed to keep the flaws in check and generally counter-balanced by the better angels. Human nature was what it was whether lived on the surface or beneath it.

By all accounts, the first few years had been terrifying and difficult as the reality sank in that they were all that was left of human kind. Doug was taken to the graveyard by Gordon, one of the Founders. It wasn't a real graveyard in the usual sense, any more than their San Francisco and Egypt were the real ones. It was basically a graveyard set, with headstones for the deceased whose cremated remains were actually at the opposite end of the settlement in one of the large storage rooms, documented and filed away for eventual burial on the surface; nevertheless, it was the place they would all go to pay their respects and remembrance for the dead. Gordon explained that there had been a series of devastating epidemics, the worst in 1968 that killed many of the children and had driven the settlement to the edge of despair—they would all die in the dark and humanity would come to a whimpering end at the bottom of a sad little burrow.

"Aunt Tawney saved us, you know." Gordon was standing before a grave. "It's kinda ironic."

Doug had talked with Gordon enough times to know that prompting was needed. "Really? How so?"

It turns out that she'd been brought into Mustard Seed at the last minute, almost as an afterthought. The logistics and planning team had determined that traditional home economics skills like sewing and cooking would be a critical part of keeping the settlement fed, clothed, clean and in good repair, so Aunt Tawney the seamstress, while not essential like some of the managers, scientists and technicians, would nevertheless be valuable, and she came with a husband, Miles, who could teach metal shop.

"We, or what was left of us, we'd lost over a hundred people to the epidemic at that point, we had no idea what it was, still don't in fact, and there was this kinda panic that was starting to set in, you could literally feel it flowing through the air and the earth."

Gordon pointed to another grave. "So the Program Manager called all of us together, what was left of us, to the Great Hall to give us a pep talk I guess, or do some kinda technical, managerial blue-sky stuff. And maybe because we were all in there or something, all together in a group like that, a big herd, one of the Future started crying, and the panic just welled up out of everybody, and we kinda... dissolved into this big...mass of trembling and moaning..."

He nodded at the grave. "And Dixon, the Program Manager, was running around trying to calm everybody down, saying that everything was gonna be ok, but you could tell from his voice and the look in his eyes that he didn't believe it. And then, and nobody knows how it started, or why, but for some reason, Aunt Tawney, and she had just lost her two kids to the epidemic, she started singing."

Gordon stood silently. Doug recognized this kind of silence. He waited. He could hear Gordon's breathing, shallow and ragged at the memory.

"We were all... just... afraid. We thought we had failed, that no human would ever again walk in the sunshine, and all of us, and the civilization we were trying to preserve, would just rot down here, with us, like rodents. And we started acting like'm, and it wasn't pretty."

Doug could hear it in his voice and see it in shoulders, and he watched as Gordon slowly began to nod his head rhythmically, as if listening to a distant tune, and then almost as a whisper, he started softly singing:

> *Abide with me; fast falls the eventide;*
> *The darkness deepens; Lord with me abide.*

He was a very old man, probably late 80s or early 90s, so his voice was thin and reedy, but you could hear the calm descend over him.

> *When other helpers fail and comforts flee,*
> *Help of the helpless, O abide with me.*

Doug stood motionless and silent as Gordon softly trailed off into another long silence, and then laughed, turned and marched toward the main corridor. "Only a few of us knew the words, so the rest of us just kinda hummed along with her for a long time."

Doug followed him out, a few steps behind since he knew that Gordon liked leading these expeditions.

They walked in silence through a curving channel, and waved in passing to Carl and Rusty who were taking photos of the chamber. They finally stopped in the archway looking down on the large flat mezzanine where the Miniature Golf Course was nestled, and beyond it Main Street USA in the distance. Gordon took in the view and caught his breath. "And every time we'd get in a state like that, which happened a lot down here, the humming would start and Aunt Tawney would get us singing again, and over the years we all learned the words, and it just became a reflex for us, like breathing."

Doug looked out over the miniature golf course where the only movement was the slowly turning blades of the little Dutch Windmill just beyond the Pyramids. "What happened to her?"

Gordon shook his head. "She was murdered."

Chapter Thirty-One

Casino Indians

The local tribe had sprouted in the early '90s as part of the bumper crop of Casino Indians that had similarly discovered their roots at the time. They were loosely affiliated with the Yomash, an ancient tribe that lived peacefully in the Central Valley until the arrival of the Spaniards. The Yomash were essentially written off by the more aggressive tribes of the Southwest as mere grubbers content with living off acorns and whatever else the Sierra foothills had to offer. They didn't even have a word for 'warrior' and were considered the dregs of the Indian food chain, kind of like personal injury lawyers in the legal profession—sometimes prosperous but without nobility or cachet. A noted ethnologist/historian once referred to them as the 'Unitarians' of the great Southwest First Peoples—able to accommodate any imposed order and willing to fight for none.

The group that Hertell was meeting that day would be content with a different selection of roots and nuts this time. They were well lawyered and had lots of ideas for Mustard Seed V2.0. It seems that by fulfilling the ancient tribal prophesy and subsequently accepting membership in the local tribe, the Founders and the Future had made themselves legally part of the tribe, subject to tribal law, and therefore had to factor tribal culture, traditions and historical grievances into any decisions about the Mustard Seed V2.0 plan: specifically there was to be a Casino, an 18hole golf course, a high-end restaurant, a coffee shop and all -you-can-eat buffet, five acres of covered parking with hookups for trailers and RV's, and a water park for the kids. They'd even gone to the trouble and expense of constructing an architectural model of their tribe-compatible version of Mustard Seed V2.0, which covered the center of the massive conference table at which Hertell, Miles, Virginia, and Kaye sat. A CAD/CAM version was up on a bay window-sized HD display on the wall, cycling through a series of impressive 3-D fly-throughs.

Opposite Hertell, sat an assortment of tribal leaders and their lawyers along with Hertell's long lost mother, Anita. Except for the cowboy boots, turquoise bolo ties and ponytails, the tribal leaders were indistinguishable from the others seated on their side of the table. An assortment of legal documents sat in front of Hertell who idly leafed through the pages and politely listened to the presentation, complete with planned capital investments, revenue projections, and fast-track zoning particulars, all of which would advance the cause of compensating historical oppression. Anita would occasionally and pointedly note the profit that those on Hertell's side of the table stood to gain.

One of the non-ponytailed suits on the other side of the table was talking about a reality-TV show concept they were exploring with a Hollywood producer,

"So what's different about this content, this project, this concept, and what really makes it truly innovative and creative and unlike anything else out there is that, this time it's about a real, and I want to stress that, a real, actual, literal, virtual parallel universe where all the TV shows are real."

The suit pointed at Miles and Virginia. "You, your whole world down there, your universe, it's all real, totally real, and yet, it's... a set, it's a giant, fabulous, beautifully lit set, and it's totally real, which sets up this magnificent, delicious cognitive dissonance in the audience, in their real world."

He rose from his seat taking on the role of an imaginary audience member. "So if that world is real, then maybe this world is all pretend, maybe my world is all pretend, and everything I thought was real, isn't, and that reality... is somewhere... else out there, beyond us? What if all this..." He looked around the conference room as if seeing it for the first time, "is fake?" He sat down and pointed at the stack of documents in front of Hertell.

"And we've tested this with focus groups in the key demographics, spiritual but not religious with adequate discretionary income, and they loved the metaphor." He caught himself. "They didn't know what a metaphor was, you know, the actual word, so we took that word out of the questionnaire and used 'meme' and 'trope' because everybody thinks they know what those mean, and they totally responded to the concept and they loved the idea."

The suit was just summarizing the production schedule and participation points when Hertell finally rose to speak.

"Well, I don't know about the rest of you, but I think I've heard enough." He looked at Miles and Virginia. "I mean do you want to hear any more, do you have any questions or anything?"

Virginia shook her head. "Gambling is a sin, so there's not much more to say."

Miles nodded in agreement. "No, I don't need to hear any more."

"Kaye, you've got a vote in this, do you want to hear more?"

"Nope. It's everything I hate anyway."

Hertell pushed the stack of documents back toward the center of the table. "Well, thanks for all the input, I can see you put a lot of time and energy into it, but we're not much interested in all this extra stuff."

He put his hands on Virginia's and Miles' shoulders. "Miles is here for the Founders, and Ginny is here for the Future, and they've pretty much got all anybody'd ever need underground already, their own world—security, purpose, human contact. We just want to move Mustard Seed to on top of the ground, with the sky and the birds and the rest of us, instead of underneath it. So people can see that this doesn't need to be the way it is, to show'm that we've forgotten some things."

The Casino Indians were evidently ready for this, but they let Anita do the talking, she stood up. "Son..."

Hertell couldn't help but laugh. "Yes Mother?" and laughed again.

"The tribe has decided," she pointed at Miles and Virginia, "and they're part of the tribe now, you're all part of the tribe, except for Kaye and me, and we're heirs to the estate just like you." She pointed to the stack of documents on the table. "The tribe owns half of the vote in this, and the three of us own the other half, and the tribe has decided that this is what needs to be done to redress historical oppression and grievances and what not, and I think we owe it to'm, and I'm sorry but you're out-voted. This is gonna happen."

Hertell sat down again and calmly pulled a document from the stack and began searching through the pages. He could smell something, it was familiar, the mysterious sweet smell of black velvet.

Anita softened, slightly. "Look, I know I've been out of your life for..." She paused for a moment for mental calculation but quickly abandoned it, "... mostly all of it, but I'm the only mom you got, and I still want you to be happy and stuff, I mean you can make your little, you know, world, up here, on the reservation, so people can come and see... what you said, the little Colonial Williamsville time capsule, or whatever it is. We won't interfere with that, that's fine, we just want the opportunity to..."

"Make heap big wampum?"

The casino Indians stiffened, and one of their indignant suits, piped up in high dudgeon, "That is very insensitive, and hurtful, and offensive, and the tribe takes exception..."

"It's been 200 years, when are you guys gonna get over it? When are we gonna be even? Why do you still need a reservation anyway? The boat people don't get one, the Hmong don't, the Mexicans don't, what makes you guys so special? What happened to the noble Indian living in perfect harmony with nature? You're just gonna carve it up and pave it over like anybody else would, you're no different, you just get to cheat dumbasses out of their rent money and call it social justice and stuff."

Hertell held up the document. "And I'm afraid you're going to have to recount the tribal vote, because according to this," he pointed to Miles and Virginia, "they get a vote now too, and everybody else down there gets a vote, the Founders and the Future, all the Generations, all of'm, and all together, they outnumber the enrolled members of your tribe by at least five hundred, so by the time they're done with you, you might not even be in the casino business anymore."

He slid the document across the table to the grim suits who were exchanging uncomfortable glances." And you really should read your own crap before you try to buffalo somebody with it."

He turned to Virginia and Kaye and Miles. "You guys ready to go?"

Kaye nodded. She recognized this behavior in Hertell, mocking, direct, unblinking, and effective. She'd been on the receiving end of it during their divorce, and hadn't really seen evidence of it since, and thought that perhaps it had been lost when the bullet entered his brain. Evidently not. But at least now she also recognized its source: he was afraid, and fear, second only to guilt, made him attack.

They were all getting into Kaye's Suburban, when Anita caught up to them in the parking lot. "Look, it's nothing personal, okay?"

Hertell laughed and opened the door for Virginia and Miles. "Yeah, I don't see how it could be."

She watched as Hertell let Virginia into the truck and closed the door for her. "You don't get it do you?"

He opened his door. "Oh I think I get it pretty well."

"No you don't." She held the door for him while he got in. She looked past him at Kaye in the driver's seat. "You don't know what you're dealing with here. Things are in motion. You think this is all by accident, some random turn of events? There are forces at work in the Universe that you are unaware of."

He buckled his seat belt. "This Universe or the parallel universe?"

Kaye started the truck.

"This one, the real one, the only one that counts; the one with real lawyers, and real politicians, and real judges. A vote's not gonna change things, a vote doesn't matter."

She looked back at Virginia and Miles. "You people don't count, all those people down under the ground don't count, they don't even exist, legally. No passports, no ID's, no birth certificates, no real ones anyway, not ones from up here, official ones, the ones that count. They're just a bunch of undocumented illegals living down there, only there's no place to deport'm to 'cause they came up out of the ground. The tribe took them in and gave them legal standing. The tribe owns them, they should be grateful, you should be grateful. We're trying to help you here. It's all right here, just take it. Why won't you take it?"

Without answering Anita's question, Hertell slammed the car door shut.

Chapter Thirty-Two

Hell On Earth

D oug learned that the Generations considered the surface, or what they believed to be left of it, to be in ruins and scourged by cannibalistic mutants, and referred to it as "Hell on earth". Which was later shortened simply to "Hell", partly because that's what they truly believed, and also partly because there was nothing else to believe. That the world had continued muddling on pretty much as it always had, was not considered.

Mustard Seed, at least for the first few years, had preserved its original, traditional government project structure, more from inertia than from intention: Program Manager, deputy program manager, various departments, and lower level section heads; however, this structure deteriorated rapidly under the stressors of life below the surface, and finally collapsed during the epidemic of 1968 since a civilization can't really be managed at all.

So they eventually recreated and then preserved the entire structure of the US Government in a way that reminded Doug of a cross between a bonsai tree and the Miniature

Golf course where he now sat with Gordon and Virginia and Hertell who had joined them in mid discussion.

They were seated on an assortment of benches, rocks and miniature versions of historic structures. Hertell was straddling the Sphinx but wasn't really part of the conversation. He was thinking about Mustard Seed V2.0 and the difficult meeting he'd had with the Casino Indians earlier in the day, but he quickly drifted off while looking at Stonehenge where Virginia sat atop one of the columns. She was talking to Doug who was seated on the Parthenon, but Hertell didn't really hear what she was saying. He was just studying her face and hands and gestures and the sound of her voice, and he just felt happy.

He looked at her, and reflected on how she'd lived her whole life in a world of forced perspective, an optical illusion like the lines that curve but don't really or the lines that look different sizes but aren't, only with her it was a world where everything that looked far away, was really close, like when she reached out to touch the airliner five miles up in the sky. Kind of the opposite of Hertell's world, where everything that seemed really close was actually far away. But something was now drawing him from his thoughts.

Gordon leaned forward and rested his hands on his knees. "And so we all knew why North did it, because she was in great pain and so he took a pillow and put an end to it. He was like a son to her, it was an act of mercy and an act of love, but it was still an act of murder, and we had no choice in the matter, he was guilty, he admitted it. He told us we had no choice and told us to do what we had to do. He said we couldn't have a murderer walking free among us. Only nobody wanted to be the executioner, so he took it out of our hands. He took care of it himself."

Doug nodded. "He committed suicide then?"

Gordon looked surprised and shook his head. "Well, no..."

Virginia agreed. "That would be a sin..."

Gordon pointed up toward the dome of rock above them. "No, North left us and went straight to Hell for what he did, he went up..."

Gordon trailed off, and then looked at Virginia in confusion. Doug could tell by their expressions that they were struggling with something. "Where did he go? North? That was his name?"

Evidently, the story of the end of the world and the fate of the surface and its inhabitants, had become so thoroughly embedded in the consciousness of the Generations that it had taken on the character of a fable; therefore, not warranting a second thought or a deeper consideration of the specifics or their implications—this is what Gordon and Virginia were wrestling with as Doug badgered them with trivial questions.

Virginia looked at Doug. "Only, I guess it turns out that Hell wasn't what we thought it was, and so, I guess North Dakota just went up into... the world."

"North Dakota? What was his last name?" Gordon and Virginia answered in unison, "Hill." Hertell dismounted the Sphinx. "Mister Frostie?"

Chapter Thirty-Three

Mister Frostie's Last Day

It had been a good day. He'd started it with his favorite breakfast of pigs-in-a-blanket at Lorene's downtown and spent most of the day in Oildale in the shady neighborhoods north of China Grade Loop. They were older neighborhoods full of grandparents taking care of grandchildren while mom and dad, if there was one, were off earning a living in Bakersfield. And as grandparents they were generally predisposed to buying ice cream for their grandchildren on warm central valley afternoons in those last precious, perfervid hours before sunset, the car-seat, and slumber.

It had been a cold and foggy winter, and spring had started rather suddenly and had caught Mister Frostie by surprise. He drove his ice cream truck randomly across town all year round, even in the winter, primarily for the curious affect the music had on people in unexpected circumstances, even though he only actually sold ice cream during the spring and summer but mostly the fall since it was always the hottest time of year.

He had no set route and just drove wherever fate led. Over the years he had developed a comprehensive knowledge of the streets and alleys and back roads of Bakersfield from Shafter down to Arvin and from Rosedale all the way out to the Li'l Pal where he'd spent the better part of the afternoon with Hertell the day before.

He didn't need to sell any ice cream at all, at least not for the money since he had plenty of that. He mainly drove around to be outside and to see people, not necessarily talk to them or otherwise interact, just to be with them. Hertell was one of the few he would actually talk to, but Hertell was a special case.

When he wasn't chiming down the streets of Bakersfield selling ice cream and picking up road kills, he spent the remainder of his time studying and contemplating the Bible. He'd come to religion under unusual circumstances. In his previous life, he'd lived in a uniformly religious community, some were more religious than others, but still on the whole it was a continuum of effortless and confident faith, only he never got it. He could see and sense the impact and effect it had on others, but he never, ever felt it himself. He envied it, even though he didn't recognize it as envy at the time.

He'd finished his business in Oildale and decided to follow China Grade Loop eastward toward the river, because it was Thursday and therefore cleaning day at all of the mansions on Yomash Lane. It had become a custom to park outside the gates of Rio Vista with his music box music playing and sell paletas to the small children of the illegals that were cleaning the empty and lifeless 7,000 square foot weekend getaways above the river. He'd stumbled upon them by accident some years before while on one of his random traversals of the back roads north of the river.

He'd stopped on the side of the road and had left his ice cream truck idling and the Mister Frostie music playing as he lit a cigarette and checked for landmarks. He could see the old wooden cross some distance away near the mouth of the canyon. He unfolded his map. His finger was on Rancheria Road and was tracing his route on the map when he sensed a presence. He looked up to see about a dozen little Mexican kids who had apparently materialized out of nowhere and were now standing quietly at the side window of his truck waiting to buy paletas, or at least his gringo version of them. He sold them what he had at a friends'n family rate of basically a dime each.

He spoke Spanish fairly well and learned that Thursday was always cleaning day so that the weekend retreats would be fresh and clean for the arrival of their owners on Friday afternoons. So he told the kids he'd be back every Thursday afternoon and that he'd bring paletas in the future.

Which is where he found himself on his last day on earth. The original kids and mothers had grown up and moved on to presumably more promising career paths, so this was a fresh bushel of kids from a new crop of illegals. He'd kept his prices down at pre-Nixon administration levels, so they often bought several each and would take the surplus paletas to their mothers and older sisters who were busy cleaning inside the gated community.

There was a new kid in line today. He'd never seen her before and figured that she and her mother were new to the group and the young daughter had merely tagged along with the other kids, not knowing what else to do. She was the last one in line and offered him a bright green hair band as barter for a paleta since she didn't have any money. He put the hair band on his wrist and then held his wrist out as if modeling it to the kids while appraising her offer.

"You know, it really kinda brings the whole outfit together, don'cha think?" But he said it in English, so none of them got it, so he said it again in Spanish. They all nodded in polite agreement. "Sí... Sí...." wanting to see the transaction approved, so he gave her a lime paleta in exchange, which they all understood without a word in the warm afternoon sun.

The kids and their paletas headed back through the gates of Rio Vista where their mothers and sisters were still cleaning. Mister Frostie drove a few more miles up Rancheria road where there was a good turn around spot. It was also a spot that had a nice view of the old rugged cross and the Lil'Pal just on the other side of the river and he would often stop there for a cigarette and a sunset before returning to his trailer for the night, but this day he stopped a little short of it for a flattened mat of fur he spotted in the opposing lane.

The sun was low on the horizon, and he had to shade his eyes from the glare as he leaned on his flat blade shovel and gave the road kill his professional assessment. It was a dirty white one, probably a Bishon Frisé or a mix of some kind, probably an escapee from a freshly cleaned Rio Vista weekend retreat. He imagined the roadkill's last few moments on earth, running up Rancheria Road with no leash, and no poop bags; nose wet, gulping in the air and the freedom and pissing on everything it could until it met the steel belted radial angels of death. It had been some time since its flattening, so it wasn't terribly unpleasant; nevertheless he'd need the square blade shovel Hertell had so generously given him to recover the remains.

It was a beautiful afternoon, the sun was just grazing the Temblors across the valley to the west, and Mister Frostie stood in the middle of the road savoring the sun on his face and that delicate silence that often settles on back county roads. For a moment he thought he could hear Mexican music. It was time to go to work. He bent over to shovel up the flattened Bichon Frisé, but a glint caught his eye. He leaned closer for a look, and then heard a short, loud chirp.

He looked back over his shoulder, but it was the chirp of no bird he recognized.

Chapter Thirty-Four

Chirp

In their defense, the sun was in their eyes and they actually did try to stop as soon as they saw what they presumed to be a CalTrans worker in a high-viz safety vest squatting in the middle of the road, shovel in hand; however, he was at most a car length away when he came into view, and the driver scarcely had time to swear and slam on the brakes before they hit him full on.

Rancheria was a lightly traveled back road, used mainly by a handful of ranchers, propane delivery trucks, illegals who tended the pot farms nestled in the inaccessible slopes of the Sequoia National Forest further to the north, and bird watchers and wildflower collectors, but only in wet years. It would also occasionally attract some eco-types in Subaru Foresters and the like bristling with mountain bikes looking for untracked places to ride without a bunch of mountain bikers rattling around ruining their wilderness experience. However, in spite of their diversity, all drivers on this isolated track were all consistent in one respect: they all tended to speed and cross lanes and assume that they could see around blind curves.

The one that concluded Mister Frostie's day was headed south. It wasn't a Subaru, but a late model Prius Wagon with two mountain bikes on top, and its interior packed full of marijuana and a couple of entrepreneurs from one of the lesser cartels—presumably a dirty Ford F-250 with a camper shell would attract more interest from law enforcement than a planet-saving hybrid studded with mountain bikes.

The Prius was going downhill in electric mode when it rounded the last blind curve before the long straightaway leading past the freshly cleaned houses of Rio Vista and on to Highway 178 beyond. It left barely 6 feet of skid marks before impacting Mister Frostie and his shovel.

They finally ground to a stop a hundred or so feet later. Mister Frostie had accompanied them for part of the trip, only most of it was while underneath the car. He lay in a jumbled mess about 50 feet behind the Prius nestled between the parallel skid marks.

The entrepreneurs sat in the car for a moment. Flaco Jimenez was playing "La Napolera" loudly on the radio as they immediately fell into a vulgar duel of bitter recrimination while quickly surveilling the area looking for any other CalTrans workers which they knew always worked in clusters consisting of one crew member doing something and the remainder either leaning on their shovels or texting on their cell phones. However, in this particular case, there were no other CalTrans workers at all, and not even a single CalTrans truck. They silenced Flaco. Perhaps this was their lucky day, no CalTrans guys with radios, no witnesses with cell phones; this would just be their little secret.

After some discussion it was decided that they would both get out of the car to drag the dead body off the road— the unspoken but reciprocal suspicion being that any other alternative would end with one being abandoned on Rancheria Road with a crumpled dead body in a safety vest in the middle of the road and a long walk to Bakersfield.

While somewhat more demanding than the routine dead Mexican in a sleeping bag to which they were accustomed, they nevertheless made quick work of moving the dead body. They cut off the tattered safety vest since it was a little too eye-catching and then dragged the body well clear of the road toward some grape fields on a low bluff overlooking the river. They left the body in a ditch at the edge of the grape field and headed back to the Prius.

Noting the Ice Cream truck in passing, their deductive reasoning led them to the inescapable conclusion that there was likely a cash box and at the very least some paletas that could be salvaged from the tragic circumstance fate had thrust upon them. They looked inside and took the cash box and a box of coconut paletas, so it wasn't a complete loss.

They drove off as the sun was setting, accompanied by "La Napolera", leaving Mister Frostie to spend the night, and the rest of his life, in a shallow ditch overlooking the Lil'Pal and the old rugged cross.

Chapter Thirty-Five

Roadkill Redux

It had been a good day, except for the very last part. Only now, it was dark. The sun must've set, but he hadn't noticed. Where had the day gone? He could see the green hair band on his wrist, but he couldn't touch it for some reason.

It was dark, but the moon had risen. He loved the moon, the real one, since it reminded him of the Zeiss moon that would mechanically arc over the Main Street of his youth, before things got complicated. It was time for his lesson. He could hear Aunt Tawny calling to him but he couldn't understand what she was saying, or if she was saying anything at all really. It was more of a sense that she was close by, and reaching out to him.

Like so many others, he'd been taught to sing and play piano by Aunt Tawny who quickly recognized his gift and moved him up the musical food chain to the Hammond B-3 organ. It was as if he could make the B-3 talk, and he always accompanied Aunt Tawny on Negro Sundays when she'd both sing and lead the choir which she did until the cancer came to torture her.

He could hear her whispering, just the way she did on the night he killed her. "Please, send me home, send me home now." Her voice was reedy and thin, ragged and torn with pain, the cancer had been eating her alive.

He looked around to see where she was but noticed that no matter how he turned his head, nothing changed. He wasn't in any pain, but nothing seemed to work. Nothing but his hand, the one just a few inches from his face, and at an odd angle, the one with the bright green hair band for a bracelet. He could move his fingers. The moon was now at his fingertips, he pinched at it and laughed to himself, though no sound actually came out of him. He had no idea where his other hand was.

He also had a gnawing sense of unfinished business, as if he'd been interrupted in the middle of something, but couldn't quite remember what it was. Wispy strands of thought would come to him at random only to loop back on themselves leaving him right back at his starting point: a flat blade shovel, a roadkill, a dirty white one, probably a Bichon Frisé or a mix of some kind, probably an escapee from one of the Rio Vista weekend retreats, Mexican music, he'd need the shovel Hertell had given him; a flat blade shovel, a roadkill, a dirty white one, probably a Bichon Frisé or a mix of some kind, Mexican music... So he cycled through this as the moon rose past his fingertips and ultimately out of view, until the irony and finality of his situation emerged—the Mexican music, the chirp, the car with the bikes on top, the surprised looks.

He had joined the ranks of his road kill, only he wasn't quite dead yet. He drifted back to his first night in Hell all those years ago, fully expecting and accepting death, only to be surprised by the outcome. It would not be a surprise this time since he knew he would not be simply melting into the biomass but would instead be flying away to be with Aunt Tawney and the rest of consciousness to a home on God's celestial shore. But for now, he'd have to be content to float in and out of consciousness as the moon crawled across the sky above his broken, torn and flattened form. He could hear her singing now, she was calling him,

> *Deep river, my home is over Jordan,*
> *Deep river, I want to cross over into campground...*

He had emerged from an escape shaft and stepped into Hell, and it was as bad as he'd imagined. He doubted he'd live for more than 24 hours, maybe 48 at best. Only it wouldn't be the mutants that would descend on him to devour his flesh for they were now all obviously long dead, scourged and scoured from the surface of the earth by the hurricane onslaught of blinding radioactive dust which was now filling his eyes and ears and lungs with ionizing radiation. He could taste it in his mouth, and he knew that ingesting radioactive fallout would just speed the process, soon his organs would fail, and he would die, if the heavy shovelfuls of brown air didn't bury him alive first. The escape shaft was filling with the radioactive dust, and he'd already resolved that he'd rather die in the open than burrowed in a shallow pit like a rodent. He pulled his sweatshirt up over his face and stumbled down a slope of some kind, though he couldn't really see it.

The sky was churning and orange, the sun was just a dull glow blotted out by the hissing folds of choking dust. He decided to move toward it and let death find him when it would. He had killed. He had been tried and convicted for it and sentenced to death, and that's what he would soon get, and he had chosen this end. And in a way it was better than what he'd expected—rather than being torn to shreds by radioactive mutants, he would instead slowly go into delirium from the radiation poisoning and then coma and then die and probably be preserved for all time in a mummified state entombed beneath tons of sterile radioactive soil. Perhaps he'd be discovered someday and mystify the archeological team of some future civilization.

He'd crawled and walked and stumbled for what seemed like hours, feeling his way up and down what must have been hills. He had lost all sense of time. He finally stopped on a hilltop when he literally butted into an old, leafless tree, possibly the last one on earth, the rest likely abraded into dust by the sandblast that was choking and rending his flesh even now. Yes, he would die on this little hill with the last tree, clinging to it to keep from being carried away by the wind, which seemed to be gathering speed and strength as if determined to grind him into meal. It was getting darker. It would be over soon.

There was a sound he recognized, a chirp, as if from a bird. He'd never actually heard a real bird before, but he'd heard plenty of them in movies and from the nature soundtracks that ran most of the day in certain parts of Mustard Seed, But, and this was what was confusing him, he was in Hell and there couldn't be birds in Hell. He slowly stirred. It was silent now, except for the sound of the bird, actually many birds by the sound of it, and he was suffocating.

He sat up with a start and tugged at the sweatshirt that had been swaddling his head through the night so that he could breathe. He was blinded by the light as he took several great gasping gulps of clean, clear, central valley air. He was burdened with several inches of dirt and struggled to gain his feet as his eyes adjusted to the bright light.

He seemed to be in a very large and well-lit hall, but there was no lighting grid and no ventilation ducts and no fire suppression piping. It was at that moment that it all came flooding back into his groggy and dusty consciousness. He was in Hell, and it was sunny and beautiful and there were birds, and that dome over his head must be ... the sky, and he was going to fall into it, and then as if drawn by a powerful magnet his arms instinctively and desperately reached out to hug the last tree on earth.

The last dead tree on earth that he'd shared the hellish night with. He hugged that dead tree like a small child fused to a parent's leg, his ragged breathing slowed and he calmed down as the fear of falling into the sky abated. The bird was chirping again, it was directly overhead. He looked up and saw the bird, and he also saw that he wasn't clinging to a dead tree at all; he was clinging to an old rugged cross.

He stood on the hilltop beneath the old rugged cross for what seemed to him to be an eternity and struggled to make sense of his circumstances—perhaps radioactive dust storms were common in the post-nuclear apocalypse world in which he now stood, but he didn't seem to have any of the symptoms of radiation sickness and except for the grit in his eyes and ears and hunger pangs, he felt fine.

Perhaps the mutants were not all dead. Perhaps the mutants had adapted to the scourging winds and would soon be emerging from their dens or nests or caves. Perhaps the mutants were all dead, but the dust wasn't radioactive anymore. Perhaps all those computer simulations had been wrong about the radioactive half-life of nuclear fallout. He considered a variety of scenarios and outcomes, but never considered that the end of the world never happened and that it had continued all these years without them.

An increasing flow of cars and motorcycles, trucks, and RVs towing boats on highway 178 finally disabused him of the notion that all the mutants were dead—the place was crawling with them. There appeared to be a river just beyond the mutant-infested highway. Rivers and streams were a fixture on some of the sets in the world he'd left below, but he'd never seen an actual river with reeds and trees and fish before. However, it was more thirst than curiosity that lured him down the hill and across the highway toward the river.

He made his way down the hill to a broad flat expanse overlooking the road and passed below what he knew to be high power electric transmission lines since Godzilla was his favorite movie and he recognized the power lines immediately from the monster's attack on Tokyo.

He reached a fence, a barbwire fence, which he recognized from Roy Rogers movies, and since it had made such an impression on him, he decided not to attempt crawling between its strands since he'd learned that barbed wire sought human flesh. Instead he followed it a short distance to a large wide opening in the fence and a dirt road framed by tall poles and topped with a sign reading "Li'l Pal Heaven".

As he reached the road, a formation of large trucks converged on his position. He froze, as he was surrounded, and there was nowhere to run. Perhaps he could pass as a mutant; he certainly looked like one, caked and chalky with radioactive dust. Several helmeted mutants approached him. They were much cleaner than he expected and from all appearances they seemed totally normal.

The head mutant addressed him, but pointed up toward the humming and crackling power lines. "We seen you comin' down from up'ere, and I tell you what Hoss, them lines up'ere are hot and some of'm are down, and hot, and you step on one ob'm, it'll cook ya, so don't go back up'ere till we tell ya it's okay."

Well at least they were speaking English and not Russian. He tried to reply, but his mouth was too dry, so all he could manage was a cough.

Another mutant addressed him. "Hey man, you ok? You look like something the cat coughed up." They all laughed in general agreement, which faded as they sensed something about their dusty foundling.

"Fine... Thirsty..." and then he coughed again. Like a gaggle of mutant mother hens, they swooped and gave him water from the Igloo strapped to the side of the truck and plied him with delicacies from a cornucopia of lunch pails—Twinkies, Ding Dongs, Slim Jims, Cokes, Marlboro's. And with that succor came the dawning realization that there was no great nuclear war, there were no mutants, and that the world had not ended.

He would later learn that the winds in Arvin, just a short distance from the Li'l Pal, were clocked at almost 200mph and over 25 million tons of soil and earth boiled two miles into the sky on that December night. Mister Frostie had risen from the earth on the night of the Great Bakersfield Dust Storm of 1977.

He'd immediately tried to explain to the PG&E workmen and later the Kern County Sheriff deputies, and in the weeks and months to follow, to a variety of Kern County mental health professionals, the circumstances under which he found himself on the surface of the planet without a social security card or a passport or an ID of any kind. He led them back to the Li'l Pal to search for the escape portal. The owner was most cooperative, and gave them complete access to the property to look for the entrance to the colossal fallout shelter being described to them by a young man, no more than fifteen years old, who, after several hours searching, had to explain that he'd wandered, literally blind in the dust storm for some time and couldn't exactly retrace his steps and that his escape tunnel had probably been filled with dirt and all traces erased by the storm anyway, but that they had to believe him since there were people living down there, hundreds of them, and he could name them all if they wanted.

He told them all the truth he had to tell, not just about the world below, but also why he'd been banished from it, how he'd killed the music teacher he loved and why, but everything he said, however truthful just made him seem more and more delusional—the OSCNOIDS power system, the gold, the Styrofoam, President Kennedy. He was committed and counseled but ultimately found to be no threat to himself or others and was eventually released, to the sunny streets of Bakersfield.

He couldn't see the moon anymore. He felt warmth, as if a thousand hands were gently touching him. Perhaps the sun was rising, or perhaps he was dead. The moon was gone now, and he could see no stars, so he was probably dead. Yes, he definitely must be dead now since he could feel himself being carried, as if by those same thousand hands. He could see now, in the distance, the old rugged cross. How fitting he thought, that the first thing he saw in the surface world would also be the last.

He laughed, not out loud, but just inside, back to his thoughts that bright morning when he rose from the radioactive dust and found himself embracing an old rugged cross to keep from falling into the sky. And while the fear of falling into that ancient sky quickly faded and rational thought returned to him that morning, the fear of falling of a different sort and in a wholly different direction had continued to stalk his thoughts, a fear that haunts all of the enlightened faithless—what if it's all true, what if all those gullible, irrational Christians were right, what if it's not just a silly fable, what if it was, and still is, and ever shall be... real? What if it's all true? He dismissed it at first, it had been a difficult night, he'd eaten a lot of radioactive dust, but faith was patient and relentless, and it gradually overtook him in the intervening years.

And now the warm hands were gently lifting him from the ditch where he'd spent the last few damaged and delirious hours of his life, and as he rose higher, he could see everything, his whole life in fact, only not in a single sequential strand like in a movie, but all at once, from all angles, connected, simultaneously chaotic and comforting.

He drifted over the streets of Bakersfield where he watched himself as a wandering prophet of sorts, only in reverse: instead of calls to repent and warnings that the end of the world was nigh, he warned that the world didn't end and that beneath their feet was a kingdom waiting to be discovered, a civilization time-capsule living beneath the pet cemetery out past the edge of town. He saw Hertell, hours old, on a blanket in the sage, where he'd found him. He drifted over his trailer, not just the trailer itself, but its whole history, how he'd searched and how God led him to it, trashed and tireless behind a gas station in Santa Fe. He drifted over the Spring Beulah A.M.E church where he could hear himself playing the Hammond B-3 organ and the choir singing...

> *Just a closer walk with thee,*
> *Grant it, Jesus, is my plea...*

He drifted over his ice cream truck on the shady streets, over all the roadkill he'd gathered up over the years, and they were rising up to meet him; no longer flattened and broken and torn, but whole and healthy and seemingly none the worse for it, and they were singing too, only not in any language and not in any words, but just their normal sounds in a beautiful, effortless harmony.

They carried him over the man on the corner who told him about all the babies who would never be born, and he could see them now, they were all around him, smiling and happy and gently bearing him, tiny babies, millions of them, like a great squirming joyous mountain, lifting him, tiny hand by tiny hand closer to Aunt Tawney who stood beside the old rugged cross in the golden sunlight with all the Saints triumphant, her arms were outstretched, she was reaching out to him, and she was healthy and whole again, and singing with all the babies and the roadkill...

> So I'll cherish the old rugged cross,
> Till my trophies at last I lay down;
> I will cling to the old rugged cross,
> And exchange it some day for a crown.

He felt her arms around him, and felt the total peace that only a small child can feel, and knew he would never worry about the living again, their anger, their guilt, their confusion, their grief, darting to and fro, or frozen in fear, because he, or whatever he would soon become, now knew what awaited them.

281

Chapter Thirty-Six

Thrift Shop

Shortly after the Bakersfield Speedway excursion and the installation of Doug as the resident geological psychologist, Hertell had set up a satellite dish above Whisper Hill and ran TV and internet cables down into the settlement to allow the surface world to be explored in relative safety. He also got some advice from the TV crews and put cameras and microphones at optimal locations throughout the colony so that the world below could be shared with the world above. There were no green plastic barns or windmills and no white sand, but it was the same idea. He wanted their hidden world to inspire the surface world.

So, in addition to Doug's lava tube excursion-based sessions, Hertell also conducted his own group sessions in the large gymnasium with the biggest HD displays, and served as docent and tour guide listening to their questions and responding as best he could.

"So you're friends with all these people...on the computer?" Jennifer was seated next to her husband Jason in the third row of bleachers with several other couples in their mid-thirties. "Where are they, where do they live?"

"Well they could be anywhere, right next door, you know, up there..." Hertell pointed up toward the surface world. "Or on the other side of the world, and you may not even know'm, and probably never even met'm..."

A chorus from the bleachers joined in. "Do you ever actually see'm... or talk to'm... or touch'm?"

"No. Not really." He scrolled through a page and clicked on a video of someone putting gas in what was presumably a new car. "I mean, there might be some photos, and maybe videos posted, but you never actually see, or talk to, or actually touch a real, physical, you know, person, in the flesh, just kinda messages and pictures back and forth pretty much."

The bleachers were quiet, as the group processed Hertell's response, so he filled the silence. "And they might not even be real people, they might be bots, computer programs pretending to be people to get information about you and for marketing and advertising and such, so you've got that too."

"So you're friends with all these people but you never actually see'm or talk to'm or touch'm, and they might not even be real?"

Hertell considered the question. "Yeah... basically."

The bleachers were silent for a moment, until Montana observed, "Then you might as well be living underground."

Hertell couldn't disagree. Furthermore, he was growing frustrated with his incremental, ad hoc and essentially artificial approach: the exposure to one new element of the modern world, when done in isolation and out of context, only succeeded in creating a cascade of additional questions and confusion which, when explained in isolation and out of context yielded the same result. It was like whack-a-mole, only he got more moles with each whack.

So Hertell decided that, just like learning a new language, that immersion, when executed in a properly controlled environment with context, guidance and explanation was the strategy to pursue. And his recent experience with the Casino Indians gave his strategy a degree of urgency.

He also had a theory, actually more of a sense, that the Generations, and particularly the Future, were possibly more ready for the modern world than any of them would have thought, because as familiar and yet simultaneously foreign as Hertell found their world, there were inexplicable similarities with things on the surface from which they'd been isolated for so many years. For example, he noticed that there was an abundance of people with J-names in their 30's and 40's among the Future—lots of Justins, Jareds, Jacobs, and Janets and Jodys, just like on the surface, as if the J-naming phenomenon of the '70s and '80s was pre-programmed into us.

It was the same for the 20-somethings, lots of Trevors, Tylers, Tristans, Taylors, Ashleys, Brittanys and Courtneys—kind of like when identical twins, separated at birth, are finally, in adulthood, reunited and it turns out they have wives with the same name, drive the same make and model of car and have identical careers, kind of like that. He had been a scientist once, a rather prominent and promising one evidently, so he conceived an experiment, to test his theory, and rather than merely, and inadequately, providing context by reviewing history as if in a diorama, he would instead have the Generations live it.

Due to the unique demographics and economics of Bakersfield, it was the home of some of the most varied and renowned thrift shops in all Christendom, with fashions and household items ranging from the current epoch back to the Eisenhower administration. And each one, and there were many, was essentially a core sample of popular culture drilled and pulled from the strata of American life of the last 50 years. While the '50s vintage items were largely gone due to a popular cable TV series and the resultant '50s-themed parties that required a certain degree of period costume, the '60s, '70s and '80s were well represented, and the '90s and beyond over represented with an excess of cheap slave labor items from China. Hertell and Doug scouted all the Bakersfield thrift stores and determined that ThriftyMart was the perfect place for a quick and safe immersion. It would be both therapy and an extraordinary experiment at the same time.

ThriftyMart was a massive affair covering several acres. He'd reserved it for the exclusive use of the entire Mustard Seed population for an entire week. The charity that ran the store was delighted with the several pounds of Oceanoid by-products offered as compensation, since, at current prices, it would cover not only the week they'd be closed to the public for the Generations and the Future, but also their entire operating budget for the balance of the year and most of the next.

In accordance with Hertell's plan, Orbin would drive busloads, in randomly selected groups of 40, to ThriftyMart over a period of days, such that they could be observed independently of one another; the immersed groups would quarantine themselves both from the groups awaiting immersion and the control group to preserve data integrity and experimental results. Hertell and Doug would observe, record, and attempt to discover their patterns of behavior in what Hertell considered to be a Petri dish of the modern world, i.e., ThriftyMart.

Since ThriftyMart was so expansive, he also set up surveillance cameras for detailed data collection and statistical analysis and also so that he could observe activities occurring outside his immediate presence and assess the more subtle indicators and behaviors, clustering, timing, movement, and so forth. However, the surveillance footage would ultimately prove to be unnecessary since the emergent behaviors were so stunningly unmistakable that the video data and statistical analysis merely reconfirmed the undeniable and obvious results.

The first group arrived at ThriftyMart where they were met by Hertell.

"Ok, you're on your own. Feel free to roam around and look at anything you want, try on anything you feel like, read any book or magazine that catches your eye, listen to any record you want, play with any toy, operate any tool or whatever, you get the idea. Me and Doug'll be lurking around as usual to answer any questions you have. We can stay here as long as you want, we'll bring in food if you get hungry, and you can have whatever you want to take with you, or if you don't want to take anything that's fine too. So... enjoy."

ThriftyMart had a reasonable organization of its artifacts: there was a shoe section, sections for gardening equipment, tools and electronics, clothing was segregated along traditional, gender-normative men-women-children lines, there was a housewares section, furniture, records, CD, VHS tapes, books, magazines, and so on; however, below this top level of basic organization, there was nothing discernible: shoes and clothing were in no particular order, not by year or style as a polyester leisure suit could be right next to grunge rock flannel right next to emo-skinny jeans.

It was as if a tornado had gone through 50 years' worth of shopping malls and deposited the debris field into neatly arranged rows of tables, clothing racks and shelving gondolas. What follows are some of the transcribed notes from Doug's Lab Notebook:

```
Day 1 Group 1—reviewed
ground    rules.    Timid
start @ 913. Clustering.
Hesitant.    Bifurcation
@929. 2ndary, tertiary at
944 and 51.
```

```
Music        started      @
1005, Beachboys. Complete
dispersion    @    1015.
Diffusion to all sections
1022, Brownian,  confirm
on    video…1330    lunch
brought in. Aggregation.
Interesting        choices.
```

Jason, Ryan, Trevor at
LP racks, many turntables
going—Moody   Blues,
Hendrix,   Vnla   Fudge,
Iron   B-fly.   Clothing
clothing clothing. Ashley
&   Morgan   in   Go-go
boots! asking   name   of
"beautiful   colors"   on
crock pots—Harvest Gold
Avocado Green... Consistent
interest/ selections all
quadrants all ages. 1715,
Disco, polyester, YMCA,
showed arm moves f/song,
whole place doing YMCA...
1800 dinner brought in...
1950   retrn   to   bus.
Definitely   done,   none
want   to   stay   longer,
Minimal artifacts, some
clothes and books.

Day   3   Group   4—same
progression   as   prior.
Check   seed   value   of
random   numgen.   May
be   sampling   artifact.
Confirm no contact with

```
unexposed groups. Miles +
many Founders most of day
with Life magazines.
```

```
Day   5   Group   9—same
progressions    as    all
prior. Sensing increased
something,    not    sure
what near end session,
consistent w/ all prior
samples, no articulation,
no    expression,    but
definitely    something
there!
```

Hertell didn't need a notebook. He was feeling exactly what the Generations were feeling. He wasn't sure if it was from the copper specks or merely from his familiarity and affection for the Generations, but he felt their joy and excitement with each discovery, the weight of each realization, and the same vague regret for what was lost.

What Hertell discovered in his experiment, and that Doug would eventually publish, was that every group of Generations and Futures, almost as if programmed or genetically destined, went through almost the exact same developmental phases, as did the surface world over the last 50 years, clothing, music, politics, culture, language, morals—in-your-face stridency, self-indulgent malaise, big-shouldered ambition, clueless plenty. Only they did it in a matter of hours, so that they had the experience but not the damaging effects—it reminded Hertell of firewalkers who walk over the coals so quickly that they aren't burned.

It was also consistent with the case studies Doug had mentioned to Hertell when he was formulating his experiment, where some poor little kid that was kept in a closet from infancy to the age of 12 and then rescued and freed into the world unable to talk or read or reason, was able, in a matter of weeks on fast-forward, to go through every developmental stage they had missed.

But there was one thing that couldn't be observed or measured or captured in the surveillance video because it was only present in the room and in the moment, and it was the same with every group and it was as undeniable as gravity. As the day progressed, and the groups moved through the decades, there was a growing presence, a feeling, faint and localized at first, but ultimately permeating the room—enough to sense, but not enough to notice, at least not at first. Hertell sensed it in the first few groups, as did everyone in those groups. It was only the repeated occurrence with each group that finally brought it into the foreground of Hertell's awareness. It was an alloy of resignation and rage, and he knew why.

He had taken the Generations and the Future through time, and had given them a better sense of what had happened, but the freshness of the memory of who they were, only a few hours before, and the recognition of what the modern world, and now they, had become, filled them with a feeling of emptiness and anger that would accompany them from ThriftyMart back to the Li'l Pal.

The experiment was over, and the last group was heading toward the Christ Victory bus.

Orbin had spent the day with them on this last trip and had put the time to good use working on the bus, scraping and wire brushing the belt of body rust that blistered and occasionally peeked from beneath the bright blue paint, and then spraying on primer from a clicker-can as he went. The Church bought the school bus at a salvage auction and it had come from somewhere back east where the salt had established the gnawing underbody cancer. So while it was junk in the wet and snowy East, in the hot arid West it had another 10 years of life in it, and even if it was held together by rust, it was only $400. He'd finished around 4pm and was sitting in the driver's seat listening to the radio when the Generations returned.

Orbin had driven each group to and from ThriftyMart over the past week, and was struck by the difference: they were chattering and happy and hopeful on the way to ThriftyMart, and were silent and sullen and cynical on the way home. He looked at Doug who was standing at the door of the bus with his clipboard, and hunched his shoulders as if to say, "WTF?" Doug returned his gaze and shrugged and shook his head. He checked his clipboard. "Peggy?" He stepped into the door of the bus and looked inside. "Is Peggy back there?" No response.

He found Peggy standing in the infant section. Hertell was standing beside her. She was staring silently at a table of Onesies. Doug approached them. "Peggy? We're leaving now.

But you can stay longer if you want and Hertell can bring you back in his truck."

Peggy was one of Doug's favorites. She had taken him once, at the end of a seemingly endless climb, to an abandoned escape tunnel, her secret place at the furthest limits of the Lava Tubes. She hadn't been to it in many years, but explained that she had run away from home as a young girl and had hidden there. She laughed at the memory. It was an odd laugh, but he was quite honored to be taken into her confidence. She was always very talkative and told Doug how she would start a puppy farm when they finished building Mustard Seed 2.0.

But she wasn't talkative today. She shook her head, and they walked out together, and as she got on the bus, she stopped in the doorway and turned to Doug and said, "I killed a baby once."

Chapter Thirty-Seven

Hosed

A nita had set to work immediately after the Casino Indian meeting with Hertell and his delegation. The tribe and its legal suits had busied themselves trying to assign blame for the flaw in the legal instrument and how to limit the damage and regroup, but this wasn't Anita's first cage fight. Thanks to the Casino Indians and their lawyers, she now had access to the politicians and the judges she'd need. She knew what to do. It was a technique she'd often used to dislodge an undesirable tenant from one of her apartment complexes, and it was all so easy.

It was mid-morning, but Hertell had been up since before dawn. It had only been two days since the ThriftyMart excursions, and the Generations kept appearing in his dreams. He would find himself awake and exhausted in the pre-dawn hours after a fitful night spent struggling up a recursive hill of his own construction; reasoning with perfect crystalline logic to himself and the Generations why the present couldn't possibly be anything other than what it turned out to be, only to find himself at the bottom of the hill again with the Generations as frustrated and lost as before.

Hertell had stayed at ThriftyMart long after everyone had left on that last day. He'd been headed for the bus when he saw Peggy standing alone, and for some reason was drawn to her side at the table, and as he reached her side, a feeling of overwhelming sadness washed over him. He stopped where he stood just a few inches from Peggy, unsure what to do and unable to speak. He heard Doug ask a question and mention Hertell's name, he felt them leave, but for some reason as the day ebbed away, he stayed and kept a kind of vigil over that field of Onesies. There was one in particular, it was a pale lemon-yellow Onesie, slightly stained, with a little blue arrow pointing to the side and the words "I'm with stupid" silkscreened on the front.

He stood in the kitchen with the stained yellow onesie in his hands, looking at it, trying to make sense of it, and why, of all the things in ThriftyMart, it was the one and only thing he'd kept. He held it up to the daylight flooding through the kitchen window, and wondered where the person was who once dwelt in this tiny stained rag. In a blinding flash, it was illuminated from within with a light brighter than the sun.

Hertell struggled to keep his eyes open to behold the miracle, and all he could make out in the blinding light was, "I'm with stupid", and then, as suddenly as it had started, the light left the little yellow Onesie, and darted mischievously across the kitchen walls and up onto the knotty pine ceiling and vanished. It was then that he saw a car coming up the driveway, sunlight reflecting off its windshield and into his eyes as it bobbed and bumped its way up the hill toward the main house.

A car pulled up in front of the house. Hertell observed its arrival from his kitchen window. It appeared to be a man and a woman in the small white car and they were presumably getting their affairs in order before pursuing their business with the Li'l Pal.

The pair introduced themselves and politely and reasonably explained that they were from county child protective services, and that there had been some anonymous allegations of child endangerment, and they were obliged to investigate, however baseless the accusation.

"It's really more of a formality, just a walk through and do a few interviews with some of the kids and some of the parents, no big deal, we should be done in less than an hour."

Hertell laughed at the notion as he felt that there was no place on earth where children were more cherished than in the world beneath the Li'l Pal, and that the best way to prove it was to take them down there to see for themselves. And thus, was set in motion the merciless snowball of good intentions.

They welcomed the pair at first, as they'd welcomed the news crews and reporters and dignitaries in those first few days after the emergence. They were proud of their world, but the interviews led to more interviews, which led to Home School curriculum assessments, which led to safety inspections, which led to health inspections, and medical exams, which led to DNA samples, and zoning reviews, and building code compliance audits, and inventories, and all manner of questionnaires. The databases were being loaded for mining.

It made Hertell uneasy, but they had nothing to hide, so the more they could reveal about themselves the sooner they could prove... he wasn't sure exactly what they were trying to prove anymore. Their innocence perhaps, but they weren't accused of anything exactly. They were just being asked to reveal enough about themselves to reveal... the next horizon to be revealed, to reveal... the next so that they could prove that they couldn't possibly be guilty of basically anything and should therefore be worthy of their inquisitor's absolution.

A van pulled up on the great warm slab and discharged a pair of doughy technicians who began unloading equipment and donning yellow HAZMAT suits.

Hertell watched them from the vegetable garden where he'd been working with Virginia and a bunch of the kids—they had landscaped the great warm slab with plants and picnic tables and luscious green sod so that, in the summers ahead, the Future could play in the sprinklers on hot afternoons and the Generations could enjoy the warm nights under the stars.

The van had driven right up on their precious lawn and left a rutted trail of mud and shredded grass. But it was of no consequence since the technicians had official business to conduct. The leader saw Hertell standing with a garden hose a short distance away, and made eye contact with him. He acknowledged Hertell with a slight lift of the chin and a vague smile that bordered on contempt as he stepped into his HAZMAT suit.

Hertell looked over at Tristan and Trevor and Travis who were staring blankly at the big ugly gash that the van had left in the great lawn they'd just finished mowing.

"Why'd they drive through the grass?" "There's no grass over there, why didn't they drive over where there was no grass?" "Why did they do that?"

More confounding questions from the Future. He felt the rage begin to rise through his body. "Because they can."

It had been so insidious, they were losing themselves to the loving care of people who neither loved nor cared, the Generations and Mustard Seed were merely a material to be processed. It had all been done with a smile and the professed best of intentions, but it was basically like the SWAT adventure some weeks before, only less honest. At least the SWAT attack was straightforward about what it was about—dominance, control and ultimately obedience— and didn't pretend that it was about anything other than what it really was.

It's funny how people respond to things—the buzzing of a bee near the head can make the dignified and brave perform a comical interpretive dance, a soft whisper can make the indifferent move closer, and a garden hose can make a pair of technicians flee in silly yellow suits.

Mustard Seed had extraordinary water pressure, and Hertell had it on full blast as he approached the van with his garden hose.

"Hey! Asshole!"

The technicians looked up in mid costume change at the approaching Hertell, and then at each other as if to confirm which one was the mystery asshole—it's not me, is it you? ...no it's not me... is there an asshole here that nobody told us about?

"Yeah! You with the chin, take your gear and your yellow costumes, and your van and get off our fucking lawn!"

The leader stood with the yellow plastic suit nestled around his ankles and held up his index finger to restore order and he pointed at his clipboard. "We have authorization to..."

The water punctuated his sentence and swept over his body to great and satisfying affect with much sputtering and ineffectual batting and slapping at the jet of water as he retreated in a mincing jig toward the van due to the yellow HAZMAT hobbles he had about his feet.

"I don't fucking care!" Hertell gave watery chase to the other technician who was already back in the van and starting it up but who nevertheless took on gallons of Sierra Nevada snow melt as he struggled to get the window up. "You're in big... mblmf... you're in deep...gngnth..."

Hertell was joined by Virginia and all the T-boys who had brought another garden hose. "Get off our lawn!"

The leader had gotten back in the van by this point and had his door closed, but the rear doors were open so Hertell and the T-boys directed their hoses into the interior until the van lurched forward and out of hose range.

The soggy technicians must have determined it to be a teachable moment as the van executed numerous donuts on the fragile sod, sending Hertell and Virginia and the T-boys into full retreat in a thudding shower of knotted mud and clumps of grass. The van then proceeded to drive through the vegetable garden and the flower garden and also managed to take out a few picnic tables and umbrellas as it made its escape from the great warm slab and down the hill. It was a scene of complete devastation resembling Woodstock the day after, and Hertell immediately gave chase in the Cushman.

While in hot pursuit, Hertell had time to wrestle with his intentions, which seemed to consist of two contradictory extremes: he wanted to hurl boulders and sticks and shout abuse at the retreating van, and he also wanted to apologize and seek forgiveness for his disobedience and for his insubordination since he knew that his behavior on the great warm slab would only make matters worse and probably much worse. But it ultimately didn't matter since the Cushman was no match for the van, which was long gone when Hertell reached the main gate.

He sat quietly in the Cushman and watched the sparse traffic on the 178 and considered his options. He could lock and secure the gate and post no trespassing signs to discourage uninvited visitors. He could try to find the name and number of the organization that was on the clipboard he'd hosed out of the asshole's hand and try to explain and apologize for the misunderstanding.

But as he contemplated the situation, a trio of massive SUVs with tinted windows pulled up in front of the Li'l Pal Heaven main gate. Evidently, the hosed van and its soggy contents had wasted no time in calling in reinforcements. The SUV's finally fell silent and the doors opened. A well -dressed young woman on a cell phone approached Hertell.

"Hi, my name is Courtney? And I work for the President? Of like the United States?"

Chapter Thirty-Eight

Owe the Future

"What's your party affiliation?" It was an odd question that confused Virginia. "What kind of party? Like a birthday party?" Courtney smiled. "You are so delightful, and so like, innocent, you know, like pure?"

Hertell, Virginia, and a handful of the Generations were assembled on the Mustard Seed Main Street USA town square with a small delegation. The answer didn't clarify the question for Virginia, so she tried again. "Or like a tea party or something?"

Courtney's face clouded and one could feel the whole delegation stiffen. "What kind of tea party?"

Virginia felt immediately sorry for the woman and her obviously blighted childhood, and tried to moderate her response. "Well, just a normal tea party with a tablecloth on the playroom floor with your stuffed animals and maybe some friends and some cookies."

Courtney and her delegation laughed. "The President is going to love that one?" Several others were assiduously taking notes and whispering to one another.

Though he'd never voted in his life, Hertell knew what they were asking. "She doesn't mean like a normal party, she means like 'Republican' or 'Democrat' type party."

There was some surprise and general amusement at the absurdity of the question. Virginia exchanged knowing looks with some of the Founders. "Oh, we're all Democrats." Several of the Future laughed. "What else could we be? We're Kennedy people after all…"

There was a gleeful silence, and Courtney held up her finger. "Give us like, just a sec?" She, and the balance of the similarly dressed delegation in blue blazers, button-down oxford shirts, regimental ties, and chinos, retreated a few steps to huddle and confer.

Even before he was shot in the head, Hertell had no interest in politics, and even less after he'd been shot in the head. He presumed that it was a great honor to be approached by a Presidential delegation. Hertell knew who the President was since he'd occasionally seen him while cycling through cable channels, but they didn't put the little 'D' or 'R' next to his name the way they would with lesser politicians, so Hertell was never exactly sure whether he was an 'R' or a 'D'. He assumed that the President was an 'R' since he was always talking about jobs and the middle class and the economy and the stock market and such, but he had no idea what the delegation or the President wanted.

It had only been seven weeks since the emergence and the SWAT team; nevertheless, Hertell felt that it would be prudent to have contact and possibly advocacy at the Presidential level, particularly after the meeting with the Casino Indians and his mother and the recent garden hose unpleasantness, so he gladly accepted the offer to meet with them.

It was an election year, and extensive focus groups and exhaustive polling data indicated that the electorate overwhelmingly considered the country, and indeed western civilization, to be seriously on the wrong track and drifting away from whatever it was that it had been, that there was a statistically significant desire to resurrect vague "heritage type" values, and that categorically, and across all demographics, the Past was the path to victory.

Courtney was a low-level, but nevertheless well-connected, and ambitious operative in the "Owe the Future" campaign machine. She'd been tracking the Mustard Seed story since it broke, as had most people since various things kept appearing on Drudge or going viral on YouTube. She also recognized an opportunity to catapult herself into the inner circle of the current campaign and into the administration if they won, and into a lucrative consultancy if they lost.

The President had been down in the polls for the past few weeks—a messy slag of financial meltdowns and burst balloons due to the disruptive impact of the Oceanoids technology since DIY OSCNOIDS kits were already selling on the internets, and an assortment of scandals, investigations, and international gaffes were dragging him down; consequently, Courtney would arrange a Town Hall meeting, so that the President could meet face-to-face with the Past, the glorious, Kennedy-era Camelot past, and show the world and more importantly, key precincts in several swing states, that the Past wants and demands exactly what the President is selling.

It would be a rogue operation since she was going around several strata of overpriced, middle-aged frat-boy experts who would either kill the idea or steal it to present as their own. She was scheduled to be one of the Millennials on the President's tour bus trolling through carefully selected stretches of the parched and fallow central valley farmlands between Modesto and Bakersfield—irrigation water had been diverted to protect a small but politically well-connected fish of some kind, so what the farmers really needed was a high-speed train. Her team would be meeting Air Force One at Lemore NAS where she would hop on the bus, ostensibly to put some local spin to the campaign talking points for stops in Visalia, Delano, and Bakersfield. She'd casually mention the time capsule of Kennedy Democrats just a few miles off the itinerary and then, as if an afterthought, float the idea of a Town Hall meeting with the Past. He was a very smart man, everybody said so, and she was confident he'd connect the demographic and polling data dots. History would write itself from there, and she would own the future.

Courtney looked up from her excited huddle, and glanced back at the Generations and then out at the Town Square setting. "And it's already like beautifully lit and ready for the optics?" She was right; it was a beautiful and well-lit afternoon on Main Street USA.

Hertell was firmly against the idea, he said that it smelled "Cynical"—literally since he had the ability to smell such things, just like those sharks that can smell a blood drop on a Band-Aid from a hundred miles away; nevertheless, Virginia and the Generations that had recently returned from ThriftyMart were quite insistent that it was an excellent idea. Hertell was troubled, but he honored their wishes. There would be a town hall meeting with the President of the United States.

Some bleachers had been set up on Main Street, and Hertell sat in the top row of the bleachers with Virginia and watched as the cameras and lights were brought in and positioned—the lights were totally unnecessary as Main Street was already beautifully lit, but evidently unions were involved. A different crew was assembling a large, circular, old-glory-themed platform on the town square where the President would soon stand, seek insights, thoughtfully consider, rationally explain, articulately summarize, and reap bushels of praise and bales of reassurances from the Past that everything was great and going in the right direction.

Hertell was happy, and thought perhaps he'd been wrong about his misgivings since the smell might have just been the smell of volcanoes because he remembered that too, and though it didn't exactly match the smell of cynical, it more or less rhymed with it—the copper specks had once given him a heightened sense of smell, like a dog's, and he'd noticed that smells would often rhyme. Which he reasoned was why dogs hang their heads out car windows the way they do, smell-rhymes, poems, only with smells not words, and he knew dogs to be great poetry lovers. But the copper slivers were no longer a part of his life as they were just a few weeks before, as if the connections and contact he had with the Generations had allowed the copper specks to finally settle into the quieter folds of his brain.

In any case, the smell of volcanoes had faded away again and now he was with Virginia, and all was well with the world. The President would soon be on their side and they'd have no more bother about Casinos and golf courses and all -you-can-eat buffets.

Virginia was sitting silently beside Hertell but he could tell she was thinking something. "Find anything you liked at ThriftyMart?"

She thought for a moment. "Yes there were some custard cups that I really liked, and an apron, and ... it's only been 50 years, we've only been gone fifty years, what have people up there been thinking?" She was looking up at the beautifully lit dome of rock over their heads.

Hertell followed her eyes, and thought for a moment. He hadn't been born until many years after they'd gone below, and during his youth he was mainly dealing with his own issues, and didn't consider himself any kind of historian or social critic if there was such a thing, and then of course he'd been shot in the head. But for the most part, from what he knew of the last fifty years, and his memory of a fraction of it, was that it didn't seem to him that anybody was thinking much of anything at all, they were just kind of living, just like him. He thought of a story that Bobby from FarmFuel told him about how you could put a frog in a pot of water and slowly bring it to a boil, so slow that the frog wouldn't even notice that it was cooking. Maybe it was like that with them, only ThriftyMart made it so they noticed.

He was thinking of a more articulate way to phrase it, but before he could, Courtney and a large contingent of Secret Service arrived and informed them that they'd need to leave so that Main Street USA could be searched for weapons and signs and hecklers and so forth since the President had had a nasty surprise from some Code Pink and Hemp Liberation agitators in Portland, and Courtney was resolved to ensure that there would not be a repeat performance—her stock had already risen in the campaign as she now had a much larger staff in her wake, not even counting the Secret Service.

The search was routine and completed quickly and efficiently, and the Generations were brought in. It was a heartwarming and nostalgic vision of Camelot. The bleachers were filling with men, women, and children wearing their 1960's finest—Camel hair and tweed and worsted gabardine, the men and boys stouthearted and protective, the women and girls starched, nurturing and aglow, the children spirited but well-behaved—the very model of a modern mythical past and the perfect backdrop to validate the Administration's spongy and bruised policies.

It was everything Courtney and her team had hoped for. "Will you look at this? It's like Mad Men only nobody's drunk or smoking or fucking anybody else's wife? It's perfect? Look at that one! She's even wearing white gloves! And a pearl necklace!"

However, despite the optics, the Past would need to be pre-briefed on the format, topics, and protocols of interacting with the President of the United States. They would also need to be rearranged so that the minorities, as there were an ample number of mixed racial pedigree, could be prominently displayed in the front few rows. Courtney and several of her favored minions took up positions on the Old Glory platform and stood for a few contemplative minutes critically assessing the Generations in the bleachers as if considering a work of modern art.

"It seems kind of out of balance." A favored minion pulled his chin thoughtfully. "I agree. Off balance."

Courtney pointed at Miles. "Could we get the African-American gentleman in the third, no fourth, no fifth row to move up here to the front?"

The bleachers seemed confused, including Miles who was sitting in the fifth row, as they'd never heard the term before. Several lesser minion facilitators were ready at the bleachers to direct the props to their optimal placement on the set. One of them pointed at Miles and gestured him to come forward to his place of racial honor in the front row. "Yes, you sir, yes this way please..."

Miles rose hesitantly, unsure that he was being addressed. "Me?"

Which triggered a chorus of affirmatives from the minions. "Yes, you sir, come take a seat up here... right up here in front..."

"But I'm not... African... were you expecting Africans down here? We didn't bring any Africans down here with us..."

Miles continued to explain the original selection process as he was led to the front row. "We have Mexicans, and some Jews, and Orientals, and Negroes like myself so that we'd have a robust genetic mix to preserve the human race and western civilization..."

The set decorators continued to rearrange the bleachers as the art critics competed to see who had the most finely tuned perceptions, subtle insights and street smart sensitivities to configure the optimal racial tic-tac-toe that would subliminally communicate social, economic, and cultural justice from all camera angles.

"We need more color over here for camera three, it looks like a Mormon choir from this angle... Need some younger faces down front for camera one... Need some X-chromosomes at top dead center from here..."

Ultimately, they all ended up essentially where they started so it was pretty much a Chinese fire drill—though Courtney couldn't say that out loud, besides time was running out and the President would soon be arriving. She stood in the center of the Old Glory platform and addressed the freshly arranged Generations.

"Ok, the President will be here soon? So we won't be able to rehearse with dummy questions? But you're all Kennedy Democrats? So that's okay?"

The Generations nodded in general agreement. "Yes... yes we are... never voted for a Republican in my life..."

It was music to Courtney's ears. "Cool, so we're just gonna..." She stopped and pointed at Hertell who was sitting with Virginia. "You're not one of'm are you? You're just the guy that found'm? But you di'nt come from down here?"

"Yes, I found them. I'm from up there not down here."

Courtney pointed off stage. "So could you like, go over there? Or something? This is just for the Democrats from down here?"

Virginia took his arm. "No, he's one of us, he can stay." Miles and some others agreed that he should stay with them in the bleachers.

"No, it's okay. The President wants to talk to you guys, not me. You're the special ones here." He stood and threaded his way out of the bleachers. "I'll be over here, I'll be watching, don't worry, you don't need me for this. This is a great honor for you. All of you."

Normally a Town Hall meeting had a well-defined process and protocol with multiple steps, reviews, risk assessments, and sign-offs to select, screen, and fluff the audience to serve up floaters for the President to knock out of the park; however, because of the unique nature of the Mustard Seed audience and the serendipity of the opportunity, and the flaccid poll numbers, it was deemed low risk and the process streamlined.

The President had been honing his key-worded answers to a set of theme-based, standardized Town Hall questions: the campaign was spending over a million dollars a week on the formulation and refinement of these policy-specific questions and their associated optimized answers—most of the expense was for the MRI's used to measure and map the neural activity of focus group participants in response to each question and answer set; they even found a few tumors.

So all Courtney and her team needed to do was to distribute the questions to the appropriate audience member—the questions were already bundled by age, gender, and race so that abortion questions would be asked by a woman, tax and national defense questions by a man, and health care by a bent and grizzled old person.

"Ok, so, you've all got your questions? So just look over your questions? And you can go back and forth and say'm out loud to each other and practice'm if you want, so that you don't, like, stumble over words and things? So... yeah, so do that?"

Courtney checked her phone and then continued. "And when the President gets here, he'll point at one of you, and call on you for like, a question? And you just ask one of the questions that we just gave to you? The ones you're holding right now? And then he'll answer you? And then you'll just keep going like that? Until you're out of questions? And it'll be great?"

Chapter Thirty-Nine

Town Hall

"First question..." The President stood in the center of Old Glory in khaki pants and a powder blue oxford shirt open at the collar and with his sleeves rolled up. He was ready to go to work. "You sir, in the third, no fourth row." He pointed at Miles.

Miles stood and stiffly read from the card he'd been given. "I am very concerned about the economy. We seem to be living beyond our means and leaving a massive burden of debt to our children and our children's children. Why can't the country balance the budget the way any family or household would, and what steps will you take to return us to our heritage values of self-reliance, individual responsibility, and a balanced budget?"

The President thoughtfully considered the heartfelt concern. "Good question." and then went on for what seemed like an hour retracing the origins of the failing economy to previous administrations, political opponents, disruptive technologies, climate change, Astroturf, undeclared wars, demographics, millionaires, billionaires, minimum wage, high-fructose corn syrup and a plethora of lesser vexations to be overcome only by principled compromise and good will to achieve universal economic justice; and then wrapped it up with a series of MRI-certified keywords and phrases guaranteed to stimulate the appropriate cerebral fold, resonate with undecided voters and simultaneously provide useful sound-bites.

The microphones picked it up first. The President was still busy talking so he didn't hear it, but everybody in the booth and in the satellite vans and broadcast centers and on the streaming internets heard it. So did Courtney, it sounded kind of like chuckling, and it seemed to be coming from the bleachers where all of the artfully arranged props were smiling in amusement; only some were shaking their heads in disbelief and others were openly snickering.

During a brief pause while the President was taking a breath in the middle of a rhetorical question, someone in the bleachers summarized the situation.

"There must be a Unicorn in there somewhere..."

The bleachers erupted in derisive laughter—there was also scattered but suppressed laughter in some of the satellite vans and broadcast centers.

Political discourse beneath the Li'l Pal had taken a different evolutionary path in the intervening years, and bore a greater resemblance to the UK Parliament replete with catcalls and mockery than to the ritualized Patty Cake of modern American politics.

From somewhere in the back row, "Ya know, I understood the individual words... But I have no idea what they meant all together as a complete thought."

More mocking laughter. "Flapdoodle!" Affirmations and shouts from the bleachers. "Poppycock!".... "The dog ate my economy!"

The President was confused, but didn't show it as he smiled and laughed as if he was in on the joke. Only he wasn't, and was looking in the direction of Courtney and her minions. It was the same smile he'd had in Portland.

Over the years, the Generations had achieved a certain level of economy and directness in matters political and were quick to detect and mercilessly denounce horseshit— which is where the Unicorn line came from: one of the original Mustard Seed Imagineers, long since gone West, had once worked with Reagan and had heard the joke on the set about an optimist and a room full of manure, only Mustard Seed gradually changed the punch line from a 'pony', something real but nevertheless unlikely to be found in a pile of dung, to a 'Unicorn' an imaginary creature unlikely to be found anywhere in a pile of anything of whatever composition. Same with the dog excuse since there were no dogs in Mustard Seed either.

The directness was due to the fact that almost all of the Founders and many of the Future had served at one time or another in congress or as President or on the Supreme Court in the bonsai US Government they had preserved beneath the Li'l Pal, and saw no distinction between person and politician. Aunt Tawney had been President up to the time of her death; Miles served two terms as President while Reagan was performing a similar service above, and then returned to useful work as a metal and woodshop teacher since there was no concept of retirement in Mustard Seed.

317

Congress was treated like jury duty, and the Supreme Court would meet once a year at the miniature golf course if there were any constitutional questions to be considered, though there never were since the entire population had memorized the constitution and no special priesthood was needed to explain to them what was written in plain English for any normal person to read and understand.

Courtney also didn't know, that, because of her severe up -speak, all of her specific directions had been interpreted by the bleachers as questions; consequently, they were under the misimpression that, after the President had called on the first person, that they were free to ask their own questions. Which they proceeded to do relentlessly, fueled and fanned by the sullen magma that had followed them back from ThriftyMart and was now spilling out.

"What is economic justice? Who's the plaintiff? Who's the defendant? What's the charge? What are you people talking about?"

Courtney was desperately flailing at the edges of the bleachers, just out of frame, trying to control the volcano sotto voce. "Next person? Next person? No! The questions on the cards? The questions on the cards? Understand?"

Exasperated, Miles turned to Courtney in an exchange caught in frame and on mic to the amusement of a few in the van and many more on the streaming feeds. "Yes, we understand the questions, but they're stupid questions and are not worth asking!"

The President was now a deer in the headlights in full vamp trying to squeeze in the MRI-sanctified words wherever he could in the onslaught of non-sanctified questions. "There are some who would let big business run roughshod over fairness and the little guy, I choose another way...to protect the middle class and working families."

And was greeted with foot stomping from the bleachers and an overlapping chorus of derision. "Are you even listening to yourself?" ... "That is complete and utter sophistry".... "Laughable jibberish".... "You ignore human nature, you're naïve, you're a child."

That was the tipping point, the President was rubbing his nose with his middle finger when Courtney stepped in front of the bleachers and motioned for the cameras to shut down.

"Mister President, Mister President, I'm sorry Mister President, I had no idea that the past was this impolite and discourteous... they are just not... civilized anymore 'cause they've been living underground for so long, they've become, like a cult of some kind, obviously some kind of religious cult."

She was immediately shouted down by the bleachers who were now largely on their feet.

Hertell had been keeping a wary eye on the Secret Service agents who seemed to be content to observe for now at least; nevertheless, he felt it prudent to join Courtney and try to calm the bleachers down.

"Okay we don't wanna talk to the President that way, 'cause he's the President and stuff."

"So what? I've been President! Twice!" followed by a chorus of "So have I!", and "and so have I!" "It gives you no right to be a casuist and sophist and not get called on it."

The campaign communications director was horrified, and inwardly gleeful to see that upstart bitch Courtney crater like this, and had switched the cable feeds to an edgy campaign infomercial the second he saw the President do the middle finger thing. The cut off and transition went off so seamlessly that he was confident most folks watching didn't even notice the change.

Felicity Spector had been preparing for her Action News At 7 broadcast, but it had been preempted by the unscheduled and impromptu Presidential Town Hall meeting. She had planned to sneak out early to see her daughter at the karate dojo, but stopped to watch the Town Hall once she saw that it was coming from Mustard Seed.

She'd done many features on the Founders and the Future in the weeks since their emergence and was quite captivated by them. She recognized everyone at the Town Hall, Miles, Virginia, Gordon, all the J-names, but was surprised when it abruptly changed from the embarrassing spectacle of the President of the United States being stumped by simple questions from an informed and demanding audience, to an inspirational film with great production values and a good beat. KERO was providing the main satellite uplink, so she checked with the Chief Engineer to see if they still had the raw feed, but it turned out it had been cut off by the remote. All they had was the inspirational video.

The town hall continued to deteriorate, but the communications director finally caught the President's eye and gave him a big double thumbs-up and shouted out "we're clear!" And congratulated himself; his quick thinking and decisive decision-making had saved the day. He was guaranteed a sinecure in the second term. The damage was minimal and would be quickly forgotten. They were safe. It would be as if it had never happened.

The President left the Gymnasium without acknowledging the Generations who were stunned at his sudden departure with a ripple of "Well fuck me dead" utterances from many.

The President didn't hear any of that as he made his way back through the halls and passageways and tunnels with his entourage past the quiet Cathedral and through the Miniature Golf Course, the gleaming gymnasium, and the Iowa cornfield, all the while issuing the most scatological and school-boyishly obscene rebuke of Courtney, his staff, the past, the present, the future, the media, the process, the electorate and a constellation of less significant life forms, swing states, key precincts, and demographics that he was resigned to courting.

However, what he didn't know was that even though they were clear of all the official cameras and microphones, they were not clear of the streaming video feeds that Hertell had set up when he brought in the internet cables for Doug's pre -PTSD therapy some weeks before.

"President Potty Mouth" was the headline on Drudge a few minutes later.

Chapter Forty

Own The Future

They pissed off the wrong people. But worse than that, they failed the attitude test.

It wasn't so much that they'd disproved the Great Man Theory by revealing the President to be... a normal person. It was more that they'd revealed themselves to be unimpressed and indifferent to the kingdom and the power and the glory of the Sovereign state. They'd lived for the past 50 years in complete isolation, and had absolutely no need for it, and specifically no dependency on it. It was simply not part of their lives. They appeared to be totally outside its control and the control of basically everybody; everybody but themselves anyway. And that could not be tolerated.

It started out as spin control for the "President Potty Mouth" incident. The press secretary stood at the podium and grimly told the sad story:

> The President went, in good faith and with high expectations, to visit a well-known and, at the time, an inspiring community from the past, a community basically that time forgot, only to

discover that what it was actually, was that it was essentially a religious cult, and possibly a violent fanatical religious cult clinging to the failed ideas and prejudices and bigotries of the past. It was an uncomfortable and possibly dangerous situation, so the President prudently but regretfully decided to end it.

Nicely done, but some of the more uppity and contentious reporters persisted.

"How does the President justify using the S-word, the B-S-word, F-word, the C-word, the M-F-word, the C-S-word, the G-D-word, the S of a B word, C-S-M-F-word, the F-P-C-S-M-F-word? And what message do you think that sends to the American people."

The press secretary considered the question and effected a concerned look on his face:

Well, the President deeply regrets using the C-word since it was clearly an insensitive and offensive word, and in fact, is completely at odds with his position on women's rights, and women's equality, and women's issues in general, and was totally uncalled for, and out of character for the president.

The President also regrets that some of the other language he used—in other words the language that was not the C-word—that he may have used language that some might find offensive, but his use of this possibly offensive language and unacceptable words merely reflected the level of frustration and deep, deep disappointment the President felt upon seeing and hearing what the past had to offer to the future. And he believes that even though it may be familiar and reassuring, that it's time to stop looking to the past for answers, but that it is instead time to start looking forward for new ideas for the American people and the people of the world. Because we owe that to the future.

A hastily assembled focus group and some MRI's had confirmed the wording shortly before the press conference. There were follow-up questions, but they were all deftly answered with variants of the responses that the campaign and the focus groups and the MRI's had feverishly crafted—listen to the question, rephrase it to address your narrative, then use the same basic answer again so you seem really consistent.

Courtney had merely stumbled upon calling Mustard Seed a fanatic religious cult while in a state of blind panic during the Main Street USA train wreck, but she immediately recognized the opportunity it presented and pursued the thread with the President on the way out as he was peppering her with frothing C-word denunciations; however, the things she said managed to penetrate the blistering torrent of abuse.

Though the microphones didn't pick any of it up since her decibel level was far below the President's, she urgently and passionately pressed her case.

"Mister President, this was a big fuck up. I admit it, and it's totally all my fault, but we can turn this on them? We can make this work for us? This is a fantastic opportunity?"

The usual protective ring of doughy, balding frat boy experts held back, and gave her plenty of room to crash and burn. They were enjoying the spectacle of watching the line-jumping little bitch go down in flames again, and again, as they made their way back to the surface and the motorcade—it was like one of those UFC best-of shows where you get to watch a brain-softening knock-out and then get to watch it all over again in slo-mo so you can see the shock wave slowly ripple over and deform the rubbery face of the recipient. They kept quiet, exchanged knowing looks and suppressed grins; one of them even had his iPhone out to capture the moment for later enjoyment. They were waiting for just the right moment to descend, shred, and devour the artless little coed.

"Mister President, if we play this right we can deflate the whole heritage-type value shtick that the Fucknose campaign is riding on, and turn the entire narrative into your favor?" Fucknose was the campaign sobriquet for the opposing candidate who actually did have a nose that looked surprisingly like a penis.

"We can wipe out the past as an issue? You wouldn't be behind the power curve anymore, playing catch-up, the other prick would. We don't have to do a whole, me-too on the past; we don't have to co-opt the past. We can just discredit the past?"

They had reached the surface and were approaching the President's SUV. Without breaking stride, the President glanced over his shoulder at his gaggle of advisers and a despondent Courtney now trailing slightly behind.

"Why didn't any of you worthless shit spinners think of this? It takes a newbie fresh out of school to think outside the box like this?" The President had once been a high school football coach and had a variety of such salty arrows in his quiver.

The worthless shit spinners stood in stunned silence for a moment, struggling to make sense of the situation as the President got into his SUV.

"No wonder I'm down in the polls." He motioned Courtney forward. "She's playing chess. You're playing with yourselves." The frat-boys silently parted and Courtney took a seat in the SUV with the President.

She would work the weekend with her team and the focus groups and the MRIs to craft the themes and talking points that the press secretary would eventually speak. She was in the first circle now; she was a player and she would now systematically, with all the levers of the kingdom and the power and the glory at her disposal, dismantle the past. It was merely a curious relic with nothing of value to offer, an obstacle standing in the way of her bright future. She would own the future now no matter what. And she would start with the Li'l Pal and the renegade past buried beneath its folds.

Chapter Forty-One

A Slight Nod

It started immediately, on all fronts and at all levels: nothing explicit, there was no specific direction given, just a general sense and acknowledgement that permission had been granted, and that an example should be made. There were no conference calls or war rooms, no encrypted emails to department managers and directors, but everyone knew what was expected of them, and each and all would pursue, plan and perform in their own way.

It seems that the good people of Mustard Seed had no license from any government agency at any level, for anything. They were operating completely outside the law: their doctors and dentists were practicing without a license, as was the barber and beauty shop; the schools were unaccredited, teachers non-union, the banks and businesses without regulation; their toilets and light bulbs were noncompliant, their ladders and step-stools without warning labels, it was a cornucopia of irresponsible and dangerous, bordering on anarchistic, behavior.

The day began with press conferences since the election was fast approaching and time was of the essence. The important thing was to get the grave concerns, serious accusations, and pending corrective actions out there and into the news cycle—the official charges, summons, and subpoenas would require weeks of Grand Jury shopping and billable legal hours and could wait until after the election—and they were all determined to outdo one another. The Department of Energy spokesman pointed to a PowerPoint presentation cycling through images of OSCNOIDS and the Choir:

> It has come to our attention that an unlicensed, unregulated, unauthorized and clearly dangerous nuclear reactor is being operated in the compound of the Mustard Seed religious... group, and we believe this represents a clear and present danger to both the innocent women and children living underground in the religious compound, basically an underground fortress, and also a serious threat to the larger community and population centers in central California and possibly the world, and the Secretary has demanded an immediate shut down and dismantling of the reactor pending a full and thorough investigation...

The Department of the Treasury spokeswoman read from a prepared statement and intoned:

It has come to our attention that the entity known as Mustard Seed, while having the outward appearance of a religious institution or sect, is not formally listed or identified as such, nor does it qualify, nor has it officially applied for 501-C-3 status; furthermore, it has failed to file either corporate or personal income tax returns from 1963 to the present; as a consequence, the Director has directed a team of investigators to investigate these allegations and make a determination regarding criminal charges, and further to stress that no one and no religious entity however unusual their origins or circumstances is above the law...

The State Department spokesperson used a partially completed portion of the Border Fence as a backdrop:

They are not economic refugees. They are not political refugees. They are refugees from the future—us, our present. They rejected our world, and now they want to take advantage of it. But just because they chose to live in the past, they are not above our laws and basic fairness. And the Secretary wants to be very clear on this, they are not undocumented workers, because they don't work— they come out on tour buses to look at us, as if we're animals in the zoo. The Secretary also believes that their mere existence here, on the surface, is insufficient, that they have no legal standing until recognized by the state, and that they are, in fact, illegal aliens in the truest sense. The Secretary also believes that they are potentially dangerous illegal aliens based on their toxic fundamentalist and extremist ideology, where men are men, and women are women—end of discussion. And the secretary has launched an investigation to investigate precedents and explore options for deportation...

In a joint statement by the Department of Defense and Justice, a chorus of spokespersons harmonized about theft and misuse of government property, since it was a government funded program after all, and disclosure of classified information, since it was classified up to the point of its discovery even though everyone had forgotten about it; consequently, the Inspector General was launching an investigation of criminal wrongdoing.

The dog pile went on all day and into the next with almost every leaf and branch of Government weighing in: Department of Agriculture, Cal-OSHA, EPA, EEOC, Fish and Wildlife, Geological Survey, and National Endowment for the Arts. The past would cease to be an issue within 24 hours of the President Potty Mouth incident, and the next few days of polling would merely confirm that Courtney's 'dis-the-past' strategy had successfully pounded a stake through the heart of the past.

It was a good strategy, and Courtney and her posse were confident they could steer the polls in their direction by discrediting the Past as represented by Mustard Seed. They knew what the polls had been saying, that there was a measurable, traceable and quantifiable desire to return to something, even though nobody was sure to what exactly; that there was a rejection of the current and palpable sense of aimless drift; and that there was an almost instinctive homing toward the hazy North Star of "heritage-type" values. But what they didn't know and couldn't explain was why there was a yearning for "heritage-type values".

It turned out that the Casino Indian media consultant who pitched the Reality TV concept to Hertell a few days earlier was actually on to something, something beyond just monetizing a phenomenon that was already present and growing on the internets. The yearning to return to heritage type values wasn't a manifestation of a deeper desire, it was a deeper desire unearthed and validated by their exposure to a stealthy tectonic of crowdsourced Mustard Seed reality TV shows that were proliferating across the internets.

What the campaign and its social media consultants and focus groups and MRI's didn't know was that those same streaming video feeds that had made the President Potty Mouth incident possible had, since almost immediately after the discovery of Mustard Seed, been feeding directly into Doug's LapsedGeologist.com website where they were tapped by thousands of RSS clients and via them to thousands more RSS clients and via them to thousands of crowdsourcing projects that lovingly whittled endless hours of Mustard Seed footage into webisodes that seemed to be scratching a full spectrum of philosophical and emotional itches.

Mustard Seed seemed to have something for everybody: Utopians and other progressives, socialists, and liberals loved the collectivist aspects of the managed community that had lived harmoniously and peacefully under their feet all these years; Dystopians and survivalist fellow-travelers, Ayn Randian objectivists, anti-globalization anarchists, and End-time Apocalyptics took comfort in the fact that with adequate planning and preparation they really could reject, retreat, shrug and safely abandon the world and the Leviathan state and hide happily beneath it until it consumed itself; conspiracy theorists, secret society and suppressed invention adherents now had an existence proof that their suspicions were correct and that there were probably many more secret Government projects like weather and mind control, and UFOs still to be unearthed; less-is-more environmentalists, back-to-nature climate change disciples, and Malthusian eugenicists heralded the obvious ability to live with limited resources and control population; right-wing conservatives and assorted leave-me-the-fuck-alone libertarians loved the self-reliance and rugged individualist aspects of the story; the faith community loved the centrality of religion and sacred song in Mustard Seed's success; the atheist and rationalist movement noted the centrality of logic, rational thinking, and Broadway Show tunes to its success.

And just like the Bakersfield Speedway National Anthem and the Double Dutch Jump Roping, many of the crowdsourced Mustard Seed webisodes had gone viral: vectored and re-vectored through personal connections and millions of email inboxes like knock-knock jokes and funny dog photographs. They were shown and discussed in PTA meetings, Bible Studies, town councils, food co-ops, and organizations of every hue and stripe.

Evidently, the past, as represented by Mustard Seed, was a major contributor to the nascent desire for a return to the heritage-type values. Values that the polls had clearly identified as crucial, in fact were directly responsible for the President's low poll numbers. The past clearly had a very large, diverse, and devoted following that didn't seem to know, or much less care about the accusations and suspicions and denunciations that were now swirling into the gaping 24-7 news maw. They had been watching and absorbing the past for weeks now and had their own sense of its value and didn't need their betters telling them not to believe their own lying eyes.

Quite the opposite in fact due to various scandals, and decades of dire warnings of apocalyptic destruction that never came to pass: the credibility of the Government, and all of its auxiliary institutions in the fourth estate, faculty lounge, and bar association, had sunk to a cold and damp nadir—to an almost soviet level of cynicism such that the assumption was that whatever the Government was saying and whatever the press was repeating, the truth was bound to be the exact opposite. For example, the Department of Energy had resolutely dismissed OSCNOIDS as a complete and utter hoax even though hundreds of thousands of DIY OCENOIDS reactors were safely and quietly pumping out electricity for houses, farms, and businesses all over the country and around the world and almost everyone knew someone who had or was building one.

Mustard Seed's grievous transgressions were trumpeted from the highest parapets of broadcast, print, and cable news for the first day, and followed by more of the same plus mockery and ridicule on snarky political comedy shows on the second day; however, the polls, at the 48 hour mark, hadn't moved at all, as if trying to decide. Courtney and her posse were confident that things would break their way on the third day, but when the 3-day rolling average polls came out, the 'own the future' campaign was even more underwater than it had been before the 'Dis-the-past' product rollout. It simply didn't matter what was said about Mustard Seed and the past, because of who was saying it.

Courtney was disappointed that the masses were either too stupid or too evil to understand the good she was trying to do them, to free them from the past and a potential President Fucknose. Fortunately, she had anticipated this since she was as cynical as the lumpen proletariat, but she'd gone to Harvard so it was different. She had in her hands all of the executive branch levers she needed to initiate stage 2 of the dis-the-past campaign. There was nothing explicit or traceable, there was no master plan nor any coordination required since the enforcement arms of the various Government agencies knew what was expected of them. All they needed was a slight nod from the right source and they would spring into action. In a matter of hours, it wouldn't matter what the polls said one way or the other because the past would be history and no longer a factor in anything.

Chapter Forty-Two

Et tu Obi

H ertell and a repair crew were laying new sod on the great warm slab—the Town Hall tectonic plate of SUVs, Semi's, busses, and lesser talus of support equipment, trucks, and satellite dishes had scraped and ground over the torn and tattered remains of the great lawn, and had effectively finished what the hosed van had started.

Hertell and his crew stopped at the approach of Orbin's Christ Victory bus, which was accompanied by two Sheriff cruisers and several white SUV's that considerately pulled to a stop just short of the lawn. Hertell asked the cleanup crew to go back inside and bring out some cookies and lemonade for their visitors. It had been a hot day laying sod, and they gratefully took the assignment. He watched as they disappeared chattering and laughing into the darkness of the pressure buffer. He then approached the formation at the far end of the great warm slab.

No one had gotten out of the white SUV's, but he could see that the deputies had gotten out of their cruisers and were leaning against them. Hertell recognized the deputies as he got closer, they were two of the first people he'd taken down into Mustard Seed. He waved to them as he approached.

They waved back and smiled, but they were troubled smiles.

Orbin had stepped out of the Christ Victory bus; he was in his Sheriff's uniform and was walking toward Hertell. It was apparent that something was wrong. He met Hertell in the middle of the great warm slab and some distance from the deputies and the white SUV's.

"Look, tell those guys that I'm sorry and everything, even though they were trespassing and stuff and totally trashed the lawn out here…"

Obie held up his hand. "That doesn't matter Hertell. They're bringing child abuse, child endangerment, and incest charges against most of the adults down there."

"For squirting some guys with a garden hose? I don't see the…"

"No, Hertell, this's nothing to do with that, this's a whole 'nother thing." Orbin had grown quite fond of Hertell. He put his hand on Hertell's shoulder. "They want to take most of the Founders and a bunch of the Generations into custody for questioning and possibly charging, and they want to take all the kids under twelve and put'm into foster care, at least for the next few weeks, maybe a month or so, until we can get this sorted out."

Hertell stood quietly, and then softly asked, "Is that what the bus is for?"

Orbin was silent for a long while, he was looking past Hertell toward the dark opening to the pressure buffer at the foot of the yawning remnant of Whisper Hill. He finally answered, "Yes."

"And they sent you to come get them?"

"Yes. And I had to call in every favor I had in the favor bank to be the one they sent. I convinced'm to let me come and do this, so there wouldn't be any... complications."

Hertell considered the news. "Complications."

"They want you too Hertell, I forget for exactly what but... they just want you outta here, that's all they want, they just want... what they want, that's all."

Hertell looked back toward Mustard Seed. "But we haven't done anything."

"I know. Nobody's saying you have, nobody's saying you haven't, they just want to prove to themselves that there's nothing going on. I guess. That's how they start these things."

"We haven't done anything, can't they just leave us alone?"

Orbin glanced back toward the SUVs. "They know you're here man. They know you exist. They can't leave you alone once they know you're here. It's a system. It can't leave anything alone."

Hertell faced Orbin and put his hand on his shoulder. "Well... Orbin, then you're gonna have to take your gun out and shoot me 'cause they... they can't have'm." He looked past Orbin toward the white SUVs and then directly into Orbin's eyes. "Fuck'm they can't have'm."

Orbin, took a deep breath, looked down and nodded his head slowly as if thinking. He rubbed his thighs and then looked at Hertell. "That's what I was hoping you'd say."

Ruben and Roy had been leaning against their cruisers and watching the exchange between Orbin and Hertell. They were out of earshot and couldn't hear anything, but they could tell by the body language that some kind of agreement had been reached which was confirmed when they saw Orbin reach furtively behind his back and give them a thumbs up. They exchanged looks and got back in their cruisers, started them up and began inching up to the SUVs as Hertell and Orbin were heading toward the big Christ Victory bus.

More cruisers began to arrive behind several large prisoner transport buses that were rumbling into view. A news helicopter was now orbiting overhead.

Hertell got in the driver seat and started the Christ Victory bus. Orbin was standing in the open doorway as Hertell fastened his seatbelt. "Well, I guess this is it then. We're depending on you." Orbin stepped off the bus. "It'll just take a while to sort things out up here. It'll just take time."

Hertell slammed it into gear. "Yeah. It's only been fifty years. What's a few more?"

"Huh?" Orbin stood looking at Hertell through the open bus door.

Hertell didn't answer and instead slammed the door and floored it. The bus roared off, tearing up the freshly laid sod as it gained speed and then heeling to the left and thundering past Ruben and Roy who were startled by the sudden change in direction.

The news copter got the whole thing; it was the shortest police chase in history, no more than a couple of hundred yards. The bus made a big circle on the great warm slab, around the white SUVs to gain speed with Ruben and

Roy giving chase in their cruisers with sirens and lights ablaze—reminiscent of wild Indians circling a wagon train. And then after one circuit the bus went directly toward the darkened opening at far end of the big slab at the foot of the excavated hillside.

In a shower of sparks and a deafening skirl of scraping metal, the bus slammed into the opening, all but disappearing as it wedged itself into and filling the entire opening like an immovable massive stopper. The only part still visible was the bus's crimped and puckered hindquarters, which read, "Christ Victory Church".

Chapter Forty-Three

Friendly Fire

They all looked up in wonder. Roy and Ruben and Orbin stood beside their cruisers and watched as helicopters filled the air: they were converging on Li'l Pal from every point of the compass rose. It was kind of a cross between the big helicopter scene in Apocalypse Now and a Keystone Cops silent movie only without the Wagner or even the tinny piano. Evidently, a number of federal, state and local agencies had decided that today was the best day ever for a SWAT team adventure. The helicopters overhead were beautifully accessorized with assault rifles and black boots.

And since they were all from separate and independent fiefdoms and realms of the kingdom with their own funding lines and separate approval chains, none of them knew that so many other agencies, administrations, services, commissions, and departments had the exact same idea and were pursuing essentially identical courses of action. They also operated on different radio frequencies with different encryption keys so they couldn't communicate with each other over their P-25's and were reduced to shouting at each other over their loudspeakers as they jockeyed and maneuvered for position while demanding that all the other helicopters yield and submit.

"This is the EPA, you are interfering with an official Federal enforcement action...

"Department of Fish and Game orders you to clear the area..."

"You are interfering with a Bureau of Land Management tactical operation and you will be fired upon if you do not immediately exit the area..."

"The Federal Communications Commission commands you..."

But none of them seemed willing to show deference to any of the others.

All of the helicopters were aglow with red laser dots from all the assault rifles they were training on one another. Two helicopters were engaged in a game of low altitude chicken trying to be the first to land on the great warm slab when a third helicopter joined the game, which is traditionally best limited to 2 participants. All of this was happening within two feet of the ground and quite disorienting to all involved: the rotor down wash was whipping up dirt and divots of sod, the barking loud speakers, and the aggressive feints and dodges of the helicopters as they jockeyed for position.

In all the excitement, one of the assault rifles accidentally discharged, and given the circumstances, the natural supposition was that they were being fired upon by the hindquarters of the Christ Victory bus.

"We're taking hostile fire from the compound!"

"We are taking fire from the vehicle!"

The helicopters immediately began returning fire to cover their retreat, spraying bullets into the Christ Victory bus, and on occasion each other, and in the resultant evasive actions the DOE chopper's tail rotor was clipped which started a chain reaction of yawing, pitching helicopters, showers of shattered Plexiglas and shards of splintered rotor blades as the three flying machines awkwardly and fleetingly embraced one another and then plummeted the remaining 18 inches to the ground in tangled heaps as the stubborn rotor blades dashed themselves to pieces and the SWAT teams scrambled out of their up-ended copters.

More helmets and boots converged on the scene since the other helicopters had immediately withdrawn to a safe distance when the shooting started and landed to discharge their troops wherever they could find room on the contested and congested hillsides. The newly arrived SWAT teams joined their bruised and shaken helicopter-borne brethren and rained fire down upon the poor, immobilized Christ Victory stopper in the hillside, and the bus was riddled and scourged with the ferocity that only employees of the Sovereign state can mete out when challenged.

The scene on the ground was even more confused as Humvees, APCs, MRAPs, Bradley's, Strykers clogged the roads and lanes of the Li'l Pal, and many simply went off road, churning over countless graves, crushing headstones and tennis balls on the way to all the action at the hollowed-out base of Whisper Hill, so as not to miss all the fun.

The FAA had declared a TFR over the Li'l Pal, as they'd done when the President was there just a few days before and advised all air traffic to keep clear, but the news copters were ignoring it since all the helicopters were on the ground now and they had the air to themselves.

Ruben and Roy had abandoned their cruisers when the helicopters began their game of chicken and had moved to safety in a gully down from Whisper Hill.

Several of the larger off-roaders reached the great warm slab and immediately opened fire on the exposed rear end of the bus with 20mm cannon, 50 cal machine guns, and a variety of tear gas munitions. Orbin tried to intervene, shouting that the bus was empty and that there was nobody there. But he couldn't be heard above the din of justice.

The hindquarters of the bus were unrecognizable now having been shredded by the continuous raking fire. The "Christ Victory" lettering was fairly obliterated except for some widely separated chips of white paint, though you could still tell the bus had once been painted a bright blue at some point in its life. But it now resembled nothing more than an anguished and distorted mask embedded in the hillside, with the eyes shot out and the mouth a ragged misshapen gash as if silently screaming.

It wasn't like in the movies where there's always a big explosion at the end with people flying through the air. Instead there was just a gradual and gentle dwindling of gunfire, and the silent and smoldering wreckage. It grew quiet, and strangely melancholy, there was nothing noble or even conclusive about it. It was just kind of sad, and kind of squalid and strangely out of proportion to all the theatrics. There were some small fires flickering from deep within the bus cave as some of the upholstery had finally ignited from all the sparking bullets and tear gas canisters. A weak plume

of smoke snaked up into the sky and eventually braided itself
with the smoke strands from the three helicopters.

Chapter Forty-Four

Jaws of Victory

"We need to... secure the PB... seal the manifold... seal it all off!"

Hertell had made it out of the bus and through the pressure buffer and manifold, across the cornfield, and into the gymnasium where he met the T-Boys returning with a platter of cookies and a tray of frosty lemonades for the visitors. They stopped mid stride, shocked at Hertell's appearance as he approached them at an uneven trot.

The T-boys hesitated. "What?... Why?"

Breathing heavily, he took a lemonade and drained it. "It doesn't matter.... just seal it off." He noted that the glass was bloody and looked down at his arms and hands.

"What do they want?"

The boys all took a step back in response to the abrupt change in Hertell's aspect and demeanor; it was as if he was visibly swelling, and then exploded, "Seal it! Now!"

The cookies and lemonades hit the floor as the T-boys sprinted up toward the pressure buffer and the manifolds.

The great bell was ringing and the Generations were gathering on the square.

349

Hertell was sitting on the edge of the Old Glory platform left over from the Town Hall meeting. He was bloody and torn from the short bus ride and his adrenaline-fueled scramble out its shattered front windshield.

He was being cleaned up and bandaged by Kaye who had been at choir practice when the bell began ringing. Most of the Founders were gathered around him.

"They're coming to take all the kids away. They're coming to take the Future and throw the rest of you in jail."

"Why?"

Hertell started to answer but fell silent to a dull rumbling that overtook the conversation. They could feel the thudding tremors through the soles of their feet.

Hertell took a deep ragged breath and let his tension fade away, and waited for the silence to return. "It doesn't really matter why. They've got lawyers, they've got judges, they've got politicians, they've got the people on the news, they've got everything. They don't need a reason, they can make up a reason."

"But why would they do that?"

Yet another of those questions that had for so long left Hertell without an answer,

"I don't know. I guess because they can."

There was shouting in the distance. It was getting closer. The T-Boys came running in, unrecognizable, covered in dust. "We sealed off the manifold... they were shooting... they were trying to blow us up!"

The original logistics planners had considered a number of scenarios, including discovery and breaching of entryways and sieges by starving survivors and mutant hordes, so all entry points, pressure buffer manifolds and major passageways in Mustard Seed were rigged to collapse if needed. And while most of the perimeter defense controls were in the main cathedral near the organ console, each choke point also had manual overrides for just such occasions as they were experiencing that very day.

The T-Boys were calmed, and the Generations gathered around the Old Glory platform and listened as Hertell repeated what Orbin had told him shortly before. Hertell had expected them to resist and put up a fight and insist that they be allowed to prove their innocence or whatever, that they be allowed to live on the surface in peace with the sun and the sky and the stars and the wind. But they didn't.

Miles nodded his head thoughtfully. "Well I guess we just came out too soon. If we're not welcome, then fine. Nevertheless, it's nice to know we're not alone." There seemed to be general agreement, especially from those who'd been to ThriftyMart. "We'll just wait a while, and come out at a better time."

Voices called out from the malt shop, "Hey! We're on TV again."

Indeed they were. And what wasn't being broadcast from the news copters orbiting Whisper Hill, was going directly to the internets from streaming video coming out of Mustard Seed—the whole garden hose incident had already been edited and posted on YouTube, looped, speeded up with the Benny Hill theme song over it, and had accumulated enough hits that there were ads on it.

The dish antenna Hertell had set up weeks before for bringing the surface into Mustard Seed had managed to survive the plague of helicopters and tires and treads and boots that had descended upon Whisper Hill, and the cables from it down into the pressure buffer were nestled in conduit piping on the ceiling of the portal. While the bus had crushed the conduit, the CAT5 cable remained intact. So, in addition to the news copter footage, the whole bus crash and lopsided gun battle was captured on the pressure buffer web cams and was already being uploaded by the Crowd-sourcing sites.

"Law Enforcement appears to be removing a barricade from the mouth of the tunnel."

Felicity Spector was in the Action News Copter, doing the play-by-play. She considered herself a professional, and she went where the story led, but she was troubled by what she was seeing. She'd spent many hours down in Mustard Seed interviewing people for various news features over the weeks since the discovery, and the notion of them attacking the police seemed totally out of character for the people she knew, much less the even more unbelievable allegations of child abuse, incest, and being an extremist religious cult that were now all over the news.

"And there's a large military tank of some kind approaching the barricade."

The SWAT teams had eventually determined that the shredded and smoldering bus posed no imminent threat and had attached tow cables to the rear axle. A massive MRAP, basically a cement truck with half-inch armor plate and foot-thick windows instead of cement, and originally designed to withstand IEDs on the quiet streets of the Holy Lands, was maneuvered into position and shackled to the tow cables.

The great warm slab was crowded with all manner of vehicles including a Segway and several motorcycles, presumably in case the bus tried to make another run for it.

The MRAP revved its engine and started backing up, its backup horn beeping. The bubbling sea of Kevlar helmets immediately parted giving the MRAP the freedom to pull the remains of the Christ Victory bus from the hillside.

Orbin noted with some irony the presence of a backup horn on an armored vehicle: blow up whatever you want with a 20mm cannon, but be careful not to back over anyone's steel-toed boot, safety first after all.

The tow cables straightened and stretched, but the Christ Victory bus didn't move. The MRAP's wheels spun, spitting gravel, grit, and what was left of the precious sod on the assembled and heavily armed spectators.

The call went out for everyone to make more room for the MRAP as it drove up to within a few lengths of the bus to get a running start at the extraction. The cars, trucks, motorcycles, and tanks were repositioned on the periphery of the apron to give the MRAP adequate Lebensraum for its mission. The SWAT teams and fellow travelers had taken cover behind the wall of vehicles in the event the tow cables snapped since a recoiling cable could easily cut a man in half. But they were totally unprepared for what actually did happen.

The engine roared, the backup horn beeped, and the MRAP rapidly gained speed across the slab and away from the obstinate bus: the cables uncoiled, stretched, and then in a sudden, shuddering metallic thunderclap, the bus broke free... kind of. The hindquarters of the obstinate bus exploded as the chassis frame, running gear, shredded tires and all, skittered out from beneath the bus while the perforated scraps of the body remained stubbornly suspended in the mouth of the portal like great ragged fangs.

Not expecting the ease with which the frame could be separated from the body, like Linus and Lucy with the football, the MRAP's inertia carried it backward into a pair of SUVs plowing them, the individuals taking cover behind them, and the MRAP itself over the far edge of the great warm slab down into the steep gully below—followed dutifully by the scraping, sparking spine of the Christ Victory bus at the other end of the cables.

The SWAT teams immediately began pouring fire into the ragged mouth of the cave under the natural assumption that the bus had been booby-trapped. The ground shook for a moment, which immediately silenced all of the small arms fire, and all was quiet as a ghostly, thick roiling cloud of choking grey dust spilled from the jagged mouth of the cave as if the hillside itself were vomiting.

There were some serious injuries now, and it would take hours to winch the MRAP out of the gully and evacuate the unfortunate few—it was payback time, now it was personal.

Chapter Forty-Five

Gopher Control

After army crawling beneath the scary looking Christ Victory bus fangs at the mouth of the portal, and satisfying themselves that there was no danger within, the authorities immediately set up a command post in the pressure buffer with tables and laptops and big screen monitors, and called for hard rock mining equipment to drill, blast, and tunnel through the hundreds of feet of collapsed manifold passages leading to the core of Mustard Seed so that they could rescue all the endangered children being victimized by the religious cult.

Lights had been set up and by nightfall the scene was reminiscent of the obelisk excavation on the moon scene in *2001:A Space Odyssey*. The mining equipment would be loaded onto C-130s to be flown from Wyoming and put into operation within 48 hours.

There was a great deal of pressure to conclude the matter quickly as the election was fast approaching and Fucknose was gaining in the polls. An FCC sniper team scouting positions at first light discovered some of the old wellheads and recognized them for what they were, ventilation ducts, and by 9 a.m. it was decided to pump several thousand cubic feet of CS gas into the vents to drive the cultists from their stronghold. At 11 a.m. they held a press conference. A PIO in full battle dress and surrounded by an assortment of concerned looking people issued the following statement:

> At 3 pm yesterday, a joint strike force coalition consisting of Federal, state, county, and local law enforcement personnel acting on warrants issued at the Federal, state, and local level attempted to take the under-age residents of the religious group commonly known as Mustard Seed, into protective custody in response to charges of child abuse, child endangerment, child neglect, sexual misconduct, building code violations, hazardous work place environment, and a variety of lesser but significant allegations. The joint forces coalition task force was met with fully automatic small arms fire and vehicle-borne improvised explosive devices otherwise known as V-IEDS causing serious injuries to multiple first- responders.

> The religious cult is now hiding in their fortified compound below ground and has effectively blocked all ingress and egress points. We are currently clearing these impediments and are in contact with the Mustard Seed leadership via

Facebook and other web 2.0 and social media mechanisms, and we hereby issue the following ultimatum. If the leadership of Mustard Seed does not release their hostages by 12 noon Pacific Daylight Time today, the joint forces coalition will commence the introduction of tear gas, a safe and environmentally friendly incapacitant, into their air supply, and will continue to do so until they release their hostages and surrender to authorities.... Questions?

"Felicity Spector Action News 29, since the people down there are sealed in, does the tear gas pose a threat to the children and elderly down there since you haven't cleared the blockage yet and there's no escape?"

There was a thoughtful pause. "We have taken that into careful consideration and deliberation, and we believe that the rescue and safety of the children outweighs the risk of accidentally killing or otherwise harming the children."

While it was true that the authorities were in communication with Mustard Seed via the internets, the communication was quite limited and Hertell and company could only connect to the command post and were effectively isolated from the rest of the world.

Evidently, several of the BLM SWAT team members, while milling about on the Great Warm Slab, had received emails with YouTube links to the Benny-Hill-Christ-Victory -bus-chase video; the MRAP-Linus-Lucy-Football prank, complete with traditional piano soundtrack, intercut with pirated Peanuts clips; and the whole helicopter-chicken-crash-battle-of-the-bulge incident which was artfully edited and accompanied by a compelling dubstep remix of "Wonderful World." with a drop that perfectly synced to the 20mm cannon fire. The BLM SWAT team immediately took their smart phones to the command post in the pressure buffer.

The incident commander watched the videos glumly. "Well, it wasn't our finest hour then was it...." He took a deep breath and cracked his neck from side to side. "Can one of you refresh the screen? I want to see how fast the view counts and comments are changing." He pointed to the closest one. "You, can you refresh your screen please."

The bulk of the IC staff was now gathered around to watch. The screen was refreshed. "Fuck! It's already got an ad." He looked up at the knot of BLM SWAT guys. "It didn't the first time did it?" But before they could answer, cell phones began to rattle vibrate, chime, bleat, and bray. A voice called out from one of the tactical consoles, "Uh we have a problem. I just got an email with another link that I think you should see..."

The big screen monitor was now filled with what appeared to be live streaming video from www.lapsedgeologist.com of the command post itself and the IC staff standing in an awkward cluster watching themselves watching themselves watching themselves on the big screen monitor.

"What the fuck!" All eyes immediately began to scour the interior of the pressure buffer looking for the web cams, and the last images to escape the command post were the distorted and grim faces of various public safety personnel looming into view and a spider-like gloved hand filling the frame, followed by blackness. They soon found the satellite dish, traced the cable down through the crushed conduit and linked the Mustard Seed CAT5 cable into the command post LAN where their firewalls were quickly configured to block all outbound and inbound traffic, except for specific IP addresses which were now being used to inform Hertell and everyone else in the Malt Shop that day that they were about to be gassed unless they came out of hiding and surrendered themselves to the protective arms of the state.

Hertell, Kaye, Virginia, and a handful of Founders sat at the counter of the Malt Shop concluding their video session with the authorities above. They'd been notified of the deadline and apprised of the consequences they would suffer if they failed to comply.

Hertell, took a sip from the straw in his milkshake. "So I guess you're gonna gas us like we're gophers or something then huh?"

"Well, that's up to you then isn't it?"

"Not really, we're not the ones that'll be pumping tear gas into the air intakes. That's pretty much exclusively you guys, and I advise against it."

"I'm sure you do."

"Where are you guys anyway, are you in the PB, the pressure buffer?"

"We're in a secure location, safe, comfortable, and so forth and so on."

"I'm sure you are." He took another sip and finished his milkshake with a noisy flourish, and then leaned closer to the webcam.

"And so are we, and again I urge you in the strongest possible terms to abandon this course of action."

"Thank you for the input. You have to the top of the hour."

The session ended and the screen went blank for a moment but was quickly filled with a screen saver slide show depicting images of natural wonders from the surface—Grand Canyon, Half Dome, beaches, deserts, jungles—presumably the IC's default screen saver, or possibly Psyops to soften the resolve of the stubborn religious zealots huddled below.

Hertell wiped his mouth, "Good milkshake," and then turned to Miles. "Sure hope those air filtration systems work."

As it turned out, it didn't really matter since the tear gas had the desired effect long before it reached the air filters.

The FCC SWAT team got a terse radio message: "Tactical One, you are authorized to deploy canisters, fire for effect. Repeat Tactical One, fire for effect."

"Roger, Tactical One, fire for effect." The six-man team was surrounded by 2-man carry transit cases brimming with CS canisters, so they donned their gas masks, selected a playlist from an iPhone, and began to pull the pins and drop the canisters down the air vents.

Similar radio calls went out to Tactical Two and Three which were positioned at other air vents several miles distant, and they immediately set about saving the children. Tactical Two formed a grenade bucket brigade to more efficiently get the most gas canisters into the air supply in the least amount of time.

The teams were about halfway through their second transit case when they began to get some broken radio messages.

"Tactical...(static)... tactical... one... (sound of shouting in the background) Cease... cease deployment... immediate...(coughing, more shouting) Stop! All Tactical Teams... (retching sounds)... Stop!

Air filtration had been one of the primary concerns of the original Mustard Seed planners and logisticians—mainly airborne radiological contaminants, but also Sarin, VX, and Mustard gas since it was assumed that they would all be used in the last, desperate, twitching spasms of humankind predicted by the Control Data 6600. However, at noon Pacific Time that day they were completely irrelevant since the air ventilation system had been designed to first route all air to the various pressure buffers, and there were over a dozen of them extending well past Mt Adelaide, not just the one beneath Whisper Hill.

The command post staff, blinded, gasping and covered in saliva, snot and vomit, came staggering and crawling out of the ragged, bus-fanged mouth of the portal—right into the lights and lenses of the TV news cameras which had been brought in to broadcast the surrender of the Mustard Seed militants.

"This is Action News Nine, and the militants seem to be surrendering...and they appear to be in full military attire..."

The camera crews were immediately shoved aside as the EPA, FCC, USGS, and DOE SWAT teams recognized the unwelcome turn of events and came to the aid of their comrades, helping them to their feet or carrying them to safely, amidst indignant exclamations of. "Gas! They've got gas! They gassed the whole command staff!" Several concerned SWAT guys donned masks and charged into the portal and down into the pressure buffer to rescue any who'd been overcome by the safe and environmentally friendly incapacitant.

Chapter Forty-Six

The Great Rat

T he choir was gathering in the Cathedral. They would typically arrive and then start with scales and vocal warm ups. Under the current circumstances, they were much less chatty than usual.

It had been three days since the teargas boomerang incident, and things had settled into something of a routine. They'd lost their internet connection, which was probably just as well since it was replete with stories about how they were just another evil, violent inbred fundamentalist religious cult. The IC's screensaver slide show of natural wonders was still on the large monitor, but other than that there had been no further contact from the surface.

It was quiet for the first two days, and Hertell hoped that perhaps the SWAT teams had decided to go out and rescue somebody else and leave Mustard Seed to rest in peace beneath the hills of the Li'l Pal. But on the third day a faint, dull grinding began, like a great rodent gnawing in some distant wall.

Hertell sat in the back as he had for almost every choir practice since he'd discovered Mustard Seed.

He stared up at the ceiling of the sanctuary and watched the distorted shadows of the arriving choir, looming and shrinking and arcing across the ceiling far above the altar and the dying Jesus. The lighting in the cathedral was quite dramatic, almost like an old *Twilight Zone* episode, key lights, sharp contrasts, deep shadows, and it made him think of Plato's cave where these people lived their whole lives chained in the cave, staring at a blank wall, seeing only shadows from the world outside, and how eventually they came to believe that the shadows actually were the real world.

The physicist in Hertell, or what remained after the bullet in his head, had always liked the Plato story since a shadow is a two-dimensional representation of a three-dimensional object—you put a sphere in front of a spotlight and you get a circle as the shadow. He'd totally forgotten what Plato's point was in the story, something philosophical no doubt, but as a physicist, and as a thought exercise, one could argue that our 3D world could theoretically be the shadow of some higher, 4+n-dimensional world beyond most people's comprehension and certainly beyond everyone's perception. In Plato's yarn, the light was from a big fire.

Hertell looked at the choir and wondered what possible source of light in this theoretical 4D, or 5D, or whatever-D world could be powerful enough to cast a 3D shadow to fill this world with mastodons and people and mountains and joy and grief and SWAT teams. It couldn't be a big fire, or a big spotlight, or an exploding sun, those were all three-dimensional too, and therefore just shadows themselves, just like Hertell and just like the choir. So the light source would have to be something in that other world, and presumably just as incomprehensible. You'd need a special kind of light to create a world as glorious and mystifying and tragic as this.

Choir practice was about to begin. He hadn't noticed, but they'd evidently finished their vocal warm-ups while he was watching the shadows on the ceiling. He would always marvel at the transformation when the choir would cease to be people and would become... he wasn't sure what. They'd be talking and normal one moment, getting pointers in phrasing, timing, expression and so on from Darlene the choir director, and then they'd start singing, and they'd become this whole other thing separate and distinct from the people who comprised it. They wouldn't really be people anymore, not while they were singing anyway, only to become people again when they'd stop for Darleen to give them notes.

Perhaps it was the words. There was no denying that the words to some of the hymns, particularly the older ones, were beautiful—silly and quaint to a thinking, rational person, redemption, salvation, life everlasting and all that—but beautiful nonetheless, and no doubt comforting to those weak enough to need them and simple enough to believe them. He'd been giving the phenomenon a lot of thought lately. Perhaps when singing those words, it's as if they're in a parallel universe where the words they're singing are true and the world they're singing about is real. It certainly appeared that way to Hertell. Then when you stop, it all goes away and you find yourself back in this world where the words are just... words again, and if only you could keep singing you'd always be there, in that parallel universe where the words are true and that world is real.

Maybe that's what it was like for the believers, where even when they're not singing those words, they're in that place with God and Jesus and angels and Santa Claus and Unicorns and Fairies and big rock candy mountains. He pitied them for believing such crap, and he envied them for it too. They were children, and he cherished them.

"Do you want to join us for the prayer Hertell?"

They asked him the question at every Choir practice, and he smiled politely and shook his head as he did every time they asked. They accepted his decision with their usual equanimity and formed a circle for the prayer. Though he had no memory of it, Hertell had been invited to many prayer circles by Kaye both before and after they were married. He'd always smile and politely decline and would eventually come to mock the practice and her beliefs.

He thought of his father's abrupt change of heart regarding religion during his last days, and wondered if one day, he too would weaken and join the procession of simpler minds turning to God upon drawing their last desperate breath in the hope that perhaps there was something bigger, something beyond this, or at least beyond them, him. He knew it to be very likely and probably inevitable since it was obviously a survival reflex of some kind, like a sneeze or a cough, a natural response to an irritant, in this particular case, death. Nothing to be ashamed of really, no more than a cough or a sneeze, since it was built into the machinery, but nevertheless such a cliché that it simply could not be indulged—like atheists who mock those who are praying for their souls, but who secretly hope that those prayers are helping and that God, if He really is out there, is listening—even though they would never give those stupid people the satisfaction.

But then again, if it's inevitable, then why wait until your last breath, what's the point of that unless you're just trying to avoid the humiliation of an I-told-you-so from simpletons. Besides he had an excuse if he wanted one, he'd been shot in the head after all. The choir began to sing.

> *Praise, my soul, the King of Heaven;*
> *To His feet thy tribute bring.*
> *Ransomed, healed, restored, forgiven,*
> *Evermore His praises sing:*
> *Alleluia! Alleluia!*
> *Praise the everlasting King.*

The grinding stopped. He'd been feeling it through his feet, but couldn't feel it anymore. He moved his feet to make better contact with the stone floor, and lightly touched his fingertips to the pew. It was definitely gone; perhaps the great rat had given up on that distant wall. Perhaps now they would be left alone to live out their lives beneath the hills of the Li'l Pal.

> *Frail as summer's flower we flourish,*
> *Blows the wind and it is gone;*
> *But while mortals rise and perish*
> *Our God lives unchanging on...*

The ground shook with a concussive jolt that was immediately followed by an overpressure shock wave that ripped through the Cathedral. The air was immediately filled with alarm claxons and sirens.

Chapter Forty-Seven

Dungeons and Dragoons

T he authorities had finally gotten the hard rock mining equipment in place in the Pressure Buffer and had been drilling and setting charges for the last 18 hours. It was slow going since they were all wearing gasmasks and NBC suits for fear of another gas attack from the cultists, but they eventually blasted a path through the manifold.

The IC's screensaver slide show of natural wonders was replaced with an IM dialog box. Nobody was in the malt shop at the time so no one saw the following message:

```
You        are      hereby
notified   that     public
safety professionals have
established  an    escape
route for the population
of  Mustard  Seed.  You
are     hereby   directed
```

to   seek   protective
custody or suffer serious
and   possibly   severe
consequences.

Hertell's ears were throbbing from the overpressure, and his nose was bleeding, but he'd made his way to the cornfield and up the wide passageway at the far end leading up to the choke point beyond. Everything was covered in gritty grey dust, which got deeper the closer he got to the surface.

He stopped in his tracks. He thought he felt a slight breeze.

It was dark up ahead. The explosion had evidently knocked out all the lighting in the passageway. The only light available was spill from the cornfield which was getting weaker as he worked his way forward in the growing darkness, feeling for the cave-in box he knew to be in the passageway.

Immediately after the blast, he'd led the stunned and shaken choir from the Cathedral and asked Kaye to take them deeper into Mustard Seed for safety and make sure everyone was accounted for. He then instinctively turned and headed up to the cornfield. He only wished now that he'd given the matter a little more thought and at least brought a flashlight.

It wouldn't be necessary. He could see tiny specks of light reflecting off the snaking walls of the passage several hundred yards ahead. He thought he heard voices, but his ears were still ringing so it may have just been his imagination. They were still far away, probably in the manifold, and by the sound of things they were trying to get past the rubble they'd just created.

Hertell was resolved to create some more for them. The passage leading from the manifold back to the cornfield was well over a quarter mile long with lots of curves and was a favorite for the golf-cart races they'd started shortly after the emergence. It would take months to drill and blast through it, which was why he was feeling around in the dark for the manual cave-in box. Which he finally found. It was a big square box with a sloped roof, like the old fire alarm boxes from antiquity. He broke the glass with his elbow and opened its little dollhouse door.

The SWAT teams were cautiously moving forward in their NBC suits and gas masks, laboring over the rubble making their way through the manifold, alert for another ambush, booby trap, or gas attack by the religious fanatics. There appeared to be a major passageway ahead, but it was effectively blocked by the blast debris. They cautiously approached and directed their flashlights into an opening big enough to see through but not big enough to fit through.

Satisfied, one of them removed his gas mask and shouted back toward the Pressure Buffer.

"Ok, we've got a way in! Bring up the equipment!"

"What?" It was a voice from some distance away in the pressure buffer.

"We got in! Bring the equipment down here!"

He was answered with silence for a moment, and finally, "What?"

Muffled advice came from beneath a nearby FCC gas mask. "TTP says you should keep your gas mask on, and you're supposed to use the radio for tactical comms."

"Go ahead and try. Radios don't work down here, Einstein. You stay here with your crystal set, I'm gonna go up and let'm know we've got these fuckers by the..."

The tactical exchange was punctuated by a siren, which was echoing from the darkened passageway on the other side of the rubble.

No one was sure what to do. "Is that one of ours?"

After 30 seconds, the siren stopped. They would now be on the receiving end of a shock wave.

The earth shook again in a trembling shudder. Dirt and small rocks jetted out of small opening and every other fissure in the rubble as if a great giant hiding within was exhaling his last breath. The SWAT team scattered and scrambled clumsily and made their way back to the safety of the pressure buffer.

Hertell had almost made it safely across the cornfield before being overtaken by the thick hissing wave of grey dust.

There was a new video session in progress with the authorities above. They'd been apprised of the latest setback beneath the Li'l Pal and were hopping mad, so they brought in Doug to try to talk Mustard Seed out.

"...So everyone is good?"

The malt shop was jammed with people, but Kaye was doing most of the talking. "Yeah we're good for at least another fifty years down here."

"You gonna stay down there too?"

Kaye had actually given the matter a lot of thought: all she had on the surface was a crappy house that had been underwater since the crash, and a cat that spent most of its time at the neighbors. Her chain-smoking parents were long dead, and her brothers all moved to Alaska and had their own lives.

"Yeah. I'm in the choir."

Doug smiled. "Everybody down there is in the choir one way or another."

"True." The rest of the malt shop voiced agreement.

"And we're staying down here, we're not coming out."

Doug looked sad and looked into the camera. "I think you've made the right decision. But we're gonna miss you up here, we're definitely gonna ...

He was interrupted by a voice from off-camera. "You want to lose your license? You want to go to jail?" The rest was inaudible.

Kaye and the rest of the malt shop watched the screen, as Doug appeared to be talking to someone off-camera. He eventually nodded at someone and then looked back toward the camera. He took a deep breath, and then seemed to sag.

Doug knew every man, woman, and child in Mustard Seed, he'd listened to their personal stories, their inner lives, their confusion, their hopes. And as he sat at the incident commander's laptop looking into its webcam, he thought about what the armed and determined agents of the state who were surrounding him had in mind for the good people of Mustard Seed.

Doug looked away from the camera for a moment, surveying the scene around him, and then looked directly into the lens.

To the authorities here assembled, your unconditional surrender and submission is the only acceptable response. You really only have one choice. They have promised that you will all be processed and placed in the custody of the most relevant agency. I therefore urge you, Hertell, and the good people of Mustard Seed that in order to preserve what remains of your lifeboat civilization and its values and its dignity, that you immediately and without reservation, shelter in place, and tell these guys up here to go fuck themselves!

With that Doug stood up and walked away leaving an empty chair. There was a muffled exchange off-camera, and the empty chair was immediately filled with a new, and very agitated presence. It was the IC, and veins were visible on his forehead.

"We are going to get you. We are going to root you out of there, every one of you, even if it takes 50 years."

A new backdrop of black BDU's and tactical vests moved in behind the IC and presumably the attached foreheads had bulging veins as well. It had all been so embarrassing. They'd prematurely announced that they'd gotten through and were about to secure the hostages, but the siren and the cave-in put some sand in their gears. This had been their 5th public humiliation: the Benny Hill Bus chase, the Wonderful World shock and awe, the Lucy-Linus-MRAP-football thing, and the boomerang gas attack featuring the IC and his whole staff crawling on their hands and knees and puking like spring break—all broadcast live and now a viral laughing stock. A price must be paid.

Kaye took it in stride. "Look, I know you have a lot of time and energy invested in this, but why don't you go find something better to do. Can't you just leave us alone?"

Since the conversation was on a closed network, it gave the IC a certain freedom of expression.

"We've got all the time in the world, and we've got all the money in the world. Nobody, and I mean nobody, can tell the EPA to go fuck off and just leave them alone..."

A chorus of overlapping voices chimed in not wanting to be left out.... "OMB... BLM... OSHA... Franchise Tax Board... HUD... Fish and Game... GSA..."

The IC turned his head to look back at the assembled team. No one in the malt shop could see the look he gave his associates, but it must have been terrifying because they immediately fell silent.

He turned back to face the screen and the malt shop. "So yes, there are multiple jurisdictions involved, and as you can imagine, a lot of stakeholders who want to see this issue resolved. So as much as you'd like us to go fuck ourselves, we're not going to do that."

Kaye tilted her head. "Come on man, there's kids down here."

The IC's momentary spasm of guilt was quickly overcome. "Well you shoulda thought of that before you gassed us down there..."

"That was your CS, you gassed yourselves, we had nothing to do with that, and we even tried to warn you..."

"Look, you're not getting away. So you might as well come out and take your medicine."

Kaye considered his comment for a moment. "Okay, so we come out and then after some court time, we all go to jail yes?"

"Maybe some of you, maybe all of you, hard to say, it all depends doesn't it?"

"But I figure you guys must be filling up a database with charges on us, yes?"

The IC prided himself on his tech savvy. "Well, a spreadsheet for now, but we may switch to an Access database so we can just sort by agency and so on and so forth. A spreadsheet, even with pivot tables won't be enough because of multiple concurrent user issues and CM and so on and..."

He trailed off. There was some snickering in the ranks. He squared his shoulders and leaned closer to the webcam. "Are you fucking with me?"

Kaye couldn't resist. "Uhh... How would I even know?" The ranks erupted in laughter, which was immediately self-suppressed.

The IC let the laughter dissipate. The vein was throbbing again. "Mrs. Daggett..."

"We're not married anymore—haven't been for a long time. Not an issue."

"Sergeant Daggett, you're in law enforcement, you know that a line has been crossed, you know how this is going to end then don't you."

"Yes I do. Some of us, maybe even all of us are going to prison. We are a danger to society, and we must be isolated from it. But look where we are, we're already underground;

we're already in a dungeon. Consider it job done. What difference does it make where we serve our time? We won't come out again for 50 years, we promise."

There was general agreement in the malt shop. "Definitely... we promise... absolutely... cross my heart and hope to die..."

The IC nodded his head thoughtfully. "Well that's an interesting perspective. And thanks for the input, but... well, there's no way to sugarcoat this, so let me just be straight with you." He leaned back in his chair and then detonated...

"Because you gotta be in our motherfucking dungeon! That's the fucking difference! It doesn't count unless your motherfucking asses are in our motherfucking dungeon!"

There was general agreement among the BDU's. "Absolutely... gotta be our dungeon... only way..."

There seemed to be a commotion near the front of the malt shop. Kaye looked back as the Generations parted to reveal Hertell standing in the doorway. He was grey and completely covered with dust, his face, his hair, his clothes, like a caveman in ceremonial ash. He silently shuffled forward toward Kaye, and then leaned down to look into the webcam.

"We'll get back to you." He closed the lid to the laptop ending the videoconference.

The IC was momentarily confused. "What the..." and then the screen went blank.

Hertell sat down at the counter between Kaye and Virginia and then spoke softly. "It didn't collapse, not completely anyway. Only part of it, most of it is still clear. It won't take'm that long to get through it. Not much more than it took them to get through the manifold anyway—Maybe a day, maybe two if we're lucky. So I'm..."

He was silenced by a familiar grinding vibration they could all feel through the floor. The giant rat was back at work.

"Feels like they're drilling again to set more charges to clear the way into the cornfield. I don't think it'll take'm long. We better have somebody get ready to blow all the passages from the corn field, Miles can we have somebody do that?" Miles nodded glumly.

Someone set a glass of water down next to Hertell. "Thank you." He drank too quickly, and had a coughing fit, explaining between spasms. "Went down ... went down wrong pipe." Kaye and several others patted him on the back to help. He recovered and shook his head. "I'm sorry for bringing all this down on you. I was hoping they'd get busy with other concerns and forget about you, but I guess they haven't. I figure we can hold'm off for a while, but we'll keep losing Mustard Seed a piece at a time until there's nothing left..."

Hertell stood up. "Miles, wait until I can get back to the cornfield, then go ahead and seal it off behind me. I think if I can surrender to'm then maybe they'll leave the rest of you alone, as long as they can put at least somebody in jail."

There was a general protest. "You didn't do anything Hertell ... you just found us."

"I squirted'm with a garden hose, and then didn't do what they told me to do, so I'm sure they can do something with that..."

He finished his glass of water, and turned to leave. "Just give me a few minutes to get up there and then blow it."

Kaye nodded her head. "Doubt if you'll be a big enough scalp for'm, they'll want all of us, but it's worth a try."

"Well just in case I am a big enough scalp," he gave Kaye a hug, then Virginia, then Peggy and shook hands with Miles and the others as he made his way out of the malt shop. As he neared the door, he heard something that caught his attention.

"Boy, it's too bad they aren't mutants. We'd know what to do then."

There was a murmur of general agreement in the malt shop... "Oh yeah, we had a nasty surprise ready for the mutants... we could definitely take care of'm if they were mutants... Yeah we'd know what to do if they were mutants..."

Hertell stopped and looked at them. "You would?"

Chapter Forty-Eight

Cleansing Waters

I t didn't work exactly as designed since it had never actually been tested, but it worked well enough.

The SWAT teams actually did resemble mutants in their bug-like gasmasks and NBC suits, and had made it into the cornfield, which didn't look much like a cornfield anymore since every stalk was covered with grey dust as was the ground and much of the ceiling. They fanned out since there were so many of them, and they brought some special radio equipment so they wouldn't have to shout so much. The lighting changed first, taking the enormous chamber from a cold ash grey to a deep and foreboding crimson. The SWAT teams sheltered in place, and radioed that the lighting had changed.

"Yes, we can see the lighting change." Which was true since the teams had helmet-mounted cameras streaming video back to the command post where the staff could observe the operation from a number of perspectives on a bank of monitors. "Continue."

They advanced to about the middle of the cornfield when the next change happened.

The leader keyed his mic. "Base, Team 3, can you adjust squelch, we're getting some feedback in our headsets..."

One of the other SWAT team guys disagreed. "It's not feedback Kenny, it's in here... and it's getting louder..."

"This is base, we hear it too, unable to identify, is there a source?"

Evidently the Mustard Seed logistics planners considered starving mutants to be particularly sensitive to sudden lighting changes and scary sounds. In this particular case, it was the sound of the giant ants from the 1950's SciFi classic *Them.*

One of the SWAT guys laughed. "You gotta be kiddin' me! It's the giant ant sound from the old movie...

"Let's cut the chatter down there..."

"It's the giant ant sound... Feets don't fail me now!"

But the laughter quickly pinched off as the sound of the giant ants was replaced by a new sound—a trickling sound at first, then a bubbling sound, and then a sloshing sound, then a rushing sound as tons of Sierra Nevada snowmelt began to wash over the cornfield sweeping soil and stalk and SWAT team up in great heaving surges, knocking them off their big black boots, filling their NBC suits and gasmasks with cool and bracing mountain fresh water.

The command staff watched their monitors in horror as their perfect tactical formations were being knocked off their feet, thrown about like driftwood, and washed out of the cornfield like so much bilge debris with the SWAT teams providing the play-by-play. "They're trying to... they're trying to drown us!... They're flooding it!"

"Recommend you egress immediately Repeat, egress, and evacuate immediately!" Which was answered with a chorus of affirmations. "Roger that... Affirmative... In progress... Jesus Christ this is cold!"

It was designed to produce a great raging torrent, with the great flooding waters putting an end to those mutants too stubborn or too stupid to flee at the scary red lights or the scary ant sound. But it was an imperfect world, and some of the valves didn't work, and some of the explosive bolts didn't blow, and some of the flumes were obstructed, so it filled the chambers and tunnels in slow, uncertain sloshes like a low-flow toilet, instead of an instantaneous, definitive flush. Nevertheless, it slowly and simply but sternly encouraged the mutants to leave the party.

The water wasn't much more than waist deep, and some of the SWAT guys were able to wade through it with some semblance of dignity, but it was quickly and relentlessly rising in irregular swells and surges, so most of the SWAT guys lost their footing, tumbled, rolled, flailed, struggled to their feet, only to be upended again as they alternately waded or bobbed along, out of the cornfield and up the recently cleared passageway, past all the hard-rock drilling equipment, and up into the manifold and the pressure buffer where it swept up all the extra SWAT gear and explosives, and duffel bags, and folding chairs, and MREs, and coffee cups and pizza boxes, and pallets of ammo and empty transit cases and communications equipment, and pushed it all out through the gaping mouth of the portal like the outwash of an RV's holding tank.

The SWAT teams settled out of the stew first, some staggering to their feet, others helped up, others simply floating along on the surges and skidding across the great warm slab as the water drained away. They vaguely resembled a swarm of giant ticks, their NBC suits bloated with water instead of host blood, but still grey with tiny little bug-like heads.

The command post staff had immediately left the command trailer to assist the excreted SWAT teams; however, the trailer was parked at the low end of the great warm slab and was swept off its stands, off the slab, and down into the adjoining gully by the wall of mud, cornstalks, and garbage.

Luckily there were no TV cameras this time.

At least they thought so.

As it turned out, their LAN had been hacked; consequently, all the SWAT helmet cam video feeds and the salty video teleconference were all streamed into the loving embrace of the internets producing a bumper crop of new YouTube webisodes, and in fact numerous channels had been set up and devoted exclusively to the evolving fable of Mustard Seed.

Chapter Forty-Nine

Law of the Land

C arl and Rusty had spent several weeks down on Main Street USA immediately after the emergence and had developed a fondness for the people down below, and saw the smearing, the resultant attack, and the ongoing siege of Mustard Seed for what it was—an object lesson on the Sovereign's power over its subjects. Rusty was particularly incensed. He had been a libertarian since Middle School and had won a total of $20k from Ayn Rand essay contests, once in high school and once again in college, and it was Rusty who had hacked into the command post tactical LAN and routed all of the streaming video feeds from the SWAT team helmet cams and the command post laptops to several hundred of the crowdsourcing sites so that all could see and hear the rescuers being washed out of Mustard Seed from multiple angles.

The "motherfucking dungeon" videoconference was all over the internets almost immediately and was quickly picked up on cable with lots of bleeps, and eventually on the mainstream broadcast Networks, but it was edited and the voice distorted so that it sounded like Kaye was the one saying "our motherfucking dungeon motherfucker!"

The IC was replaced, but the problem remained, these stubborn people from the past had not yet been brought to heel. The election was nearing and the President was sinking in the polls, dragged down by the siege of Mustard Seed and the constant stream of embarrassing videos—if the Government couldn't even root some religious nuts out of a gopher hole, then what else was beyond its competency, and maybe it shouldn't be able to tell us what kind of light bulbs we can have or how much water can be in a toilet flush or anything else of consequence. Maybe it should just leave us alone; maybe those Mustard Seed people were onto something.

The Feds had taken command after the Lucy-Linus-Football- MRAP incident claiming jurisdiction based on the number and severity of Federal violations—any thought of resistance from the other jurisdictions quickly evaporated when it was pointed out that all the military equipment sported by the state and county players was a gift from the Federal Government. Justice owned this hot potato, and it got hotter and more embarrassing since they'd taken over—Justice had crawled, crying like babies, out of the earth; Justice had washed out of the earth like so much tangled sewage. Justice was now officially a laughing stock, and a new IC couldn't fix that. This defiance of authority could not be borne, the legitimacy of the whole system was at stake, and decisive and forceful action was needed.

President Potty Mouth was seated in the conference room on Air Force One somewhere over Nebraska on the way to a campaign stop in Florida. A gaggle of advisors was exploring options and eating pizza. Courtney was not one of them as she'd left the campaign to spend more time with her family. One of the spongy frat boys wiped his mouth and pounded the table.

"Okay. Executive Order. And we can do this. Just issue an executive order declaring that Mustard Seed is now a Federal Prison, and then it is our motherfucking dungeon—stroke of the pen, law of the land, how cool is that!"

The President pulled his chin and nodded. The other frat boys, seeing this, immediately warmed to the idea and had suggestions.

"Yeah, try'm in absentia, sentence'm for a few hundred years..."

"Put up cyclone fencing..." "A little razor wire at the top."... "Like a garnish!"

"Signs and guards" ... "Plug the hole and seal'm in."

"Yeah. Definitely gotta dump a butt load of concrete in the hole so they can't get out..."

Satisfied that they'd all gotten their oars in the water, they throttled back. The President had been nodding his head the whole time, which was good. He was clearly thinking about it. They returned to their pizzas to leave room for questions from the leader of the free world.

Instead, a voice came from behind them. "Yeah, not a bad idea, it could work."

The frat boys turned from their pizza to appraise him. He was seated on the couch. He was very old and had spook written all over him.

Carl rubbed his crew cut and smiled at the frat boys. "But it's still just a damage-limiting operation, and you'll still look like clowns." He had been summoned since he was the one that had closed the DD254 on Mustard Seed and knew the most about it. "You need to conclude this, permanently, definitively."

"That's what we're doing, we're gonna bury them alive in a dungeon. Our dungeon!" Several high-fived each other. "Our motherfucking dungeon!"

He took off his glasses. "'Alive' is the operative word here." He proceeded to fog and clean a lens. "If we don't see them, and let me emphasize that, see them with our boot on their neck, if we don't see them in orange jump suits, or slouched in court, or dead and draining in the pan, it doesn't matter whose dungeon they're in."

He checked the lens, and continued cleaning, emphasizing each syllable. "You need to send a clear message that this type of behavior, or actually misbehavior, will not be tolerated, at least not in this administration."

Satisfied with his cleaning job, he put his glasses back on. "I know every shaft, every vault, every chokepoint down there, and it's a very impressive facility. I've met every single one of the people down there, and I personally like many of them, probably all of them in fact." He leaned forward and put his hands on his knees. "But I love this country, and I have a sworn duty to protect it, and its institutions. And leaving those people to continue life as they are, content, ungoverned, without consequence, sends... a message to... well, to everybody, domestically and internationally."

Carl had been late to the party. He was just outside Yountville when the story broke on Drudge and thus the top-secret classification issues were immediately made moot—whatever Mustard Seed was and for whatever reason it had been classified top-secret back in 1963, it was now public knowledge, and the bell could not be un-rung. It was a long quiet ride back down to Bakersfield for Carl as he considered his options in closing out the DD254 on this long forgotten and now formerly top-secret program.

It would be an easy one, shouldn't take more than a day or two: some quick interviews with the principals, collect documents if there were any, piece together the events, personnel, and timeline, complete, sign, and file the DD254 and go home. But it ended up taking weeks as Carl and Rusty got to know the world below and the people in it.

The President finally spoke. "So, what's your suggestion?"

Chapter Fifty

Choir Practice

"**D**o you want to join us for the prayer Hertell?"

As was his custom he smiled politely and shook his head. The choir had gathered for practice in the Cathedral, and they warmly accepted his decision, as was their custom.

It had been a little more than a day since the cleansing water incident, and it had been quiet—so perhaps the great rat had found another wall to gnaw. There was no contact with the outside world at all now, even the SWAT team's IC's screensaver slide show of natural wonders had disappeared. They seemed to have lost interest.

Hertell watched the prayer circle form and wondered how long it would take for his perceptions to adjust to life in the world of false horizons and forced perspectives where everything that looked so far away was actually quite close and often within reach. And as he thought about movie sets and facades and what was real and what wasn't, the copper angels began to stir, only instead of hearing mastodons or clicking trilobites, he could hear Mister Frostie singing.

It made him happy. The voice was far away, but it was unmistakable...

Precious Lord, take my hand
Lead me on, let me stand...

He wondered what it must have been like for Mister Frostie. Cast into the world, a stranger in a strange land, wandering, knowing that comfort and love and home were so close. Unable to convince those he now walked among that there was a precious little world beneath their feet...

I am tired, I am weak, I am worn;

Unable to tell all those he'd left below what he knew to be true, that the world was still out there, with sun and moon and sky, that they weren't alone, that the world hadn't ended but had gone on without them, a real world of trees and grass and dogs and doors that went into rooms, and not just sets and lights and sound effects.

Through the storm, through the night,
Lead me on to the light:

And he'd been wrestling with something since the Casino Indian meeting. It was something that the Hollywood producer had said, and it had been lurking at the edges of Hertell's thoughts since then and would only come forward in quieter and contemplative moments. And the distant voice of Mister Frostie had brought it all into focus for him.

Take my hand, precious Lord,
Lead me home.

Perhaps there really was a parallel universe where all the TV shows are real and we're all pretend. Certainly possible with current Cosmological theories.

When the darkness appears
And the night draws near,

Perhaps this world really isn't anything more than just a set, a pretend place on a sound stage with lights and costumes and props, and we're all in a movie that writes itself. Shakespeare and Elvis and Plato said as much in their own way.

And the day is past and gone,

And perhaps the real world is actually, virtually, literally the one the choir is singing about, and when they're singing, that's when they're actually in that world, and that's what Hertell had been seeing in them all this time.

At the river I stand,
Guide my feet, hold my hand:

It was illogical, it was irrational, but it was possible.

Take my hand, precious Lord,
Lead me home.

Hertell felt warmth in both hands.

He thought he might be bleeding again. He looked down at his left hand. There was something in it. It was a woman's hand, and he was gripping it, tightly. He looked up and saw Kaye. She was looking at him. There were tears in her eyes, and he couldn't remember ever seeing such joy in her face before. Confused, he looked up. He was standing in the prayer circle, and all eyes were on him, and all with a look of general astonishment.

It had started out quite softly before the prayer had begun, a lone voice from the back of the darkened cathedral. It grew louder and stronger as it came closer. It was Hertell. It was as if he were being carried toward them, and they all saw it for what it was: a miracle, a small one, a routine one, and one they all recognized, a man falling into faith, the miracle of a man accepting everlasting life for the mere asking.

Hertell stood in the prayer circle, holding the hand of the only woman he had ever loved, trying to make sense of how he got there.

"Uhh... did I interrupt something? I think ...

He never got to finish that sentence.

Chapter Fifty-One

Bunker Buster

T he HTSF was configured to trigger upon reaching the first void it penetrated. The B-2 had taken off from Whiteman AFB, but rather than heading east to visit a Uranium centrifuge bunker in Iran, it instead took a short flight west to the Li'l Pal, and released the GBU-28 bunker buster bomb from about 50,000 feet over Tehachapi. The crew would be back to Whiteman in time for lunch. It was Sloppy Joe Day at the Ozark.

It took some doing, but an executive order had been issued identifying Mustard Seed as a suspected terrorist organization; another executive order temporarily suspended posse comitatus so that the military could assist a domestic law enforcement action; and a third authorized the DoD to support a designated federal law enforcement entity. The FAA issued a TFR to keep all air traffic out of the area during the operation.

There were still some i's to dot and t's to cross, but everything was in order and the legal precedent for killing Americans had been long ago established in Afghanistan, Sudan and the like; this was a regrettable but necessary step to ensure national security, so they were bullet-proof and no amount of pissing and moaning from preppers in fly-over country would change that.

The GBU-28 penetrated the earth at the precise coordinates and at the precise angle that had been programmed into it. In less than a heartbeat, tongues of flame shot out of all the well heads that Hertell Senior and the wildcatters had drilled back in the '50s, the same ones that had earlier been filled with CS canisters by the SWAT teams. The shockwave from the air vents shattered the empty transit cases that littered the area and blew the shredded black plastic debris down the hillsides.

The flames were just an instantaneous effect, and the air vents immediately issued plumes of grey dust which quickly settled into streaks on the hillsides, and were followed soon thereafter by black, acrid smoke. The SWAT teams had been directed to clear the area, so they were never in danger but remained at a distance to provide perimeter security in case any survivors tried to surrender. They hooted and high-fived each other as the dark smoke snaked up into the windless sky.

There would be no web cam footage this time since the hacked tactical LAN had been replaced with a high security, encrypted network enclave. Instead, there was a press conference, which opened with a compelling video of B-2's in flight, the scary fanged jaws of the Mustard Seed portal, and injured SWAT team members being loaded into ambulances.

The new, improved IC stood before the microphones and read from a prepared statement:

At approximately 11 am Pacific Daylight time today, a joint rescue task force attempted to breach defenses of the designated terrorist organization, commonly known as Mustard Seed, in order to rescue the under-age hostages and others we believed were being held against their will. A high-technology and environmentally friendly kinetic effects system, commonly known as a bunker buster bomb, was directed at a vulnerable area of the facility where it penetrated and detonated as expected; however, we believe that due to the defective construction of the underground fortress, as cited in numerous building code violations, that the bomb, rather than facilitating the rescue of the terrorists, instead resulted in the collapse and destruction of their subterranean habitat and the subsequent loss of all of its inhabitants.

Listening devices have been deployed, to detect signs of life, and so far there have been none. Based on this evidence, we have concluded that there are no survivors, but we will continue to monitor the site and take appropriate action if signs of life are detected.

The rescue portion of this operation is now officially terminated, and recovery operations will commence pending the results of a cost-effectiveness analysis.

We deeply regret the loss of life, but we also want to stress that no individual or organization, regardless of its religious affiliation, is above the law.

Questions?

"Now that's a clear fucking message!" "Yeah, it says, do not... fuck... with us!" "Or you die! Game over!"

The campaign staff was gathered around a bank of TVs on the President's "Owe the Future" Bus somewhere in western Pennsylvania. The President was on one of the screens giving a campaign speech in the adjoining community college gymnasium because senior staff thought it best for him to be otherwise occupied during the Mustard Seed press conference so he could keep his distance from the incident and appear more unconcerned and Presidential since the leader of the free world simply doesn't have cycles to waste on Jesus freaks in a gopher hole. The leader of the free world's sound was off, but it looked like it was going well. The only screen with the sound up was the Mustard Seed presser.

The IC's speech had been extensively tested, and the MRI's all looked great, and judging by the questions that were being asked, it was all going according to plan. All the questions from the press followed the narrative they'd tested and refined with the MRI's—the perfect combination of confusing sentences and big words to make it sound complicated and therefore best left to the Government.

One of the frat boys pointed at the screen. "Aw look, it's that Christian bitch..."

"Would Muslims get the same treatment?"

"Turn off the sound; I don't have to listen to that skank."

A different reporter asked, "What about Scientologists?"

The sound was turned down, but as it turned out, it would have been better to leave it up, because in the ensuing quiet, an anguished voice came from the back of the bus.

"Uh oh... Uh oh... This is not good. Not good at all."

Chapter Fifty-Two

The Last Word

T ime passed and other things had taken over the news cycle. There was a new President whose nose vaguely resembled a penis; a new war had started over in the Holy Lands, the stock market had crashed because of Oceanoids and then recovered because of Oceanoids; there was a major national security leak that not only tied together every conspiracy theory ever whispered on late night radio—crop circles, suppressed inventions, grassy knolls, Area 51, Chupacabra, weather control, UFO's—but also revealed a seabed of Governmental corruption, cynicism, stupidity, and deceit stretching back to the Kennedy administration and present in every subsequent strata of accumulated political sediment; and there was a new phone coming out.

Since Hertell Jr. had died intestate, the property went to the state and was then taken over by the Federal Government under an executive order issued by the new President—presumably an atonement of sorts for the prior administration's enforcement excesses. It was eventually declared a National Cemetery, and the old wooden cross was removed due to the wall between church and state and to avoid lawsuits from the ACLU.

So Mustard Seed and the sad fate of its inhabitants had faded from the headlines. Nevertheless, their double-dutch jump roping video was still racking up views on YouTube, one of the crowdsourcers developed a "Duck-And-Cover" app that had nearly a billion downloads worldwide, there were Singing Christmas Specials on TV again, and the buoyant, hopeful songs of Vera Lynn were sampled, looped, and auto-tuned to fill countless earbuds the world over—the trap cover was haunting but strangely uplifting.

But remarkably, even though Mustard Seed was no longer before peoples' eyes as it once had been in its last days, it was now definitely behind their eyes: it had become embedded in the public consciousness like a fairy tale, or a fable, or a myth, only these people and their world had really existed, and in spite of their sad fate, the fact that they did exist and once walked among us, was silently and patiently reassuring, like Santa Claus and the Tooth Fairy and maybe even Heaven and Life Everlasting.

A new system was being tested to serve as a backup to GPS since it was continuously being hacked and spoofed. It was a kind of new improved version of LORAN only using Schumann Resonance frequencies down around 30Hz and below. It was a very clever idea that recognized that there was essentially a big spherical void surrounding the earth between the surface and the ionosphere about 30 miles up. This big spherical void acted like a massive, but silent, church bell that had a resonant frequency of about 7.5 Hz. A frequency far below what people can hear but strangely the same frequency as human alpha brain waves, and by tinking the "bell" at specific intervals you could determine geolocation.

Renato had recently been divorced by his wife, so he had a lot more time to devote to his passion which was amateur radio astronomy. He'd been a ham operator since puberty and had met his wife at an ARRL convention, but evidently, she wasn't as into it as he was. He was curious to see if he could detect the signals of the new GPS system, so the challenge was to set up a receiver with enough sensitivity to detect the really, really, really weak signals. Since his wife had moved out, he finally had time to address the challenge. Now that he wasn't distracted with his wife and her ceaseless demands for interaction and eye-contact, it was actually pretty easy: an old PC and a DSP card for the receiver, a 300-foot wire for the antenna, preamp and the spectrum software. He'd been talking to another amateur radio astronomer named Niall in New Zealand, who was also recently divorced, and doing the same thing only with different equipment so they could cross-check their results, though it wasn't actually talking in the usual sense but rather blogging with some auxiliary email for the longer technical discussions and IM for the shorter ones.

Renato was a physicist by day, and got an IM from Niall while trying to explain something to some stupid rocket scientists at NASA. He didn't even bother to say excuse me since they probably wouldn't have understood that either. He looked at his phone, the message said.

```
"las twordc ame in"
```

Renato texted back, "k"

The signal had been coming in over the last few weeks a character at a time in standard International Morse code. It wasn't a natural signal like lighting and atom bombs that can also can ring the great big silent church bell. But it was definitely man-made and was most likely the new system's equivalent of a traditional "Hello World" test message. They both thought the first character was of natural origin, but after the second character and then the third, it was clear that it wasn't random lighting strikes or nuclear bombs shooting off in the Holy Lands.

Renato went home at the end of the day and directly into his wife's old room, which was now his lab, and looked at the computer screen with the last word on the message. He knew it to be the last word since it ended with "SK" for end of transmission. The full message read:

```
"Kicking and screaming,
born this day, Hertell
Daggett III. Mustard
Seed."
```

One More Thing

(Actually two)

I hope you enjoyed reading *Dog Logic,* and if you did, ***please*** leave a review. Reviews really help, and they can be as short as you want (longer too if so inclined). Since you're reading the print edition, here are QR codes for your smartphone or tablet that will take you straight to the appropriate *Dog Logic* review page...

Amazon

GooglePlay

Barnes & Noble

Kobo

That Second Thing

And if you haven't already downloaded the free audiobook edition, point your smart phone or tablet camera at the QR Code below...

Audiobook

The audiobook is a great companion piece to the novel and a whole new way to experience the world of *Dog Logic* -- sound effects, music, the works. It'll also get you ready for the next book in the *Dog Logic Triptych: Water Memory*, which picks up the story 10 years after the end of *Dog Logic*:

> *The earth's magnetic poles have reversed and civilization has just had its clock reset to the great cosmic flashing 12:00am from almost a million years ago, and humanity, and everybody in it, is pretty much forgetting everything it learned since the last time. Everybody except Hertell, who decides to start civilization over again, and try to get it right this time. What could possibly go wrong?*

To Alison, because I keep forgetting we're not the same person

About Author

Tom Strelich was born into a family of professional wrestlers and raised in Bakersfield, California. His plays include *BAFO (Best and Final Offer), Dog Logic,* and *Neon Psalms.* Honors include National Endowment for the Arts grant for playwrights, Kennedy Center Fund For New American Plays award, and Dramatists Guild/CBS New Play Award. Strelich has one screen credit, *Out There* (Showtime). His first novel, *Dog Logic,* (loosely based on the play - same setting, same characters, epically different story) has won several awards.

CPSIA information can be obtained
at www.ICGtesting.com
Printed in the USA
JSHW011920190723
45070JS00006B/175